Shall Never See So Much

Gerald Gillis

BookLocker.com, Inc.
2010

This book is dedicated to my wife, Debby.

Together we've raised wonderful kids, traveled to far-off places, and been blessed in ways too numerous to list. You have stood by me and supported me in everything I've ever done. You have the heart of an angel, and I love you for who you are and what you mean to me. This one's for you, babe!

Author's Note

Shall Never See So Much is a work of fiction, an historical novel. The subject is the Vietnam era, and the settings include the combat zone as well as the home front. In the main, the story is set in the first half of the year 1968—one of the most chaotic, challenging, and dissonant periods in the history of the United States. It is an account of America at war, not only with a foreign enemy in a strange, distant place, but sometimes even with itself. For the more than one-third of today's American populace who had yet to be born by the war's conclusion in 1975, it may be useful to know that the nation's current discomfort and divisiveness over sending (and then keeping) U.S. troops in harm's way is hardly without precedent. The Vietnam era sliced hot and hard into the cultural and political fabric of this country, with a sharp edge not seen since the Civil War.

The overarching theme of the novel stems from my belief that the human spirit is fundamentally heroic, despite the darker facets that are always there, always crowding out the more virtuous. The valor of American troops that was so frequently displayed in Vietnam was every bit as noteworthy as any of their wartime predecessors in uniform. Likewise, the efforts of those who strove unselfishly and in good faith to put an end to the conflict provided an important counterweight to the national discourse, sometimes at their own peril. It is my hope that readers will fully discern this theme in the pages that follow.

A sizeable portion of this novel is a story about U. S. Marines. That choice was intentional, given my own previous service with the Marine Corps. Time spent in Marine green reaches well beyond active service and becomes a lifelong affiliation. I am no different than the many others with whom I share the same bond.

With regard to the history, it is also my hope that readers will find a responsible and realistic depiction. Robert F. Kennedy is one of modern history's most compelling characters, and his impact upon the course of events in 1968 was profound, to include his sudden loss. I have attempted in every way to portray RFK with what I believe to be an appropriate and deserved respect.

Several individuals merit a nod of appreciation in assisting me with this undertaking. Sally and Tim Degnen were the first to provide me with important feedback and encouragement from their reviews. Atlanta radio host J.J. Jackson was helpful in reaching back and uncovering the popular music of the period. Phillip Massengill, M.D., kindly offered important medical information and helpful explanation. My uncle and long-time mentor, Henry Hughes, implored me to keep the project moving forward, often at those very moments when my motivation was flagging. Suzanne Akins, my daughter, enthusiastically contributed her many talents and insightful counsel in a number of categories. My heartfelt thanks to all.

Gerald Gillis
Marietta, Georgia

"The weight of this sad time we must obey;

Speak what we feel, not what we ought to say.

The oldest hath borne the most: we that are young

Shall never see so much nor live so long."

--William Shakespeare
King Lear

PART ONE

January – February, 1968

CHAPTER ONE
Ashau Valley, South Vietnam

The sudden eruption of small-arms fire seemed to snatch away the available air from the already anxious U. S. Marines in the column. Twenty-four-year-old First Lieutenant Tom Flanagan licked his parched lips and strained to see ahead in the green shroud of vegetation. The tired Marine needed little reminder that enemy soldiers were almost always in his midst, even in the remote, dark places that otherwise seemed untouched by any sort of human intrusion. Hence the putrid, misty jungle became a cocktail of clamor that included, in order, the burst of gunfire, the shrieking flight of startled birds, and the shouts of men involved in a death struggle from an up-close, whites-of-the-eyeball range. Fragments of leaves that were shot away by the flying bullets floated softly to the ground. The rising smoke of the gunfire was visible through the oblique light shafts angling down through the jungle canopy. From up ahead, a frantic shout for a medical corpsman by an unseen Marine carried with it an urgency that all other Marines within earshot recognized as ominous. It was barely forty seconds into the fight before the final shots echoed away like the receding shadow of a cloud.

As Flanagan crouched beneath the weight of his field pack, with his muscles as tense as bowstrings, the young Chicago native could feel his heartbeat pounding at his temples as if trying to escape. He overheard radio traffic that the short fight had produced one dead Marine and at least three dead North Vietnamese Army soldiers (NVA). Since other Marines could be heard shouting orders up front, Flanagan sensed that things had yet to be fully sorted out. His platoon, along with the rest of Fox Company, 2nd Battalion, 5th Marines, 1st Marine Division, was stalled along a narrow east-west jungle trail deep within the infamous Ashau Valley.

Flanagan leaned his trim, athletic, six-foot frame against a tree and gulped the warm water from his canteen. His almond eyes were fixated on the map he held until he noticed his own trembling hand and the sweat from his chin splattering onto and rolling off the map's laminated surface. Flanagan poured canteen water over his short brown hair as he fretted over the Ashau and the visceral dread associated with the mere mention of its name; about the hardcore NVA who roamed beneath its triple-thick canopy; about the harrowing and often grotesque stories of those who had survived in there, and the haunting memories of those who hadn't. Of all the adjacent geography he had thus far trod in Vietnam—the rugged mountain peaks of the Annamese Cordillera chain to the west; Hue, Phu Bai, and the sandy shores of the South China Sea to the east—it was the Ashau, seventy-five kilometers south of the demilitarized zone (DMZ), that was clearly his least favorite.

There was a sudden stirring up ahead. Flanagan heard the sounds of men struggling with a load, their labored breathing interspersed with an occasional profanity. He then noticed the damp red hair of the dead Marine who was being carried to the rear in a poncho by two of his comrades. Once again here was the inexplicably strange yet natural sight in a world that was difficult to fully grasp and impossible to describe. There were the shots, the shouts, and then the bodies. Always, at the end of the sequence, the bodies were broken, sometimes horribly mangled, sometimes just pale and still. And they were always young, always just kids. The dead Marine's red hair reminded him of his sister Kate, which in turn reminded him of her anti-war politics and her dovish fiancé, all of which he despised and considered as evidence of Kate's serious lack of substance. He spat out a mouthful of warm water and muttered a barely discernible, "Screw it," when his bear-like platoon sergeant appeared at his side.

"My sentiments exactly," said Staff Sgt. Dennis Jankowski, age forty-three, his helmet wedged between his arm and his large torso, a stubby unlit cigar jutting from the corner of his mouth. Jankowski swiped his hand through his wet salt-and-pepper hair and accepted the canteen from Flanagan. "What the hell's happening up there?"

4

"Not sure," said Flanagan. "Either they ambushed us or we surprised them."

Jankowski took a drink and placed the cigar back between his stained teeth. "Ain't no ambush," he said, shaking his head and glancing up the trail where idle Marines knelt and faced outboard. "Too goddamn short and too little following on. I'd say we probably surprised the little shithooks."

Flanagan shot a weary glance at Jankowski. "Surprise isn't something we generally do to the little shithooks."

Jankowski laughed softly, his shoulders and upper body shaking in that manner common to people of his large physical size. "Point well taken," he said with a nod.

Flanagan's radio operator, a freckled-faced Oregonian named Wenrick, handed over the handset of the PRC-25 radio that was strapped to his back. "It's Bayou Six," said Wenrick.

Flanagan took another quick sip of water before keying the handset. "This is Bayou Three, over."

"Be advised that we're holding here until we can get some supporting fire up the trail," radioed the company commander. "Set your people in and report to me at the forward command post, over."

"Roger, out," replied Flanagan, who then turned to Jankowski. "Skipper's gonna blast the trail up ahead. Set 'em in."

Jankowski placed his helmet on his head and then turned and called out in a deep, gravelly voice, "Gimme the squad leaders. Chop-chop! Squad leaders up."

Flanagan moved out along the trail with Wenrick close behind until they reached Capt. Robert Tanner, a tall, prematurely balding, twenty-eight-year-old, Yale-educated native of New Orleans, near the front of the column. Tanner had dropped his pack and was down on all fours, hovering like a hawk over the documents recovered from one of the dead NVA. For weeks now Tanner had been sharing with Flanagan and his other platoon leaders the concern from headquarters over the supposed large enemy troop movements throughout Vietnam. And since hard evidence had been scarce, Tanner glanced up at Flanagan, raised his eyebrows, and winked.

"All kinds of arrows and unit designations scribbled over this damn thing," Tanner said calmly. "Multiple units—looks like infantry, signal, demolition, medical; all moving west to east, linking up with other units to the north and south. Hell, it appears that the whole friggin' NVA army just might be out here in the Ashau with us, gentlemen."

Tanner's tone was flat and unemotional. Tom Flanagan glanced at his counterparts from Second and First Platoons, Lieutenants Kevin Riordan and Dave Espy, respectively, and Sgt. Jeff Auer, the leader of Weapons Platoon. Lt. Walt Davies, the Executive Officer, was also listening in.

Flanagan moved in closer for a look.

"From where we are," said Tanner as he swept his hand along the map, "some of these same trails could be used to break out to Hue and Phu Bai. Good cover and concealment, good avenues of approach, the ability to mass once everybody's where they're supposed to be. They could bring a whole lot of hurt to a whole lot of different places. I don't quite know what to make of it, tell you the truth, but this friggin' terrain's dense enough to hide gallons of the little bastards, even though we're only seeing 'em a few pints at a time. But if we're getting all this 'movement' that headquarters keeps talking about, then we could be on to something big here, gents, something boocoo big. This map convinces me that somebody sure as hell thought this stuff through. This is hardly amateur work here, gentlemen. No sir, not this. Charlie's got his shit *wired* if he's about to come at us with this."

Flanagan sensed an uneasiness creeping into Tanner's typically unruffled demeanor. He also noticed Lt. Riordan's forced grin and Lt. Espy's hard swallow.

"If the boys from Hanoi are up there," Tanner said, rising and dusting the red dirt from the knees of his trousers, then pointing east, up the trail, "then let's see if we can bust 'em up a little and make 'em pay for leaving these nice maps and this good scoop with some hapless little snuffy in the rear."

Tanner again glanced at Flanagan and winked.

As Tanner folded the maps away and then made ready to radio his findings to headquarters, Riordan inconspicuously leaned toward Flanagan and whispered out of the side of his mouth, "What the hell does 'hapless' mean?"

"Standby for the artillery," Tanner called sharply.

Flanagan, Wenrick, and the others took up positions off the trail. Soon the dull thud of the first two 105mm howitzer rounds being fired from a nearby Marine artillery fire base could be heard. Flanagan listened as the rounds shrieked overhead with a sound resembling that of a large sheet tearing, until the shells impacted up the trail with two deep, successive crunches. He then heard the uplifted dirt and jungle debris as it cascaded back down through the trees.

Flanagan overheard Tanner shout, "Follow 'em on up the trail," to the nearby forward observer. Over the next five minutes, Flanagan counted nearly two-dozen explosions as he lay face down in the stench of the rotting foliage a few meters off the path. He silently worried about a mistake—the short round that might land in the midst of the friendly position and blast him and his fellow Marines into little more than a pink mist. Thank God it didn't happen often, but then again there were lots of rounds fired in-country, *lots*, and the fog of combat inevitably raised the odds that one would stray off its course. And it was much worse with the air-delivered stuff. Napalm was horribly unforgiving, and the red-orange-black inferno played to every man's most deeply hidden fears.

Proper skin care can sometimes be a bitch in this part of the world, Flanagan thought as he raised his head enough to see a large brownish-black beetle crawl across his hand. He started to grin but then felt his front teeth sticking to his upper lip. His head ached again, and he wondered if it might be caused by the arduous physical and emotional strain he was constantly enduring. Maybe it's caused by some strange allergy or some peculiar infection from some godawful Asian plight. Or maybe, he thought, it's because he's scared one-third to death over what the other two-thirds might be like if and when he and a chunk of Russian steel meet in the final act that sends him home in one of those silver metal containers he'd often seen lined up on the runway in Da Nang.

It was a struggle beyond belief, he pondered. Survival in Vietnam was unlike anything he could've ever conjured up in even his wildest imagination. No amount of training could have ever prepared him for what it was actually like, or what he knew it would be like over the next seven months. He was good at his job—he'd already received the Bronze Star for his intrepid leadership during which his platoon had torn into and defeated a significantly larger enemy force. And he had the respect of his troops and fellow officers. He knew that other junior officers looked to him for guidance, and his opinion was often sought on a variety of topics. But he struggled in the field as did everyone else. He got bone tired, hungry, thirsty, hot, cold, irritable, horny, homesick, and scared stiff, sometimes all within the span of an hour. Death, misery, and suffering were all around him, like the dense jungle that enshrouded him, and he knew he was always only a breath away from eternity.

Die you Marxist assholes, Flanagan thought with a surge of hormonal aggression. It really *was* him or me, he reminded himself once again. This is Vietnam, where the Marines had trained him to come and fight; where killing was the mission and bodies were the scorecard. It was early January, 1968, the date or day of the week of which he was uncertain. But if he could make it to August, he knew, August 14th to be exact, then his tour would be completed. If he was to make it through his thirteen-months of combat duty and wake up to his Rotation Date and get back home again to Chicago, alive and with everything attached and in good working order, then it was the other guy who would have to do the dying for *his* country. Not just today, but the next day and the day after that and every day thereafter until he was finally on board the Freedom Bird and headed back to The World. His mission was to survive, to live long enough in this nightmare of a place by killing the other guy with better efficiency than the other guy could do in return. He reminded himself again to concentrate on just one hour at a time, knowing that those hours would accumulate into days and those days into weeks and eventually into months. And then finally, *finally*, he'd wake up one morning and go the hell home.

No sooner had the artillery barrage lifted when scattered small-arms fire broke out at the tail of the column, to the west. "Dammit!" Flanagan mumbled under his breath. "They're trying to pinch us on both ends."

"Keep shelling the same position," shouted Capt. Tanner to the nearby forward observer as the CO calmly stood up to get his bearings under the watchful eyes of Flanagan and the others nearby. "Seal this east flank and keep 'em off me while I get a handle on the other end."

Under Tanner's orders, Flanagan immediately moved his platoon off the trail and deployed to the north. By the time he had his Marines in place, no more than one-hundred meters from the trail, the firing ceased as the enemy seemed to evaporate into the silent jungle. The short firefight had left two additional friendly wounded, and a blood trail left behind by the NVA.

Flanagan and his men waited as twenty minutes of steady artillery pounding discouraged any further enemy movement. Once the fire was lifted, Flanagan placed his platoon on the point of the company and moved without incident several hundred meters to the east to an area suitable for a landing zone.

After a Marine CH-46 chopper had come in late afternoon to retrieve the wounded, Tom Flanagan, helmetless but with his flak jacket still wrapped around his torso, sat alone in the bottom of a freshly dug fighting hole. It was dusk, and the evening air was damp and still. Flanagan's platoon was spread out and positioned inside a line of trees to the north of the clearing. He leaned back and relaxed as he cooked his C-ration meal of beans and franks—the first time he'd had hot food in three days, and while it was still only C-rats, it was nonetheless hot, and hot almost always meant better.

Lt. Kevin Riordan, chow in hand, walked up to Flanagan's position and peered into the hole. Riordan was short and stubby, with thinning dark hair and the thick chest and heavy arms of a weightlifter. Flanagan glanced up at his friend and Basic School classmate and motioned him down.

They sat beneath the ground surface amid the odors of freshly dug earth, hot C-rations, and unbathed infantrymen. Flanagan's radio operator, Wenrick, with whom he shared the hole, was elsewhere visiting a buddy.

"Heard anything from Chicago lately?" Riordan asked as he began heating his own meal.

"Only that my baby brother's freshman year in college is already a bummer, and my kid sister's in D.C. working with an ad agency and living in sin with a dipshit, pussy lawyer student."

Riordan frowned. "Bet you're crazy about that."

"You bet I am," Flanagan said with a frown. "I can't think of my sister as anything but a colossal failure now. She's wasting her life living with this spineless ass and trying to stop a war she knows nothing about but thinks she understands better than everyone else, including those who are deciding on the policies and those of us who are actually fighting these little Commie bastards. She thinks it's a bad war serving a bad purpose; therefore, by extension, anyone involved in its conduct must also be bad. She's always had strong opinions about the things she really cares about—both of us are alike there—but this friggin' war has shown a side of her that I have a hard time recognizing. She now thinks I'm a complete warmongering asshole and she's convinced that this entire Vietnam episode is going to wreck the country. And she believes in her gut that the people who share her convictions are the only ones who can save us, thank God. It's hard to imagine that she and I sprang forth from the same parents. She turned on me like a mongoose the day I told her that I'd joined the Marine Corps, and we haven't passed a civil sentence between us since."

"And I'll bet she knows her boyfriend isn't your favorite person, right?" Riordan asked.

Flanagan grinned slightly. "I've hinted at that, yeah."

They both laughed.

"What do your parents think?" asked Riordan.

"Of what?"

"Of you being a Marine and her being a protestor, and splitting the family apart?"

Flanagan sighed. "They don't know *what* to think. And they don't dare take one side or the other, at least not where it's apparent to Kate or myself. I think they're like a lot of others nowadays—they just wish this whole Vietnam thing would somehow vanish into thin air. Just wake up one morning and it's peace on earth and goodwill toward men, even toward the friggin' Communists. But they also know that it won't go away, and that their son and daughter will likely be at odds over this for a long time to come."

"My guess is the whole *country* will be at odds over this for a long time to come," added Riordan.

Flanagan sighed again and shook his head in resignation. "Yeah, you're probably right."

"What about Jill? Any word from her lately?" Riordan asked.

Flanagan tensed slightly. Jill Rohrbach, the middle of three daughters from a loving, tight-knit, southern Wisconsin farming family, had been the love of Flanagan's life, and to whom he had nearly proposed marriage. Blonde, blue-eyed, poised beyond her years and smart enough for ongoing academic honors, Jill was intent upon a career as a public accountant. The German-American beauty queen had fallen for the baseball-hero Flanagan while both were in their junior year at Northwestern. For well over a year they were inseparable, and their love for each other seemed deep and genuine. Flanagan had purchased Jill's engagement ring and was planning a proposal to her at third base on the baseball field, at night with their friends and his teammates conveniently out of sight. His plan suddenly unraveled when a seemingly innocuous disagreement somehow escalated into a nasty, bitter feud from which neither seemed willing to back down.

He and Jill failed to reconcile before Flanagan soon thereafter finished school and immediately reported to Marine officer's training at Quantico, Virginia. Still deeply in love with Jill, Flanagan blamed himself unmercifully for allowing the couple to divert out of their marriage trajectory after their future together had seemed so certain and so inevitable for so long.

"Nope, nothing," Flanagan answered, looking away.

"Does she have another guy now?" Riordan asked in a softer tone.

Flanagan shrugged self-consciously. "I don't know," he answered, his voice trailing off.

Both men shifted uncomfortably.

"Enough about me," Flanagan said finally. "What about you? Heard anything from Boston?"

Riordan drew a deep breath and paused for a moment. "My best buddy from the neighborhood got shot to pieces down in Dak To with an Army airborne outfit; he's been medevaced back to The World. My favorite professor in college has turned hippie radical. He's got a beard and hair to his ass and dresses like Jesus. Oh, and one of my former girlfriends—one of my favorites, too, a dark-haired beauty with huge knockers and a butt like a basketball—has up and married a soul brother. I almost shit a crab cake when I found out. How could she do that? How could she be so stupid?"

Flanagan stopped eating and stared at Riordan. "What the hell's the matter with you, man?" Flanagan asked in disgust.

Both officers suddenly heard the heavy footsteps of Wenrick as the young radioman approached on the run.

"There's a problem at LP Two, sir, to the north," Wenrick said breathlessly as he kneeled down and thrust the radio's handset down to Flanagan.

"This is Bayou Three. Advise your situation, over," Flanagan said calmly, though he could feel his pulse accelerating rapidly.

The only response the listening post offered in return was three successive clicks of the handset, indicating a need for silence. "I ain't *even* liking this," Flanagan mumbled. He immediately dispatched a runner to the command post to alert Capt. Tanner. With Sgt. Jankowski's assistance he put his platoon on full alert before he gathered a four-man fire team and, along with Wenrick, left the company perimeter for the listening post.

Flanagan quickly alerted the two Marines at the listening post that he was en route to their position. In addition to the potential presence of enemy soldiers, Flanagan tensed over the thought of his two fatigued and scared Marines up ahead with their fingers on the triggers of their weapons. It was barely light enough to distinguish movement, and clear identification would thus be made more difficult. By the time Flanagan and his five Marines had carefully covered the three-hundred meters to the listening post, they were bathed in sweat.

"There's been lots of movement, sir," the corporal whispered in a distinct Southern drawl when they finally linked up. "NVA regulars, and lots of 'em, on the trail and heading east. For sure there's a couple of rifle companies, maybe more. They've got crew-served weapons, bandoleers, rockets, full packs—just a whole shitpot full of 'em. And they may still be down there for all I know. God almighty damn, sir, I ain't never seen that many live damn gooks in one damn place in my whole damn life."

Flanagan attempted to calm himself with a deep breath as the perspiration dripped steadily from the tip of his nose. He strained to see ahead in the dark. There was nothing—no sights, no sounds, no vibrations. He briefly considered the possibility of pushing ahead, nearer to the trail, but the prospect of stumbling headlong into a battalion or, worse yet, maybe even a full regiment of NVA held little appeal.

"We'll stay put, right here. Pass the word: Full alert for the next two hours, then fifty percent until first light."

Flanagan overheard the corporal's slow exhaling before the young Marine crawled away and disappeared into the darkness.

Flanagan remained awake with half his Marines and all of the insects for most of the chilly night. The jungle could be a damp and cold place after sunset, especially to men already moist from exertion. When he finally did succumb to his fatigue only two hours prior to first light, Flanagan was awakened by Wenrick after barely an hour of sleep.

"Sir?" came the whisper, followed by two quick shoves on the shoulder. "You awake, sir?"

Flanagan's body jerked and stiffened. Instinctively he felt for the M-16 rifle beside him. "What? What's the scoop?" he whispered back hoarsely.

"They're on the move again," said Wenrick.

Flanagan sat up, braced by his elbows, and waited for his head to clear. He was cold and stiff. His mouth tasted of early morning slime, and his neck, shoulders, and back ached as if he'd been stuffed into a lunch pail to sleep. He noticed the stale odor of the rubber poncho he had used to ward off the chill, then the familiar stench of the jungle, and he was suddenly hit with the grim reality of his and his Marines' situation. The heavy-eyed fog quickly lifted from inside his head, like steam off a coffee cup.

The corporal belly-crawled to Flanagan's side. "Sir, they're no more than fifty meters to our right front," he said in a whisper. "I'm telling you this place is shitty with gooks, Lieutenant."

"Everybody awake?" asked Flanagan.

"Yessir."

Flanagan wiped at his face with a dirty hand, then took a deep breath and glanced out into the dark jungle. "What the hell's going on here, Corporal?"

"Wish to hell I knew, sir."

"How close can we get?"

This time it was the corporal who took the long, deep breath. "Close as you want, sir, I guess."

"Then let's move. You and me and Wenrick, and the rest stay here."

Before leaving the position, Flanagan crawled around to each man, and to each man his whispered message was identical. "Listen up: Nobody moves, sleeps, smokes, talks, or farts, or it's your ass and my ass and everybody's ass. There's a blue friggin' horde of 'em just up ahead, so for crissakes don't do anything to stir 'em up. And if we somehow get discovered and you hear firing ahead, hold your own fire until you see us or hear us, then move up to cover us coming back into the position. As soon as we're all in again, we'll *didi mau* back the same way we came."

Each man acknowledged his understanding.

Flanagan followed the corporal as the three Marines crawled out slowly, carefully, to a point where the NVA soldiers could be heard as they moved on the trail, some sixty feet ahead. By the time Flanagan and his Marines were in place, wide-eyed with pounding hearts and a trepidation that grabbed at and squeezed hard at their innards, there was just enough light to see the outline of the enemy troops through the thick undergrowth. Flanagan strained to see as the uniformed NVA unit moved single-file along the narrow path, their weapons slung, their pith helmets and full packs camouflaged with foliage. They were moving west to east, briskly, with good discipline and interval. The thick jungle mostly absorbed their footsteps, but what little noise emerged was the unmistakable sound of infantry on the move—serious soldiers embarked upon a serious mission.

The Marines stayed in position for a half-hour, waiting perhaps ten minutes after the final NVA soldier in the column had disappeared before Flanagan gave a hand signal and they began crawling back to their original position.

"Send it in the clear, Wenrick: Tell 'em we're on our way back to the perimeter, and that we've had more movement on the trail. Estimate an enemy battalion with full gear, on the march heading east, looking like they're trying to get somewhere in a hurry."

Wenrick immediately keyed the radio and sent the message. Word was radioed back to Flanagan to return to the company position immediately.

Something's up, Flanagan kept thinking on the way back to the perimeter. Something big. He'd just seen more NVA in the open than he'd ever seen before. He noticed the quick glances from his Marines as they attempted to measure their leader's reaction to the large enemy troop movements. They, too, knew that something treacherous was taking shape.

Though there had been conflicting reports for the past several weeks, each Marine knew with certainty that unusually large numbers of enemy soldiers were now in the same geographical space as they. And, with an inevitability that left each Marine with a baseball-sized knot in his belly, a confrontation of major proportions was developing with all due haste.

Flanagan felt a sudden chill.

"What the hell is going *on* here?" he mumbled under his breath again.

CHAPTER TWO
McLean, Virginia

Kate Flanagan, age twenty-three, sat quietly off to the side, listening and absorbing. More than one admiring glance had already come her way as she sat up straight and attentive, an occasional smile highlighting her striking facial features. She scanned the bright, warm living room that had been converted into an assembly hall, of sorts. There were more than a dozen people crowded together, all seated except one and often all talking at the same time. They ignored the occasional forays of two dogs—one a huge black Newfoundland named Brumus, the other a cocker spaniel called Freckles—and several small, pajama-clad Kennedy children chasing about in a whirlwind of giggles and barks. The haze of cigar smoke was thick, and several of the men held after dinner drinks of coffee or Irish whiskey (or both) up and away from the little feet and the marauding paws. At first Kate had been put off by the outward bedlam of it all, but the more she observed, the more she scrutinized the interactions of the participants, the more the entire setting seemed in perfect accord.

Kate watched as Robert F. Kennedy, the former Attorney General and current United States Senator from New York, turned and glanced over at the proceedings from where he stood across the room with a telephone to his ear. Kennedy had thus far said little, preferring instead to listen and ponder and occasionally ask a question as the debate carried on around him, almost as if he wasn't there.

She leaned forward with interest when her host began to speak.

"Look guys, hear me out on this one. I've been silent all evening, but I can't hold my tongue any longer or I'll choke on it. I've got only one thing to say, one thing only, and it's this: I swear to God that if Bob Kennedy's not occupying the White House in January of Nineteen Sixty Nine," the young staffer exclaimed, now wide-eyed with passion, "then we may as well throw up our hands and give up on this two-hundred year experiment with American-style democracy. And if we do that, if we fail to get him elected, then by God we should *all* walk to the gallows with a look of shame on our faces."

One person applauded and called out, "Here, here. A nice revolutionary touch, Dan."

Another raised a snifter of brandy into the air. "Sixteen-hundred Pennsylvania Avenue or the gallows. Has a nice democratic ring to it. Give me Kennedy or give me . . . "

Kate chuckled out loud.

Another more mellowed advisor called out, grinning, "Good grief, Dan. Sit down and have a cup of black coffee."

Things were buzzing at Bobby Kennedy's Hickory Hill estate. Kennedy still stood alone in a far corner of the room, head bowed, his white shirt wrinkled and unbuttoned at the collar, the telephone still affixed to the side of his face. He seemed to be straining to hear, turning away from the others, sometimes nodding or shrugging and sometimes offering a few words. He gestured occasionally and then ran his fingers through the hair that fell over onto his forehead. Mostly he remained composed and quiet as he listened to the steady stream on the other end, the source of which Kate had deduced to be his brother Teddy.

Ethel Kennedy occasionally popped into the room to offer a few suggestions or make a point or counterpoint, then just as quickly disappeared.

The arguments proceeded.

Pro: RFK's got to announce for the Presidency; McCarthy doesn't represent the poor, the disadvantaged; LBJ doesn't represent anyone anymore; someone has to end this terrible war; someone's got to bring the American people together again.

Con: RFK can't announce; LBJ's not as vulnerable as he might seem, especially given the power of the incumbency; it would be politically much more the wiser to wait until '72; Vietnam will likely dissipate under its own weight, but even if it doesn't, the country will be far more favorably inclined toward a Kennedy candidacy in 1972 than in 1968.

Dan Marinelli, age twenty-six, a full-time member of Bobby Kennedy's congressional staff, sipped from a coffee cup and then leaned over to whisper to the attractive young advertising professional he had invited to the meeting.

"Care for a little fresh air, Kate?"

Kate smiled and nodded. While she had never been easily awed, she had likewise never before witnessed such a scene or been in such prominent company. "Sure," she answered as she shook her red hair from her eyes and reached for her wool coat on the back of the chair.

They went out a nearby door, out onto the porch that was partially illuminated by the inside lights. The late-January night was brisk, and the fresh night air burned Kate's nostrils as she inhaled the first few breaths.

Dan lit a cigarette and took a long pull. Lean and angular at six-foot three, he ran his hand through his dark hair and turned to Kate. "Okay, tell me what you make of all this."

Kate folded her arms against her chest to ward off the stiff evening chill. Tall at five-foot eight, with the long, slender features of a dancer, she cut a striking figure with her shoulder-length red hair and her probing, dark-brown eyes that projected not only her propensity toward warmth and friendliness but also her seriousness and inability to suffer fools. "I've always been interested in the 'behind-the-scenes' stuff of national politics," she answered, her breath vaporizing in the air. "And I can say with complete certainty that this is all very, very fascinating."

Kate glanced up at the winking stars in the ink-black sky above. She wondered if their alignment favored another Kennedy candidacy, perhaps another Kennedy administration. Or, she mused, might there be something even more surprising, more unforeseen, or perhaps more ominous in the offing. She pondered briefly about how her Marine brother would react if he could see her now, visiting at the home of Robert Kennedy and listening to a high-level political-strategy discussion that involved many of Kennedy's closest advisers.

She smiled at the thought as she twisted a lock of red hair around her index finger. "I'm a little surprised they'd let you bring an outsider in when they're talking such heavy strategy," Kate said with a self-conscious grin.

"I told everyone you'll be with us soon, so it's no big deal," said Dan with a nonchalant shrug.

Kate's eyebrows quickly raised. "I beg your pardon?"

Dan grinned. "I told 'em to get used to seeing you around, that you were going to hire on and help us. That's why they're not worried. I've already cleared you. You're one of us. Sorta."

Kate stood in silence for a moment, her confusion evident.

"So, I suppose we should nail it down, right?" Dan pressed.

"Nail it down? Nail *what* down?"

"That you'll come to work for us. You will, won't you?"

Kate laughed. "No, Dan, I will not. I have a full-time job already. Remember?"

"I remember."

"And you still haven't told me how you managed to find out about me and get my name," said Kate.

"Look, I've gotten to know a lot of people in this town. I have a lot of sources, I really do. And so I asked a gentleman I greatly respect to give me the name of the best young ad pro around, and he immediately told me about you."

Kate gave him a sideways glance. "I've only known you a few days but I've already concluded that you're an incredibly accomplished liar, I swear."

"It's no lie, really. Now that I've met you, I can tell he knew exactly what he was talking about."

Kate shook her head in disbelief, suppressing a grin.

Dan shrugged. "Let's see now: Chicago native; Phi Beta Kappa with a degree in journalism from a small liberal arts college in central Illinois; the middle of three children; headstrong, independent, creative, insightful; a real, honest-to-goodness hotshot in a town full of hotshots and hotshot charlatans. How's that for a quick thumbnail sketch?"

20

Kate finally grinned. "Everything after the city, college, and family stuff is highly debatable, especially the 'hotshot' part."

"He's gonna go, Kate," Dan said, moving slightly closer and lowering his voice. "He's gonna do it, honest to God. And when he does, we're gonna need your talents. The country's gonna need your talents. The whole world's gonna need your talents."

Kate held out her hand to stop any further approaches. "A bit more dramatic than necessary, but I think I get your point. And maybe it's just me, but have you noticed there's nothing near a consensus in that room, from the people closest to him?"

"He'll go," Dan said confidently. "There's just no other solution. He's *got* to, and he damn well knows it."

"Oh?" Kate said as she blew into her cupped hands. "How can you be so sure?"

"I just know, that's all. Your fiancé Harold—"

"Everett."

"Yeah, Everett. He wants you to join him in Gene McCarthy's camp, right?"

"Correct."

"Please don't do that. We need you a helluva lot more than they do. We can win, Kate. Our guy can win," Dan said emphatically.

"So can McCarthy."

"Only if Johnson turns blue and falls over clutching his chest. And only if Bob stays out."

"Dan, you don't have a candidate yet. And I'm not leaving my job," she said firmly, pausing to measure his reaction. "So please, let's get back inside. It's freezing out here."

She turned and started back toward the door. Dan quickly crushed out his cigarette with his foot and followed after her.

"Kate, wait."

"Look," she said, slightly irritated, "I appreciate the invitation, I really do. And even though it's been an extremely interesting and invigorating evening, I'm not about to stop and start my professional life on a whim. It's a moot point, I'm afraid, and besides that, it's cold out here and I'm freezing my young—"

He reached for her, stopping her, then turned her toward him. He gently, tentatively took her hands in his, which she immediately pulled away.

"You know as well as I do what's at stake here," Dan said. "You've even got a member of your own family at risk."

Kate winced slightly. "Sorry, but I'm not seeing where my other family members fit into all this."

"I was in the Army in Vietnam just a year ago and I know from personal experience that this war's like a cancer. And it's spreading faster each day, each week. I saw how it's eating our country's young, and the sooner it ends, the better."

She took a step back. "Listen, here's the way I see it: McCarthy'll get us out of Vietnam, even if he does nothing else. And come to think of it, that'd be entirely enough for one measly little politician to accomplish. So there it is, Dan. There you have it. I'm glad I could clear that up for you tonight, although the setting is a bit ironic, I have to admit."

Dan Marinelli chuckled and shook his head in polite disagreement. "If McCarthy were to do well in the primaries," he said, again speaking in a soft, conspiratorial tone, "Johnson would then be exposed and weakened, and Bob could emerge out of the smoke and rescue the Democratic Party. Nixon's likely to be the Republican, and we know from before that he's beatable. Then it all comes down to winning the national election and then ending the war."

"That simple, huh?" Kate asked, her eyebrows arched.

"Not quite, but you see my larger point. It all reduces down to this: The country can't take another four years of Lyndon Baines Johnson. Period, exclamation point."

"What about those people inside?" Kate countered. "Some say now, some say later. Others say they're not sure. Even if he entered and won all the primaries, the opinion in there is still divided on whether he'd actually be elected. You told me yourself that the Senator's own brother is telling him to wait until Seventy Two, that LBJ will be reelected. His own brother!"

"Yeah, okay, but—"

"Yes, that's right," came the unmistakably rich Boston accent of Robert Francis Kennedy, walking up alongside wearing an unzipped leather flight jacket and holding a cup of hot steaming coffee.

Kate turned toward Kennedy. Even in the dim light his familiar face appeared tired, Kate thought, as if he were aging beyond his forty-two years.

"My brother told me again, too, just now," Kennedy said. "He's very convincing, I have to say. And very consistent. I certainly know where he stands, and I suppose I have some idea on where you stand, Dan. Perhaps you have an opinion on all of this, Miss Flanagan. Care to make a contribution to this friendly quarrel?"

It suddenly struck Kate that she was standing face to face with the reigning member of America's First Family—the familiar toothy grin, the hooded blue eyes, the shock of hair, the casual stance with one hand thrust into the pocket of his trousers—and when she finally opened her mouth to speak, nothing came out.

Bobby Kennedy immediately raised his hand slightly, as if to shrug off the question. "Listen, I'm glad you could join us tonight. I don't know how much good any of this has done you," he said, pausing and then grinning boyishly before adding, "I'm not even certain how much good it's done me, but I'm glad you could stop in and be with us. I hope you'll come back and visit again."

Dan cleared his throat. "I was just trying to convince Miss Flanagan to join the staff, Senator. She's the one I told you about earlier, the one who works for the D.C. ad agency and came so highly recommended. We could sure use her to help get our message out."

"Yes, I remember. And are you having any success?"

"Modest, at this point. But there's hope," said Dan.

"Yes, well, I suppose there's always hope."

There was an awkward moment of silence before Kate suddenly blurted out, "So, are you gonna become President of the United States?"

Dan Marinelli swallowed hard; Bobby Kennedy grinned self-consciously; and in spite of the cold, Kate Flanagan was suddenly tingling with warmth and flushed with embarrassment. All she could hear in her head was the sound of her own voice, repeating the question she now wished she could somehow reel back into her possession.

"Only if I can't become Emperor of Rome, I suppose," Kennedy said, smiling. "I wish it were that easy."

Kennedy finally turned and walked slowly back toward the door. He paused before stepping inside and turned back toward the pair, another grin uplifting his face. "And they call *me* blunt and ruthless," he called out. "If you should decide to join us, Kate, and I hope you do, then my guess is you'll fit right in."

* * *

Dan Marinelli drove Kate back to the fashionable Georgetown townhouse she shared with her law-student fiancé.

"God, I can't believe I said that to him," Kate mumbled in disgust when Dan pulled over at her address. "The only full sentence I spoke to him all evening, and it had to come out like that. I should've just kept my big mouth shut."

Dan laughed as he slid the blue Camaro's floor shift into park. "Don't think anything of it. He loved it."

"Well, it doesn't matter," Kate said as she reached for the door handle.

"Hey, hold on. What do you mean, it doesn't matter?" Dan asked.

"It doesn't matter because I won't be changing jobs," Kate said firmly.

"Why not?"

Kate took a deep breath and exhaled slowly. "I have a job, Dan. We've been over all of that. And besides, I—"

Dan reached across for her hand.

"—also have a fiancé," she said in an aggravated tone, avoiding his touch.

24

Dan shrugged. "I hope he knows how lucky he is."

Kate reached for the door handle. "Thank you for such a memorable evening, but I really must be going."

"Wait," he said, touching her arm. "Tell me about your brother in the Marines."

"What about him?" she asked after a brief silence.

"Tell me where he is in Vietnam; tell me what he's like; tell me what he's written to you about what he's doing and seeing over there."

Kate gave a resigned sigh and shook her head. "I'm afraid we don't communicate a lot."

"No? Why not?"

"Because," Kate answered defensively, "my older brother and I aren't in contact anymore. We disagree on a lot of things, on *most* things, and it's gotten worse over the last couple of years."

"Yeah? Like what?" Dan pressed.

"Like the war," Kate answered quickly.

Dan nodded but otherwise remained quiet.

Kate's expression hardened. "I've lost a lot of the admiration I used to have for him. He's mocked me and my beliefs. He's questioned my sincerity, my motives. He takes issue with just about everyone and everything in my life. I've all but given up on our ever having a normal relationship again."

Dan remained silent.

"It's sad, but my brother and I have almost nothing in common anymore."

"Have you been open to listening to him?" Dan asked after pausing.

"Of course. I just remember that he couldn't wait to tell me he'd volunteered for the Marines so he could get overseas and 'blow away some gooks' and get the war over. He was so arrogant about it, so cocky. He knew my feelings about the war, and he rubbed it in my face all the harder. Told me I must be a 'goddamned pinko commie' when he found out that Everett and I took part in the protests at the White House and the Pentagon." She sighed. "This was the same Tommy that I'd always looked up

25

to—the athletic star and the academic star and the one all the guys wanted to be like and all the girls wanted to be with. He was the one who could fill up a room just by walking into it. He was my big brother, my protector, my standard of excellence that I knew I'd always have a hard time meeting, no matter how hard I tried. But now, Tommy seems like the world's biggest asshole to me."

"How does Tommy get along with your fiancé?" Dan asked tentatively.

Their eyes met only briefly before Kate looked away. After a pause, she cleared her throat and turned to face him.

"Let's make sure we understand what's happened here tonight, Dan. It's important to me that you know how to interpret all of this."

Dan gave a confused look. "Interpret?"

"Yes, interpret. And here are the specifics. Number one: I have nothing further to say about my relationship with my brother, or for that matter about my brother's relationship with anyone else. Number two: I have no intention of leaving the agency. I have a good job and a good future with a good firm, and I don't want you to think that I'm anything but happy with what I'm doing with my professional life. Number three: I'm engaged to be married, and I don't want you to think that I'm anything but perfectly happy with *that* part of my life, too. And number four: Even though we've known each other only a few short days, I appreciate your interest in me, I really do, although I'm not at all sure whether it's personal or professional, which is neither here nor there. But, based on what I've just explained and what I'm certain a man with your great intuitive powers can read between the lines, I suppose the proper conclusion would be that there's very little need for you to contact me again."

Kate heard Dan's sigh, then glanced over and saw an expression of disbelief pulling down on his face.

"My God, I think you've just told me to take a hike," he said in a pained voice.

Kate looked away.

"Well?" he asked.

"Well what?"

"Is my 'interpretation' correct?"

"Your words, Dan. Not mine."

"Dammit, you can help us, Kate. You can make a difference and be part of something bigger than either of us. And you'd be doing your brother and a bunch of others like him a world of good, too. And I can make that happen for you bright and early tomorrow morning."

Kate stared ahead and said nothing. She thought about reaching then and there for the door knob and abruptly ending the conversation, but she remained seated.

"You may never again have a chance like this the rest of your life," he continued. "Twenty years from now you'll look back on this time and place and kick yourself if you let this opportunity get away. We've got exactly the right man at exactly the right moment in this country's history. Everything he's ever done in his entire life has prepared him for this. He'll use his experience and his insight and his capacity to grow, and he'll provide us with the leadership this country desperately needs. It's our job to help him get to the Oval Office. He'll do the rest once he's there. You can be part of something that can change the world, Kate. *And as an insider*, for crying out loud! So for God's sake don't let this slip away."

She turned and faced him, but still said nothing.

"When I came back to Brooklyn from the Army last year, I honestly didn't know *what* the hell I'd do. I really thought that my best moments had already passed, that the rest of my life would be spent just going through the motions. Can you believe that? I'm only twenty-five and yet I'm thinking that maybe I've peaked as a productive human being. But when I got lucky and eventually hired on with Bob's senatorial staff, I knew right then and there that my life was really just beginning, that now I'd be able to hit a lick that would end up making a difference, and probably a very big difference."

Dan grinned, but Kate sat expressionless.

"And what you mentioned earlier about not being sure whother my interest was personal or professional, well, let me assure you that I'm greatly interested in what you can do to help us advance our political agenda," he said, pausing and then adding in a softer voice, "and honestly, the fact that you're a beautiful, intelligent, alluring woman is something that I've hardly noticed."

Try as she might, Kate couldn't hide her smile.

"So, Miss Kate Flanagan, when can we meet for lunch and discuss your job change?"

Kate laughed. "I've already given you the answer. Besides, I'm going to Chicago to visit with my family for a few days."

"Great. It'll give you some time to get away and think about things. Chicago's a terrific town, and a good Kennedy town, to boot. And please be sure to give your family my regards."

"I'll be sure and do that," Kate said as she opened the car door.

Dan smiled. "Can I walk you to the door?"

"Nope. That won't be necessary."

He leaned toward her, and as he did he reached for her hand, taking it and kissing it gently. "You've been absolutely wonderful company tonight. *Buona notte,* sweet Katherine. I'll be in touch soon."

CHAPTER THREE
Near Phu Bai, South Vietnam

Tom Flanagan was tapped softly on his lower leg after a short, deep, one-hour nap. He opened his eyes and tried to focus, then turned slightly to see who was standing nearby. Flanagan had been out all night on an ambush patrol, the results of which had been nothing more than the usual edginess, blackness, and biting insects. The steady stream of unsettling jungle noises had contributed to the utter exhaustion he'd felt when the welcomed dawn had finally broken.

"Sorry to have to wake you, sir, but the Skipper wants to see you pronto," said Capt. Tanner's radio operator, a skinny lance corporal named Bohannon who was leaning down at the foot of the impromptu poncho shelter.

"What's up?" Flanagan asked.

"I dunno, sir. Alls I was told was to go find Lieutenant Flanagan and tell him the Skipper wants him at the command post ASAP."

Flanagan sat up and adjusted his eyes to the light. It was just past noon in the Fox Company position about a kilometer southeast of Phu Bai, along the western banks of the Song Giang River. It had rained earlier, and Flanagan's utilities were still damp from the downpour. At least now he didn't stink as badly, he reasoned as he yawned and stretched and caught a quick sniff. But the stink never fully went away out here, he knew. There was a letter nearby from his mother, explaining, among other family particulars, how sister Kate had been approached by Robert Kennedy's people about hiring on with them. He'd felt the urge to write back and suggest to his mother that Kate was beyond repair, that she had become a long lost lamb searching for the bright lights, that faith healing or folk singing or maybe even Hollywood itself would probably find its way onto her agenda at some point. Sleep and now the summons from the CP had dulled his impulse to respond, however, and instead he folded the letter away and stuffed it into his pack. He pulled on his boots, grabbed his M-16 rifle, and made his way to the cleared area in the trees where Capt. Tanner had established his command post.

Flanagan found the CO sitting on an ammo crate, writing a letter and drinking a cup of coffee from a green C-ration can. "You wanted to see me, Skipper?" he asked as he propped his weapon against a tree.

Capt. Tanner motioned for Flanagan to take a seat on the ground alongside. "Yeah. I've got a proposal for you."

Flanagan sat down with his legs crossed. "You're gonna cut my hair and send me to Vietnam, right?" he asked, stifling a yawn.

"No," said Tanner, chuckling. "Someone's already beaten me to it. What I have is a lot more distinguished."

Flanagan waited patiently for Tanner to finish with his letter. He greatly admired Tanner, and saw in him everything a Marine officer should be. Tanner was tough, fair, brave, intelligent, and both technically and tactically sound in his profession of arms. He had come to trust the captain, trust him with his own life and the lives of his Marines, and strove every day to become more like him. Tanner's easy Southern manner belied the steel beneath the surface, and Flanagan had yet to see his CO in a situation where Tanner seemed anything but in complete control. Tanner was easily the best Marine with whom he'd ever come into contact, as good as any Marine in the Corps, he was certain.

"I'll get right to the point, Tom," Tanner said, tossing the letter aside and turning his attention to Flanagan. "There's a spot open on the Battalion S-3 staff, and the Operations people have expressed an interest in you. The major himself asked me if you were available, and since you're the senior platoon leader in the company—you're just barely senior to Kevin Riordan—then I'll ask you if you'd like to leave Fox Company and join the S-3 shop."

Flanagan's expression revealed his complete surprise. "Why me, sir?"

Tanner smiled. "You sure as hell must've done something to impress Major O'Leary. Or maybe it's just you Irish types sticking together. Whatever the case, it's clear to me they'd like to have you on board. You're highly regarded throughout the entire battalion, Lieutenant, so I'm not surprised that people are interested in you."

Flanagan quickly tried to recall what he might have said or done that would've come to the S-3's attention, but nothing specific came to mind. He could only speculate that since Major O'Leary read all the after-action reports of the 2nd Battalion units, he'd likely come across Flanagan's name in a Fox Company report or during a meeting of the battalion CO's staff. "I don't know what to say, sir. I'm happy commanding a platoon in Fox Company, and I sure as hell like working for you. But I'm flattered that the major and his people would ask about me. What would you do, Skipper, if you were in my position?"

Tanner glanced quickly at Flanagan and then looked away. "Remember, I'm a grunt commander—a lifer, at that—so I'm not sure you should use me as the most objective source of guidance on this. It basically all comes down to the choice of either staying in the field as a platoon leader, or going to battalion as a staff officer. You'll be working in Operations, coordinating missions and supporting fires and all that good stuff. If you want out of the bush, then here's your chance. All you've got to do is say yes, simple as that. The orders will be cut today and you'll be on your way. You've got to decide here and now if this is something you'd like to do."

Flanagan hesitated. His chances of surviving, he clearly knew, would be improved by taking the staff billet. Vietnam was everywhere a dangerous place, but no place more so than out in the bush with the daily grind of the grunts.

"You've got, what? Seven months left on your tour?" Tanner asked.

"That's affirmative, sir."

Tanner nodded and stared at Flanagan for a brief moment. "You're damn good at your job, Tom. And I think you have the potential to get a helluva lot better. You know your Marines, and they know you, and by now they've gotten accustomed to your leadership style. I don't know what the future holds for the conduct of this war, but I've got a feeling in my gut that all hell's about to break loose. It's hard to explain, but I've just got a feeling that the status quo around here is about to be turned upside down. And if things do change, if the NVA really are massing for a major offensive, then the best place for the best leaders will be out here in the boonies where the ass-kicking takes place. Don't ever confuse the low opinion some people have of the infantry with the lack of importance of its mission. Wars have always been, and always will be, decided in the end by the little green man who jumps in the hole and *kills* the enemy bastards. When everything is said and done, history tells us that the end will be decided on the ground with the grunts at close range. When the bad guy sees that the U. S. Marine maneuvering toward him will soon enough fire a burst into his cranium, then things become more negotiable. You see what I mean?"

"Yes sir, I do," Flanagan said with a nod.

"If the leadership in infantry units is bad, then Marines die. It's a universal truth. But when it's good, when Marines are well led, then they're the most effective fighters this world has ever witnessed. Another universal truth. You agree?"

"I agree, sir," Flanagan said with another nod.

"So you can't have one without the other. Axiomatic, as we highly educated assholes are fond of saying. As a company commander, if I expect to field a combat-effective rifle company, then I myself have to be damn good and I've got to have damn good platoon leaders and squad leaders and fire-team leaders— hell, good *leaders*. Otherwise, Charlie's gonna quickly notice our shortcomings and let us know in his own indelicate style just what bad things come to units that don't have their shit together. Right?"

"Right, Skipper."

"And if we're gonna end this war with a victory in the field, then it'll be done with grunts, by grunts. And when it's all over, the grunts that are left standing go home and live to fight another day."

Flanagan nodded once again.

"On the other hand," Tanner said, his tone softening as he glanced down at his fingernails, "I certainly wouldn't blame a man if he had a chance to do some good, interesting staff work and serve with a group of excellent Marines. And hell, it wouldn't be like you were going off to the rear and joining up with the friggin' finance pussys or something. You'd still be assigned to an infantry battalion, and you'd have a chance to learn about a lot of good stuff, for sure. And Major O'Leary's one squared-away Marine, no doubt about it. No sir, I wouldn't blame a man for jumping on a chance like this one."

Tanner paused for a moment, rubbing his chin and then slapping at an insect crawling across the leg of his trousers.

"This is all on the level, right sir? You're not kidding or anything like that?" Flanagan asked in a tentative tone.

"Of course not," Tanner replied with slight irritation.

Flanagan paused briefly and then suddenly burst out in loud laughter.

Tanner scowled. "Just what the hell's so funny, Lieutenant?"

"May I speak openly, sir?"

Tanner paused briefly, then answered, "You may, yes."

Flanagan, still grinning, cleared his throat. "I just want to compliment you on the truly outstanding hustle you just laid on me. It was by any objective measure a real work of art, sir."

"Hustle? Hell, I was just giving you the benefit of my wisdom and experience," said Tanner, trying hard to suppress a grin. "I can see now that it's all fallen on deaf ears."

"No, sir, it didn't fall on deaf ears, I assure you. And I appreciate knowing that you want me to stay in Fox Company," Flanagan said.

"That's affirmative, I want you here. But the matter also involves someone senior to me who wants you, too. And since you can't serve two commanders, you're gonna have to make a choice. And you have to choose now. So what's it gonna be?"

A thousand different images raced across Flanagan's mind, including one with the metal caskets he'd often seen lined up on the Da Nang tarmac. When he looked away for a moment and then glanced back at Tanner, the CO was smiling, almost laughing.

"Having a hard time with this?" asked Tanner.

Flanagan took a deep breath and nodded. "It's tempting, sir, I have to admit. But I've gotta ask you again, Skipper. You've got a wife and two kids back home, and if a billet like this opened up and the officer-in-charge was asking for you by name, would you give up your command and take it?"

Tanner frowned and took a sip of coffee. "Hell no," he growled, "but I've already told you that in this case I'm not objective worth a damn."

"And you're convinced the gooks are about to stir things up?"

"I am, yes," Tanner said confidently as he tossed out the remainder of the coffee from the cup. "And when it happens, it'll be a damned interesting time to be a troop leader in Fox Company, 2nd Battalion, 5th Marines."

Tanner grabbed a nearby canteen and rinsed out the coffee cup. He then got up and reached for his pack and, after a moment of searching its thick contents, held up a pint bottle of fine Tennessee whiskey. He poured a shot into the tin cup and presented it to Flanagan. "Here," he said, still grinning, "we'll have a little celebration drink."

"Celebrating what, Skipper?" said the confused Flanagan as he accepted the drink.

"Your decision, what else?"

"But I haven't made a decision yet."

"Then make it now," Tanner ordered, holding the bottle. "Battalion needs to know ASAP. And so do I."

Again the images paraded across Flanagan's mind—his family, his friends, Jill Rohrbach, the girl he'd almost married, his classmates, his parish priest back home, his favorite teacher. Then there was the smell of the hot dogs at Wrigley, the chilly air-conditioning and the sticky floors of his neighborhood movie house, the always stirring sight of the deep blue waters of Lake

Michigan, the laughter of his family at the dinner table. There was *life* on the other side of this living hell, and he damn well wanted to see it, smell it, and touch it all again. Then he saw in his mind's eye the faces of his Marines, heard their voices and laughter, and remembered their unimaginable, unselfish bravery in action. Together they had walked long distances, been parched by the interminable heat, kept wide-eyed awake at night, been rained on, shot at, gone days without food and long hours without water. They had grieved together when some had fallen. Together they had comforted those who had been told in terse letters from girlfriends that the romance had ended. And each had shaken the hand of a close buddy going home, with an unspoken brotherly love so intense that only men bonded by such inexpressible common experience could ever hope to understand. Flanagan had signed on to do his duty, and then he had decided to command Marines. He had his command, had his Marines, and if what Capt. Tanner said about the escalation of the war turned out to be true, then his Marines—*his* Marines—would be left with another leader.

"Thanks for the offer, Skipper," said Flanagan, feeling a strange sense of relief. "And please pass along my thanks to Major O'Leary. But I'm staying right here," he declared with a point toward the ground he was occupying.

Tanner moved forward and poured another shot into Flanagan's cup. "In that case, Lieutenant, you'll have the pleasure of a full load."

Flanagan nodded and held his cup toward Tanner. "Nothing quite as good as being in the bush with a full load."

"To Fox Company," offered the smiling Tanner.

"To Fox Company," answered Flanagan.

* * *

"You did *what*?" Lt. Kevin Riordan shrieked when he had listened to Flanagan's account of his meeting with Tanner.

"I turned it down," Flanagan said as he sat on the ground with Riordan, away from the nearest of their Marines. "I don't want to be stuck back there in S-3 sticking colored pins in a goddamn map and reading reports of what my old platoon was doing. That's not me. Besides, Skipper says he thinks the shit's about to hit the fan, and I want to be out here when it happens."

Riordan gave a disgusted look. "You're friggin' crazy, man. You could've split from out here and lived to tell about it. If they come at me with the same offer, all you're gonna see is assholes and elbows, I swear to God."

Flanagan turned and looked squarely at Riordan. "It's not gonna be you, Kevin. The Skipper said he didn't plan on it being anyone else in Fox Company if I didn't want it."

Riordan's expression immediately soured. "Those bastards," Riordan said with a taut jaw. "I'll go to the Skipper myself and find out what the hell's going on."

"Might not do you any good to go and make an ass of yourself, pal."

"Why? What the hell are they gonna do to me? Cut my hair and send me out with the friggin' grunts?" Riordan said in disgust.

Flanagan chuckled.

"Dammit," said Riordan, disgusted. "Why the hell wouldn't they give me a crack at it? I deserve it. I rate it the same as you. Why wouldn't they make me the same offer?"

"I don't know. He didn't tell me why."

"If they'd made me the same offer, I'd be out of here without so much as a 'kiss my ass,' I guarantee it."

"I just hope I'm doing the right thing," Flanagan said with a loud sigh.

"The right thing? Damn! You're friggin' looney, man. Looney! Hell, you wouldn't know the 'right thing' if it raised up and bit you on the head of the dick, I swear."

Flanagan laughed. "If I get zapped, then it's a great comfort to know you'll be standing over my corpse calling me 'looney' and telling me I could've avoided the whole thing."

"And I'll say it with a straight face and a clear conscience, I shit you not."

After several moments of silence, Flanagan picked up a small twig and tossed it at Riordan's leg, saying softly, "You wouldn't leave either, you lying piece of dung. I've known you long enough to know you better than that. I know how you whine when you're in garrison, and I know how solid you are out in the bush. You can't shit me and get away with it. We go back too far."

"I *would've* left, too. You don't know, man. You just don't know," Riordan said in a soft tone, looking away and sighing. "We're gonna get our asses shot off out here, Tom. It's a simple matter of probability because there are *way* too many bullets and shells and rockets chasing *far* too few grunts. I can feel it in my gut, man. There's a world of hurt out here, everywhere you go. Why hell, the life expectancy of a goddamn grunt lieutenant in the goddamn Marine Corps in goddamn Vietnam is roughly the same as that of a friggin' bird flying three feet off the pavement on a Massachusetts freeway. It's just a matter of time before all that's gonna be left of either of us are a few measly feathers and a greasy pink stain on the goddamn deck."

Flanagan winced, then chuckled at the description. "Oh three forever," he said in reference to the Marine Corps designation of 03 for the infantry occupational specialty.

"Yeah, right. Oh three for friggin' ever," said Riordan with a disgusted shake of his head.

Suddenly there was shouting behind them, and they both stiffened when they heard their names being called.

"Over here," Flanagan called loudly,

One of Riordan's squad leaders came at them on the run. "They need both of you at the CP, sirs. Something about some shit coming down."

"Where?" Riordan asked.

"Don't know for sure, Lieutenant. Only word I got was that the radios were humming to beat all hell and that Charlie was hitting several places on further up the river."

Flanagan glanced quickly at Riordan and caught his friend's eye for a split second before they both got up and sprinted toward the CP.

CHAPTER FOUR
Chicago

John and Elaine Flanagan welcomed their daughter Kate for a long-weekend visit to their suburban Arlington Heights home. As they took their dinner in front of the new Zenith color-console television, Kate heard the complaints of the middle-aged couple about how they were still adjusting to having the big split-level house all to themselves. Kate's younger brother, Chris, had gone off to college in Iowa and thus far had shown little inclination to come home for a visit. Kate noticed that her mother, Elaine, a New England native and a registered nurse who practiced in a nearby suburban Chicago hospital, clearly seemed more preoccupied and tense than when she'd last visited. Elaine's red hair was cut short and parted in the middle, and her face seemed thinner and more deeply lined now. On the other hand, her father, John, a native Chicagoan and a professor of American history at the downtown campus of a large state university, still seemed as stoic as ever. John's dark hair was now graying around the temples, but otherwise the Navy veteran of World War II still looked his usual self to Kate.

Kate glanced around at the familiar surroundings—the furnishings, the layout of the room, the soft colors, her father in his favorite easy chair—and then noticed again the house's own signature odor of mothballs, furniture polish, and oak logs burning, one that she was certain she could select out of a lineup of a million others. She missed her parents' home, much as she had when she'd left for college, as she had when she had first left for Washington, D.C., and a career in advertising. And as long as her parents remained here, she had concluded, she would always feel like a little girl again when she came back to the house and all the many memories it kept safely on deposit for her.

Kate settled back with her parents and their roast-beef dinner as the Friday night news coverage of the war's major events unfolded. She and her mom sat together on the large sofa, while John, wearing his usual gray cardigan sweater, was ensconced nearby in his well-worn recliner. Kate could glance out the window and see the high winds and snow flurries as the January temperatures dipped into the teens. A warm fire crackled in the fireplace, and Walter Cronkite, with his fatherly tone and venerable manner, the ubiquitous teletype in the background, was staring straight into the Flanagans' living room as he broadcast the *CBS Evening News.*

And there was lots of it.

Kate listened to the account of the 90-ton electronic intelligence ship *Pueblo*, with its U.S. Navy crew of 83, having been seized several days earlier by the North Koreans for what the Communists claimed was an intrusion into their 12-mile territorial waters, and for the Navy's carrying out of alleged "hostile acts." Shots had been fired from North Korean gunboats, and at least one U.S. sailor was feared dead. The ship had apparently been taken to Wansan in North Korea, where the American crew had disappeared into a perilous, foreboding captivity.

President Johnson, meanwhile, was calling up 14,000 reservists.

"My God!" gasped Elaine. "Another Asian war? That's all we need."

John held up his hand to silence his wife as Cronkite continued. A grim-faced Arthur Goldberg, the U.S. Ambassador to the United Nations, was asking for an urgent meeting of the U.N. Security Council despite the fact that North Korea was not a United Nations member.

"Good for you, Artie," Elaine declared. "Give 'em some more of that 'until hell freezes over' stuff. Do you think we'll bomb 'em, John?"

John shook his head and muttered, "Not yet, no. And by the way, the 'hell freezes over' reference was from Adlai Stevenson, back during the Cuban missile crisis."

"I knew that, for cryin' out loud," Elaine replied indignantly.

Kate grinned.

Cronkite continued. Several Congressmen were demanding immediate, firm, unspecified retaliation. This was nothing short of an atrocity in international waters, they charged, and it was a deliberate provocation that must not go unanswered. Things were undeniably buzzing on the Hill, as if there weren't enough important agenda items already on the table. In other news, Sen. Robert F. Kennedy said at a National Press Club luncheon that he wouldn't oppose LBJ under "any foreseeable circumstances."

Kate coughed slightly and shifted in her seat when she caught her mother's glance.

"Is that true, Kate?" her mother asked. "I thought they were telling you he was certain to run."

Her father also turned and glanced in Kate's direction.

Kate swallowed and shrugged. "I really don't know for sure."

They turned back to Cronkite. Gene McCarthy gave another low-key speech to an auditorium full of highly-charged college students. Richard Nixon gave a highly-charged speech to a ballroom full of low-key Republican functionaries. And there were the usual protestors at the White House, carrying placards and shouting, *"Hey, hey, LBJ, how many kids have you killed today?"*

"They ought to be ashamed of themselves," blurted a disgusted John. "That's the President of the United States they're talking about."

Kate grinned again.

In still other news, the U.S. Army's strategic reserve had fallen to one division. And U.N. Secretary-General U Thant said that meaningful peace talks in Vietnam would be possible only if the U.S. would unconditionally stop the bombing. Reaction on Capitol Hill had been mixed. Then from Vietnam came correspondent Dan Rather's report.

Kate remained seated when Elaine promptly got up and left the room. John pushed back his tray and watched with interest as the nightly videotaped carnage began to roll: There was a short, vicious firefight in a tree line near a rice paddy. There was a medic bandaging the bloody leg of a frightened young soldier from the

1st Infantry Division—the famed Big Red One—who with trembling hand was smoking a cigarette and trying hard to appear nonchalant through the pain and shock. There was the medevac chopper coming in for dead and wounded GIs in a whirlwind of red dust and rotor wash. There was a short piece showing the contorted bodies of several dead enemy soldiers. And there was an after-action report from a crew cut young officer of about the same age as their son Tom who spoke in the clipped, acronym-filled vernacular of the military. Then there followed a report from Gen. Westmoreland's headquarters on the current state of the war. There was an assessment from current Secretary of Defense Robert McNamara, as well as comments from McNamara's newly-named replacement, Clark Clifford. And finally there was a protest scene of draft-card burning from student demonstrators on a California campus.

Kate grimaced and shook her head in disgust. John waited to see if there might be something on the Marines, the 5th Marines to be specific, but when the coverage ended he called to Elaine and she returned to the room.

"So?" Elaine asked as she took her seat on the sofa.

"Nothing this time," John answered. "Tonight they covered the Army."

"Surely you don't expect to see Tommy on television, do you?" Kate asked.

"Who knows?" Elaine answered. "Where's Tommy's company? What's the name of that place, John?"

"Quang Tri, I think," John answered as he reached for a map of Vietnam atop the adjacent coffee table. "But he's operated out of, let's see, Dong Ha, Da Nang, Phu Bai, Con Thien . . . and yeah, here it is, that Ashau place he mentioned in his last letter. Ashau, not Quang Tri. He gets around, that boy."

"Wish to God he'd get around to coming home," Elaine said with a sigh.

"He'll be home this summer," said John.

Kate pondered briefly what it would be like with her older brother back home again. She remembered all too well how

Tommy had grinned and told her that if at any time she needed him to come and take care of that "candyass" Everett, whom he had also taken great delight in at first calling "Eveready" before finally settling upon "Neveready," that she need only call him and he'd quickly be there. Neither did it help that Everett was in fact scared out of his senses by Kate's older brother, and considered Tommy's behavior reprehensible and his outlook symbolic of all that had gone into dragging the United States into the Vietnam imbroglio in the first place.

"I wish it could be sooner," said Elaine.

"I'm not so sure," Kate said a bit more loudly than she'd intended, drawing immediate stares of rebuke from her parents.

"What do you mean by that?" John asked with a curious expression.

"It means, Dad, that I'm just not sure I want Tommy back home again, telling me how big a mess I'm making of my life."

"Would you rather he stay in Vietnam, then?" her father pressed.

"No, I don't mean that," answered Kate. "I just think that, I mean, I don't know *what* I mean. Just forget I said anything."

"Why in God's name can't you and your brother put your differences aside and get back to being members of the same family again?" her mother asked.

"Mom, please," Kate said in a dismissive tone.

John gave her an impatient look. "He's your brother, Kate. And he's off fighting in a war, doing his duty. You would do well to remember that."

"He's my brother, yes. And he's off fighting in a war. But doing his duty?"

"He's doing his duty, Kate, yes," Elaine said sharply. "I don't like this war any more than you do, but I'm not going to blame it on the young men being sent over there by our government to fight it."

"I'm afraid our ideas over what constitute 'duty' differ slightly," said Kate.

John jerked slightly and turned toward her. "If my generation had felt that way, you might be using chopsticks to—"

"It's not the same, John," countered Elaine. "And that's nothing against what Tommy's reasons were for joining the Marines. But it's just not the same."

"It is in most ways," John said softly.

"Except that we've got a kid in this one, and that's changed *everything*," Elaine said firmly.

John stared across at his wife for a moment, then removed his glasses and looked over at the fireplace, remaining silent.

Elaine turned toward Kate. "I've never in my life been so sick to my stomach over something, literally, every single waking hour, as I have over this, and it began the day he called us from Quantico and told us he'd gotten his orders to go over there. It's like morning sickness, except that it doesn't go away when morning does."

Elaine leaned back and placed her hand over her mouth, fighting back the tears. Kate reached over and took hold of her other hand.

"Tough day today, nurse?" Kate asked, guessing that she'd probably treated a young man about Tommy's age with a serious illness or injury.

She nodded, her eyes misty.

"Anything I can do?"

"Go bring your brother home," she said with a forced laugh.

"Tommy's gonna be okay, dear," John said. "You've gotta believe that, and keep on believing it, like we've talked about all those times before. I keep telling myself that Tommy's gonna be fine, that he's gonna make it out of there, and it helps, it really does. You can't let it wear you down, Elaine."

Elaine drew a deep breath and cleared her throat. She looked away and said softly, "I just can't help it. This stupid war's gonna—"

"Elaine."

"This stupid war's gonna wreck our whole family, and I'll be damned if—"

"Elaine, stop."

"Kate's struggling with it; Chris is being affected by it. He may end up having to go himself, God forbid—I really worry about Chris—and for cryin' out loud Tommy's *life* is threatened by it. It's almost too much to bear, I swear. It's almost more than I can deal with."

"We're just like a lot of other families," said John. "We're not alone in this. We have lots of company."

"And it's your child, too, who's been sent over there by our government to that worthless little Asian place to risk being killed."

"There's a reason, Elaine. It's not a foolhardy concept that free people sometimes have to fight to preserve their freedom," John said firmly. "You know that. And you also know that I don't like Tommy being over there any more than you do. I swear to God I wish we could somehow win the war tonight and get all those kids out of there first thing in the morning, but I'm afraid I just don't see a quick resolution to this thing. It's never easy, never pleasant, but sometimes I'm afraid it's necessary."

Kate could feel her own temperature rising, but she fought off the temptation to join in yet another of the long list of arguments she'd had with her father on the matter of Vietnam. Instead, she held onto her mother's hand and kept her silence.

"John, how many days in your entire life before this stupid war started were you concerned with what was happening in that little nothing of a country?"

"It's aggression, pure and simple. They're a partner of ours in a security treaty and they've been invaded. The damned Russians are testing us all over the globe. A few years ago it was Berlin, then Cuba. Today it's Vietnam and maybe even Korea again. Tomorrow it'll be someplace else."

Elaine exploded. "They're *peasants*, for crissakes. They wouldn't know what to *do* with California even if they could somehow figure out how the hell to *get* there."

John smiled slightly and then turned serious again. "The Soviets have missiles pointed at us that number in the thousands, and they're not happy unless they're trying to intimidate us or involve us in a shooting war with one of their proxies. You know that."

Kate felt her mother lean back hard against the sofa.

"I *don't* know that," said Elaine. "I've never known a Communist, never known one in my life as far as I can tell. All I know is that my boy's gone to war with some peasant mother's boy, and it seems to me that both she and I stand to lose everything and gain nothing. And it's absolutely scaring me to death."

"Our country's at war, Elaine. We've been through it twice before in our lifetimes," John said softly.

Elaine took a long, deep breath. "It's not the same, John. You just can't use that comparison here. It's not the same and dammit, you know it."

"We're at war, the nation's at war. It *is* the same."

"It's the same only in that our American boys are fighting in some godforsaken far-off place. Apart from that, there's nothing similar. No Pearl Harbor. No declaration of war. No full-fledged draft. No rationing. No bond drives. No nothing of the sort. My goodness, John, you're the historian. You ought to be able to see that."

Kate saw her father wince, then heard her mother's own sigh of remorse.

"God, I need a cigarette," Elaine said, standing and looking about the room. "And maybe even a drink."

"Finish your dinner, Mom," said Kate.

"Maybe two drinks."

"Mom."

"Maybe more than two," she called, leaving the room again. "Where the hell are my cigarettes?"

Kate couldn't help but notice the despondent expression on her father's face. "She has her good days and her bad. We both do," he said with evident concern. "You're seeing one of the bad ones, I'm afraid."

John took a deep breath and leaned back in his chair. "I'm starting to believe that this war's influence on the American people will be more like the Civil War than anything we've seen since."

"How so?" Kate asked.

"Well, for starters, in the way it's turning family members against one another," John said, staring hard at Kate.

Kate sighed loudly and shrunk back into the sofa, only barely hearing Walter Cronkite as he summed up his newscast with, "And that's the way it is, this Friday, January Twenty Sixth, Nineteen Sixty Eight."

CHAPTER FIVE
Washington, D.C.

It was an unusually bright Saturday morning in Georgetown as Kate Flanagan sat at the kitchen table of the upscale apartment she shared with her law-student fiancé, Everett Beckwith Hollingsworth, III. Everett was busy discussing by phone the details of a planned Eugene McCarthy rally scheduled for later that same day in a downtown D.C. hotel, while Kate listened as she snuggled inside her thick tan robe. Everett spoke in animated terms about how the anticipated success of Sen. McCarthy's presidential bid was now "assured" with the onset of the violent, large-scale Tet Offensive now raging throughout Vietnam.

"It's ours now," he kept saying, always following with a satisfied laugh. "This plays right into our hands. We couldn't have scripted it any better if we'd been granted a wish by a genie."

Kate sipped her coffee and eventually found herself staring in deep thought at the red checkerboard pattern of the tablecloth. Her mother had called the previous evening from Chicago, anxious to discover if Kate had any recent word from her brother Tommy in Vietnam. She had explained to her mother that word from Tommy was the *last* thing she'd expect from him.

"Then try writing *him!*" Kate's mom had exhorted.

"Mother, if we have nothing to talk about when we're sitting on the same sofa in the same room, then why all of a sudden do you think we should be discussing things under *these* conditions?"

Kate had heard her mother quickly counter with, "It's precisely *these* conditions that damn well ought to make you want to know more about your own brother's condition. I am really, *really* disappointed in you, Katherine."

Only a few more words were spoken before the phone had gone dead on the other end. God, Kate thought, sighing. What's happening to our family?

Kate tried to imagine what might be happening with Tommy, where he might be, what he might be doing, what danger he might be exposed to. She considered, but for a brief moment, the possibility of his being killed in action, and how she might go through the rest of her life regretting the fact that their differences were still smoldering when Tommy drew his last mortal breath. She wondered if Tommy's specific aggravation with her, or perhaps even his general aggravation with her body of liberal beliefs, might prompt him to do something ill-advised and actually become the direct *cause* of his undoing. And, given that, she wondered if the responsibility for her brother's loss would thus become hers, as much, if not more so, than the enemy combatant who actually pulled the trigger. Whatever else she thought of Tommy, she just couldn't imagine him dead. Not yet; not so young. But she clearly knew that other sisters in other places were thinking the same thoughts about their brothers, and some were no doubt having their worlds shattered by receiving the terse notifications from the Department of Defense that began with the dreaded, "We regret to inform you . . . "

Kate drew a deep breath and closed her eyes, trying to visualize exactly how a reconciliation might be accomplished, what form it might take, what result it might achieve, who else might be needed to bring it about. She was constructing in her head the opening sentence of a letter to Tommy—a peace overture of sorts—when Everett finally got her attention from where he stood several feet away with the phone to his ear.

"Kate! For God's sake, would you do me a favor and look this way, please?"

She looked up bleary eyed, emerging from her trance.

"We're all set for six o'clock, over on M Street. You're going, right?" he asked.

"Uhhh," she mumbled halfheartedly, eyebrows raised, taking a moment to regain her bearings. "Honestly, I really haven't given it much thought. At six, you say?"

"Yes, it's at six," Everett replied with annoyance after covering the phone's mouthpiece.

Kate shrugged and looked away. "Yeah, okay, I'll go."

Everett stared at her a moment longer before eventually hanging up the telephone. "So," he said, hands on hips, "what is it?"

Kate ignored him and instead got up and poured herself another cup of coffee.

"I asked you a question, Kate. Do you plan on giving me the courtesy of a reply?"

"Nothing's bothering me," she said snappishly, turning and adding, "and don't come at me with that lawyer bullshit."

"Forgive me for asking," Everett said, shrugging. "But just for the record, that 'lawyer bullshit,' as you so succinctly put it, will no doubt over the course of the next thirty years or so make me a well-deserved fortune, make *us* a fortune. And you're still not telling me what's bothering you."

Kate returned to the table. When she looked up she saw Everett staring back at her, running his hand through his light brown, thinning, shoulder-length hair and then straightening his wire-rim glasses. She looked at his face and remembered how they'd met by pure happenstance seven months earlier in a Georgetown restaurant; how he was now in his second year of law school after having taken an undergraduate degree in literature from the Ivy League alma mater of his father and grandfather; how at her own age of twenty-three, his student deferments and political connections had thus far shielded him from military service. Four months from their first meeting, she remembered, Everett had succeeded in convincing her to move into the expensive, well-appointed Georgetown apartment he had taken in anticipation of just such an arrangement.

"I don't care to talk about it," Kate said after several moments of silence.

"Should I leave you alone, then?"

"Yes," she answered quickly. "I think that would be best."

The telephone rang again. "It's your brother Chris," Everett called out.

Her younger brother, it seems, was also interested in finding out if Kate had received any news from Tommy. When

Kate suggested that Chris call home and inquire, that she'd thus far heard nothing from Tommy and furthermore didn't expect to, Chris laughed and said that nowadays talking to his parents was unpleasant to the point of comparing it to a "bad trip."

"Once they start jacking me about my grades, it's over," he confessed. "And it's always in the first two or three sentences. You know, right after, 'Hello Chris. How are you?' It completely bums me out."

"Then make better grades," Kate suggested.

Chris chuckled and said, "Up yours too, sis."

They made giggly small talk a while longer before Chris finally became serious. "The news stories say the Marines are in some hellacious fighting at a place called Khe Sanh. They're surrounded and can't get out. Have you heard of it?"

"Only briefly. Why?"

"Because it's supposed to be really bad, with lots of guys getting messed up. There's a dude up here in one of my classes who's a vet, and he gave me a funny sort of expression when I told him my brother was a Marine lieutenant over there. I asked him what he meant with the look he gave me, and he said the Marines are bad enough as it is about taking casualties, but Marine lieutenants are notorious for their casualty rates. He told me I sure as hell *ought* to be concerned about Tommy, especially if he's at Khe Sanh. Jeez, Kate, I hope he hasn't been sent there."

Kate drew a deep breath and shook her head. "So do I, Chris. God, so do I."

* * *

Kate looked out at the cavernous ballroom of the M Street hotel. It was packed mostly with young people, many of whom would often break into the spontaneous chant of, "*We want Gene. We want Gene.*" Placards and balloons were everywhere, and there was a series of speakers at the podium whose enthusiastic, amplified voices were inevitably louder than was necessary by at least half. There were sign-up tables for volunteers to work the upcoming primaries, sign-up tables for contributors, tables with political materials, and tables piled high with buttons, bumper stickers, and the like. There was as much energy in the room as there were multi-colored decorations and banners. Kate noticed Everett working the room with polished ease, as if he knew virtually everyone in the crowd. She could hear many calling out his name, from which there would proceed a routine of handshakes and backslapping with the gentlemen, and an occasional hug from a lady.

Kate also noticed something else about the rally, something nagging inside her that she'd chosen not to discuss with Everett. She noticed that she felt more distant, more emotionally detached than before. For the first time she seemed less a part of it, more an observer than a willing, active participant. Even the pictures of Gene McCarthy himself did little to stir her political passions. She'd heard the message and the chants before, often, and she'd been driven and sustained by the campaign's themes, but now the whole thing seemed to be wearing thin on her. She had seen it all played out before, many of the same people, much of the same sloganeering, all to be seen and heard in one place only to be taken someplace else and repeated again the next time.

Maybe Marinelli's right, she kept thinking. Maybe Bobby Kennedy's the only one who could pull together the diverse Democratic coalition and still keep an energy about him throughout a long campaign.

Kate stood alone off to the side, dressed casually in white slacks and heavy black sweater, looking about for a ladies room after a third glass of punch.

"Hi, Kate. Great to see you again."

Kate turned to see Dan Marinelli, who was grinning broadly in his jeans and blue blazer. "Dan, what in heaven's name are you doing here? Do I take it there's been a recent conversion?"

He leaned forward slightly, nearer to her, and spoke in an exaggerated whisper. "Nothing of the sort, I assure you. I was just in the area and decided to," he said, pausing and shrugging innocently as he looked around, "you know, see how the hotel handles one of these things. Who knows, we might want to use it for one of our shindigs someday."

"So," Kate said, raising her voice as the chanting began anew, and making a sweeping gesture at the large crowd, "what do you think?"

"We want Gene. We want Gene."

Dan shrugged nonchalantly and leaned close to her, answering, "It's an okay venue, I suppose, for something as modest as this."

Kate laughed loudly.

"Heard anything from your brother lately?" Dan asked.

"No," said Kate, grimacing. "You're the third person to ask me that in the last twenty-four hours. I haven't heard from Tommy, so I have to assume everything's okay with him."

"We want Gene. We want Gene."

"Vietnam's not a very good place to be these days," Dan said.

Kate frowned. "It's my understanding that it's *never* been a very good place to be."

"Good point," he answered with a nod. "Listen, can we slip out of here and grab a cup of coffee?"

"We want Gene. We want Gene."

Kate turned and cut a quick glimpse toward Everett, on the far side of the room, where she could see him leaning over one of the tables in an animated conversation with an attractive young lady. She turned back and nodded to Dan, saying almost in a shout, "Yeah, okay. I'll meet you in the coffee shop as soon as I deal with the punch."

Dan had coffee and donuts waiting for her in the nearby shop.

Kate slid into the corner booth. "What happened to you?" she asked, pointing to the discoloration beneath Dan's left eye.

"Touch football, Kennedy-style. It's like a rite of passage, a test of survival," Dan said with a chuckle. "And I thought the Army was tough."

Dan sipped his coffee and looked directly at Kate. "So, tell me why you're here."

Her eyes widened. "Look who's talking, Marinelli. C'mon, you're kidding, right?"

Dan grinned. "I really do love your spirit."

"No, no. Don't change the subject. I'm here because I was asked to come by my fiancé, and I accepted. Now tell me why *you're* here?"

He shrugged. "Because I wanted to see you."

"Yeah, right."

"It's true. And because I wanted to let you know that we're still hoping you'll join us. You're still considering it, aren't you?"

"I've given it some more thought, yeah."

"Outstanding," he said with a pleased smile. "That's what I came here hoping to hear. I sort of thought the appeal might grow on you. As talented and adventurous as you are, you *need* a major challenge. And I think you'd find that in the role we'd give you. Besides, how are you ever going to know where the edge is unless you're willing to go over it once in a while?" He nodded and then shrugged. "Got any questions that I can answer for you?"

She pushed the red hair away from her eyes. "Is Kennedy any closer to making a decision?"

Dan nodded. "As a matter of fact, next week he's giving a major speech on the war in your hometown of Chicago. We've already lost sixteen-thousand Americans in Vietnam, and now that the fighting's spread in such a big way, if Johnson escalates this thing like all the military brass are calling for, then there's no telling what the final number will rise to. Bob McNamara's with us—has been for some time, thank God—but he's leaving, and I'm afraid Clark Clifford's simply going to fit in with the rest of the old crowd when it comes to expanding the war."

"When will he announce?"

"I don't know. Soon, I hope."

"*Will* he announce?"

"Yes, I'm certain of it. I just can't tie it to a specific date yet. But he's gonna go, like I told you before. Whether he likes it or not, he has to get in, especially now."

Kate was skeptical, and her expression quickly reflected it.

"He'll go," Dan said. "And it won't be too much longer before he announces. We need you with us, and the sooner you can make the change, the better. Let's be honest here: Gene McCarthy's got some interesting points to make, but in the end he's just a pretender, and nothing more. Like I've told you before, the crucial difference is that Bob can win."

"McCarthy's *not* a pretender. He's mobilized the country against the war like nobody else has. He's got real momentum."

Dan shrugged and nodded. "I'll admit that he's providing a voice and a platform where not much existed before, but he can't get into a long campaign with Lyndon Johnson and win. His star may be bright now, but it'll fade later. And if he's established as the movement's chief spokesman, then the movement will fade with him. He goes down and it goes down with him. That's the big risk. And we all lose as a result."

Kate became quiet as she pondered her response, all the while keeping her eyes fixed upon Dan. She was about to open her mouth to speak when Everett suddenly approached the booth.

"Well, hello kids," he said, deliberately passing his gaze back and forth. "Mind if I join you?"

Kate overcame a slight rush of embarrassment and said quickly, "Dan Marinelli, I'd like you to meet my fiancé, Everett Hollingsworth."

Dan wriggled out of the booth and accepted the outstretched hand of Everett. Everett then slid into the seat beside Kate and sat back with his hands in his lap, quietly studying Dan.

"You look familiar for some reason," Everett said. "Have we met before?"

"I don't think so."

Everett turned to Kate. "Do you two work together?"

Kate and Dan both grinned.

"Not exactly," Kate answered. "Dan's on Senator Kennedy's staff."

"Kennedy, as in Robert Francis or Edward Moore?" Everett asked, turning and staring at Dan.

"The New York version."

"Ah, yes. Inside every Bostonian is a New Yorker just dying to get out. Did he send you here to check on us?"

"No, of course not."

"Hmm," Everett said in mock confusion. "I'm not sure whether that's good or bad."

"I came on my own."

"As a spy?" asked Everett in mock alarm.

"No, not at all," Dan said with a slightly embarrassed laugh.

"So, if Kennedy didn't send you and you're not spying, just what business do you have here?" Everett asked, removing his glasses and wiping the lenses with a handkerchief, all the while keeping his eyes fixed upon Dan.

"It's not business, really. I'm here for the coffee and donuts."

Everett smiled and wrapped his wire-rimmed glasses around the front of his face. "I can see that, thank you. I was just curious why someone from the Senator Robert Francis Kennedy staff would favor us simple McCarthyites with an uninvited but not necessarily unwelcome visit."

"McCarthyites are hardly simple. And besides, we're on the same side, you know."

"Only technically, and then again only marginally so. Apart from that, the differences are staggering," Everett said, following with a chuckle.

"Staggering?"

"Precisely," Everett said.

"We both want to end the war," said Dan.

"But no doubt for altogether different reasons. Again, the measurement's in miles, not millimeters."

"The end of the war means the killing stops. What other reasons do you have?" asked Dan.

"Reasons that Bobby Kennedy probably couldn't comprehend in a thousand years. Reasons that deal with political, societal, institutional concerns."

"Wow, I knew you guys were deep, but I didn't realize you were *that* deep?" Dan said with a wrinkle of his brow.

"Not surprising."

"So, it's survival, then. You want to end the war for reasons of survival," said Dan.

"Simplistically, yes. I suppose that's accurate," Everett answered, sniffing.

"Who's specific survival? Yours?" asked Dan, leaning forward slightly.

"A good start, to be sure. You bet your sweet bippie."

Kate shifted uncomfortably.

"What about the ones already over there, already at risk?" asked Dan.

"Them too, yeah. And you, as well. Now that I've met you I wouldn't want to hear that you've gone over there and met your ultimate demise," Everett said.

"Already been, thank you."

"Ah," Everett said, smirking. "Then I'm relieved beyond measure."

Kate reached for a glass of water.

"I'm surprised you could be a Kennedy supporter," Everett said. "If you'd bothered to study the background of the Vietnam involvement since the late Fifties and the early part of this decade, you'd see that the Kennedys' hands aren't exactly disinfectant clean when it comes to culpability. What started as a misguided little adventure by elite American military specialists has grown into a one-way ticket to national oblivion. I assume you're aware of that little morsel."

"What do you know about Vietnam?" Dan asked in a biting tone. "I can handle a lecture on political candidates and their positions on the issues, but don't come at me posing as an authority on the war. My sense is that you know next to nothing about what's really going on over there. "

Everett paused a moment, then chuckled slightly. "You're absolutely correct. I know as little about Vietnam as I know about the surface of the planet Neptune. But enough to know that I wouldn't care to find myself in either place," he answered smugly.

"A trip there might do you some good," Dan cracked. "And I mean Vietnam, not Neptune. A year in the bush and you'd gain some insights that you'd otherwise never gain in, say, a thousand years."

Everett remained quiet for a moment, finally saying, "I don't think so. I haven't yet detected any such wisdom in anyone I've met who's been there."

Dan glanced over at Kate before deciding against pressing the matter any further. He smiled at Everett and softly said, "Miles, not millimeters. Right?"

"Very good," said Everett. "And since we started off talking politics here, I seem to remember that your man Senator Kennedy has gone from one position to another on the war. First he was a hawk, now he's a dove; first he was one of the sponsors, now he's one of the antagonists. From proponent to opponent, he's made it look easy. But surely he must have his reasons, huh?"

"Of course he has his reasons," Dan said, his voice still calm but with his jaw beginning to tighten. "He's lived and learned."

Everett smiled. "Speaking of which, I do hope that *you've* lived and learned by visiting a McCarthy function," he said in a voice thick with sarcasm.

Kate cleared her throat and interjected, "I think maybe it'd be a good idea to change the subject."

"I think maybe it'd be a good idea for me to take my leave," Dan said, starting to slide out of the booth. He glanced again at Kate and then dropped two dollar-bills on the table. He extended his hand to Everett. "Pleased to meet you. And I wish you and your candidate well in the coming months." He then leaned across and offered his hand to Kate. "Nice seeing you again, Kate. Remember to wear a helmet during those touch football games."

With that, Dan turned and left.

"Touch football games?" asked Everett, turning toward Kate. "What touch football games?"

Kate fingered the thin silver necklace around her neck, grinning slightly. "Oh, it's not important."

"Then what the hell did he mean?"

"Nothing, Everett."

"Kate, dammit, are you hiding something from me?"

She gave a look of hurt. "Would I do that to you, sweetest?"

"Kate, I'm asking you once more: Do you or do you not have something to tell me?"

"I believe I warned you about using that lawyer stuff on me."

"Kate!"

"It's only one small item. That's all, really."

"Yeah?"

"It's not a big thing, really, it's—"

"Kate, dammit!"

"Okay, here it is: I've made a decision," she said with a shrug.

"You've made a decision. And?"

"I'm changing jobs," she declared conclusively.

"Yeah? On the level?"

"On the level."

"And that's it? That's all there is to it?"

"That's it."

"Full disclosure?"

"There you go again. But yes, full and complete disclosure."

Everett seemed relieved. "Yeah, well, okay then," he said, getting up from the booth. "Why didn't you tell me earlier?"

"Because I've just now decided," Kate answered as she slid out of her seat. "Before, I wasn't sure. Now, I am. I feel like a great burden's been lifted off my shoulders. I feel free for the first time in weeks."

Kate spread her arms as if making ready to take flight.

"That's terrific, but I thought you liked your job. Has something changed to make you not like your job?"

"No. I do like my job. I mean, I did. It's just that I've been offered something much more meaningful and far more challenging."

"Yeah?"

"Yeah," Kate replied.

"More meaningful and challenging, huh? Does that also mean more responsibility and greater authority and higher pay, all those sorts of things?"

Kate wrinkled her nose. "Well, I'm not sure yet."

"You're not sure? Kate, what the hell are you talking about? What are you getting yourself into? Shouldn't you know what the basic—"

"Don't worry. I know what I'm doing."

"But how can—"

"I said I know what I'm doing," she said abruptly.

Everett shrugged. "Well then, congratulations, I suppose."

"Thanks."

"So, who are you going to work for?" Everett said nonchalantly as he dug into his pocket for some loose change.

"Senator Robert Francis Kennedy of New York," Kate replied as she turned and walked out.

CHAPTER SIX
Hue, South Vietnam

I t was a cold, overcast, fifty-degree day, just after dawn on Sunday, February 4th, as Lt. Tom Flanagan stood alone at his Fox Company position at the Hue University complex. To the right of his platoon sector was Le Loi Street and the Perfume River; on the left was 1st Battalion, 1st Marines. To the front, barely two blocks away, were the NVA, in buildings, behind walls, and on rooftops—concealed positions with overlapping and deadly fields of fire. To the rear were the buildings of the Military Assistance Command-Vietnam (MACV) complex. Flanagan knew a vicious fight was in store, and he had been horrified to find out that the Saigon government had decided to restrict the use of supporting arms at Hue in an attempt to preserve as much of the ancient city as possible. As had been explained to Flanagan and his fellow officers, the Rules of Engagement for Hue stipulated that no artillery or naval gunfire would be permitted in support of U.S. forces, and only limited use of jets. Apart from the several Marine tanks, Ontos, and Mechanical Mules with their mounted 106mm recoilless rifles, the Marines' supporting arms would consist primarily of the small arms and crew-served weapons the infantry companies would carry into the fight themselves.

This must be as bad as it can get, Flanagan thought as he glanced out through the haze at the enemy-occupied buildings to his front. He wished for what seemed like the millionth time that he would suddenly awaken to find that the entire nightmare had dissipated like a rising gas, with the monumental relief that would follow. But then he heard the gunshots in the distance, and knew that it was all too real.

He remembered how the urgent call to Fox Company had come on January 31st from headquarters: Stand-by to board the trucks that are en-route to your position for transport back to Phu Bai, for re-supply and re-fitting in preparation for immediate assignment to Hue City. He had then learned that Hue, the third largest city in South Vietnam, was under siege by what had begun on January 31st as an assault by an estimated 9 NVA battalions, and that by February 4th had grown to 14 battalions—a total of 6,000 well-equipped, hard-hitting enemy soldiers. He had coon many of Hue's population of 140,000 out on the roads as refugees, knowing that still others were caught in the midst of what was quickly developing into a bitter, pivotal confrontation.

It was bad all right. And it definitely wasn't a dream. Flanagan listened with his platoon-leader colleagues as Capt. Tanner briefed his officers from a bullet-scarred, single-story University building that had been reclaimed from the NVA two days before. Brass shell casings still littered the floor, and several blood-encrusted bandages had been left behind by the enemy.

"Our objective is the Treasury and Post Office complex," said Capt. Tanner, halting to sip lukewarm coffee from his canteen cup. "It's well defended, it's surrounded by an eight-foot wall, and the Treasury building itself is thickly constructed, as you might expect."

Flanagan glanced up from a road map of Hue that he had found in a nearby Esso gas station, and cut a quick glance at the others.

"Hotel Company will be on our right flank," Tanner continued, "and will advance to the Public Health building, secure it, and provide supporting fire for our assault. Golf Company will be in reserve."

The platoon leaders stole another quick glance at each another, knowing as they did that Golf Company had been shot to pieces over the previous two days and had already been reduced by more than a third since its arrival into Hue.

"Expect the resistance to be strong, gentlemen. We'll use all the support we can get from the tanks and recoilless rifles. Use as much smoke as you need to mask your movements. Make sure your people check their gas masks before we move out, in case we have to gas them at the objective. We'll evacuate the wounded back to the MACV dispensary where we can then medevac them to Phu Bai or elsewhere, if needed."

Tanner took another sip of coffee and studied the faces of his subordinate commanders. "Are there any questions?"

"Do we need prisoners, sir?" asked Lt. Dave Espy of First Platoon.

"We always need prisoners. If they leave some feckless little snuffy behind and we have a chance to snatch him, then by all means do so. But our first priority is to kick Charlie's ass out of Hue, and we'll do whatever it takes to do that. My simple military mind tells me that as close as we're gonna have to get to Charles, the only prisoners you'll likely have a chance at getting will be the boocoo damaged ones."

Espy and the others nodded.

"Any other questions?"

There were none. Tanner stood and glanced at his watch. The starting time for crossing the line of departure was yet another hour away, and the platoon leaders were dismissed to make their preparations.

"What the hell does 'feckless' mean?" Lt. Kevin Riordan asked of Tom Flanagan once they were outside the building.

Flanagan laughed, accepted Riordan's good-luck handshake, and then spent some time with Sgt. Jankowski going over the orders and organizing the squads. Flanagan was tense, and as hard as he tried not to show it, he was certain the old veteran Jankowski could detect it.

"We'll do fine, Lieutenant," Jankowski said at one point. "These are damn fine troops, and they'll do their jobs." Jankowski then smiled, showing his stained teeth. He removed his cigar and thrust it in Flanagan's direction for emphasis. "And I'll go so far as to personally guarantee it."

Flanagan mingled among his troops as they loaded their magazines, cleaned their weapons, or merely rested themselves on the asphalt parking lot that the platoon occupied. The men were well aware that Golf Company had been badly hurt the day before, and that their turn was now coming for the difficult attack upon a fortified objective. But Flanagan also sensed that his men wanted this fight, that they wanted their chance to get face-to-face

63

with this elusive enemy who so often before had seemed so deadly and yet so invisible, who had killed Marines with snipers and booby traps, unseen and often unexpected. The troops wanted payback, and on this day it seemed a certainty that they would have their chance. The grim men of Fox Company had specific designs on killing as many North Vietnamese soldiers as they could find before the day ended.

"God go with us," Flanagan said as he turned away and crossed himself.

Fox Company left out at the appointed hour with Riordan's and Flanagan's platoons in the lead, Espy's platoon following in trace accompanied by Capt. Tanner and the command post. A two-story Catholic school building and adjacent courtyard stood between Fox Company and the Treasury building. The NVA opened fire from the Treasury complex as soon as the Marines were in sight, and the wall surrounding the school's courtyard provided cover from the small-arms fire. The firing became intense, and several Marines were hit in the initial fusillade.

"We gotta blow us a hole in this friggin' wall, Lieutenant," Jankowski screamed over the noise of the gunfire.

Flanagan nodded. "Do it," he screamed back.

Jankowski moved everyone away and then arranged for a Marine with a shoulder-fired 3.5-inch rocket launcher to blast a hole in the wall sufficiently large enough to move the troops through. The Marine gunner then immediately moved inside the courtyard, took aim, and blew another hole in the adjacent wall before both he and his loader were shot dead in a torrent of bullets.

"Get through there and get to the other side," Jankowski screamed as he started pushing Marines through the opening. "Cover 'em, people. Give 'em some cover. *Go, go, go, dammit!* Get through there."

Flanagan heard a rifle round strike the wall just above his head as his turn came to duck through the hole and start his sprint to the opposite wall. The enemy AK-47 rounds were flying overhead with such frenzy that it gave off the sound of buzzing bees. Grenade explosions began reverberating as the Marines closed the distance to their NVA adversaries. Wenrick carried the radio on his back and stayed near to Flanagan, while both men carried M-16 rifles in an attempt to look as indistinguishable from the others as possible.

The Marines kept up the firing at the Treasury complex, which was itself surrounded by an eight-foot wall. A Marine squad leader from Flanagan's platoon suddenly grabbed a 3.5-inch rocket launcher, positioned himself in the hole in the near wall, and fired three rounds into the Treasury wall and gate, blowing a hole in the concrete and destroying much of the metal gate. The Marine, a black sergeant E-5 from Los Angeles named David Douglas, then left the wall and ran past Flanagan with the launcher still in his grasp.

"I can get some clear shots from up there," Douglas shouted, stopping and pointing to the schoolhouse to the rear.

Flanagan glanced back and saw at least a dozen windows on the building's second story. "Okay, but don't stay in one place for long. Keep shooting and moving, and I'll get you some ammo up there."

Douglas nodded as he and his loader took off running, keeping low and holding on to their helmets as they rushed away. By the time Douglas had entered the building and climbed the steps to take up a firing position in one of the rooms, Flanagan had two other Marines following close behind, ferrying rocket ammunition. Flanagan saw Douglas looking out a window and choosing a target from among the many rifle flashes coming from across the street on the second floor of the Treasury. He saw Douglas fire three rounds from one room, run to another, fire once and then move again, repeating this sequence until Douglas had fired perhaps thirty rocket rounds.

Flanagan then directed a squad to move across the street, under fire, and take up positions against the Treasury wall. The firing from the enemy troops picked up considerably, a virtual hailstorm of steel thudding against the wall and street near the crouched Marines. Fragments of chipped concrete showered the men as they remained under cover, and they became unable to advance any further. Flanagan could make out sketchy radio reports that Riordan's men were keeping the pressure on the Post Office complex, but the resistance there was also strong.

With one hand atop his helmet and the other gripping his M-16, Flanagan sprinted to the schoolhouse for a better look. All the while Sgt. Douglas kept up his continuous firing of the 3.5 rocket launcher. Enemy bullets occasionally ricocheted around inside the room with Flanagan, Douglas, and his young loader, but it wasn't until an enemy B-40 rocket came whooshing into a room the three of them were in the process of vacating that the momentum of their attack was halted. Douglas was violently slammed forward into the hallway by the force of the blast, into Flanagan. Flanagan was then smashed into an adjacent wall, thinking for a moment that he might be near death, as explosion, collision, and concussion rendered him deaf and disoriented. His head cleared in time for him to see Douglas struggling to regain his feet, while the young Marine serving as the loader, who was still in the room, gasped once, then twice, then sighed loudly before finally dying from the fragmentation wounds to his head, neck, and chest.

Flanagan finally raised himself to a kneeling position and glanced about at the rays of sunlight shining through the thick smoke and dust. He took a quick inventory of his major body parts and noticed some bleeding on his hand, but otherwise he seemed relatively unscathed apart from the ringing in his ears. A corpsman quickly arrived and worked over the fatally wounded loader for several moments, then finally gave up and wrapped the arm wounds of Douglas and the hand wound of Flanagan.

"You wanna be medevaced to the rear, man?" the corpsman asked Sgt. Douglas when he completed the wrapping.

"You gotta be shittin' me," Douglas answered, almost in a snarl.

Flanagan got to his feet and had one last look at the body of the loader, took a deep breath and steeled himself, then leaned outside a rear window and shouted for a Marine to come upstairs and grab some ammo and follow Douglas to another window. Within a few short moments Douglas was once again firing across at the Treasury. Flanagan sent two M-60 machine-gun teams to the schoolhouse to set up their weapons and begin pouring a steady stream of fire at the Treasury. The red tracers were soon darting above the heads of the Marines outside as the gun growled deeply and spit its spent cartridges out onto the floor.

Flanagan picked up another radio report where, on the right flank, the Hotel Company grunts had taken the Public Health building after a short fight, and had taken up positions atop its roof. He noticed when they began firing over at the Treasury/Post Office complex where much of Fox Company remained pinned against the courtyard wall.

The fire team from Flanagan's platoon that had been pinned down against the Treasury wall took a casualty when a Marine attempted to wriggle through the hole and press on to the building in the assault. The NVA shot him in the head, and as the other Marines pulled him from the hole, it was clear that the wounded American was only barely alive. Flanagan and others nearby watched in awe as the team leader, who had been unable to make the original crossing with his fellow Marines, suddenly climbed through the hole in the courtyard wall and dashed across the street. Marines along the courtyard began shouting for heavy covering fire at the Treasury building. The team leader made it to the other side, then slung the injured Marine over his shoulder and made another mad dash back across the street, again under heavy fire, and pulled his wounded mate to cover through the hole in the courtyard wall. But it was too late, and the grievously wounded man died before he could be evacuated to MACV.

Flanagan glanced back and saw the protruding 3.5 rocket launcher in the schoolhouse. "Sergeant Douglas," he called with a shout.

Douglas looked down at Flanagan. "Yessir?"

"Get down here. We're gonna gas 'em and then go over into the attack, and I'll need you and your tube down here."

Douglas nodded and immediately disappeared inside. Flanagan then noticed Major O'Leary, the Battalion S-3, who was busily rigging a tear gas launcher with a power-cell battery. The industrious major, who had left his battalion-headquarters post to get nearer to the fighting, had somehow scrounged a live battery in the middle of a major firefight.

"Will it work?" Flanagan shouted.

The major nodded. "Bet your ass it'll work."

Capt. Tanner, who had been busily working out the assault plan from his vantage point in the schoolhouse, went over the plan with Flanagan and Riordan who by then had joined Espy, Auer, and Lt. Davies, the XO, in the schoolhouse. The plan called for Riordan's platoon to attack the Post Office, Flanagan's the Treasury. Espy would move his platoon up and support Flanagan. Tanner confirmed reports from the platoons that showed Riordan's men had suffered three dead and six wounded; Flanagan's losses were six dead and eight wounded—one third of his people—while Espy's platoon had suffered one dead and two wounded. Most of the wounded had refused evacuation, and all but the three or four of the most seriously injured were still at their posts.

Tanner dismissed his platoon leaders and then awaited word from the major that the gas launcher was operational.

Meanwhile, Flanagan watched from the schoolhouse when, from below, Sgt. Douglas fired several rounds through the courtyard hole and blew a second hole in the Treasury wall, then blew down the oak entrance doors to give the Marines access to the building itself.

"It's a go," Tanner radioed Flanagan after ten minutes. "Get everybody in their gas masks, get the smoke out, and wait for word from me to move out."

Suddenly an NVA machine gun from Flanagan's right flank opened up on his men against the schoolhouse wall. Two Marines were hit, then three, then four. A round hit near enough to Flanagan to spray concrete debris into his eyes and mouth. A Marine standing three feet away was struck in the lower abdomen and shouted, "Oh God, no!" before falling backwards against the wall and screaming in agony. A Golf Company team to the rear of the schoolhouse quickly sighted a 106 recoilless rifle onto the building and silenced the machine gunner with two blasts.

Flanagan's men loaded their weapons and then took off their helmets and fitted the rubberized gas masks over their faces. Once everyone was ready and in position, the major and another Marine operating the launcher began sailing the gas capsules into the Treasury complex. The white riot-control gas was soon drifting up and around the firing positions of the NVA, who had no masks to protect themselves from the disabling gas. Smoke grenades were thrown into the street by the Marines to conceal their movement, and soon thereafter the radioed order from Capt. Tanner took Fox Company into the attack. Sgt. Douglas fired off dozens of rounds at the Treasury building from the open courtyard while Flanagan and the rest of his Marines squeezed through the holes in the courtyard wall, crossed the street in a sprint, squeezed through the holes in the Treasury wall, and moved up in the assault against the compound. The Marines were gasping and sweating profusely inside the gas masks, but they advanced steadily under the enemy's sporadic fire.

Flanagan was close behind when the first fire team ran through the blasted doorway and into the Treasury building. There was lots of battle debris inside, concrete rubble and shell casings were everywhere, and Flanagan could hear footsteps as the NVA hurriedly vacated the building to the rear. An NVA soldier in a pith helmet and carrying an AK-47 was running helter-skelter down a staircase within six feet of Flanagan, the sight and proximity of which momentarily startled Flanagan and thus gave the enemy soldier the first opportunity for a quick shot. Before the young Vietnamese could fully raise his weapon and fire, his head suddenly exploded into a red mist from the well-aimed burst of a Marine M-60 machine gunner. Flanagan was sprayed with blood and brain tissue as the man tumbled forward and fell over at an odd angle, his legs and one arm underneath him.

The platoon began a room-by-room clearing of the building, and two M-60 gunners firing wildly from the hip hosed many of the rooms before other Marines would enter. Flanagan watched as one wounded NVA soldier attempted to crawl away from his pursuers, only to be ripped apart by fully automatic bursts from three different directions.

Payback time, Flanagan thought briefly. He also knew there would be no enemy prisoners taken in the Treasury building.

After forty minutes of tense searching, radio and verbal reports from his squad leaders eventually confirmed to Flanagan that all the rooms in the Treasury building had been cleared. He then left the platoon in the care of Sgt. Jankowski, who set up defensive positions to defend against the possibility of an NVA counterattack. The men were eager to remove their gas masks, and only a residual amount of the gas irritant remained. Flanagan was soaked with perspiration when he walked outside and checked on the wounded, some of whom were ambulatory and already walking back toward the dispensary. Others were being made ready for the trip on stretchers after receiving first-aid treatment from any one of the several Navy corpsmen who worked over the wounded of all three platoons.

There was lots of blood, sterile bandages, and bags of plasma, and Flanagan noticed the strong medicinal odor in the immediate area that crowded out the cordite and diesel fumes. The corpsmen worked calmly and efficiently, and only occasionally would a corpsman raise his voice and call out, "I gotta get this guy movin' to the rear, pronto," to a nearby radio operator.

Flanagan walked among several of the grunts who were receiving treatment. He leaned over a seriously wounded Marine who was laid out on a stretcher with a bloody dressing covering his head and eyes.

"This is Lieutenant Flanagan. Can you hear me?" he asked softly.

"Yessir," came the weak reply.

"You were one hell of a Marine today," Flanagan said softly.

"Thanks much, sir. You weren't half-bad yourself."

"Get yourself well because I want your young ass back out here with us in this wonderful Southeast Asian paradise."

Flanagan noted the faint smile.

"Mind if I have a little convalescent leave first, sir?" the wounded Marine asked.

"No," Flanagan said as he patted the man's boot. "Matter of fact, I insist that you do."

Flanagan walked among the others, offering encouragement to the more seriously hurt and lightly joking with some of the lesser wounded.

The corpsman assigned to Flanagan's platoon, HM3 Al Fackler, most often referred to as "Doc," put the finishing touches on the facial dressing of a wounded Marine. When he spotted Flanagan, Fackler lit a cigarette and stepped away with the lieutenant from the impromptu aid station.

"Your hand okay, Lieutenant?" asked Fackler, glancing down at the bandage.

"It's fine. What's the report?"

"Three more WIAs, no KIAs in the compound assault," Fackler said as he picked at a piece of tobacco on his tongue.

Flanagan nodded, looking exhausted. "I'll need a list, Doc."

Off to the side, a tank and a mechanical mule were setting out in the street to ferry some of the more seriously wounded back to the MACV aid station. The wounded Marines were literally piled atop one another, and several corpsmen were up on the vehicles with their patients, holding aloft the clear plastic bags of plasma. There were lots of bloody bandages on lots of damaged young heads and bodies, and the sight of it momentarily stunned Flanagan.

"Good God in heaven," Flanagan muttered aloud.

Fackler took another drag. "Be the longest list we've ever had since we've been working together, sir. We've never had a day like this before."

Flanagan gave a resigned shake of his head.

"Did you hear about Lieutenant Riordan?" asked the corpsman.

Flanagan tensed. "No. What?"

"He got dinged by a sniper when they were clearing the last building over there," Fackler said with a point toward the Post Office complex. "The way I heard it, he went down and nobody could get to him for several minutes. First wound was a femoral artery, gunshot, and they hit him a couple more times in the lower torso while he was out there exposed. By the time any of the grunts could get to him, he was KIA. He lost a shitload of blood with that leg wound."

The news sucked the air out of Flanagan's lungs, and he suddenly felt sick to his stomach. He struggled to take a deep breath, and thought for a brief moment about going over to take a look at the body to confirm its identity. Maybe it's a mistake, he thought. Maybe it's not Riordan. But he knew all too well. He needed no confirmation. There was no mistake, and only with considerable effort did he eventually calm himself. He had work to do, he kept reminding himself. His men were watching and counting on him. He had no time for emotional outbursts or grief-stricken overloads or anything of the sort. He had to shake it off, quickly, since there was still a dangerous enemy close at hand. But he kept glancing over in the direction of Riordan's platoon. "Dammit," he finally sighed under his breath, feeling his eyes moisten.

"I gotta get back, sir. Got a few more to wrap," Fackler said as he crushed out his cigarette.

"Don't forget my list."

"Aye-aye, Lieutenant."

Dave Espy, his M-16 slung over his shoulder, spotted Flanagan in the street and walked over alongside his fellow platoon leader. "Hear about Kevin?" Espy asked.

"I just did, yeah. Has he already been taken to the rear?"

"No. He's still in the street over there, underneath a poncho. There's nothing sticking out but his jungle boots. Hard to believe, isn't it?"

Flanagan drew another deep breath. "Yep."

"Jeez, I can't believe he's gone," Espy said, shaking his head.

Flanagan gave Espy a quick, hard glance. "It won't stop with Kevin. This friggin' place is gonna be covered up with a lot more flesh before it's over."

Capt. Tanner approached in a fast walk. "We're staying here for the night, gentlemen. Sergeant Magee's taking over for Lieutenant Riordan, and I want a briefing from each of you in twenty minutes in the CP I'm setting up in that single-story building over there," Tanner said with a point toward the Post Office complex. "Twenty minutes, gents."

Tanner started to walk away, then stopped and turned back. "Hell of a job today, men. Fox Company's been bloodied, but dammit, Fox Company owns this little piece of Hue City now."

Flanagan gave a tired nod to Espy and then left to rejoin his platoon.

* * *

It was midnight before Flanagan was finally able to take off his helmet and flak jacket and sit down to some needed rest. He claimed a room on the first floor of the Treasury as his, and one of his resourceful Marines had even left a cot in the room for him. Another scrounged item, a candle, provided enough illumination to see the shell casings, chipped concrete, and other debris scattered about the floor. Flanagan sat on the cot and leaned against the wall, reflecting on the day's violent events he had witnessed at such a close range.

An hour at a time, he kept thinking to himself. Just one hour at a time.

He was about to rip open his C-ration meal when the burly Sgt. Jankowski tapped on the open door. Jankowski held out a paper sack, a puckish expression on his face.

"I come bearing a gift, Lieutenant," Jankowski said as he opened the sack and brought out two cans of American beer.

Flanagan smiled. "How the hell did you come across those?"

"I'm a man of influence," Jankowski said as he produced a can opener from the pocket of his utility trousers and then proceeded to punch holes in the tops.

"I only wish there were dozens more," said Flanagan after accepting the warm can with its sudsy contents bubbling over the top.

Jankowski smiled and took a long gulp. "Everything in its own time, sir."

Flanagan quickly washed down the cold ham-and-limas with the warm beer. Jankowski, who sat on the floor nearby, leaned back against the concrete wall and lit one of his cigars. He ran a hand through his graying hair, belched, and looked up at his platoon leader who was sitting on the cot.

"Any word from the Skipper on replacements?" asked Jankowski.

"He said Battalion's doing all they can, but not to expect any until they actually show up out here with their weapons in their hot little hands."

Jankowski blew a cloud of cigar smoke, then took a deep breath and exhaled slowly. "I hope the little bastards up the street aren't somehow reinforcing."

"That's a comforting thought," Flanagan said after a burning sip of the beer.

"We'll find out soon enough. By the way, sorry to hear about Lieutenant Riordan. It's never easy to get word that a buddy's gone down."

Flanagan nodded. "I suppose you've experienced that once or twice, huh?"

Jankowski glanced away momentarily and then removed the cigar from his mouth. "More times than I would've preferred, yessir. It's not the part of this job that I enjoy the most, for damn sure."

"What *do* you enjoy most about your job?" Flanagan asked.

"The troops, the grunts in the field."

Flanagan smiled slightly.

Jankowski puffed on the cigar again, then flicked an ash off to the side. "If you don't mind my saying so, sir, I made the landing on Okinawa in Forty-Five, I froze my ass off at the Chosin Reservoir in Fifty, and this is my second tour with the grunts in Vietnam. So wouldn't you agree that I'm a combat veteran of some authority?"

"I would, yes."

"And that I ought to know what I'm talking about when it comes to knowing something about the nature and character of combat troops?"

"For sure, yes," said Flanagan, nodding.

"Then believe me when I tell you that these troops are as good as any I've ever seen, as good as the *best* I've ever seen. No difference, really. Different eras, maybe, but basically the same in all the important ways. Hell, one generation used to listen to Frances Langford and now this one listens to Janis Joplin, but when it comes to guts and pride and combat effectiveness and good Marine Corps shit like that, these kids are right up there at the top. Nearly every one of 'em had the look of death in his eyes today, that dazed friggin' look when a man figures that today's the day he buys the farm. I saw it on Okinawa at Shuri Castle, I saw it in Korea, and I damn well saw it today. But they stayed out there against that friggin' wall and kept firing, and when it came time to attack, by God they moved up without hesitation. Sergeant Douglas with that three-five was *some*thing, I swear to God, and that kid Steiner who went after his wounded man across the street, under some kind of bad-ass fire, and hauled his man out of there even though the kid was so boocoo messed up he wouldn't live another hour—shit, alls I can say is I'm glad I wasn't one of them poor damn gooks who had to face these troops today. I've been in this business a long time, and what I saw today will stay with me for the rest of my life. I ain't shittin' you, Lieutenant, those Marines were beautiful today, absolutely beautiful."

"I know," said Flanagan in a voice thick with emotion. "I ordered some to their deaths." He paused, then added, "I remember reading about the Duke of Wellington saying that there was nothing so dreadful as a great victory—except a great defeat. Today, I can fully understand what he meant."

"You give orders and men fight and die. You did outstanding today, sir. I thought you were better today than I've ever seen you. You seemed to be everywhere at once, but mostly out front leading your Marines. And your Marines responded to your leadership. The fact is, Lieutenant, we faced the bastards in a vicious fight and we won. And you were in command of a platoon that was doing a shitload of the winning."

Flanagan nodded his appreciation. "Still, some of my men died today."

Jankowski shrugged. "It's like my ole granny used to say: 'You're gonna have some of that.' Always have, always will. You can't command men in battle and not expect some to get hurt. It's gonna happen, and you know as well as I do that it's all part of the gear that comes in your pack."

"I understand that. I just wish I could somehow be perfect, where every one of my perfect orders provides the perfect result."

Jankowski drained the last of the beer from the can and belched again. "You figure out how to get like that, Mister Flanagan, and your days out here as a shave-tail lieutenant will be gone forever," he said, prompting laughter from both.

* * *

After the candle had burned away, Flanagan used a flashlight, its red lens attached, and propped it against his gear so he could see to finish the letter he was writing to his sister Kate. It was two o'clock in the morning, and he had been so completely exhausted, so fatigued from the enormous stress of the day and the gallons of adrenaline that had gushed through his veins, that he'd had great difficulty in falling asleep. His relationship with his sister had been wretched for some time, the effects of which had strangely nagged at him more in the past few days than at any other time he could remember. He sensed that he needed to reconcile things with Kate, that he needed to make the effort now and not have the bitterness linger another day, and the early-morning quiet of the Hue Treasury building seemed the right place and the right time.

"So, I know you're going to think that I've gone absolutely spastic, but I feel strongly that the thing for me to do is to break the ice and tell you that I'm sorry for all the things I've said and all the things I've done to hurt you. I wish I could have better accepted and dealt with your beliefs, but like so many other things, I have to confess that I just didn't try very hard. And I hope someday we can be together again so I can tell you to your face that I love you, and that you mean a great deal to me as my sister and my good friend (and maybe you'll have gotten rid of all those screwy beliefs by then, huh?). Really, I hurt when I think about what we've missed over the past few years, especially when I remember what we had for so long when we were growing up. No matter what happens to me, I will always love you and Chris and Mom and Dad, and consider myself fortunate for having been blessed with such a wonderful family. Please pray for me, Kate, for I don't know what's in store for me here. I only know that there's more death and suffering in this place than I could ever adequately describe. I have a feeling in my gut that I haven't felt since I've been over here, and if this turns out to be the last correspondence we have, heaven forbid, then please know that I did the best I could, as best I knew how. And that all of you, but especially you, Kate, are on my mind and in my heart. May God bless and keep you, Tom."

He pushed the letter aside, leaning back and letting his thoughts flow to his family, and of the safety and comfort they were thankfully enjoying. He thought of what else might be happening back in The World, and how removed America's citizenry was from the horrors of Vietnam. He found it ironic that new heart transplant procedures were occurring in South Africa and the U.S., designed to save and maintain life, in stark contrast to the military procedures now occurring in Hue where the singular objective was the taking of life. He remembered hearing recently that the Packers had won the second Super Bowl over the Raiders, and how large numbers of football fans would have invested great emotion and attached great significance to something that now seemed so detached and trivial to him.

He smiled when he remembered the frigid day at Soldier Field when he and his father had agonized over the hated Packers beating his beloved Bears, in what now seemed like another life, a hazy memory of a happy innocence he knew he'd never know again. He folded the letter into the envelope, turned out the flashlight, and slept peacefully.

Finally.

* * *

The next morning, Monday, February 5th, Flanagan learned that his platoon would again be on the attack. The objective, the Cercle Sportif, was a country-club building complete with verandas, 1930s furnishings, and plush green lawns stretching all the way down to the river. He also learned that the assault plan to take down the objective had Dave Espy's 1st Platoon and his own 3rd in the lead, with Sgt. Magee, replacing the deceased Kevin Riordan, and his 2nd Platoon in the rear with Weapons Platoon. A network film crew would also be along, assigned to Flanagan's platoon.

Flanagan also noticed for the first time since the Fox Company Marines had entered Hue City, that the putrid odor of dead, decaying bodies was being spread about by the steady winds as a reminder of the killing zone the entire city had now become.

As if anyone needed a reminder.

Upon command, Lt. Flanagan moved his squads through a blown-open gate and across the open lawn leading into the Cercle Sportif building. Resistance was moderate, and the platoon was soon in the building with only two wounded still left on the grounds. Several running gunfights broke out between the Marines and the NVA, and each of the rooms had to be painstakingly cleared of the stubborn defenders. The fighting was intense at first, and the bullets were flying in such volumes that proper control and coordination became difficult.

"Fire in the hole!" shouted a Marine.

The M-26 grenade exploded with a flash and a boom only twenty-five feet from Flanagan, peppering him in the face and arm with its small slivers of hot shrapnel. Flanagan had watched when one of his own troops had attempted to toss the grenade inside an open second-floor doorway, but the throw had been high and hard and the grenade had instead ricocheted off the concrete and bounced back down in the direction of the Marines, bursting in mid-air.

"You okay, sir?" called a startled Marine.

"You stupid shit, I'm on *your* goddamn side," Flanagan said gruffly.

"Jesus, I'm sorry, sir. You okay?"

"I'll be fine," Flanagan said as he put his fingers to his face and glanced at the sticky blood on his fingertips.

"You're hit, sir," said Wenrick. "Corpsman!"

"Forget it, dammit," Flanagan snapped. "Just keep moving."

Blood streaked down Flanagan's face from the wound just beneath his right eye. Several open wounds on his right forearm also oozed. He ignored his condition and pressed on, maintaining radio communications with his squads, keeping visual contact with adjacent units, and trying as best he could to control the unfolding events. Any sort of control was complicated, however, since the confusion generated by the swift pace of events seemed to coalesce into a blur of gunfire, shouting, movement, and smoke.

The noise inside the Cercle Sportif was deafening. Frequent explosions were continuously rocking the building, and all but the loudest voices of the combatants were audible over the clamor. Marines were succeeding in clearing the premises room by room, and several NVA were cut down as they attempted to escape out the rear of the building. Dave Espy's platoon was inside the building and handling the left sector, Flanagan the right. Flanagan overheard radio reports that Golf Company was also having success in subduing the enemy in the adjacent library building, and Hotel Company had quickly secured the hospital. When Flanagan radioed Capt. Tanner and asked if he should continue in pursuit beyond the immediate objective, Tanner radioed back for him to secure the building and consolidate his platoon into a defensive posture.

At one point Flanagan turned and noticed the film crew peeking inside the building, camera ready, and then quickly withdrawing when gunfire and shouting erupted nearby.

Capt. Tanner radioed from his CP just outside the building that an aid station was soon to be set up on the bottom floor. Several Fox Company Marines were already being brought into the building to receive treatment.

Flanagan was on his way to confer with Sgt. Jankowski when a sudden bright flash accompanied by a loud *whoosh* preceded an explosion in a second-floor room that sent smoke and debris flying out into the open area. Flanagan was knocked backwards into Wenrick and both men tumbled part of the way down an old wooden staircase, breaking portions of the railing in the process.

"Son of a bitch!" Flanagan overheard from a nearby Marine who, like Flanagan, was trying to get to his feet and clear his head. The dust was thick enough to taste, and broken glass from the blast had slightly wounded several others. Flanagan coughed and took several more dusty breaths before pulling himself to his feet.

"Where the hell did that come from?" Flanagan shouted hoarsely. "Anybody see it?"

"Forward," came a reply. "Right front."

"Get something on the bastard. Keep his friggin' head down until we can get him with something heavier," called Flanagan. "Get on him, dammit."

"Get a machine gun up here."

"Hey I need a blooper up here. Gimme a blooper."

"Hurry hurry hurry. C'mon, quickly!"

Flanagan radioed Capt. Tanner, who passed along the message to Golf Company. Marines were already sighting rocket launchers and 106s at the building where the flash had been observed.

Someone screamed "Corpsman!" and Flanagan arrived with Wenrick and Doc Fackler just in time to see Sgt. Jankowski, sitting upright and braced against a wall, looking in disbelief at his own exposed intestines that he held in his trembling, bloody hands. Jankowski looked directly into Flanagan's eyes, moaned, then coughed and said with clenched teeth, "Damn it all," before his eyes suddenly rolled back and his head fell forward.

"Dammit, no!" Flanagan exclaimed as he and the corpsman attempted to revive the mortally wounded Jankowski. The explosion had ripped him apart at the midsection, grotesquely, and Flanagan instinctively knew Jankowski was beyond help.

The corpsman quickly leaned over Jankowski and listened for signs of breathing. There were none. Jankowski's pupils had rolled upward, and his head was limp in the hands of Fackler.

"C'mon, man," Flanagan called out in half-plea, half-shout.

The corpsman worked Jankowski into a prone position and breathed into his mouth. He rose up and gave Jankowski's chest two rapid thrusts, then leaned forward to listen for breathing. Jankowski's face was china-pale, his eyes staring out weakly at the darkness.

"C'mon dammit," Flanagan called out as his eyes began to fill with tears. "Please. Don't let go."

"It's no good, sir," the corpsman finally spoke after several more attempts at detecting a pulse.

Both men stood back and looked down at the horrible mess that only moments before had been the veteran platoon sergeant. Several other grunts gathered in the doorway to peer in at the scene. Someone came in with a wooden door, and the men wasted little time in lifting Jankowski's body and carrying it out of the room.

"You need some attention, too, Lieutenant," the corpsman said as he opened his bag for a swab and a sterile dressing.

Flanagan started out the door until the corpsman grabbed his uninjured arm and pulled him to a sitting position. "Stay where you are, sir."

Flanagan gave off a deep sigh. "This isn't really happening," he said faintly.

"Say again, sir?" Doc Fackler asked, leaning forward.

"Nothing. It was nothing."

Flanagan suddenly turned and vomited a mouthful of bile. He coughed for a moment, then leaned back against a wall. He took out his canteen and rinsed the foul taste from his mouth.

"Can I give you something for pain, Lieutenant?" Doc Fackler asked.

"No, I'm okay," Flanagan answered quickly.

"You sure?"

Flanagan nodded. "Somebody get Sergeant Douglas up here ASAP," he called out as Fackler began cleaning the facial wounds with an antiseptic. Several shouts of "Sergeant Douglas up" rang out through the building.

Soon thereafter Sgt. Douglas came running up the stairs and entered the room, holding his M-16 by the handle.

"You wanna see me, sir?" the sergeant said.

"Take a seat," Flanagan said with a fresh bandage underneath his eye. "You got the scoop on Sergeant Jankowski, right?"

"Yessir."

"And you're aware that you're next in line, the most senior man?"

"Right, sir. I've already been in touch with the squad leaders," Douglas answered confidently.

"Good, because you are now the platoon sergeant, as of this instant. I'll expect you to get busy and provide me with a report on the condition of the squads, the number of wounded and walking wounded, the deployment and the gaps in the fields of fire. I need to know how much ammo we have, how much water we need, and what kind of fighting condition our Marines and their equipment are in."

Sgt. Douglas gave an "Aye-aye, sir," got up and quickly started off when Flanagan suddenly called him back.

"Yessir?"

"Keep your friggin' head down," Flanagan ordered.

"Will do, sir."

"One other thing," Flanagan said, wincing slightly at the tightness of the corpsman's bandage on his arm. "Keep everyone on their toes. We should all know by now that these assholes aren't going to go quietly. "

"No problem, sir."

"One last thing: I want you to know that I've got full confidence in you. You're gonna be one damn fine platoon sergeant." Flanagan looked up and smiled weakly, adding, "Get the hell out of here and go see about my platoon."

Douglas gave a determined half-smile and nodded his thanks to Flanagan before quickly heading back out the doorway.

"Got some big shoes to fill," the corpsman observed.

"Yeah," said Flanagan, nodding and thinking of the old warrior Jankowski.

* * *

"Can we get you to say that on camera, Lieutenant?" asked the network reporter after the area had been secured.

It was dusk, and things had grown considerably less hectic. Some Marines were eating their C-rations while others were lounging around outside the building. Somewhere a tape player was playing *The Girl's All Right with Me*, and a few youthful American voices could be overheard singing along.

"Say *what* on camera?" snapped Flanagan.

"About what went on today, about in general how it's going here in Hue. You know, just a situation report, more or less. Will you agree to that?"

"No specifics, dammit. You understand that?"

GERALD GILLIS

"Right, no specifics."

"No tactical stuff, no casualty figures, no unit stuff. Nothing the Commie pricks could hear on an American news broadcast in Peoria and telephone back to Cuba and Moscow and on over to the little bastards in Hanoi. You know how quickly that kind of stuff moves around the world nowadays. It's a matter of days and hours now, not weeks."

"Yeah, yeah, I know. No specifics, Lieutenant."

Flanagan looked ahead at the camera and sound men, both of whom were Asian and, like the American reporter, dressed in jungle utilities. "You guys have been a pain in my military ass all damn day."

The crew grinned, except the reporter. "So, Lieutenant, what do you say? Will you do it?"

Flanagan sipped the canned Coca-Cola that the sound man had scrounged and given to him. It had a metallic taste, and it was warm, but otherwise it was a divine little piece of Americana. He looked at the reporter, standing in front with a pleading look on his face, and thought of the remote chance that someone back in Chicago might watch the evening news and see him, alive and mostly well in Hue City. Who the hell knows what else might happen? he thought. Who the hell really knows?

One hour at a time, he thought again.

Flanagan finally nodded his consent, and as soon as the newsman began his line of questioning about the day's events, sporadic small-arms firing started from up ahead, out of immediate range but nevertheless causing the reporter to duck and temporarily lose his train of thought. Flanagan stood straight and unflinching, sipping his Coke, and several black Marines who were casually watching nearby grinned and slapped hands.

" . . . As I was saying, Lieutenant, what was represented with today's action in Hue . . . "

CHAPTER SEVEN
Washington, D.C.

Kate Flanagan found a parking spot on the street—an unlikely but nonetheless welcome piece of good luck—and smoothly slid her dark-blue Mustang in on the first try. She got out into the blustery cold and walked the single block to the Georgetown restaurant, and though she was stylishly dressed in business attire with long coat and scarf, it was hardly enough to shield her from the gusty, mid-February wind. It was shortly before noon on Friday, and the crowd at the popular eatery was already building. Inside, she was met by Dan Marinelli and a half-dozen other Bobby Kennedy staffers—four males and two females. Dan greeted her warmly and then quickly made the introductions, and each of the others received Kate with smiles and enthusiasm. The group had a drink at the bar, after which they were escorted to a cozy private dining room in the rear of the building. It was Kate's final day with her current advertising-agency employer, and she had earlier that same day tactfully declined the managing partner's offer of lunch in what she knew would be his last-ditch effort to salvage her for his firm.

Come Monday morning, she realized with both excitement and apprehension, she would become a full-fledged member of Robert F. Kennedy's senatorial staff.

They were all seated, and after ordering lunch, each of the Kennedy staffers proceeded to give Kate a brief sketch of their respective backgrounds. All, it turned out, were well educated—half with master's degrees and one with a law degree—and apart from a single Californian they all hailed from the East. Some assisted in speechwriting; some did background research on issues; some drafted legislation; some answered the immense quantities of mail; some scheduled appointments and maintained RFK's itinerary. They were all alert and fashionably dressed, all poised and composed, all with about the same length in hair, and all with a tendency to laugh loudly and frequently.

The group enjoyed a relaxed lunch, and Kate was impressed over how much of her own background the others seemed to know. Senator Kennedy, it was explained, was returning that day from a trip to New York, and the staffers were all eager to find out the results of the meeting RFK had held with several of his most trusted advisers.

"Might be soon," Dan whispered to Kate, followed by a wink. "Might be *real* soon."

By the time lunch ended and the table had been cleared, all eyes seemed to settle upon Dan. "This is gonna be great," he said with excitement in his voice. "This is gonna be momentous; historic, even. Just think about *this*, ladies and gentlemen: Now we've got a lifelong Democrat, a Chicagoan, a proven advertising pro, and a redhead, each of which we needed and all of which we've been lucky enough to find in the same person. The circle is now complete. And so I say to each of you, press on, and let's get going with our move from the Senate Office Building to the White House."

There was laughter and applause, and almost on cue the waiter brought in a bottle of champagne on ice. Kate was the first to be served.

"So, moving right along, if I may have your undivided attention," Dan said from his seat at the head of the table after tapping a spoon against a glass. "Kate, since I've already briefed everyone on your background in great detail and with meticulous accuracy, there's very little need for you to review the specifics, that is, unless you simply feel the need to take the floor and state it for yourself in the unlikely event you don't trust the picture of your impressive record that I've already quite ably painted."

"Good grief, was that one sentence or fifteen?" asked a staffer.

"Did you really serve time in San Quentin, Kate, like Dan told us?" asked the lawyer staffer. "For something as relatively minor as grand theft auto?"

"I thought it was possession and distribution," asserted one of the female staffers.

Kate offered a good-natured laugh and joked, "It was nothing as piddling as that, I can assure you."

"Amend the record, Kate," said another to laughter.

"Hell, disavow the record, Kate," said still another to still further laughter.

"Please, just a minute here," Dan shouted at the others before turning to Kate. "I had intended to offer you the floor before I was so rudely interrupted. However, the offer still stands. The floor is hereby yours, Miss Flanagan. Take it if you like."

Kate smiled and nodded graciously. "I feel no such need, Dan, and I'll take my chances with the record as it now stands. Thank you just the same."

"In that event," Dan said, pausing suddenly when he noticed the door to the room opening.

Everyone else in the room stopped and looked back toward the door.

"In that event," said the grinning Bobby Kennedy as he walked into the room unaccompanied, "in the little time you've known her you've probably succeeded in doing irreparable harm to Miss Flanagan's opinion of me specifically and all of you in general."

The group remained seated.

"Please, keep your seats everyone," Kennedy said with an exaggerated motion of his hand.

Dan quickly stood. "Actually, Senator, we had already decided to sacrifice Kate's opinion of you and concentrate instead on bolstering our own images."

"Bolstering? Or perhaps salvaging?" Kennedy asked.

"Bolstering, of course," said Dan.

Kennedy unbuttoned the jacket of his gray suit and accepted a glass of champagne from a staffer. "Then you'll need quite a bit more of this," he said, chuckling and pointing to the single bottle. "Perhaps a bit more time, too, like a month and a half," he said, pronouncing the last word as *hoff* in his Boston accent.

Kennedy stepped around the end of the table and extended his hand to Kate, who quickly stood. "Nice to have you with us, Kate. Sorry I missed you the other day when you were in the office. I just wanted to stop in and tell you that I'm happy to have you as part of our staff."

Kate swallowed and appeared slightly flustered by Kennedy's attention. "I'm very happy to be here, Senator. Thanks for stopping by."

"A toast," called Dan, prompting the others to stand. "To our newest member. I toast the arrival of Kate Flanagan and the many talents she will bring to our lofty efforts."

"Here, here."

Kennedy took a sip and placed the glass on the table. He glanced at his watch and ran his fingers through his hair. "I'm late already," he announced as he buttoned his jacket and glanced over at Dan. "See me when you get back, okay?"

Dan nodded. "Right, Bob."

"See you later, everyone," Kennedy called with a wave as he turned to leave. "See you soon, Kate."

With that, he was gone.

The others chuckled when they noticed Kate's wide-eyed expression of incredulity. Kate blushed and reached for a glass of water.

"You'll get used to it," one of the female staffers sagely advised, adding, "sorta," which drew an instant uproar.

The luncheon eventually broke up and nearly all the staffers left the restaurant to return to work. Dan leaned over from standing alongside Kate and asked, "Can we have a quick drink before you leave?"

Kate glanced at her watch and frowned. "Dan, for goodness sake, it's my last day and I can't go back there sloshed."

"Okay, coffee then," he quickly countered. When he saw Kate glance down again at her watch, he added, "Fifteen minutes, and that's it. I promise."

Kate drew a deep breath and quickly contemplated whether she should return to her old boss or have coffee with her new one.

"Fifteen minutes, Dan, please. I've got several things to wrap up before I walk out of there for good."

Dan nodded his agreement as they went into the bar and took a small corner table, alongside the windows. A waitress quickly brought the coffee that Dan had called out to his bartender friend.

"So," Dan asked as he stirred the sugar into his coffee, "tell me how you think it went today?"

"I'm really impressed with all of them," Kate answered without hesitation. "And I was especially impressed to get the 'high-level' visit. I wasn't expecting that."

Dan grinned mischievously. "Good."

"You didn't have anything to do with it, did you?"

"Me?" he said, shrugging innocently. "Do you really think I have that kind of influence?"

"Yeah," Kate said with a grin, twisting a lock of her red hair around her index finger. "I think you probably do. And I really appreciate it."

"I'm glad you enjoyed it. Tell me, what has your guy Edward said about it?"

"It's Everett."

"Yeah, him."

Kate chuckled. "I think he would've handled it better if I'd told him I was going to work for Richard Nixon." She thought briefly about telling Dan of the ensuing arguments they'd had, some of which had been quite heated, but she chose instead to say nothing further.

"And your parents? Did you tell them?" asked Dan.

"Yes, of course."

"And?" said Dan, leaning forward.

"They're fine," Kate answered before pausing and adding, "mostly."

"Mostly?"

"I think my dad's a little put out with me," Kate said with a slight shrug.

"Yeah? Why?"

"Oh, he's not always pleased with the way I choose to live my life."

Dan turned his head slightly in what Kate knew was a request for elaboration.

"Don't worry," said Kate. "He'll still claim me as his daughter."

"I didn't mean to," Dan said, his face reddening, "I mean, I didn't—"

"Look, it's okay. My father would probably prefer that I not live with my fiancé or have a job on Bobby Kennedy's staff, but he'll be okay."

"Live with *a* fiancé, or *this* fiancé?" said Dan.

Kate looked at her watch and announced, "I'd better be leaving."

"No, wait," said Dan, touching her arm. "Tell me about your Marine brother. Where is he now?"

She drew a deep breath. "We found out he's in Hue."

Dan's expression immediately changed.

"Is it that bad?" Kate asked.

"Well," Dan said, suddenly measuring his words, "I suppose it could be worse."

"Yeah? Where?" asked Kate, eyebrows raised.

Dan paused a moment before answering, "I'm not sure. There are lots of bad places in Vietnam right now, but Hue City's gotta be right up there at the top, based on what I'm seeing and reading."

She let out a sigh. "Damn it all, and he's been hurt already."

"How so?"

"He was on television," said Kate.

"You're kidding! In a hospital?"

"No, being interviewed. I didn't see it, but my mother called and she and my dad had seen him and she was completely bummed out because he was bandaged on his face and arm."

Dan exhaled loudly. "He could use a few prayers, Kate. But you already know that. I'll offer a few from my end, for what it's worth."

She pushed the coffee aside and looked away, outside the window. She took a deep breath, her lips pursed tightly together, and when she turned to face Dan, her expression was resolute.

"I've been thinking a lot about this lately. Night and day, all night and all day, sometimes, especially since this Tet-nightmare thing started. Some of it has become clearer to me, and I've come to terms with some of the things that Tommy holds dear, some of his beliefs and the way he sees things in general. But still, a lot of it is unclear, and I'll never understand how Tommy or anyone else could actually want to take part in a war, in killing other human beings. And I'll do everything in my power to bring a stop to the killing, which, among other things, has caused me to leave my job and join you and the others. So I suppose it all boils down to the fact that Tommy made a decision to do what he thought was the right thing for him, just like I made my decision to do what I thought was the right thing for me. And if Tommy now finds himself in a bad situation in Hue, then I have to remember that first of all he's put himself in Vietnam of his own free will—*his own free will, dammit!*—and if Hue or any of those other bad places are on the list of possibilities, then he's accepted that as being part of what he volunteered to do, part of doing what he determined was the right thing for him to do."

Dan crushed out a cigarette but otherwise said nothing.

"Tommy and I will probably never see eye to eye on much more than a handful of things—a few basic family matters, maybe, but maybe not—and I suppose I'm prepared to live with that and I'm sure he is, too. He's told me as much, as a matter of fact."

When Dan sat absolutely still and made no response for several moments, Kate finally leaned forward and said firmly, "So that's that. Any other questions about my brother?"

"No more questions," Dan answered softly. "I wish your brother well, and I hope he comes through this okay. I pray to God he does."

* * *

Kate arrived back at her townhouse at seven. The managers and employees at her ad agency had set up a conference room with booze and snacks, and late in the day thcro had been a going-away party in her honor. She had been fine until several of her closest colleagues, after several glasses of wine, had been moved to tears, and from that point on, against a determined effort to do otherwise, Kate had been become an emotional train wreck. She had pulled herself together at the end only long enough to start crying anew when she finally got into her car and started the drive home.

Everett was away, and she felt exhausted and headachy when she came into the kitchen to fetch some aspirin and a glass of water. She noticed a letter addressed to her on the table, the return address of which showed it being from "1st Lt. T. M. Flanagan, USMC," and included his unit name and an FPO of San Francisco. She stared at the letter for several moments, water glass in one hand and aspirin in the other, trying to imagine what additional emotional jostling she would incur by the time she'd finished reading it. Her curiosity finally got the better of her when she ripped open the envelope and opened the folded pages.

She quickly read through the two handwritten pages, stained in places with the dirt and grime that the Marine on the other end had worn and lived with. Her first impulse was disbelief, so she finished it once and started through it again for confirmation. Her heart raced as she pictured her brother in her mind's eye and associated the words she read with the sound of his voice. He was actually apologizing—something he hardly ever did, ever, but this time without condition or equivocation—and he was all but announcing to her in a renewal of their previously sacrosanct brother-sister privilege, his apparent belief that the wartime circumstance of his own death might soon be upon him, that this letter was his attempt at setting things straight while he still had some time and some life left in him. Kate pictured in her head the boy Tommy with the gap-toothed grin; flashed ahead to Tommy the Little Leaguer; then the boy scout in his new uniform; the crew-cut high school grad in cap and gown; the confident college student; the college baseball star who had drawn the attention of big-league scouts; the wise, indefatigable older brother she'd known and loved in what seemed now a previous life.

She thought of Jill Rohrbach, and wondered if she and Tommy had corresponded since their last meeting before Tommy had left for Vietnam. She was reluctant to contact Jill, even though she remained certain that Tommy still loved her and intended to reconcile with her once he came home. The agony she knew that Tommy had endured over the break-up with Jill caused her even more tears as her mind kept racing through the flashing mental images of her brother.

Suddenly all the pain and bitterness of the recent past evaporated into a hot, flushing rush of adoration and forgiveness. And then came the fright.

"Oh dear God," she said, almost in panic, raising the letter to her bosom and holding it close as she gasped for air and envisioned a flag-draped coffin in a cold Chicago cemetery. "Oh God, no! Please, no!"

Could it be that he's now dead? she kept thinking. Is he dead already?

"Oh no," she said in a quivering, child-like voice of anguish.

Is someone about to knock on my door or call me on the phone and tell me my brother's dead? her inner voice was shouting.

"Oh dear God, no."

The tears started flowing again, and she quickly took a seat at the table. She alternately raced through moments of anger, despair, hysteria, and guilt. She wondered if she should alert her parents—her father if not her mother, at least. And Chris. And others. But to what? And would Tommy approve? She was disoriented, as much in the news itself as by the sudden, unexpected reversal of the status quo, and she wanted desperately to avoid violating Tommy's resurrected trust.

She took several deep breaths and kept repeating, "It's okay. Everything's really okay."

She fought hard to regain control, and she momentarily panicked anew when she heard the opening of the front door of the townhouse. She felt relieved when she heard the sound of Everett's voice.

"Kate, are you home?" Everett called from inside the doorway.

She tried to say, "In here," but her voice broke into a gurgle.

Everett walked into the kitchen smiling broadly, his eyes bright, as if he had something so important to announce that it was dripping from his tongue. But when he looked down and saw her tear-streaked face, her reddened eyes, her look of distress and sheer exhaustion, and the water and the aspirin in the center of the table, he immediately froze.

"Oh shit. What's happened?" he said tentatively, turning pale. "Tell me what's happened."

She sat up straight and took a deep breath. "It's been one bitch of a day, as you might've noticed," she answered, even managing a slight smile.

"I've noticed, yeah. Has there been a disaster or something?"

"No, there's been no disaster."

"Is everyone okay?" Everett asked.

"Everyone's okay. For the moment, anyway."

"What do you mean?"

"Everyone's okay. That's all I meant," Kate said.

She felt herself calming, and she extended her hand which he immediately took and began stroking.

"Care to tell me about it?" he asked in a soothing tone.

"It's okay. Things are fine. I'm fine. Everybody's fine."

"Kate?"

"I'm a little tipsy, and I had a scare."

"A scare? What kind of scare?" he asked.

"Nothing. Everything's okay, really. It's just been a really heavy day, that's all. I've left my job and some wonderful friends.

I've met with my new associates. I've heard from my brother in Vietnam. I think I'm just exhausted from all the—"

He pulled her to her feet and embraced her. "Jesus, Kate, you scared the living hell out of me. Please, for crissakes, don't ever do that to me again."

"What?" asked Kate.

"That. Scaring me to death."

She pushed away from him slightly. "You're acting like you want an apology or something, when I thought *I* was the one having the hard day."

She noticed his look of embarrassment before he reached for her again.

"No apology necessary," he said softly.

"I should think not, at least not from me."

"Then let me offer my apology," he said.

"Thank you."

"Anything else I can do for you?" he asked.

"What've you got in mind?"

"I'm at your service," he announced. "What do you feel like doing? Eating? Drinking? Going out? Catching a movie?"

"No, none of that, especially drinking," she said with a giggle.

"Anything else, then?"

She began rubbing her temples.

"Two aspirin and a glass of water," she said, which he immediately picked up from the table and handed to her.

"Anything else?"

She gave a catty grin. "As unlikely as it seems, yeah, there is one thing I feel like doing."

"Yeah? What?"

She parted her legs and pressed against the front of his thigh. "Use your imagination. I've had an emotionally demanding day and I want something soothing."

"I'll have to use more than my imagination, in that case."

"Then start using."

He held her in his arms. Her shoulders and back were taut with tension, and she felt him reach up with one hand and begin gently rubbing her neck. She sighed, seeming to melt in place, and it wasn't long before her tightness began to ease. He began kissing her neck, her ear, the side of her face, and she felt his hand underneath her skirt, on the firm roundness and cleaved middle of her buttocks. She moaned slightly and responded by tightening her hold upon him and kissing him passionately. Her head still ached, throbbed even, but there was enough pleasure beginning to surge through the rest of her to mask the otherwise annoying pain. They stood in the middle of the kitchen, locked in embrace, enjoying in every way the warmth, scent, taste, and feel of one another as they moved along on the path to ecstasy. She allowed him to unbutton her blouse, and in a matter of moments they were both bare from the waist up, her smooth milky-white breasts pressed hard against his chest. Her breathing came quickly, and the delicious warmth of his hands upon her soft skin was all the more arousing. "Let's go back to the bedroom," he whispered.

"No," she replied, her voice husky. "I'd rather stay here."

He pulled away a moment and glanced at the table, then the floor. "Are you sure?"

"Yes," she said as she reached for him. "Right now. Right here."

The telephone rang with startling unexpectedness. Everett gave an exasperated sigh as Kate flinched and immediately pulled away from him. He noticed her suddenly changing expression.

"Let it ring," he suggested weakly.

"I can't," she replied as she reached for her blouse.

"Dammit," Everett mumbled under his breath.

Kate quickly slipped into her top before reaching for the nearby phone in the kitchen. She swept the hair out of her eyes and began buttoning her blouse, the phone propped against her cheek and shoulder, when she answered with a soft, "Hello."

Everett then saw a look of wide-eyed astonishment overtake Kate as she stopped and grabbed the telephone with both hands.

It was Jill Rohrbach on the other end.

CHAPTER EIGHT
Hue, South Vietnam

The sky was as gray as beach sand, with a column of thin black smoke rising in the distance from a previous airstrike.

Lt. Flanagan, with radio-operator Wenrick walking alongside, guided on a north-south Hue street on the south side of the railroad tracks. To his right-front was the Tu Dam Pogoda, and to the far right was the Phu Cam Cathedral. He could glance over and see Espy's platoon on the left, and he knew Magee's platoon was in the rear. Up ahead, but out of sight, Flanagan knew that Hotel Company was moving toward them in what was expected to be a pincer movement to flush out any enemy troops. The now dreadful, ubiquitous odor of putrefying bodies, only partially buried in open graves and rubble, seemed thick enough to wear, close enough to reach out and grab by the handful.

"This is one stinkin' son of a bitch," Wenrick said as he and Flanagan walked along with rifles at the ready in the center of the platoon column. "*Damn*, this place stinks!"

"Be happy it's you doing the smelling of them," Flanagan countered as he kept his eyes forward on the street ahead, "and not the other way around. Keep looking at it that way and before long the place will start to smell like a botanical garden."

Wenrick grinned. "Never thought of it like that before, sir. From dead gook to botanical garden—now *that's* one hell of a trip."

Flanagan kept glancing from side to side. So far, so good, he thought as his men moved deliberately up the road. "That's why you have me here, Wenrick. I take care of the big things and point out the little things. The American taxpayer expects no less of me, and I will not let them down. I'm just trying to earn my keep."

"By the way, sir, did you get to see Walter Cronkite yesterday morning?" asked Wenrick.

Flanagan gave a curious glance toward Wenrick. "No. Where?"

"He was with some of the top brass over on Le Loi Street. He even had on a helmet and flak jacket, and he was smoking a pipe."

"No shit?"

"No shit, sir. And I saw him—the real live dude himself," Wenrick said with evident pride.

"I'd heard he was here."

"Yessir, he's right here in Hue City with us grunts."

Damn, Flanagan thought with slight amusement. Walter Cronkite, the man himself, right here in Hue for a look of his own. Flanagan chuckled, thinking that Hue would be a real surprise, a real eye-opener to Cronkite if he gets close enough to smell the powder. Or the bodies. How about that! Walter friggin' Cronkite.

The Marines kept moving.

Flanagan thought briefly of his family, of Jill Rohrbach, of what Kate's reaction would be to the letter he'd sent several days earlier. He had done the right thing, of that he was certain. And deep down he knew that Kate would respond generously. She had a tough exterior, much like their mother, but underneath he knew Kate to be sympathetic in matters involving the family. Maybe soon he would hear from her, he hoped. And maybe when her letter did arrive, he thought with dark amusement, he'd still be around to read it.

One more hour, he silently prayed.

Up ahead, Flanagan saw an NVA soldier suddenly emerge in full view from behind a building and fire a B-40 rocket into the advancing column. The enemy soldier then quickly ducked back into an alley before the Marines on the point could take him under fire. The rocket detonated with a bright flash and sprayed razor-sharp metal fragments into the bodies of several Marines. Immediately thereafter another NVA from a second-story window to the right-front opened up with an AK-47. When the NVA soldier with the launcher came out again to fire the B-40, he was literally shot to pieces with a fusillade of M-16 rifle fire from the advancing Marines. He fell over backward with the rocket launcher on top of him.

The enemy firing intensified, and the Marines quickly moved off the street. Flanagan moved quickly to his left to get to the cover of a house, once there turning and reaching behind him for the radio from Wenrick. But Wenrick wasn't there. When he looked out into the street, three Marines, including Wenrick, were on the ground and exposed. Bullets were kicking up the dirt all around, and Wenrick rolled, aimed, and fired his weapon on full automatic at the window. Flanagan heard his young radio operator growl "Shit!" as Wenrick fired a full magazine and rolled to his side to retrieve another from his belt.

"Gimme some cover fire," Flanagan shouted to the men up ahead. "We gotta get 'em off the street. Cover, cover."

Flanagan heard another AK-47 join in the action from a building adjacent to the first, to the left-front, and a running firefight was now underway.

"I'm hit," Flanagan heard Wenrick scream in a desperate voice. Wenrick rolled and faced Flanagan, then reached down and felt his leg. Flanagan saw the bloody leg and the look of fright on Wenrick's face.

"Stay down," Flanagan screamed back.

Flanagan then recognized the two distinct *thunk* sounds as NVA mortars joined the action. "Incoming. Incoming."

"I'm hit," called Wenrick.

"Stay down, goddammit," Flanagan called in return.

The mortar shells impacted off to the side, away from the downed men in the street. Flanagan and two other Marines suddenly made a rush to the street under covering fire. Flanagan grabbed Wenrick's outstretched hand and pulled him thirty feet across the street to safety behind the single-story building. A bullet struck the plastic canteen on Flanagan's hip and punctured it near the bottom. The water soaked through onto Flanagan's utility trousers and caused him to think he'd been wounded in the buttocks as he felt the shock and the moisture. He quickly glanced around and saw the dark spot. He knew for sure he was unhurt only when he grabbed at the spot and saw water on his fingers.

"Corpsman."

Wenrick was hyperventilating as Flanagan reached into his radioman's first-aid pack and pulled out a sterile bandage. There were several nasty punctures, the bleeding thick but not abnormally so, and the wounds were on the outside of the mid-thigh between the knee and hip. Flanagan took out his combat knife and quickly cut away the trousers.

"Does it look okay, sir?" asked the anxious Wenrick. "How does it look?"

Flanagan began tightly wrapping the wound. "It looks like you've been hit, Wenrick. It's not too bad and you aren't about to die. Take a deep breath and lay back. We've got some decent cover here."

"Shit!" the young man growled with clenched teeth as the pain began to grow.

"What've you got, Lieutenant?" called Doc Fackler as he ran around the corner holding onto his helmet.

"Radioman, semi-fucked up, one each. No morphine yet. What else have you got up there, Doc?" Flanagan said calmly as he finished the dressing.

Fackler looked at the dressing and then prepared a morphine injection for Wenrick. "Two WIAs. One fragmentation and gunshot through and through; one fragmentation only; both stable, but I need to get back to the gunshot."

The firing continued. Flanagan got the radio pack off Wenrick and called in a quick situation report to Capt. Tanner, then took reports from each of his squads. Sgt. Douglas was with one of the squads up ahead that was steadily maneuvering for an assault upon the closest of the sniper locations.

"Gotta go, Wenrick. You can have sick call for the rest of the day, but I'll need your shot-up ass back out here tomorrow."

Flanagan then heard another pair of *thunk* sounds from up ahead.

"Incoming!" Flanagan shouted out to his Marines. "Where the hell is that coming from? Gimme a blooper up here. Somebody get some shit on that brick building up there. Up there, up ahead. Hurry up, dammit, put something *on* it. Get down, *get down*. Incoming!"

Flanagan leaned over Wenrick and protected him with his own body as Fackler covered his head with his arms and curled into a fetal position alongside. The two rounds exploded in the street, just twenty meters from their position, scattering debris and sending an echo reverberating off the concrete walls. Flanagan coughed through the dust and then looked down at Wenrick's pale, sweaty face, and winked. He could tell from Wenrick's eyes that the injured Marine could already feel the morphine easing the pain in his leg. Flanagan propped up Wenrick's head with a helmet liner.

"Thanks for coming out there for me, sir," Wenrick offered with an admiring grin. "I knew you wouldn't leave me out there."

Flanagan nodded and picked up the radio's handset. "Roger that, I want those automatic rifles silenced. Get the three-five up there and blast 'em out, and then find those tubes. There's half a klick between us and Hotel, so the tubes have gotta be in there somewhere. But watch yourself, they'll be covering the tubes with ARs. And be aware of Hotel's line of fire."

Flanagan stood and made ready to leave. "Get 'em to the rear, Doc. We've got an LZ about three blocks back, in a parking lot."

"Will do, sir."

"Keep your head down, sir," Wenrick called out.

Flanagan grabbed the radio gear and carried it alongside him as he left on the run to get closer to the firing. He called back to Capt. Tanner and found out that Hotel Company, on the opposite side of the enemy enclave from Fox Company, was also under mortar and small-arms fire. One of the NVA snipers had already been killed, and Sgt. Douglas was in the final stages of directing a squad in overtaking the other.

Flanagan ordered a Marine with a 3.5-inch rocket launcher to fire four rounds into the second building before a squad rushed inside to find a mangled NVA soldier taking his last gasping, wide-eyed breaths. Flanagan then consolidated the platoon on a line and began directing a sweep forward in search of the mortar tubes when, seemingly out of nowhere, two Marine F-4 Phantom jets showed up overhead and made rocket-firing runs into the NVA positions. The sudden presence of the aircraft took Flanagan and his Marines by complete surprise. The Phantoms came screaming in low and perpendicular to the axis of the Fox and Hotel Companies' advance.

"Hold up, hold up!" Flanagan shouted and radioed to his advancing Marines. "What's going on?" he radioed back to the CO. "Who the hell called for air? What the hell is this stuff doing here without me knowing about it, goddammit?" he screamed at the top of his lungs to the nearby aerial observer, a Marine lieutenant. "Who called the goddamn air? I've got people out in the *open* here."

"I thought you got the word," the AO called back.

"What friggin' word?" Flanagan shouted, the veins in his neck bulging. "Who the hell was supposed to give me the word? I almost walked my people directly underneath that goddamn air."

The AO quickly began separating himself from Flanagan.

"What the hell kind of screwed up plan was *that*?" Flanagan called with a parting shot.

Small arms could still be heard ahead, and Capt. Tanner soon radioed for Flanagan to halt his platoon in place and await further orders. The lack of coordination with the tactical air momentarily broke up the advance, but no Marine casualties were encountered as a result.

Several minutes passed before Flanagan finally calmed down.

"Hotel's got 'em," Sgt. Douglas speculated with a confident nod when told by Flanagan of Tanner's order. "If they don't already have 'em, they've got the little bastards cut off."

The two men shared a quick drink from Douglas' canteen before Capt. Tanner arrived in their position.

"Hotel's cut off the mortars, so we're gonna stay here and prevent any escape until they mop things up on their end," Tanner advised. "The snafu with the air happened when the S-3 didn't get the word to us quickly enough. Why, I don't know, and I'll take that up with him as soon as I see him again. Hotel knew about it, but we obviously didn't until it was almost too late. Anyway, the important thing is that Hotel's got 'em in a headlock."

"What about the wounded?" asked Flanagan.

"We brought 'em up with us, and we've got a medevac on the way in. It's picking up some wounded from over at the Citadel now, and it'll be over here most skosh. Did we take any more casualties when we took out the two positions?"

"Negative, Skipper," Douglas answered.

"Then we'll get ours out ASAP."

Flanagan turned the platoon over to Sgt. Douglas after seeing to the positioning of his people. He then walked a block to the rear area where Wenrick and the others were stretched out on the living room floor of an abandoned residence. One man was seriously wounded with shrapnel wounds to the legs and abdomen and a gunshot wound to the upper arm. Doc Fackler held an IV bag above the semi-conscious man. The two others were propped up and smoking cigarettes. Flanagan heard someone outside shout "chopper" and then heard the distant thumping of the rotor blades.

"Good luck, men," Flanagan said as he reached down and shook the hands of both the lesser injured.

"I wouldn't take anything for it, sir," Wenrick said as he took Flanagan's hand in his. "I'd damn well follow you anywhere, Lieutenant."

Flanagan nodded his thanks, then leaned over and touched the arm of the seriously injured Marine, a Native American. "Hang in there, Sixkiller. Good luck back in The World."

The man nodded slightly and squeezed Flanagan's leg. Several other Marines came inside the house and helped Fackler remove the wounded to the nearby landing zone. The CH-46 came in low from across the Perfume River, settled down amid a blast of rotor wash and red smoke, quickly took on the wounded, and then pitched forward nose-down in a gradual right-hand turn toward Phu Bai, to the south. Flanagan watched as the chopper eventually receded into the low-hanging fog behind a trail of dark exhaust, the steady pop-popping of its rotors becoming more pronounced the further out it got.

* * *

The day's action was over by early afternoon. At dusk Flanagan and several others attended a Mass conducted by Father Armbrester in an old, shell-damaged cathedral. Later, Flanagan and Sgt. Douglas found a spot in the soft grass outside the cathedral to sit down and cook their C-rations meals. It was mostly dark, and the weather was cool and dry. Several other 3rd Platoon Marines sat nearby, soon joined by a half-dozen black Marines, all of whom were unaware of the nearby presence of Flanagan and Douglas. The men were grubby, their uniforms dirty and torn in places, their faces grimy, some of their limbs, heads, and faces bandaged. Dark blood stains, their own or perhaps that of a buddy, were visible on many of the green uniforms.

"Walter Cronkite ought to come over here and eat some of this tired-ass shit," Flanagan overheard from one of the Marines. "The dude would say good-bye to the Nam in a hurry, man, and be back on that Freedom Bird. He'd be bookin' from this crazy shit."

Flanagan and Douglas glanced at one another and grinned. The others nearby laughed.

"There it is, man. Why would he want this cold greasy shit when he could snap his fingers back in The World and have a steak and a glass of wine? The dude ain't no fool."

"No damn gook's gonna blow his ass away back in The World, neither. The damn gooks don't give a shit about Walter Cronkite, man. He comes out here and ole Charlie might say, 'Here, newsman, how'd you like this B-40 rocket up your big-city New York ass?'"

Everyone laughed again.

Flanagan continued to listen quietly as one of the Marines, a veteran M-60 machine gunner from Pittsburgh named Maddox, nicknamed Dog (short for Mad Dog), was busy sparring with a new replacement, a young white private named Renner.

"Renner, what did you tell me about playing football in college, man?" Dog asked.

Flanagan looked over and saw Renner nod tentatively, all the while eyeing Dog with suspicion. "Right. I played two years at Boise State."

"Boise what? There ain't no damn state named Boise," said Dog. "Where the hell is that, man?"

"It's in Idaho."

"Idaho? Is that over around Lake Erie?"

They all laughed, especially Dog. All except Renner, that is.

"Renner, you ain't big enough to have played ball in college, man. How much do you weigh?"

"About one-seventy."

"Shit," said Dog with a sneer. "You're maybe one-fifty, tops. No damn new guy's gonna come in here and jive the Dog, man. One-fifty and no more, and that ain't no bullshit."

"The dude says he's one-seventy, Dog. Are you calling the man a liar?"

"I am if he says he weighs one-seventy."

"Well he says it, man. And he says he played some ball down around Erie. Renner, what've got to say, boy?"

Renner remained silent.

"The brother says he doesn't believe you, Renner. He says you aren't being truthful. He says there ain't no such thing as a Boise State. And he says you weigh one-fifty, tops."

More laughter, again except from Renner.

"Good thing the lying dude ain't Pinocchio," said Dog, grinning broadly, "or his nose would be longer than his damn dick."

"Shit," said another, blowing bits of cracker out of his mouth as he spoke. "I'll bet his nose is *already* longer than his damn dick."

"And he's got a pug nose, too, man."

SHALL NEVER SEE SO MUCH

The heckling went on for several more minutes. Flanagan noticed that Renner seemed uneasy and was about ready to get up and walk away when one of the black Marines suddenly tossed a small box of C-ration cigarettes in his direction.

"Here, Renner," said the man, smiling. "You earned these, man."

"You're all right, Renner," Dog declared with a big grin, "for a blue-eyed brother from Boise."

Everyone laughed, including Renner, who didn't smoke but accepted the gesture just the same.

Renner's confidence returned and he happily joined in the conversation by asking the others about Fox Company's and 3rd Platoon's command structure. Sgt. Douglas cut a quick glance toward Flanagan, acting as if he was ready to call attention to themselves and thereby end the discussion. Flanagan raised his hand slightly, directing Douglas to remain silent.

"So what's Captain Tanner like?" Renner asked.

"The Tan Man," said Dog, grinning, "he ain't got no flies. The dude's got his shit in one bag, man, and that's all a man can ask for out here. He goes about his business and doesn't hassle his people. He can be a hardass when he needs to be, but he doesn't screw with the troopies like some other CO's do. Nah, man, I ain't got nothing but respect for the Tan Man. He's a damn good Marine."

Others either nodded or voiced their agreement with Dog's assessment.

"What about Lieutenant Flanagan?"

There was some uncomfortable shifting and coughing among several Marines. "Good man," Dog finally said, prompting the others to agree, but with noticeably less enthusiasm.

Sgt. Douglas shot another quick glance at Flanagan.

* * *

"Gentlemen, it's official. Fox Company's crossing the river and going in at the Citadel."

Capt. Tanner sat with his feet propped upon a stack of ammo boxes that ho'd converted into a makeshift desk. Flanagan and the other platoon leaders were seated on crates and folding chairs in the single-story University building. Tanner confirmed the rumor that had been floating around the South Side for days, that at least one rifle company from 2/5 would be sent over to reinforce the bloody struggle going on at the Citadel, and indeed there was some talk that the entire battalion might be used. He explained that word had finally come down that only one company would be utilized, prompting each of the Fox, Hotel, and Golf Company commanders to volunteer their respective units. Fox Company had thus been chosen to join the fray while the remainder of the battalion continued as a security force on the South Side.

"This time tomorrow morning we'll be along the northeast wall someplace," Tanner said confidently.

* * *

It was cloudy and dry on Friday, February 16, when Flanagan and his platoon boarded the Navy landing craft with the rest of Fox Company for the trip up the Perfume River to the northern corner of the Citadel. He was acutely aware that Friday marked the fourth consecutive day that his fellow Marines inside the Citadel had been battling what was estimated to be two NVA battalions. He was also aware that the friendly Army of the Republic of Vietnam (ARVN) and South Vietnamese Marine units had forgone their active status and essentially moved from offense to defense in what was politely being referred to as a "down tempoing" of their operations. Flanagan had even received word that the ARVN had resorted to looting much of Hue, and that the U.S. command had even given "shoot to kill" orders to deal with the ARVN looters. The ARVN weren't fighting, and the Marines weren't the only ones in Hue who knew it. The NVA controlled the northeast and southwest walls of the Citadel, and Flanagan could easily see the enemy flag as it flew defiantly from atop the Imperial Palace.

It was hardly any surprise, then, that when Flanagan looked across the river at the Citadel and heard the sound of the gunfire, smelled the odor of smoke and death and diesel exhaust in the air, he had the kind of empty feeling in his gut that had become all too familiar since he'd arrived in Hue City. The South Side had been no piece of cake, he knew, but this Citadel mission was going to be something altogether different. The NVA were hard and willing, and the stories coming out of the Citadel very clearly registered with the men that a lot more American blood would be required before the NVA would quit the city, if indeed quit was even an option their adversaries would be allowed to consider.

One more hour, Flanagan kept thinking.

Fox Company had come across the river at eight in the morning. By ten, Flanagan and his men were patrolling an area within the Citadel, near the northeast wall, that was littered with spider holes from which the NVA would frequently pop up and fire at Marines. Buildings and houses provided protection for other enemy troops, and a large, damaged tower along the northeast wall was also being utilized by the enemy with machine guns and automatic weapons.

Flanagan's 3rd Platoon moved into the area interspersed with spider holes and immediately set about finding the NVA and destroying them in their holes by aggressively, almost defiantly attacking them with grenades and gunfire. Once they killed the enemy troops, the Marines pulled the limp bodies from the holes and laid their AK-47s beside them, then moved on to the next. They found and killed at least a dozen enemy soldiers, and their forward progress stalled only when they were caught in a sudden crossfire from two buildings to their left and right front.

"We've got a man down in the open," called one of Flanagan's squad leaders. "And we can't get to him."

Flanagan and his new radio operator, Vasquez, ran from the cover of a thick tree to a small, four-foot wall where the squad leader and his men were crouching and firing away at the targets ahead. The wounded Marine was writhing on the ground in the fetal position perhaps twenty meters to the front of the wall where Flanagan and several others were crouched.

"It's Dog," said the squad leader. "He was moving his gun up to give us some flank cover."

A Marine suddenly scaled the wall but was shot in the head and upper torso and killed before he could take a step beyond. He slumped back toward the wall, and was caught and pulled down by a fellow Marine.

"Son of a bitch!" came an anguished cry from down the wall.

Mortars began exploding nearby, and another man was wounded. A Marine with an M-79 grenade launcher stood up from the wall and calmly fired four well-aimed shots at one of the buildings before he himself was hit and knocked down, his helmet flying backward when he hit the ground.

An NVA soldier who had been missed during the earlier sweep rose from a spider hole behind the Marines and fired a burst at the men crouching behind the wall. Another NVA appeared from behind a building to the rear and made ready to fire a B-40 rocket before he was shot and killed by some 1st Platoon Marines. The NVA soldier in the spider hole succeeded in wounding two of Flanagan's men before the 1st Platoon Marines quickly silenced him with shower of hand grenades.

Flanagan looked around and saw nearly as many men on the ground as he saw firing. He immediately called back to Sgt. Magee of 1st Platoon and told him to pull up closer and seal his backside. "Keep 'em *off* me back there," he radioed in a shout.

The artillery of Marine 155mm howitzers and the 5-and 6-inch shells of a Navy cruiser in the South China Sea helped suppress the enemy fire long enough for Flanagan to move a squad of Magee's men forward to provide covering fire for a continuation of the assault once the barrage ended. The men hunkered down behind the wall, reloading their weapons, grabbing a quick drink from their canteens, glancing over at the condition of the several wounded being treated by the corpsman.

Dog was still down, to the front.

Flanagan shouted "Cover me" and suddenly jumped over the wall and dashed forward to the side of his grievously wounded machine gunner. Dog was unconscious, with gunshot wounds to the head, leg, foot, and groin, and Flanagan himself felt a sudden sharp pain at the base of his neck, along his left shoulder, much as if he'd been hit with a solid punch. He was momentarily knocked off balance, and he struggled mightily to pick up the big man in a fireman's carry. His own wound burned and bled down his arm, but he finally got Dog up onto his other shoulder. He felt Dog's body shudder when two more bullets struck it, then he heard the sickening sound of a bullet striking a head as blood and bits of Dog's brain sprayed onto Flanagan. He fell to one knee, holding onto his wounded man, then rose and continued running, his adrenaline pumping so fast he thought it might squirt out his open wound in a stream, expecting any second to be hit and knocked down, probably even killed. He could see his own Marines standing behind the wall and providing a covering fire which nearly deafened him. He felt nauseous and exhausted, and he kept wondering if he were taking the very last of this lifetime's final few breaths. He could hear little over the noise of the battlefield except his own gasping and his constant repeating of the phrase, "Oh God, oh God, oh God."

He could see one of his men standing and shouting something unknown to him, presumably directing Flanagan toward him with the rapid hand motions he was making. Flanagan was functioning on automatic now, seeing everything in slow motion, aware only of the enormously heavy weight of Dog's body on his shoulder and the smoky, almost surrealistic appearance of the battle site. The gunfire and shouting seemed to merge into a long, continuous cacophony that was no longer earsplitting. He gave way and finally surrendered his ability to think and lead and process multiple pieces of information at once, and moved instead on sheer instinct toward his man who was still standing and making hand signals and providing him with guidance and direction.

Flanagan finally reached the wall and literally threw Dog's limp body into the arms of two Marines, then was himself forcefully pulled over the wall and dropped to the ground by another. His neck ached, and he was bathed in his own and Dog's blood such that when the corpsman arrived, he didn't immediately know where to start in assessing Flanagan's condition. Flanagan reached his hand up to the base of his neck and felt the bullet's entry and exit holes. The corpsman, whose eyes had been searching up and down the platoon leader's bloody face and upper body, then began his treatment.

Flanagan sat breathless as the corpsman went into his bag for a dressing. He leaned back against the wall, the sounds of battle still reverberating all about, and found himself suddenly and uncharacteristically unsure as to which gripping, powerful emotion he should give in to: Shouting out with clinched fist his defiance and his relief at having survived in the face of near certain doom; or, breaking down and weeping uncontrollably at the dead and dying Marines all about him. He took a deep breath, braced himself against the growing pain of his wound, and, with clinched teeth and eyes filling with tears, yielded in part to both.

The artillery was lifted fifteen minutes later and the energized Marines under the direction of Sgt. Douglas immediately went over into the assault on the two buildings, supported by 2nd Platoon on the right.

"You're a hell of a mess, Lieutenant," said Doc Fackler as he applied a dressing to Flanagan's injury. Fackler then gave him a morphine injection and wiped his face clean with a damp dressing. "It's a nice one, though. Clean, through and through, and it doesn't look like it took anything but a little meat with it."

Flanagan's throat was parched, and he took a sip of water that he had difficulty in swallowing. "What about Dog?" he asked in a hoarse gasp, already knowing the answer.

"Nope," Fackler said with a businesslike finality. "Dog's bought it, sir."

Flanagan looked up and saw Capt. Tanner standing above him. Tanner then kneeled down beside his platoon leader.

"Get him ready to go out, Doc," Tanner ordered.

"No way, sir," Flanagan protested. "I'll stay in the field with my platoon." He made an attempt to stand but fell back wobbly against the wall.

He looked up to see Tanner glancing over at the corpsman and making a jerky, thumbs-up motion akin to a baseball umpire. The CO nodded and repeated, "Yep, get him ready to go." He then leaned near Flanagan and said, "Tom, I'm sending you to the rear, and I want you back just as soon as you're fit. But until that time, can Sergeant Douglas handle the platoon in your absence?"

"Yessir," Flanagan said, nodding. "No doubt in my mind he can handle it until I get back."

"Okay," Tanner said with a slap at Flanagan's leg. "That's what I needed to know. Good luck, Tom. Take care and I'll see you when you get back."

With that, Tanner was over the wall and gone.

In less than ten minutes, most of the firing in the immediate vicinity had ceased. Flanagan then began to see many of his 3rd Platoon Marines returning to the wall after the firefight. Nearly all of the platoon's black Marines stopped by, most saying very little but some nodding at Flanagan, while others were content just to make eye contact. Dog's blood was still visible all over Flanagan's utilities.

Vasquez, Flanagan's radio operator, came back and in a tearful voice told the groggy, reclining Flanagan that he was sorry the platoon leader had been wounded, and that Lt. Dave Espy of 2nd Platoon had been killed in the final assault.

Flanagan closed his eyes a moment, then looked up and nodded at Vasquez. "Thanks for letting me know," he said softly.

Sgt. Douglas came over just as Flanagan was about to board a Mechanical Mule for transport back to the aid station at the ARVN headquarters. Douglas helped Flanagan to the vehicle, then braced him as he climbed up and took a seat on the side of the Mule.

"Hurry up and get back, sir," Douglas said.

Flanagan gave a weary nod. "Keep your head down."

"I will, sir. I want the chance to serve with you again."

Flanagan arrived at the aid station at ARVN headquarters in ten minutes. An hour later and after a short hop aboard a CH-46 Sea Knight with a full load of other wounded Marines from Hue City, he arrived at the bigger aid station at Phu Bai. He stretched out on the cold floor of a Quonset hut at Phu Bai as he waited behind the more seriously injured Marines for his turn in the x-ray unit. He was cold and thirsty, and while his pain was steady, it was not unbearable. He heard the soft crying of a nearby Marine, the pleading prayers of another. There was a loud moan further away, followed by a profanity. A corpsman soon arrived and stood over him, leaning down for a look at his dog tags and then writing something on a chart.

"Need anything, Lieutenant?" the corpsman asked.

"A drink of water," Flanagan replied. "And maybe a blanket."

The corpsman nodded and stepped away.

"And probably a platoon," Flanagan mumbled softly as the images of many of his dead and wounded Marines flickered through his mind.

PART TWO
March – May, 1968

CHAPTER NINE
Washington, D.C.

"**I** am today announcing my candidacy for the presidency of the United States. I do not run for the presidency to oppose any man, but to propose new policies . . . "

It was ten o'clock in the morning, Saturday, March 16, 1968. Kate Flanagan watched from a seat in the rear as Sen. Robert F. Kennedy, in blue suit and red-and-blue tie with gold PT-109 tie clasp, stood resolutely before a packed room which included his wife, Ethel, and nine of their ten children, along with a sea of reporters, photographers, Kennedy backers, and tourists. The scene was the old Senate Caucus Room where his brother John had announced his own candidacy on January 2, 1960. What had been widely anticipated was now official: Robert Kennedy was in the race for the nomination of the Democratic Party. His aim, for all intents and purposes, was a reclamation of the White House, and he was now satisfied that he could bring about precisely that.

Kate listened as Kennedy spoke of the "disastrous, divisive" policies, and the necessity of changing the men who made them. He spoke kindly of Eugene McCarthy, whose stunning March 12 primary victory in New Hampshire had legitimized the anti-war message in the United States. He spoke of Lyndon Johnson's loyal service to his brother, and noted that while his own and LBJ's policy differences were profound, those differences were more ideological than personal. He spoke of entering the Nebraska, Oregon, and California primaries in May and June. He tried to deal with and diffuse the popular "ruthless" characterization, for he clearly knew that his late entry into the race would be viewed as opportunistic. Finally, he took questions before ending the session and then entering with his family into the crush of people who instantly surrounded him, who wanted to be near him, to touch him, to shake his hand.

Kate tried to steer clear of the bulging crowd as the people jammed close to Kennedy on his way out of the building, out into the corridor, down the staircase, and on to the waiting cars. The press was set to follow him to National Airport where he was to board a commercial flight to New York so he could walk in the St. Patrick's Day Parade there. Kate watched it all from a distance, never having seen anything quite like it, astonished at the commotion that swirled around the newest presidential contender.

Meanwhile, with the candidate en route to New York, the campaign's status quo was taken up in a meeting in Ted Kennedy's Senate office. It included a group of relatives and 1960 campaign vets, along with several younger staff members from what was referred to as the "Kiddie Corps," to include Dan Marinelli and, for a brief time, Kate Flanagan. There were issues-related positions to establish, policy proposals to flesh out—the vaunted Kennedy campaign machine and logistical structure did not yet exist—and there was much work to do in establishing an overall organization and then assigning specific tasks. Kate listened while it was explained that many of the advisers and veterans of the previous campaign would be working for expenses only, as opposed to the full-time staffers, and a smooth working relationship was rightfully viewed as essential in avoiding (or at least minimizing) the hurt feelings and bruised egos that would otherwise detract from the campaign's overall effectiveness.

Kate joined in the discussions, since there were seemingly tens of thousands of details to attend to. There were people and places and functions to put together like a giant jigsaw puzzle. There was the reconciling of the demand for campaign funds with its corresponding supply. There were statements to make, speeches to write, advertising to buy, volunteers to recruit, local pols to contact, and, most importantly, voters to reach. Amid all the myriad items under consideration, Kate paused at one point to consider the fact that there was once again a Kennedy running for president, again the eldest son, this time more controversial than before. She knew with certainty that no one else in American politics could come even remotely close to the celebrity and mystique that this family and thus this individual still maintained over a nation still profoundly affected by November, 1963. She surmised that for those observing from a safe distance, this entire matter of Kennedy's candidacy was absorbing; to those on the periphery, it was electrifying; and to those finding themselves very deeply within it, as was she, it was epochal.

And indeed for those within it, she concluded as she regained her concentration, it was cause enough to get down to work.

Kate Flanagan left the meeting after an hour and called home to Chicago from a pay phone at a popular Massachusetts Avenue bar. Several of her Kennedy-staffer colleagues were there, and the events of the day were being properly and enthusiastically commemorated. "It's official now," she kept telling her mother. "Now it's all the way with RFK." Her parents, who had watched the televised proceedings, seemed genuinely excited for her. "And I'll get to be a part of all this," she said more than once, as if to convince herself. "Wow, it's really happening. Can you believe it? It's really happening." When Kate's mother informed her that her brother Tommy had been released for duty after recovering from his injury, Kate's eyes began to tear. "This is a *really* great day," she said. "The only thing that could make it better would be to have Tommy on his way home."

Kate had never told her parents, or anyone else for that matter, of her brother's letter to her when, in the depths of his despair at Hue, he had written her of the vision he'd come to have of his own imminent death. It had passed, Hue had passed, and somehow Kate felt that the worst was over for Tommy, no matter what else stood in his path before his tour in Vietnam would be completed and he would be able to return home. As well, the worst was now over in their stormy brother-sister relationship, which she had detailed in a long letter of reconciliation to Tommy after he'd been hospitalized.

When her mother asked about Jill Rohrbach, who had called her Chicago home and asked for Kate's contact info in D.C., Kate mentioned only that Jill had asked about the latest news from Tommy, and to confirm that she still had his correct overseas mailing address. On the other important topic she and Jill had discussed, Kate said nothing.

Kate joined a dozen others and seated herself at a long table where the pitchers of beer nearly equaled the number of people. Some of the men smoked cigars as they leaned back with ties loosened and enjoyed the company and the late-afternoon buzz. Several of the women slipped out of their shoes and sat barefoot in their business attire. When Dan Marinelli arrived shortly before five, the group greeted him with a round of applause, an announcement of "Here come da' judge," a full mug, and the sole remaining slice of pizza which by that time had cooled considerably.

Marinelli glanced around at the condition of the table, summoned a waiter, and proceeded to order considerably more pizza. "Bring us more beer, too," he added with a shrug. "Hell, we're just getting started."

"Sock it to 'em, Danny boy."

The others gave Dan little time to get into the swing of things before they began pressing him on the details of the meeting. Everyone had an opinion on everything, a standard issue but in this case fueled all the more by the afternoon drinking, and Dan soon realized that his wisest course would be to steer around or avoid altogether the matters of business until first thing Monday morning.

"No more shop talk," he finally declared to little avail. "I'll bring everybody up to speed at Monday's staff meeting."

He then turned and whispered to Kate, "But you, Miss Flanagan, are gonna need to be in Indiana first thing Monday morning, so I need to go over a few things with you in private."

Dan rose. "You liberal Democrat intoxicated patriotic buffoons will have to excuse Kate and me for a few moments while we work out some primary details."

"Primary to whom?" asked a staffer.

"Primary to the presidential aspirations of one Robert F. Kennedy."

The group cheered boisterously.

"All the way with Robert F. Kennedy."

"That doesn't rhyme."

"Okay, then. All the way with Senator Robert F. Kennedy from New York via Massachusetts."

"All the way with Bobby and family."

Dan smiled and waved his hand in dismissal. "You people are incorrigible."

"Hey, isn't that the proper name for a blimp?"

"No, it's *Hindenburg*, actually."

Dan pointed the way to a corner table as Kate stood. "Let's get away before someone thinks we actually belong with these hooligans."

"Hooligan: Isn't that someone from the Isle of Hool?"

"Indian Ocean, right?"

"No, Gulf of Siam."

"Ahhhhsoooo," several said in exaggerated Asian accents as they quickly stood and bowed ceremonially to one another.

Dan and Kate were still laughing when they seated themselves at the table several feet away. They declined another drink and instead ordered coffee.

"Can you leave on Sunday for Indiana?" Dan asked as they awaited the coffee.

Kate shrugged. "Yeah, I suppose so. For how long?"

"A week, for sure. Maybe two."

Kate hesitated slightly before nodding. "Yeah, okay. What do you want me to do?"

Dan sighed and rolled his eyes. "God, we've got a ton of stuff to get done in a short amount of time. I want you to go to Indiana and give us a report on what we'll need to do to win if we enter it."

"He's going to run in Indiana? He didn't mention it this morning."

"I know, and deliberately so. We're gonna hire a pollster and see what the numbers there tell us, and then Bob will make a decision. Governor Branigin's running as a stand-in for LBJ, as a

Favorite Son, and McCarthy will be there, of course. If we go, then dammit, we've gotta win. And if we win, we can knock McCarthy right out of this thing by June and face it off alone with Lyndon Johnson in California."

"Okay, so what do we expect in Indiana?" Kate asked.

"It's insular; they may have a tendency to look at Bob as a 'ruthless' carpetbagger, as the ultimate Yankee," Dan said with a resigned look. "We'll do well with blacks, the Slavs, the Poles, the poor. But we know up front that Labor'll be with Branigin, and the campuses will be with McCarthy. The only chance we'll have, if we go, is to have a huge saturation effort in the media and then get Bob there to as many places as possible. He plays well enough in person to help with the 'ruthless' nonsense, when people can see his qualities for themselves. But remember, Nixon beat Jack Kennedy in Indiana in Sixty by almost a quarter of a million votes. Hell, George Wallace got nearly a third of the vote there in the Sixty-Four primary."

Kate's eyes widened. "We have ourselves a challenge."

"We do indeed. But if we decide to go, and if we can get Indiana's Vance Hartke from the Senate with us, and if we can get Bob to Indiana frequently enough, and if the people there will give us an open ear and an open mind, then we can win this thing. And as we continue to win the primaries—and we'll damn well need to win 'em all—we'll have enough momentum going into California."

Kate smiled. "So, tell me how I fit in with all this?"

"Go to Indiana. Scout around. See what the media's saying there about us. Get with the ad agency and get a handle on the number of television outlets in the state. Go to the statehouse in Indianapolis and find out exactly what papers will need to be filed for entry into the primary."

"Will anybody else be there?"

"Pierre Salinger's planning on making a trip, I think, for at least a couple of days. And maybe some of Ted's people from Massachusetts. I'll let you know who, where, what, et cetera, as things develop."

"The old timers are coming back in, right?"

"You bet. Stephen Smith and Ted will be running things, best I can tell. Ted Sorensen, Kenny O'Donnell, Dick Goodwin, Fred Dutton, Frank Mankiewicz, Salinger—they're all in for the long haul. Walinsky and Greenfield will still be doing the bulk of the speechwriting. One or two others from the old days may join us yet, but we've got to get humping with what we've got. It's less than ninety days until the California primary."

"Okay," Kate said with a nod. "Who do I report back to, and how frequently?"

"Talk to me," Dan said with a point toward himself. "And daily."

"Will you be coming to Indiana?"

"Maybe later."

Their eyes locked for an instant before Kate turned away. She reached for the cup of coffee and asked, "Will my airline ticket be waiting at the counter?"

"Yes. Check with United. It's Indianapolis via Chicago. There's also a rental car for you at Indy. Oh, I almost forgot," Dan said, reaching into his pocket and producing a wad of twenty-dollar bills. "Here's five-hundred bucks cash for your hotel and meals and stuff. If you need more, call me and I'll wire it. Or you can use your own funds, in which case I'll reimburse you when you get back."

"Okay," said Kate as she accepted the cash. "I'll call you when I get up there."

"If Bob decides to come to Indiana, I want you there to meet him. And I'll want you to brief him on what you've found. He'll ask a lot of probing questions, and I want you to give him straight, honest answers. Use the same approach with Ted or anyone else in the organization. We'll have a lot at stake if we jump into the Indiana primary, and I trust your judgment, so call it like you see it. Okay?"

"Yep, okay."

Their eyes locked again, but this time Kate didn't turn away. Dan reached across and touched her hand. Kate glanced down quickly, then looked back at Dan, but otherwise remained unmoving.

"I told you earlier that you could be a part of history if you quit your job and joined us. Remember?" he asked, his tone rising.

Kate smiled. "Of course I remember."

"Well, then," he said, sitting up straight and puffing out his chest, still touching her hand. "Let's go make some history."

They both smiled.

* * *

"Two weeks?" Everett asked in evident pique. "Kate, where are you going that you have to be away for two weeks?"

"I'm going away on business. That's all I want to say."

Everett placed his hands on his hips and scowled. "I knew this arrangement wouldn't work, dammit."

Kate chuckled. When she went into a hall bathroom, closed the door, lowered her skirt and proceeded to relieve herself, Everett walked over and stood outside the door.

"You can't tell me where you're going?" he asked.

"Yes, Everett, I can. But I'm choosing not to."

"That's not fair. I'll worry about you."

"No need. I'll be fine. Now get away from the door and allow me to pee in private," she said.

"I will not. I'm only asking that you be truthful with me."

"I'm being perfectly truthful with you already."

She heard him sigh dramatically. "Screw Bobby Kennedy, that opportunistic little son of a bitch," he mumbled.

"I heard that," said Kate.

"I meant it, too."

The toilet flushed. When Kate opened the door a minute later, Everett was still standing in the doorway.

"Look, I don't want to jeopardize our relationship over this silly game of politics," he said. "But I was afraid of this, and I don't like the way this is starting out. Bobby Kennedy's been a candidate for less than eight hours, and we're already having problems dealing with it."

"You're the one having problems dealing with it. I'm quite content with the arrangement, I can assure you."

"Kate, dammit, I can't accept—"

Kate moved to him and wrapped her arms around his neck and kissed him. As he pushed closer to her, she heard his breathing become deeper and she felt his hand moving over her rear. When she pulled away quickly and stepped back, he almost lost his balance.

"Don't lecture me on what you can or cannot accept," Kate said firmly. "We're not working toward the same political objectives here, and now it's more than just a fantasy for me. You'll have to get used to it if you're going to stay with Gene McCarthy. My aim—our aim—is to put Bobby Kennedy in the White House. And I won't let Gene McCarthy or any of his followers get in my—our—way."

"God, you're as ruthless as he is."

Kate laughed and started to walk away.

"You're going to Nebraska, aren't you? Or maybe California. Huh? Are you going to California?"

Everett followed her into the bedroom. "I know. You're going to Oregon, right? Or Indiana? That's it. That's where you're going. You're secretly going to Indiana, right?"

Kate pushed Everett out of the bedroom and closed the door.

"So, it's Indiana, is it?" he called from the hallway. "Well, you're not gonna win, dammit. You people can't come in at the last minute like this and expect the American people to be fooled by your guy's rank opportunism. That's just crap and you know it. It just won't wash, I guarantee it. We'll send him back with his little tail between his legs to New York or Massachusetts or Washington or wherever the hell it is he comes from nowadays. Did you hear that, Kate? I said you're *not gonna win!*"

* * *

125

Sen. Robert F. Kennedy was mobbed at the airport in Indianapolis on March 28, 1968, when he flew into the city to file the necessary papers for the primary on May 7. His earlier March itinerary had already featured appearances and speeches In Kansas, Georgia, Alabama, Tennessee, and California, and his visit into Indiana was his initial foray into this all-important primary state. The poll commissioned by his campaign organization had shown the day before that Kennedy was running close behind Gov. Branigin and ahead of McCarthy. Hence, the decision by Kennedy to run in Indiana was a calculated gamble, and it was all too clear that a victory was essential to build the requisite *momentum needed by the time of the California primary.

Kate Flanagan was waiting at the airport for the Kennedy entourage to arrive. She had arranged for several cars and a police escort to take the party to the downtown Capitol building. Robert and Ethel Kennedy and Bill Barry, RFK's security man, climbed into the back seat of the waiting Cadillac. With Kate in the front, the driver slowly pulled out behind the lead motorcycle cop.

"How are you, Kate?" Kennedy asked as he waved at bystanders along the way.

"I'm fine, Senator. I welcome you and Mrs. Kennedy to Indiana."

"Thanks, and thank you for all the good information you've been sending back to Washington. Dan's had some nice things to say about you and the work you've been doing here."

"That's an understatement," added Ethel. "Dan really thinks you walk on water."

Kate blushed slightly.

"Actually he thinks we both walk on water," Kennedy said, grinning, "but for altogether different reasons, I think."

Kate grinned and blushed again.

"See what you've done," Ethel admonished in jest.

"I know, I know," Kennedy said, turning and looking outside, occasionally waving at bystanders. "Next time I come to Indiana, she'll have a Volkswagen beetle waiting for me. Promise me you won't do that to me, Kate."

"I promise, Senator. And in addition to that, I'll even promise you that I'll never disclose to Dan the fact that, of the two of us, you're the one who really can't walk on water."

Ethel erupted in laughter; Kennedy grinned and nodded his acknowledgment.

"And in return I promise I won't tell Dan about your complete lack of self-confidence," Kennedy replied, still grinning.

There were people and signs along the way, and there were reports of a sizeable crowd waiting at the statehouse. There were enough black faces along the way to lift Kennedy's spirits as he gazed outside throughout a silent period of perhaps five minutes. At one point just before reaching the statehouse there was a man in overalls holding a sign that caught Kennedy's eye. It read *Farmers for Branigan.*

"I can win the farm vote," he said as if attempting to convince himself. "I should easily get the farm vote. Just look at my breakfast table. Look at all the milk and the bread and the eggs, all the jam and the cereal. Enough to keep the farmers busy for another generation, at least."

Ethel smiled.

"Maybe two generations," he added softly.

"I understand you have a brother in Vietnam, Kate," Ethel said. "And that he was recently hurt."

"That's right," Kate answered with a nod. "He was wounded in the battle for Hue."

"What's his condition now?" Kennedy asked.

"He was evacuated to a hospital, but he's doing much better."

"What has he had to say about the war?" asked Kennedy.

Kate winced. "Honestly, he doesn't say much about the war itself. He's seen a lot of fighting, but I don't know if it's changed his mind about what he used to think was the 'rightness' of the war."

"It just might," Kennedy said softly.

"I just wish he could come home," Kate said with a sigh.

"Yes," said Kennedy. "I wish they all could."

Kennedy shook his head in disheartenment and lapsed into another period of silence before he finally leaned forward and asked, "So now that you've been here a few days, Kate, do you think Indiana's winnable?"

"Yes," Kate answered immediately. "I'm a lot more convinced today than I was on March 18th, the day I arrived here."

"Why? What's made you more convinced?"

"The polling numbers are encouraging; the editorials aren't exactly affectionate, but they're not vicious, at least not yet, and I consider that a positive; and if we come into Indiana with momentum, looking in every way like the winning team, and then promote our cause and make the television appearances and generally get our message out there en mass, then I think the potential's here for us to score big with the part of the electorate we'll need to win."

Kennedy nodded thoughtfully.

"On the other hand," Kate said warily, "if we come in here with little or no momentum, and then can't generate any once we're here, then I wouldn't expect Indiana to be very kind to us."

"Of course not," said Kennedy.

"But," Kate said, adding a slightly self-conscious grin, "I think I'm starting to develop an instinct for this kind of stuff, and my instinct is very definitely telling me that we're gonna win."

Kennedy sat back against the seat and said softly, "Good. That's good. That's very good."

By the time the Kennedy party reached the Capitol, there was a crowd estimated at 4,000 waiting for the candidate. Kate followed along as Kennedy, with Bill Barry and Ethel close behind, moved slowly through the pressing throngs. Kate was taken aback by the crowd's strong need to be close to and actually touch Kennedy. She noticed that with some, it was the unbridled excitement that goes with celebrity watching; with others, it appeared almost as a reverence, a near hypnotic state in having seen him and a near disbelief in having heard his voice or touched his hand or clothing. For his part, Kennedy moved along unhurriedly and obliged the people whose hands were touching his hair, arms, shoulders—any part of him that they could reach out and grab.

After the papers were filed and Kennedy had delivered a short speech to the people from the steps of the Capitol, the party returned to the airport where the next leg of the trip involved stops in New Mexico and Arizona.

"See you soon, Kate," Kennedy said as the car delivered him to his chartered jet. "Thanks again for all you're doing."

Kate smiled. "I should be the one thanking you for all you're doing."

He grinned and waved, and was gone.

Kate closed out a few loose ends in Indianapolis before finally returning to the airport in the late evening for her commercial flight back to Washington. Dan Marinelli had earlier told her that he wanted her to return yet again to Indiana to work with others in the organization on the many tasks that lay ahead now that the decision had been made. Dan had sounded tired, as if he'd been operating on too little sleep, but his enthusiasm was still evident.

"We're gonna win Indiana!" Dan had virtually shouted into the phone. "And you and I are gonna have a helluva good time enjoying it when we do."

Kate settled into her window seat and relaxed as the jet accelerated and rolled down the runway for the trip home to Washington. If the past several days were any clue, she was already enjoying her job far beyond anything she'd ever imagined. And she looked forward with an almost childlike glee to her first full-blown political campaign. She was part of the Kennedy team now, enthused about and immersed in her work, proud of her candidate and his causes, satisfied that something considerably better awaited America, and excited that she would be a part of it. This was heady stuff, to be sure, and Dan had been quite right about this being the chance of a lifetime.

She sat back and smiled contentedly. She became satisfied that nothing in her life would ever be the same after such a transforming experience as this. She wondered briefly over how many people in the working population were as enthralled with what they were doing as was she. She loved it, every part of it, and it showed.

She'd never felt better in her life.

CHAPTER TEN
Quang Nam Province, South Vietnam

Lt. Flanagan's 3rd Platoon found the spot from the map coordinates. It straddled the Song Vu Gia River in the area near Dai Loc and Duc Duc referred to as the Arizona Territory, and it was hardly a pretty sight. There were eight American bodies on the ground, some already badly decomposed, the result of a VC ambush a week earlier.

"Get 'em bagged," Flanagan ordered his platoon sergeant, Sgt. Douglas, as they both stood off to the side and up from the prevailing wind. "We'll move them over to the clearing as soon as we hear the chopper. Everybody else set-in and provide three-sixty security. And keep an eye open for across the river. The little people are out here with us, I guarantee it."

Flanagan shielded his eyes from the bright mid-March sun as he glanced across the muddy river at the trees and undergrowth on the far side. He worried about snipers anytime his men were halted, and he could imagine a lone enemy soldier across the river taking dead aim on the forehead of an unsuspecting Marine. Then, too, he worried about snipers when his men were moving. Snipers and booby traps were the unseen and often deadly adversaries so typical to the grunt's life in the bush, and stood in stark contrast to the street fighting the men had so recently experienced in Hue City.

Flanagan kept looking for movement on the river's opposite bank as he used Vasquez's PRC-25 radio to request a helicopter. Nothing moved; nothing appeared unusual; nothing drew any unwarranted attention. He could hear the gurgling of the river current and smell the sour mud of its banks, but otherwise nothing struck his senses as especially noteworthy. And it was precisely that, the lack of noteworthiness in an area so lush with danger, that suddenly bothered him. Yep, he concluded. There's a bad guy in there somewhere. Maybe a sniper; maybe a scout. But somebody's in there, for certain.

"You okay, sir?" Sgt. Douglas asked when he saw the pale Flanagan remove his pack and take a seat on the ground near the river bank.

"I'm fine, yeah. Get those KIAs bagged and let's be ready to beat feet out of here as soon as they're extracted."

Flanagan leaned back and rested his aching body. It was brutally clear that he'd lost a large portion of his conditioning during his nearly three-week stay in the hospitals at Phu Bai and then Da Nang. His neck and shoulder muscles throbbed incessantly, and the pack straps made it an exercise in sheer misery. He gulped two more Darvons that Doc Fackler had given him, chasing them with warm water from his canteen and hoping that someday very soon he would feel up to the demanding duties of his job.

"They're ready," Sgt. Douglas called once the dead Marines had been zipped into the vinyl body bags.

Flanagan nodded and remained seated.

"Some of the bodies were mutilated," Douglas said in a subdued voice when he came over and stood next to Flanagan. "Charlie messed 'em up bad, the assholes. Sliced all of 'em up, and even cut the dick off one Marine and stuck it in his mouth."

Flanagan quickly glanced up at Douglas but said nothing. The VC mutilated the bodies for our exclusive benefit, he thought. Charlie wants to get inside *our* heads. He's leaving *us* a message, a calling card. *We're* the ones he's screwing with, not them, not the dead. Besides, the relatives of the dead Marines wouldn't see the evidence anyway, so the aftereffect back in The World would be limited. No, it wasn't the surviving relatives that the VC wanted to intimidate with their barbarity. It was the grunts who'd come back out after their dead; the handlers at the morgue back in the rear who would prepare the bodies for shipment home; and all the other people that those people would talk to about what they'd seen the VC do to the bodies of young American fighting men. The VC were absolutely devoid of scruples or conscience, Flanagan knew, and they plied their trade in terror and stealth and shock with an efficiency that was often outright chilling to all but the most severely hardened Americans.

"Maybe we can return the favor some day," a nearby Marine was overheard suggesting.

Flanagan winced and stiffened. "Knock it off, dammit. We're in the business of killing 'em, and that's it. I find out somebody's mutilating dead gooks or taking 'souvenirs' of their body parts, it's gonna be their ass, plain and simple." Flanagan then turned to Sgt. Douglas and said sternly, "Make *damn sure* everybody understands that."

Sgt. Douglas responded with, "Aye-aye, sir."

"Chopper," someone nearby called out.

Sgt. Douglas supervised the removal of the bodies to the adjacent clearing while the other Marines remained in their positions. The CH-46 settled rear-first into the clearing in a blast of wind and flying debris, its engines running the entire time, and took on the vinyl-encased bodies of the eight dead. The chopper then nosed forward and banked toward the northeast after Flanagan had signaled a thumbs-up to the cockpit crew.

"Saddle up," Sgt. Douglas called as he walked among the men. "First squad on the point. Keep your intervals and your eyes open for booby traps. And I want good noise discipline at all times. Let's move, people."

Flanagan went over the patrol plan in his head again, which included a section of the river to the south for a distance of approximately three-thousand meters, then turning west and covering another thousand meters for a rendezvous at dusk with the remainder of Fox Company. The entire rifle company would then stay out in the field for one additional day before being transported back to Da Nang for a short rest break.

Flanagan also remembered Capt. Tanner's lecture on the fact that since nearly every unit in the regiment was re-fitting after Tet, the need for diligence and alertness had never been greater.

Train them good, Tanner had instructed Flanagan; train them right.

Flanagan was near the front of his platoon column as it moved single-file along the river bank. Vasquez, carrying the radio, was positioned directly behind him, with Sgt. Douglas further to the rear. Flanagan had deliberately placed on the point a lance corporal named Joseph Lupo, nicknamed Monkee, not so much for reasons of resemblance as for his preference in rock groups, and who also hailed from Flanagan's hometown of Chicago. Lupo had previously been a discipline case for Flanagan, but after distinguishing himself in the fighting at Hue by earning a Bronze Star and two Purple Hearts, he had settled down to become one of the platoon's most trusted and able performers.

The platoon kept a deliberate pace in the warm afternoon heat. Flanagan noticed that the foliage along the river bank was dense enough to provide shade without unduly restricting the visibility ahead and to the side. He also noticed that the undergrowth was thick with clinging vines and broken tree branches. He was busy untangling his foot from one such vine and didn't immediately notice when Monkee suddenly stopped and crouched, unmoving, with his fist raised as a signal to those behind.

Flanagan strained to see what was happening up ahead, but he could see nothing unusual. He quickly glanced at his map to make certain that he could fix the platoon's location in case something developed. Two tense minutes passed before the man to Flanagan's immediate front turned and touched the collar of his utility shirt, indicating Monkee's request for the platoon leader to move up. Flanagan turned and motioned with his head for Vasquez to follow, and they both started up the column in a crouch.

"It's our lucky day, sir," the dark-haired, dark-eyed Lupo said in a low voice as he pointed to an object dangling from a tree fifty meters ahead. "Little shitasses thought they could pull one over on the Monkee, but they're full of bad rice today."

Flanagan wiped the sweat from his eyes and squinted hard at where Monkee was pointing. "I don't see jackshit, Lupo. What the hell are you looking at?"

"It's a rocket round, Lieutenant, hanging upside down up there. See the fins? See it hanging from that tree?"

"Which friggin' tree?" asked Flanagan, staring ahead at the thick growth.

Lupo put his right hand, palm out, about two feet in front of his face and closed his left eye. "If you put your index finger on the trail, the tree with the rocket round in it will be just off your little finger."

Flanagan followed with Lupo's hand-measurement technique.

"See it now, sir?" asked Lupo.

"Ahhh," Flanagan said as soon as he recognized the distant form. "Isn't that a kick in the ass? They've left us a puzzle."

Monkee's self-satisfied grin suddenly disappeared. "Sir?"

Flanagan turned and looked across the river. "Have you seen any movement across the river? Anything at all?"

"No sir, nothing. But I've mostly been looking up ahead."

He turned back to the rocket round. "Can you see any wires?"

Monkee stared ahead, moving his head about for a better view. "No sir. Could be command detonated, though. Could be wired where we can't see it, on the other side of those vines."

"What kind of dumbshit VC would hang a rocket round up in the air for a patrol point to see at a distance that's outside the bursting radius?" pondered Flanagan.

Monkee pondered for a moment, then nodded thoughtfully. "Yeah, okay. I get it. They *want* us to see it so we'll deviate."

"Could be," answered Flanagan.

"We can't offset but one way—away from the river—and they'll blow the shit out of us as soon as we move away from this thing," Monkee said forcefully. "They've got something in there that we can't see, and it's probably bigger than this friggin' rocket round. Maybe a 105 round, or maybe even a 155. They think we'll see this thing and move over to avoid it "

"A very logical deduction, and I agree entirely," said Flanagan. "Now we've got to choose between offsetting and walking into something we *can't* see, or walking ahead toward the rocket round that we clearly *can* see."

Monkee's face contorted into a frown.

"What if," Vasquez said, stopping to swallow, "they really *are* dumbshits?"

"Then if we choose to walk ahead, we get a mouthful of Chinese steel," Flanagan said calmly.

Monkee took a deep breath. "You want me to walk up there, sir, and test out our theory?"

Flanagan looked out across the river. "You saw nothing on the other side of the river, right?"

"Affirmative, sir. But like I said, I was paying a helluva lot more attention to what was in front of me than across the river."

"Understood," Flanagan said with a confident nod of his head. "Charlie's over there watching, and that gives us another option. And no, Lupo, I don't want you or anybody else walking up there and testing out our theory."

Flanagan noticed when Monkee and Vasquez glanced at one another.

"Here's what we're gonna do," Flanagan ordered. "We'll stay put right here. If I can get some air out here, we'll hit the tree line on the opposite side of the river. We can get a blooper on that rocket round up ahead and get rid of it, too. And if the other surprise is far enough over there on our right flank, far enough away from where we are now, then it really shouldn't give us any trouble even if Charlie cranks it off before we can zap him first."

Monkee and Vasquez grinned at one another before Flanagan turned and started back down the column, toward Sgt. Douglas.

It took twelve minutes for the Huey Cobra gunship to arrive on station. Flanagan was in direct contact with the pilot, and once the target was established with a white phosphorous round and the friendly position identified to the crew, the gunship made several low-level passes with rockets and miniguns. The tree line on the opposite side of the river erupted in flashes and grayish-black smoke, and the Marines from 3rd Platoon poured its own small-arms fire on top of the furious attack by the gunship. Flanagan also directed a Marine with an M-79 grenade launcher to destroy the rocket round suspended from the tree on their side of the river. Nothing else detonated except the M-79 rounds fired by the friendlies.

After three passes, the gunship pilot circled the target area and then radioed to Flanagan that nothing appeared to be moving within the tree line or hedgerows. Flanagan thanked the gunship crew for their efforts and released them for return to their base at Chu Lai.

"Okay, Lupo," Flanagan called as he stood. "Let's move out."

The men were wary as they moved past the spot where the rocket round had been flaunted, but nothing developed and the column passed without incident. Flanagan felt relieved the further away they got from the scene, but he felt especially encouraged that a killer booby trap had been avoided, and that perhaps even the booby-trappers themselves had been destroyed along with their device. Later, Lupo was rotated from the point and replaced by one of the newer men when the platoon was within a thousand meters, commonly referred to as a *klick*, of rejoining the Fox Company position. "Get 'em some experience," Capt. Tanner had ordered Flanagan and the other platoon leaders on the previous night. "The only way they can learn it is to do it. Don't take any unnecessary risks, but let 'em get their hands dirty."

"You got a full magazine?" Flanagan asked the young, apprehensive point man as the platoon made ready to move out after a rest break of fifteen minutes.

"Yessir."

"We're only a klick away from our company position, to the northwest. But this is the Arizona Territory, and we're still very definitely in Indian Country. Pay attention to what you're doing up there," Flanagan said calmly.

"Yessir."

Sgt. Douglas came to the front of the column and examined the man's gear and weapon, then nodded and slapped him on the helmet. "We're playing for keeps out here, Marine. Head up, eyes open."

Flanagan gave Douglas a wink as the latter passed on the way back to his position in the column.

Flanagan quickly noticed that the new man on the point was erratic, at first starting his pace out far too slowly and then speeding it up too quickly and recklessly. At Flanagan's suggestion, the squad leader moved up and admonished the new man, telling him to move more naturally. The point man eventually steadied, and his pace soon normalized.

The platoon had traveled perhaps five-hundred meters when the young private on the point was killed instantly when he failed to see a well-disguised trip wire that caught the toe of his boot, consequently detonating an artillery-shell booby trap. The man following next in line was gruesomely blown apart at the waist. Flanagan was knocked backwards by the blast of the flashing orange ball, but recovered his senses quickly enough to hear through badly ringing ears the screams of the hideously wounded man just ahead.

"Corpsman!" someone was already calling.

"Spread out," Flanagan shouted. He radioed his squads to take up defensive positions and then radioed Capt. Tanner that an apparent booby trap had exploded on the point. There was no gunfire, only the screaming of the wounded Marine. A priority medevac was requested, and Flanagan glanced about for an LZ.

"Check around your immediate area for more," Flanagan heard one of the squad leaders shout. "Don't anybody move off to the side."

Doc Fackler joined Flanagan up ahead, reaching the wounded man only to see the exposed intestines and the bloody stumps where the man's legs had been. His powder-darkened face and arms had been burned by the powerful blast, his white eyes wide and frightened. Flanagan watched as Fackler gave him an immediate injection of morphine, then attempted to push the man's innards back into place to reduce the exposure. Flanagan looked over at the body of the point man, slumped against the base of a tree in what almost appeared as a normal resting position.

"Anything moves out there, blow it away," came another gruffly shouted command from a squad leader.

Flanagan's ears were still ringing as he stood over the busy Fackler and looked down on the wounded man. The air was thick with cordite and the coppery smell of blood. Flanagan glanced to the side and noticed the injured man's severed legs about twenty feet away, one of the jungle boots still on a foot.

"Oh no," the man wailed in a half-cry. "Oh God, somebody help me, somebody do something, please. Momma! Oh God help me."

Fackler administered another morphine injection, and Flanagan knew immediately that Fackler's unspoken but clear prognosis was clear, that in making the man as oblivious as possible to his pain, the corpsman was essentially doing all he could reasonably do.

The wounded man suddenly looked up at Flanagan and, with a face mirroring equal parts desperation and confusion, reached out and took Flanagan's hand. He then said in a pleading, breaking voice, "Help me get to my feet, sir. I'll be okay if I can get to my feet." The man then blinked and made a moaning sound, becoming instantly limp, and as he did so Flanagan held onto his bloody hand a moment longer before finally stepping back away from the ghastly scene to compose himself.

"*Dammit!*" the grim, tight-jawed Flanagan repeated several times as he moved through the position.

"I've got the medevac locked on," Sgt. Douglas said when he saw the pale, shaken Flanagan. "I found a place on the map a hundred meters to the east. I've got a fire team already headed that way."

Flanagan nodded. "Let's get moving." He then walked back to the corpsman, who was still kneeling over his horribly injured patient. "We need to move him, Doc. We've got a medevac on the way."

Fackler felt the man's wrist for a pulse, then his neck, then leaned over and listened to his chest. The corpsman raised up after several moments and announced, "He's KIA, sir."

Four Marines went out with the medevac chopper—two dead and two wounded. All but one of the four had been in-country less than eight weeks. Flanagan barely knew their names, and now he was sending them away, two temporarily and two forever.

Flanagan returned his platoon back to the Fox Company position by dusk, as planned. But he was arriving, as on other days and in other places, with several fewer in his ranks.

* * *

Flanagan's 3rd Platoon remained in the company position to provide security while 1st and 2nd Platoons patrolled the adjacent terrain. It was late morning, and the knob of small connecting hills that the position occupied provided good visibility into a surrounding countryside that was checkered with glimmering rice paddies to the east and south, dotted with hedgerows and moderate forest in the immediate area, and covered with thickly jungled mountains to the west. Since it had rained the night before, Flanagan and his troops were drying their clothes and their gear in the warmth of the clear blue sky and bright sunshine.

The shirtless Flanagan sat atop a bunker and sunned himself in relative leisure. From a nearby bunker came the sound of a transistor radio playing *Tighten Up*. He scanned out over the surrounding terrain, its differing shades of green and brown conveying a serenity and radiance that contrasted so harshly with the dangers he knew were within. How could it seem so tranquil and yet be so deadly? he pondered. For many Americans, Vietnam was a hell on earth, but it didn't look like hell, at least not from a distance. Yet when he remembered back to the recent overcast, cold, drizzly days of Hue, and the death and stench that was so much a part of it, he wondered how much worse a real hell could be than what the Marines had faced and endured there. It was yet another in a long list of incongruities that was so much a part of Vietnam.

In some ways he felt as if he'd been in Vietnam forever, that when he tried to remember some of the details of life back in The World—what an order of McDonald's fries tasted like; the exact sounds of his parents' voices; what it would be like to walk down Michigan Avenue without having to be alert for snipers; what it was like to be with a young American woman with long hair and round hips and big boobs—it all seemed to blur as if part of another life.

With his weapon near at hand, Flanagan turned his attention to the four letters he had received after the re-supply chopper had come and gone—one from his parents, one from his sister Kate, one from the parents of Lt. Kevin Riordan, and much to his surprise, one from Jill Rohrbach.

He read Kate's letter first.

"You wouldn't believe how exciting it is to be working on Senator Kennedy's staff. I can't wait for you to get home so I can personally introduce you to RFK. You'll change your mind, Tommy, about what this country needs in its political leaders as soon as you have a chance to meet him and talk with him. I really believe my 'screwy beliefs' would rub off on you after a short while. Who knows? It might just be the best thing that ever happened to you (and me). And I think you'd really like the staffer I work closest with, Dan Marinelli, who also served in Vietnam. You two would get along famously, I think. Hurry up and get back home so we can have some of those wonderful times again that we've had so often before. Please be careful and know that I'm praying every day for your safe return. Write soon. Always, Kate."

Maybe Kate will help end the war and bring us all home, he thought in amusement as he examined his pale skin for sunburn before slipping back into his utility shirt. But until that time, he knew, Charlie would still be out there, armed and exceedingly dangerous.

He then read the letters from his own parents and the parents of Kevin Riordan, who had written from Boston thanking Flanagan for his kind remarks about their son who had died at Hue. The Flanagans and the Riordans were all dealing with the war as best they knew how, albeit under different circumstances now, and Flanagan thought briefly that perhaps his own role as a participant might in some alternative way be easier than that of being a parent and sending, and then losing, a son to war.

Flanagan let out a deep breath and stared at the letter from Jill, his first from her since arriving in Vietnam. The sight of the letter inundated him with confounding impulses—hurt, anger, disappointment, guilt, affection—but then Jill's familiar handwriting brought back a rush of fond memories. The letter was unscented when he opened it and held it to his nose. He breathed it in anyway, slowly, deeply, his eyes closed, as if enticing his brain to find still another Jill-related connection. He hadn't seen her in months, but there was little about her that he couldn't replicate in his mind as his curiosity, along with his arousal, grew.

My Dear Tom:

I hope this letter finds you safe and well. I understand from Kate that you were recently wounded, and I hope you have recovered fully and are out of any danger. I pray that you will return home safe and sound.

Tom, I don't know of any easy way to communicate this to you, so I suppose the best way is just to let you know outright that I've become engaged to be married. I've met someone who lives and works in the Milwaukee area, as I do, and we've decided to get married in October. I wanted you to find this out directly from me, but I only wish I could tell you personally rather than in a letter being sent to you in Vietnam.

I won't bore you with a lot of details about my life, but I passed the CPA exam and I'm working as a staff auditor for a Big Eight accounting firm. My fiancé, Branson Atkinson, works as a staff auditor at a competitor Big Eight firm. He is a good man, Tom, and has many of your great qualities. It would mean a lot to me to know that you wish us well with our marriage plans.

Please know that I think of you often, and I want only the best for you. My family sends their best wishes, and I enjoyed recently speaking by phone to your Mom and Kate. I told only Kate of my engagement, and asked that she write nothing to you about it until you had heard from me.

Please be safe, Tom. And thank you so much for all the warm, wonderful memories I have of the time we shared together. You will always be important to me. God bless.

Love, Jill

Flanagan swallowed hard and glanced around to see if any of his men were watching. He wiped at his eyes, then reached for his nearby canteen for a drink of water. The lump in his throat felt as if it had been propelled there by a cannon shot. He noticed his accelerated heartbeat and his rapid, shallow breathing, much as if he were under fire in combat. *Dammit Jill*, he kept thinking. How could you *do* this?

"Disturbing anything, sir?"

Flanagan sat up straight, cleared his throat and turned to see Sgt. Douglas approaching. "No, not at all. I was just wishing I was back in Chicago getting laid."

"Is that one wish or two?" asked Douglas.

"It's two, but I'd settle for an either/or."

"Ah. Well I'm sure you're really happy to see me showing up here and blowing your daydreams away with the business of the Marine Corps."

Flanagan took a deep breath and shrugged. "I suppose the Marine Corps is paying me to take care of its business, not mine. What've you got, Sergeant Douglas?"

"Are you okay, sir?" said the observant Douglas. "I can come back it you'd like."

"I'm fine," Flanagan answered self-consciously. "Tell me what you've got."

Douglas nodded, then handed Flanagan a map. "I was talking to Sergeant Magee and Sergeant Sinclair last night about what they've been seeing in this general area, and I think I may have found a good ambush spot. I just thought if Captain Tanner wanted an ambush mission, that we might have something we've already given some thought to."

Douglas took a seat alongside Flanagan and pointed to a specific area on the map to the southwest of their present position. "There's a trail here, but there's another trail that intersects at this spot that isn't shown. We've got a four-way intersection here, and it'd be easy enough for the gooks to hide their troops in the trees and lay low until night, then get out and move in the open. There's plenty of cover and concealment nearby. We know they're using the river, and it makes sense that they'd also be using this trail network. Both First and Third Platoons have been over that terrain during daylight hours, and Magee and Sinclair said they'd seen evidence the gooks had been there recently. One patrol saw footprints; the other saw discarded clothing—uniform articles, not farmers' stuff. And they saw human shit just off the trail. We might be able to catch 'em at this intersection and bust some caps on 'em. Maybe get a little payback for what they did to us yesterday. Anyway, I thought I'd bring it to you in case the Skipper might be looking for a good spot."

"Looks good," Flanagan said as he studied the spot. "I'll let the Skipper have a look."

* * *

"Beautiful. Absolutely beautiful," Capt. Tanner said with a wide grin as he studied the map with Flanagan. "Tell Douglas I'd give him a week off in Tahiti if it were left up to me, but a day or two in Da Nang might have to suffice."

Flanagan grinned. "It's the thought that counts."

"Right. And my thought about this ambush is that you ought to take your platoon out tonight, set the ambush in, and wait until first light to return if nobody shows up. Give me a list of artillery targets, and we'll lay 'em in."

Flanagan nodded. "Aye-aye, sir. We'll be there by first dark."

"Good hunting, Tom."

* * *

The platoon reached the ambush site with barely enough light left to select the most suitable location. The south side of the trail afforded a slightly higher rise in the terrain, so Flanagan spread his Marines along the path for a length of sixty meters. Two claymores were then employed at oblique angles on the flanks of the position. Flanagan and Sgt. Douglas had earlier decided to bring the platoon to the field without the burden of their heavy packs, with only their flak jackets and soft covers to go with their ammo and canteens. They had been in position no more than fifteen minutes when suddenly a near-horizontal rainstorm turned loose in a pelting squall. Their ponchos were back in the rear with their packs, useless to them, though it hardly mattered as quickly as the storm had arisen.

Damn it all, Flanagan thought as he sighted out over the barrel of his M-16. He had situated himself and Vasquez at the midpoint in his line of troops, with prearranged radio codes with his men on the flanks to warn him of any movement on the path. But now their visibility was significantly restricted, and the fury of the pounding rain masked all the other noises of the night. The rain took away their eyes and ears and drenched them into a steady succession of drips, and after a while the cold achiness made each man attempt to narrow his shoulders and hunch himself forward in an effort to bring himself underneath the bill of his saturated cover.

But it only got colder and achier as the time went slowly by.

Flanagan started to feel sluggish, his neck and shoulders were aching steadily, and no matter how hard he tried to concentrate on the mission, on the preplanned artillery targets, on the radio codes and call signs, on the enemy's possible avenues of approach, on their travel speeds and troop strengths and the firepower potential they could deliver to him and his Marines, his eyelids nevertheless became heavy and his head began to nod forward. He eventually became limp, his mouth open and drooling, before he finally removed his soft cover and turned his face up into the rain, breathing deeply and letting his face be splashed. Finally, almost desperately, he willed the drowsiness out of his head.

Flanagan sat up slightly and glanced to either side. He could barely discern the form of another man, although Vasquez was close enough to reach out and touch. It was dark and wet and spooky, but the monotony and the ensuing fatigue it invited seemed to outweigh everything else. Flanagan was certain that at least half his men were sleeping, maybe more, from catnapping to comatose, and he was left to hope that their quick reactions and youthful reflexes would bring them into the fight quickly if and when the first shots were fired.

It became increasingly miserable and cold. Flanagan tried mightily to avoid thinking of Jill, amusing himself instead by visualizing a sunny, sandy Florida beach with plenty of bikini-clad young beauties. It didn't work, but it did help that his heavy sleepiness dulled his full range of senses. He fought back by realizing that he was in charge, that he was the single individual in a group of nearly forty Americans who alone decided many small things and several big things, such as the conditions under which these and other men might fight and subsequently die. Here they were, far away from home and family, in the cold rain, on the wet ground, ostensibly without sleep, scared, tired, alone, their muscles aching, their bowels perpetually loose, their inevitable rashes itching and perhaps even bleeding, still hungry even though they'd eaten their last meal out of a can, wearing the same clothes they'd worn for more than a week, and, if that wasn't enough, in grave danger of being wounded or killed by a crafty, stealthy, dangerous enemy. And most, if not all, were having difficulty concentrating.

What a great deal, Flanagan concluded. Who could ask for anything more? Soft beds, clean sheets, warm women—a thing of the past. That was then; this is now. Reality these days is a rainy rice paddy, where a man's free to be outdoors, smoke cigarettes, cuss, spit, shoot rifles, and kill people. What's a little Asiatic combat amongst friends, anyway? he thought, as much in disgust as amusement.

The time passed with a dreadfully slow tempo. He glanced at the luminous dials of his watch and saw that it was six more hours until first light. He went over in detail every likely ambush scenario he could envision, and the resultant actions required of him as the platoon leader. He was bothered, as usual, by the idea of an enemy force of large size choosing this night and this place to make their presence known, in which case he and a lot of others would never live to see the sun rise. Otherwise, he felt confident he could manage events to his own satisfaction.

Then five more hours.

He went over the names and faces and duties of all the men in his platoon. He had made it a point on the previous day to spend some time with the new guys, to learn their names and find out enough tidbits about them to retain at least one or two pertinent items in his memory. Their hometowns; their training levels; their strengths and weaknesses; their family situations, to the extent that he knew them; their overall abilities as Marines. Satisfied, he then reviewed the old-timers in the same fashion.

Then four more hours.

He played an entire Beatles' concert in his head. He liked the old stuff best, from '64 and '65, and tended to represent those songs in his concert list in far greater proportion to the more recent releases. The new stuff seemed different, way too hippyish, and the change in the Beatles' music and appearance had been faster and deeper than he would have preferred. Why couldn't they just stay with the old stuff in the old style? Why did they have to change everything so radically?

He was glancing at his watch after the last song of the show, just as the Fab Four were taking their bows to the screams and the applause, when the claymore to his far left exploded with a deep, frightening *boom.*

Before he could raise his weapon and point it at the trail, the claymore at the opposite end of the trail also exploded. The gunfire from the Marines immediately poured forth onto the ambush area. Flanagan looked out at the trail for signs of the enemy, for muzzle flashes from their weapons, but saw nothing. When he fired a burst, his night vision was instantly impaired from the flashes of his own M-16. The firing was furious for perhaps twenty seconds, then became sporadic for another thirty seconds before Flanagan and Sgt. Douglas began shouting, "Cease fire."

Sgt. Douglas shouted, "Anybody hit?"

There was a weak, "Yeah," and then one of the squad leaders, a corporal named Hobart, called out, "I need a corpsman over here."

"Corpsman up."

Sgt. Douglas stood up and called to another squad leader, Corporal Easton, to "get a fire team on the trail and let's see what we've got. Listen up people, we're putting friendlies on the trail so hold your fire."

Flanagan called out to the team on the trail, which by now included Sgt. Douglas. "What've you got out there?"

"We got one KIA," came the reply.

"Anything on the body? Any papers?" Flanagan asked.

"Tits," came the answer.

"Say again?"

"It's a female gook. And she's boocoo messed up."

"You gotta be shittin' me. Is there a weapon?" called Flanagan.

"Affirmative. An SKS."

"Has it been fired?"

There was a delay of several seconds before the voice on the trail called out, "I don't think so. The weapon's still on safe."

Sgt. Douglas found Flanagan in the dark. "What do you make of it, Lieutenant?"

"A local VC. Not part of a big unit moving through here, I wouldn't think. And any more stragglers out here would've heard by now that they've got company."

"Right. And booked."

"Yeah, they're gone," Flanagan said as he made his way off the trail and found Hobart and his wounded Marine.

"He's gunshot, Lieutenant. Just below the elbow," said Doc Fackler. "The bone's likely fractured but the bleeding's under control."

"We're two klicks from the company position. Can he make it back with us?"

"Yessir," the wounded man spoke up.

"Yeah, I think so," agreed Fackler.

Flanagan glanced at his watch and saw that it was still just under three hours until daybreak. If he stayed, the need to change positions was critical. It was still rainy and dark, and the likelihood of another encounter was low. The platoon had been in the ambush location for over seven hours, fired two claymores and hundreds of rounds of small-arms ammo, and all they had to show for it was one dead Vietnamese female and one Marine who had been accidentally shot by another Marine.

Flanagan took a deep breath and wiped the water from his eyes. "Vasquez, send a message that we're coming back in, and that we've got one Victor Charlie KIA and one friendly WIA. No further contact anticipated this position. Send it now."

"Right, sir."

"Sergeant Douglas?" called Flanagan.

"Yessir?"

"Get 'em up and ready to move out."

"Aye-aye, sir. What about the VC girl?"

"Take the weapon and leave her on the trail," Flanagan answered, and then mumbled, "Let's get the hell out of here."

Several nearby Marines overheard the platoon leader and voiced their agreement with a "roger that."

* * *

Dearest Jill:

I have received your letter of March 25. I sincerely appreciate your thoughtful consideration in letting me know directly of your engagement.

I congratulate you and Branson, and wish you both the very best.

I am deeply sorry for our estrangement, and take personal responsibility for failing to try harder at bringing us back together, and then keeping us together. I'll regret for the rest of my life that I had to learn this lesson the hard way.

I don't know what else I can add, my dear sweet Jill, other than to let you know that I still love you dearly, and on some level, always will.

Love Always, Tom

CHAPTER ELEVEN
Indianapolis

Kate Flanagan leaned back against the headboard of her hotel-room bed. She kept glancing out of the corner of her eye to the bare wall beside her bed, certain that she was seeing something dark moving about in the same spot where moments before she had been startled by what she guessed was the largest cockroach in Indiana. She held a can of Coke in one hand and a package of cheese crackers in the other—her dinner for the evening—as she watched while the President of the United States was introduced to a prime-time, national-television audience. The speech was being carried live by the networks, and Lyndon Johnson wore a particularly somber expression as he began his remarks.

"Good evening, my fellow Americans:

"Tonight I want to speak to you of peace in Vietnam and Southeast Asia. No other question so preoccupies our people. No other dream so absorbs the 250 million human beings who live in that part of the world. No other goal motivates American policy in Southeast Asia . . . "

Kate listened, alternately glancing at the nearby wall, and as she did so she briefly entertained the idea of Robert Kennedy appearing on television, as president, in a prime-time address to the nation. She made a mental note of the obvious visual contrasts—from LBJ's tired eyes and heavily lined face to RFK's youthfulness and vitality. President Johnson, Kate thought, seemed absolutely exhausted, as if he'd aged twenty years in the previous five. All the more reason, she concluded, for the change that she and many others were working so hard to bring about.

" . . . Tonight, I have ordered our aircraft and our naval vessels to make no attacks on North Vietnam, except in the area north of the demilitarized zone where the continuing enemy buildup threatens allied forward positions and where the movements of their troops and supplies are closely related to that threat. . . "

Kate wondered how Tommy and his fellow Marines might receive such news. She giggled when she imagined his incredulous expression and his disapprovingly salty language. She glanced over at a group of photos she had pinned to a piece of cardboard atop her nightstand. There was one of her and Tommy, together in Chicago, while they were still in college. It seemed so long ago since she'd last seen him.

". . . With America's sons in the field far away, with America's future under challenge right here at home, with our hopes and the world's hope for peace in the balance every day, I do not believe that I should devote an hour or a day of my time to any personal partisan causes or to any duties other than the awesome duties of this office—the Presidency of your country.

"Accordingly, I shall not seek, and I will not accept, the nomination of my party for another term as your President . . . "

"My God!" Kate said aloud in wide-eyed astonishment, failing to notice the return of the cockroach.

* * *

"So what did he say?" Kate asked as she spoke on the phone the next day, April 1, from her cramped Indianapolis office to Dan Marinelli who was in New York with the Kennedy entourage. "Was he ecstatic? Was there a big party? Did it sound like New Year's Eve?"

"I swear to God, Kate, all he said was, 'Well, we can forget about Johnson,' and then he got busy on some other stuff."

"That's all? No jumping up and down? No shouting with glee?"

"Nope, none of that. And if you knew Bob Kennedy like I do, well, you'd know that his reaction was typical. The entire strategy suddenly turns on a dime—everything changes with one announcement, as if all the pins have been pulled out of the map—and Bob shrugs it off and gets down to working on some of the campaign details with the people he feels most comfortable with. He was in perfect character."

"What was your own reaction?"

"Jumping up and down. Shouting with glee."

Kate laughed.

"By the way, I've seen the television spots you helped come up with, and they look terrific. We'll have some good stuff to put in front of Indiana before this thing's over. We'll bury McCarthy in our first head-to-head if all goes according to plan. Now that Johnson's out, we'll step up the pace and schedule some things in Indiana to help with that. I'll get back to you with the details. And we'll have to wait and see how Vice President Humphrey plays out, but obviously we think he'll jump in in Johnson's place. Not sure when he'll formally announce, but he'll be there, we expect."

"He's beatable, too, don't you think?"

"Hell yes. Did you guys lease the space in Indianapolis over the old movie theater?"

"Yeah, we did. The theater's showing *Gone with the Wind*. There's something prophetic in there somewhere. Maybe it's the thing with the Johnson announcement."

"Hell, Kate, maybe it's the Johnson presidency."

They both laughed uneasily.

* * *

Kate was waiting with several others when the chartered plane finally landed at Weir Cook Airport. She had been informed earlier of the breaking story out of Memphis that Dr. Martin Luther King, Jr. had been assassinated there. She saw the shocked, haggard Robert Kennedy step off the plane and immediately get into a closed car with Fred Dutton. Ethel was being sent to a hotel, and Kate and a handful of youthful volunteers climbed into the last vehicle in the motorcade and pulled away with the police escort.

"What's going to happen now?" one of the young female volunteers asked.

"I don't know," was Kate's terse answer.

"Will there be a riot?"

"I don't know. Do you want to get out?" Kate asked.

The young woman did not answer. The driver glanced at Kate.

"Tell me now if you want to get out. I need to know right now," Kate pressed.

Still, there was no answer from the young woman.

Kate had been told that the mayor of Indianapolis had thought it a bad idea, but Robert Kennedy was going to the ghetto anyway on April 4. The appearance had been scheduled in a largely black area considered too dangerous by the police, but an enthusiastic crowd was expected nonetheless. What hadn't been anticipated, what couldn't have been foreseen, was that Kennedy's visit was now coinciding with news of the King assassination.

Kate and the others couldn't help but notice when the police escort peeled away from the motorcade as soon as it entered the ghetto. By the time the Kennedy party reached the site, it was clear that the mostly black crowd of a thousand or so had not received word of King's death. It was windy and cold, but there was applause and a generally festive atmosphere, with Kennedy banners and signs throughout the crowd, as the candidate climbed onto a flatbed truck in a parking lot.

Kate maneuvered her way to a spot near the truck, her hands trembling and her mouth dry from the fear that had risen up from deep inside her belly. She glanced around at the crowd and thought momentarily of being a white person in a black ghetto with a presidential candidate in the very midst of what was about to become devastating news for these and millions of others. She took a deep breath and attempted to calm herself, but she felt powerless and out of control. She silently prayed—desperately prayed, actually—that the crowd would remain under control, but she remained unsure. She glanced up at Kennedy, hoping that he could somehow maintain his hold on the crowd, but she felt an ominous fear of such piercing intensity that she had to fight hard not to be overtaken by it.

The grim, misty-eyed Kennedy, dressed in black overcoat, asked to speak immediately. "I have bad news for you," he said in a wavering voice as he spoke into the microphone, "for all of our fellow citizens, and for those who love peace all over the world, and that is that Martin Luther King was shot and killed tonight."

A tremor of disbelief surged through the crowd, and some screamed, "No!" but it was also clear that a full comprehension did not immediately reach everyone. Kennedy seemed to sense it and with his words and tone he attempted to ease the pain and the bewilderment that began to spread over the crowd like a mountain fog.

Kate took a deep breath, then another. Her knees were trembling, and she suddenly felt weak, as if she might faint. She momentarily lost her balance, but as she did she was firmly braced by the arm of a gray-haired, bespectacled black man who had seen her falter and caught her before she fell over.

"You okay, young lady?" he leaned over and asked in a loud but genteel whisper.

Kate forced a smile and answered, "Yes, thank you," and as she did so she reached out and grabbed the truck body to steady herself. In a few brief moments she succeeded in finding her inner calm, and her rapid pulse began to moderate. As she looked around she could see the hurt in the eyes of the young and the old, who only moments before had shown such hope and happiness. She saw the tears, the anger, but above all, the shock and disbelief. She suddenly realized she wasn't alone, that there was fear and helplessness blanketing the entire crowd, enough so that she quickly felt bonded to them more by their similarities than by their differences. She turned and listened to Robert Kennedy, finding comfort in his conviction and his presence, sharing her grief with the others and accepting their grief as her own, no longer threatened, no longer terrified

". . . What we need in the United States is not division; what we need in the United States is not hatred; what we need in the United States is not violence or lawlessness, but love and wisdom, and compassion toward one another, and a feeling of justice toward those who still suffer within our country, whether they be white or they be black . . ."

Kate looked out at the sea of faces, so many reflecting the same feelings that she herself was registering. Her legs still trembled, but she began to regain her composure.

". . . Let us dedicate ourselves to what the Greeks wrote so many years ago: to tame the savageness of man and to make gentle the life of this world.

"Let us dedicate ourselves to that, and say a prayer for our country and our people."

* * *

By the time they were all back at the hotel, none in the Kennedy party, not even the grizzled veteran campaigners, could ever remember a more effective and eloquent message from their candidate. The circumstances had been nothing short of extraordinary, as was obvious, and RFK had been up to it in every way. Kate observed the inner workings of the team as several schedule changes were made to accommodate a Martin Luther King funeral, and contact with Coretta Scott King, King's widow, was quickly made. Kennedy's offer of assistance was accepted, and a charter plane was arranged for transport of Dr. King's body from Memphis to his Atlanta home. A speech in Cleveland scheduled for the following day would still be made, but afterwards the candidate would be free to attend King's funeral in Atlanta.

Dan Marinelli showed up in Indianapolis late on the night of the 4th and checked into the hotel where Kate and the Kennedy entourage were staying. Dan immediately found the suite where a late-night strategy session was taking place with several senior Kennedy insiders, and upon entering the smoky room he noticed the fully-dressed Kate Flanagan curled up sideways in a chair in the far corner of the suite, seemingly sound asleep.

But Kate was merely resting her tired eyes, and she was still listening to all that was being said.

Dan stowed his luggage to the side and immediately became a part of the discussion: Scheduling matters; the likely successor to Dr. King, and the need for a coalition with the black leadership; the latest polling numbers from Indiana; the latest from the McCarthy camp; the latest from LBJ's peace overture to the North Vietnamese; and the likely impact upon the Democratic Party mix of Hubert Humphrey's entry.

It was late, and the events of the day finally began to wear on everyone.

"But let's not forget what's happened tonight," Dan finally said. "We've had another political assassination in this country, and our guy's security has got to be Priority Number One from this point on. As much as I'd like to think otherwise, surely to God there's some idiot out there who'd love to take a crack at Bob Kennedy."

The others offered their silent agreement.

"He won't do it," said an aide. "He won't put up with being screened off from the public. How can we protect him when, damn it, he won't protect himself?"

"We've got to, that's all there is to it."

"But how?"

The door suddenly opened and in walked Robert Kennedy, his tie loosened, accompanied by his cocker spaniel, Freckles. He nodded at Dan and the others and then noticed Kate in the corner chair.

"Has she heard from her brother lately, the one in Vietnam?" Kennedy asked.

"He's doing well," Dan answered. "Kate told me he's even scheduled some time off for himself in Australia. His R & R should be coming up soon."

"What's R & R?" someone asked.

"Rest & Recreation," Dan answered, then smiling and adding, "and everything it implies."

Kennedy found a hotel blanket in a nearby closet and walked over to cover Kate. Kate's eyelids quickly opened, and after a moment she raised her head and smiled.

"Why, you're not so ruthless after all," said Kate.

Kennedy grinned. "Don't tell anyone."

* * *

From her Indianapolis office Kate read the newspaper account of the King funeral in Atlanta on April 7, which put to rest the civil rights leader but not the civil unrest in America that followed in the wake of the assassination. There were riots in 110 cities; 39 deaths; 2,500 injured; and 75,000 National Guardsmen in city streets throughout the country. Washington, D.C. was under curfew, and smoke and flames had at one point been visible from several sections of the city. She read where Robert Kennedy had an opportunity in Atlanta to meet with several black political and entertainment figures, but it was clear that race relations in the United States were badly frayed. For Kate, it was also clear that a unifying message was greatly needed, desperately needed, a message that in her own opinion a growing number of the American people, both black and white, were beginning to feel that Robert F. Kennedy was uniquely qualified to offer.

Kate was right there as Kennedy stepped up his Indiana campaign with appearances all across the state, along with saturation advertising throughout the electronic media. The Wabash Cannonball train traveled the state and delivered the candidate and his family to many of the rural sections, and eventually came to be playfully known among the reporters covering the Kennedy campaign as the Ruthless Cannonball. She grew accustomed to Kennedy's staccato delivery, his often trembling hands, his statistical sorties, his self-deprecating humor, his conviction, his right fist pounding into his left palm, his wrap-up with George Bernard Shaw quotations (which the press used as a signal to scurry to the buses), and his genuine need for contact with the public. She watched closely as his personal qualities and his celebrity combined to move him steadily up in the polling numbers, and there was reason for optimism among the Kennedy team that with less than a month to go before the May 7 primary, the Indiana campaign message was indeed having the intended effect.

Kate continued in her advertising work for the campaign, as well as filling in in assorted other roles as the needs of the campaign dictated. She rode the train for several days as it made the stops at the depots of the many small towns, the names of which she'd mostly never before heard. She was doing good work, valuable work, and her stature as an accomplished professional had grown considerably among the senior Kennedy advisers and the candidate himself. She was going home to Georgetown most weekends, although the separation had caused a strain in her relationship with her fiancé. They were often at odds, arguing over small things and not speaking altogether on their bigger differences. There was now an evident tension between them, seemingly perpetual, sometimes slight but more often abounding. Her disjointed personal life notwithstanding, the work she was doing and the fulfillment she was receiving from it was as satisfying to her as anything she'd ever experienced.

Even her improved relationship with her brother Tommy, albeit long-distance but otherwise genuine and heartfelt, had served to buoy her spirits and improve her outlook over the shape of things to come. He had survived the wounds and horrors of Hue, of Tet, and he would be home in several months and out of the awful meat grinder that Vietnam had most assuredly become. The news of Jill Rohrbach's engagement had also wounded him, Kate was sure, but she also knew he would survive that, as well.

Things were mostly good, her life had purpose, had meaning, and she was enjoying It to the fulloct.

* * *

Dan Marinelli and Kate were having a late dinner together in a corner booth of an upscale Indianapolis restaurant. Even though they spoke often by phone, they saw one another only occasionally, and usually briefly, on the campaign trail. This was their first such face-to-face contact in weeks.

"More wine?" Dan asked as he held out the bottle of Bordeaux.

"I've had a full glass already, but yeah, sure," Kate answered with a shrug as she took another bite of the succulent prime rib.

Dan poured a full glass.

"You're going home this weekend, right?" he asked.

"Yep. My fiancé's been complaining about my being away for what seems like forever."

"I don't blame him. I'd complain, too, if I was engaged to you and you were gone all the time."

She smiled.

"I know darn well what you're gonna say, Kate. Don't say it, please. I left myself wide open, I know. But don't say it."

"Don't say what?"

"Don't say that if you were engaged to me, you'd *want* to be gone all the time," Dan said with a grin.

"I wasn't going to say that," Kate replied.

Dan sat back, chest extended. "Good, because if you were engaged to me, my dear, sweet Katherine, the truth is you'd *never* leave."

Kate immediately reached over and removed the bottle of wine from Dan's easy reach.

"It's true," he said, chuckling. "It comes from the heart, not the grapes."

"Hah. Another sip of wine and I'm afraid you'll be proposing."

"Actually I do have a proposal to make," Dan said.

Kate's eyes widened and she pointed to her full mouth as a signal for Dan to remain quiet until she could speak. When she finally did speak, she said curtly, "No proposals from you tonight, Marinelli. Neither personal nor professional."

"So you won't let me ask if you want to go to Nebraska, then Oregon, and then California, and do what you've been doing so well here in Indiana?"

"No, I will not. Not tonight," Kate said, reaching for her wine.

"Why not?"

"Because I promised Everett that we'd have a full-blown discussion of my work and my travel schedule this weekend, that's why not."

"What does 'full-blown discussion' mean?" Dan asked with a confused expression.

"It means exactly that."

"Look," Dan said with exasperation in his tone, "Everett's a McCarthy supporter, and apparently a damn lonely one, at that. He doesn't like your politics or your travel away from Washington, so when you have your 'full-blown' talk, will it come as a shock when he tells you that he wants you to change jobs and stay home with him? I mean c'mon, where's the epiphany here?"

Kate winced slightly but said nothing.

Dan immediately poured himself another glass and topped off Kate's, emptying the bottle.

"What do you do in your spare time here?" he asked after a brief pause had dissipated the tension.

Kate smiled. "I've become a television addict. If I don't get to see *Mod Squad*, or *Julia*, or *Mission: Impossible*, then I'm miserable. And I watch Carson most nights, at least for a while."

"Go to any nightclubs?"

"Sometimes, yeah. There's one a couple of blocks from here that's pretty decent," she said.

"Want to get a drink there tonight?"

Kate hesitated a moment before answering, "Yeah, I suppose so."

"Great. Speaking of night clubs, I saw a super band a few weeks ago in a joint up in Milwaukee. It's a bunch of long-hairs who call themselves the Chicago something-or-other. They've got a really good, snappy groove. Brass and everything, really a nice sound. Who knows, maybe they'll make it to the big time one day and I can tell everyone I was there when they were just getting started."

"Maybe you'll invite them to the White House someday," she said with a giggle.

"Good idea. I'll make a note of it," Dan said with raised index finger.

After dinner they walked the few blocks to the nightclub and took a table furthermost from the stage and the dance floor. They ordered drinks—beer for Dan and a rum and coke for Kate—as the band cranked out the soulful R & B tunes in rapid succession with plenty of ear-splitting volume. A sweating, pompadoured singer in a loose, flowing shirt and outrageously tight flared pants poured out his heart to the energetic few on the compact dance floor. Kate noticed as Dan's eyes took the measure of every female in the place, and he seemed particularly taken with a tall, full-bosomed blonde in her mid-twenties who danced often, each time with a different partner.

Dan became quiet as he concentrated on the dancer.

"Why don't you go over and ask Elke to dance?" Kate asked almost in a shout over the loud music when she also noticed the woman looking over at Dan with growing frequency.

"Who?" asked Dan.

"Her," Kate said with a point. "Miss Bavaria."

"Nah," he said, shrugging.

"Oh go ahead, Dan. Don't mind me. Ask her before she comes over here and asks you first."

"She's a good dancer, isn't she?"

"Oh, you bet. She can do it all," Kate answered with a full scoop of sarcasm as she watched the lurching, ungraceful motions. She finally mumbled, "Peggy Fleming she ain't."

The young woman stepped to the Pony, the Jerk, the Swim, the Boogaloo, the Mashed Potato, and the Frug. She made it a point on several occasions to walk near to the table of Dan and Kate, always with an inviting smile for Dan, as she returned to the nearby table she was sharing with two other young women.

Kate smiled as she passed nearby. "Probably does a nice polka, too, wouldn't you think, Hans?"

"Do you know her?" Dan asked, leaning toward Kate.

"Hardly a chance," she answered with a sneer.

Kate glanced over and saw the woman smile and wave at Dan as she sat back and smoked a cigarette.

"It's your lucky night," Kate cracked.

When the band suddenly went into *My Girl*, Dan rose and extended his hand to Kate.

"You're exactly right," he said with a grin.

Kate hesitated a moment before she finally pushed back from her chair and took Dan's hand. He led her to the center of the dance floor and then took her in his arms, slowly but steadily pulling her closer to him.

"Remember, I'm engaged," Kate offered when the going got a little too close at one point.

"Oh, I remember," he replied, backing off and sounding slightly dejected. "At this point, the phrase 'engaged to be married' as it applies to you has about the same intrinsic appeal to me as does the phrase 'turn your head to the side and cough.'"

Kate couldn't hide her smile.

The song ended and the dancers offered up their applause as Dan escorted her back to the table. Kate refused the offer of another drink.

"Really, Dan, I've got to be leaving. I've got an early meeting with the ad agency in the morning."

Dan stood. "Then I'll walk you to your room."

Once they entered the hotel lobby Kate expected that Dan would say his good-byes from there, but when he stepped onto the elevator with her she realized he was taking his escort duty literally. The elevator stopped on the seventh floor and Kate and Dan walked the short distance to her room. Dan waited in the hallway while Kate opened the door to her room and stepped inside. She turned and faced Dan, bracing the door open with her elbow.

"Thank you for the dinner and dancing. And thank you for seeing me to my room. That's very considerate of you."

"You're very welcome. And I thank you for your delightful company. I'm glad we finally had the chance to spend some time together."

There was a clumsy, brief pause before Kate said, "Well, I really should turn in for the night."

Dan reached for her hand, held it a moment, then smiled and said with a chuckle, "Pleasant dreams, Fraulein Flanagan."

CHAPTER TWELVE
Sydney, Australia

Flanagan bolted upright in the bed, his mouth dry and his heart pounding, his eyes desperately searching the darkened room. His instinctive first impulse concerned the location of his weapon, and he felt a surge of near panic sweep over his already glistening body when he reached out and failed to feel the familiar contours of his M-16 rifle. The NVA were there— *right there!*— and they were there in large, horrendous numbers. He wanted to scream, to shout out a warning that there were enemy here, there, everywhere, and he felt again for his weapon. Still, it wasn't there. What was there instead were the soft contours of the rumpled sheets, the hump of a fluffy pillow, the steady drone of the air conditioning, and the barely visible profile of a television set directly across from his bed. It was only then that his head cleared enough for him to realize that he was in a hotel room in Sydney, Australia.

Vietnam, thankfully, was several thousand miles away.

"Damn!" he gasped, his heart feeling as if it were pumping hard enough to give him aerial flight if only he'd spread his arms. He took in a deep breath and sat back against the headboard. His night vision quickly returned, and he could look around and make out the furniture and the clock radio on the nightstand next to the bed. It was three o'clock in the morning. He tasted salt from the sweat that had trickled into his mouth, and the bed was damp underneath him. It took several minutes before he calmed, and by that time he was awake to the point that sleep no longer interested him.

He flicked on the light. There were newspapers everywhere—in the chair, on the floor, at the foot of the bed. He'd bought every English-language paper he could find so he could consume all that was going on in Sydney and Melbourne and Glasgow and New York and London. There really *was* a world that existed beyond Vietnam, that carried on with its business and operated its airports and printed its newspapers and booked its hotel rooms. Things really *were* normal away from the death and stench of Southeast Asia. People really *could* be nice to one another; they really *could* be pleasant and friendly, without worry over incoming or booby traps, without concern over the dangers of the dark, without the abnormal and the bizarre having somehow been convoluted into the routine.

This really is Australia, he kept thinking; and more importantly, this really isn't Vietnam.

* * *

The place was loud and smelled of smoke and perfume. Flanagan had consumed lots of beer, and he had even bought a few rounds as his gift to several complete strangers that had engaged him in conversation. He hadn't felt so rich and handsome and urbane, and quite so drunk, in such a long time that the entire experience had a freshness to it that kept him occupied. Over the course of the four hours he remained in the club, he'd met and spent time with at least a dozen people, but after a while he had settled into the company of three Australian girls and two American guys. The Americans were in their mid-twenties, and had described themselves to Flanagan as exchange students from Spokane. The girls, locals from Sydney, were in their early twenties.

Afterwards the six of them walked a short distance from the nightclub to a dingy apartment in a modest residential section. They climbed a flight of stairs and came inside the split-level structure, and while the others settled onto the tattered couch and chairs, Flanagan stumbled slightly as he stood upright and gazed about the dwelling.

"What the hell's this?" Flanagan asked as he looked around at the walls that were festooned with psychedelic posters.

"Groovy, huh?" said the young woman with whom he had left the club. Aimee had brown hair that was long and flowing and parted in the middle. Her delicate features were silky smooth, her oval face accentuated by the granny glasses and the beret she wore. She was unadorned without make-up of any sort, and she looked and acted much older than her twenty years.

"Let's have a drink," said Carl, a heavyset and full-bearded American. "Got any of that whiskey left, Jerome?"

Jerome, a skinny black American with an Afro and goatee, reached toward a coffee table and picked up a cigar box into which dozens of pre-rolled joints had been stashed. "The whiskey and the wine are in the kitchen, Carl. Me, I'm having a little herb."

Carl got up and half-staggered to the kitchen while Jerome passed around the cigar box to the young women.

"Care to join us, Tom?" asked Aimee, holding the box toward him.

"No thanks. I'll stay with the booze," Flanagan said as he followed Carl into the kitchen.

There were several knocks on the door as others, male and female, entered the apartment. It was one o'clock in the morning, and the party was picking up momentum.

Soon the large open area downstairs was bustling. The well-worn albums of such favorites as Bob Dylan and Joan Baez were played, sometimes skipping, sometimes repeating until the phonograph's arm was nudged. Flanagan sat on the floor, off to the side and alongside Aimee. A bottle of white wine, half a loaf of stale French bread, a couple of joints for Aimee's use, and a half-dozen Three Musketeers were within easy reach. A robust discussion among Carl, Jerome, and several others was starting to draw the remainder into the center of the room like metal filings to a magnet.

Carl was physically the largest person in the house, and who in Flanagan's opinion struck a stereotypical resemblance to a motorcyclist. He wore an old leather jacket and had unkempt long hair and a scruffy beard. Carl was busy lecturing on the evils of what he kept referring to as "The System."

"It's rigged, man," Carl claimed in a gravelly, nasally voice. "It's gotta be torn down and rebuilt. If you've got money in America, man, then you've got influence. And if you've got influence, then you can buy off anything or anybody in the goddamn system— the courts, the pigs, the politicians, the—"

"The Army," interjected Aimee.

"Yeah, right. Especially the friggin' Army," said Carl, nodding his agreement.

Flanagan turned and glanced at Aimee with the questioning look of how any such young Australian woman could come to know anything about an army, any army, much less an American version.

"It's not only rigged in favor of those with money," chimed in Jerome, "it's rigged in other ways, too."

"Right on, man," agreed Carl. "And it'll never get any better until we throw out all those bastards and start over again from the ground up."

"Which bastards?" Flanagan asked.

"All of 'em," came the answer in unison from several others.

"And who do you put in their place?" asked Flanagan.

"Timothy Leary," came one answer. "Or maybe Jim Morrison."

"H. Rap Brown," came another.

"Batman."

"Ho Chi Minh."

"Dr. Benjamin Spock."

"Mahatma Ghandi."

"Che Guevara," came a shrill female voice over the others from the direction of the kitchen, evoking laughter. "Che forever!"

"What about Bobby Kennedy?" asked Flanagan.

"You gotta be shittin' me, man," growled Carl amid the grumbles of others. "He's not any different than the rest of those assholes."

"Except he's richer," added Aimee.

"And therefore, by definition, more influential," added Jerome.

"Right," said Flanagan, "that's my point. Maybe he can use his influence to do some good."

"Like his brother did during the Bay of Pigs?" asked Jerome in a calm, detached tone. "What you so obviously fail to understand is that people like Bobby Kennedy and his cronies in Washington are the *cause* of the shit the world's in."

"Then what's the answer?" Flanagan asked, shrugging.

"Turn everything over to the people," Jerome replied, becoming animated. "The power, the money, the influence—everything, man. That'd be a start. You're familiar with Camus, right?"

Flanagan hesitated a moment before answering, "Sure."

Jerome smirked, then nodded. "Then you understand when he writes about the alienation that results when people feel they can't control and master their own fates. Poor people are pushed into urban centers of hopelessness, called housing projects, and forgotten about. And as long as they stay there and don't make any noise, don't make any demands, why, they're invisible. Out of sight, out of mind. You dig? But the moment they complain about having nothing—no control over their destinies, no money, no recourse, no justice, no hope—then they become the embarrassment to society that society doesn't otherwise recognize and doesn't otherwise claim. And the faces are the same, whether it's Bed-Stuy in New York or the backwoods of Mississippi. Same faces, just different places. There's too much Wall Street, too much Main Street, and not enough back street."

"Right on," echoed several others.

"Too much Wall Street," continued Jerome. "America's industrial elite play the stock market—the nationally preferred and universally condoned method of gambling—and hope to benefit from the labor of workers who are solely responsible for the firm's profits which, to be sure, those workers will never, ever see or share in. Not in their entire lives, man. And so the rich retire to Florida and the workers either drop dead or keep on working. I ask you, where's the justice here?"

"Are you a Marxist, Jerome?" Flanagan blurted out, quieting the others as the rippling effect spread over the room.

169

Jerome smiled calmly. "What makes you think I'm a Marxist?"

Flanagan stiffened. "You seem to have difficulty with a lot of the normal American stuff."

"That's because so much of the normal American stuff is shit, man," growled Carl. "Pure, unadulterated shit."

Jerome regained the floor after raising his hand slightly. "The man's asked me a question, and he deserves an answer. The question being, Am I a Marxist?" Jerome paused and chuckled slightly, his eyes at first lowered, then turned slowly toward Flanagan. "I prefer to think of myself as a revolutionary."

"Ah," said Flanagan with eyebrows raised and head slightly tilted to the side. "Then you no doubt remember what your friend Camus said about every revolutionary ending up either an oppressor or a heretic."

Jerome frowned and looked away.

"Nothing wrong with Marxists," called Carl.

Flanagan shrugged. "I don't know any Marxists myself," he said, pausing and then adding, "but I've shot a few." He stifled a grin. "It was nothing personal, mind you."

"It beats money-grubbing capitalists," called someone nearby.

"Or imperialists going around bombing everyone who doesn't agree with them," shouted another.

"Good God!" shrieked an exasperated, wide-eyed Flanagan. "Is it the weather here in Sydney, or are you people *always* this friggin' happy?"

Jerome smiled despite his growing annoyance. "We're always happy to get to listen to a naive honkey like you tell us everything's just dandy with the world, especially when we know otherwise. Sure, man, we're just happy as pigs in shit. Can't you tell?"

Aimee sent a message through her expression and body language for the others to relax and back off a bit.

"What the hell's that flag doing here?" Flanagan asked, scowling and pointing to the red-and-blue flag with the yellow star that was nailed to a hallway wall.

"That's the flag of the NLF," Carl answered in reference to the National Liberation Front, the political entity of the Viet Cong. "The oppressed patriots, the ones on the right side."

"I know whose goddamn flag it is," Flanagan snapped. "Do you know anybody in the NLF?"

"No, but I can sure as hell sympathize with 'em," said Carl.

"How so? Would you be willing to fight beside them?" asked Flanagan

Carl stared hard at Flanagan. "I just might, yeah."

"I don't believe you," Flanagan said, staring back at Carl. "Not for a minute. I sure as hell don't see a fighter when I look at you."

Carl stiffened. "Oh yeah? Then what is it you see, man?"

"A friggin' sympathizer, whatever the hell that's supposed to mean," Flanagan said, smiling and adding, "and a mighty goddamn ugly one, at that. But definitely not a fighter."

Carl shifted his legs, as if he were about to stand. Flanagan's expression instantly hardened as he, too, shifted his feet. Aimee raised her hand and shook her head, and Carl sat back.

"You can display something like that when American guys your own age are fighting and getting messed up and killed over there by people fighting under that same flag?" said Flanagan, pointing.

"If those dumbass Americans fight over there, man," Carl answered, his voice rising, "then they deserve whatever they get. If they want to go over there and take their guns and napalm and drop it on the villagers and their rice fields and their ancestral homes, then goddammit as far as I'm concerned they all deserve whatever they get!"

A few others voiced their agreement.

Flanagan tilted the wine bottle and took a drink. "Did I happen to mention that I'm a U. S. Marine Corps lieutenant down here from Vietnam on R & R?"

"No, but it wasn't like we didn't know what your bag was, man," said Carl.

"Talk about being out of place," Flanagan said with a chuckle as he leaned over and kissed Aimee on the cheek, then removed the black beret from atop her head and placed it on his own. When he took another long gulp from the bottle, the beret promptly fell off behind his back. "A damned *good* wine, certainly, a very nice Australian white," he muttered to no one in particular, licking his lips, "but I wouldn't go so far as to call it a great one."

"Slow down," Aimee admonished in a soft whisper after reclaiming her beret.

Flanagan turned to Aimee and grinned. "My sister's working for Bobby Kennedy and I'm a Marine down here from Vietnam," he said, belching in mid-sentence and then wiping his mouth with his hand. "Let's see now: I'm a naive honkey from an old-fashioned family, we've got a little money invested on Wall Street, it's Friday night and I'm in Sydney friggin' Australia in a room with a lot of dope, a bunch of free thinkers, and one ugly-ass sympathizer. We've got a lot in common, don't we, gang?"

Aimee took the bottle away when Flanagan struggled to his feet and staggered off to the bathroom, mumbling, "Yeah, man, a whole shitload in common. Even got a goddamn gook flag in here."

The party eventually broke up, but only after Flanagan had passed out in a corner of the main downstairs room where he remained until dawn. He awoke around seven, underneath an old blanket but still freezing, stiff from the hard floor and nauseated by the odors of stale smoke and dirty carpeting, among others. He thought briefly about going upstairs to wake Aimee, to square things with her before going back to his hotel room, but he wasn't entirely sure what he'd find up there; or whom; or in what combination. Besides, his head throbbed like he'd been hit with a hatchet, and his stomach was queasy to the point of imminent nausea. When he got up and started to walk toward the door, he was met by Jerome.

"I suppose you've guessed by now, huh Marine?" asked Jerome in a tentative voice.

"What? That story you gave me about you and Carl being students?"

"Right, that."

"Yeah," said Flanagan. "So what the hell *are* you?"

"We're just trying to be free and have a good time, man."

"You're deserters, aren't you?" asked Flanagan.

"What makes you say that?"

Flanagan shrugged. "I never thought for a minute that either of you was adroit enough to be an exchange student."

"We deserted, man, yeah," confessed Jerome, gazing down. "We came here on R & R four months ago and met these chicks and never went back."

Flanagan started around Jerome. "Then I hope they catch you both and string you up by your pubic hairs. Now get the hell out of my way."

Flanagan opened the door and started out.

"Are you gonna let 'em know, man? Are you gonna tell 'em we're here?" called Jerome.

Flanagan started down the stairs, then stopped. "You chose this for yourself, and you knew you wouldn't be able to stay in one place for very long. I'm as disgusted about having spent my time with you as I'm sure you are about me. You know what I think of you, and about what you've done. And you probably assume that I'll turn you in as soon as I get the chance." He grinned and said, "If I were you, I'd keep moving," and then turned and walked away.

* * *

Flanagan was up and out of his room by nine, had a breakfast of ham and eggs in the hotel restaurant, and afterwards walked across the street to a department store. It was cool inside, almost chilly, and there was something about the store's interior that was familiar to him, something that very much reminded him of Chicago's chic Michigan Avenue stores. Maybe it was that particular, almost regulation smell that all the finer retail stores seemed to share; maybe the way the saleslady lightly re-folded the loose garments on a table; maybe the way the floor shined and the bells chimed. It was definitely familiar to him, even though in other ways it felt odd and distant.

He bought gifts: A dress shirt and new wallet for his father; a London Fog jacket for Chris; a blouse, silver necklace, and silk scarf for his mother; a gold charm bracelet and a book of poetry for Kate. He thought briefly about sending Jill Rohrbach an early wedding gift, but he quickly dismissed the impulse. He looked at men's suits and still recognized the styles, though the neckties were wider. Some of the more popular colognes were new to him, and he sprayed the mist of several into his hand and one in particular across his face. He liked a couple, but most he dismissed outright with an unflattering "French Whore" designation.

He looked at golf clubs in the sporting goods area, and there were even a few baseball gloves on display. In Australia even, he thought with American pride. When he picked up a fielder's mitt, a nice Rawlings Ron Santo model, he tried it on and relished the splendid fit and the familiar leathery odor. He was immediately taken back to his childhood, to Little League games and trips to Wrigley Field with his father; to his days at Northwestern where he had started three years on the baseball team and went on to play an All Big Ten-caliber third base; to the fun and camaraderie and tradition that he associated with the grand ole game. He could almost smell the beer and the hot dogs, the freshly cut grass, hear the sound of the vendors calling out to the crowd, and he could think of no amount of money that he wouldn't have given on the spot to be back once again at Wrigley, with his dad, underneath the blue Chicago sky, the wind blowing in hard off the lake, kicking back and acting like a kid again in the presence of thousands of others doing exactly the same thing.

He put down the glove and left. Thoughts of American baseball while in an Australian department store while on leave from Vietnam were beginning to cause his mental circuit-breakers to trip. And tripping of any sort, he solemnly vowed, had absolutely no place on this excursion.

Flanagan had a large shopping bag full of packages and was making his way toward the store's exit when he noticed an attractive young saleslady behind the perfume counter. She glanced up as he was walking by, and he quickly noticed from her name tag that her name was Pamela.

"You seem to have been everywhere in the store but here," she said with a lovely smile and a soft, endearing Aussie accent. "Surely you might consider finishing your shopping with a gift of perfume for her."

Flanagan stopped and smiled in return. "Surely. How utterly stupid of me."

"Ah, a Yank. What brings you to Australia?"

He moved closer and rested his shopping bag on the floor beside him. She was in her early twenties, of medium height and slender build. Her light-brown hair was cut in bangs, accentuating her round cheekbones and soft dimples. Her blue eyes were bright and alive, large without being obtrusive, alternately coquettish and fixed, at once a striking, compelling, arresting attribute. Her painted lips were full, framing her lovely smile. And when she did smile, her entire face seemed to transform its individual features into what Flanagan judged to be a virtual work of grandeur.

"I'm sorry," he said sheepishly. "What was the question?"

She giggled. "What brings you to Australia?"

"I'm taking a little time off from my regular job," he said with a slight grin.

"Yeah? Regular, as in U.S. military?"

"Yep, that's it."

"Vietnam?" she asked with a slight turn of her head.

"Afraid so, yeah," Flanagan said.

175

Her eyebrows arched. "In that case, Yank, welcome to civilization."

Flanagan laughed. "Thanks. And my name's Tom. Tom Flanagan."

"Nice to meet ya', Tom Flanagan. I'm Pamela Whitestone."

Flanagan extended his hand and Pamela gently took it. Hers was without question the softest hand, the prettiest face, the finest, most sensuous female package he'd laid his eyes on—or his hand, or anything else for that matter—in more months than he cared to remember.

"Speaking of perfume . . ." he said, grinning.

"Yes, Tom. What would you like me to show you?"

He grinned boyishly. "All of 'em. I want you to show me every single item you've got back there. And if you have any others anyplace else in the building, I'd like to see those, too," he said, glancing at his watch. "And I have no other place to be, so there's no need to feel rushed."

Pamela laughed out loud. "That's very cute. Very well done, it was. But seriously, where would you like me to start?"

Flanagan shrugged. "So what's your favorite, Miss Whitestone? It is *Miss* Whitestone, isn't it?"

"It is, yes. And I prefer Shalimar, actually. Shall we begin with it?"

"Yes, Shalimar. Perfect."

Pamela showed Flanagan two additional selections before he brought the matter to a close by purchasing the Shalimar.

"Lovely choice," Pamela complimented. "Will there be anything else for you today, Tom?"

He took a deep breath. "I suppose not."

"All right," Pamela said as she rang up the sale on the register. When she returned in a moment with his change and his receipt, Flanagan leaned toward her and lowered his voice. "Pamela, is there a place where we could, you know, maybe meet this evening for a drink?"

"There are literally hundreds of places where we could meet for a drink," she said. "Sydney has no end to such places, believe me."

He stood in silence for a moment, with a look on his face that said, that screamed, *Yeah? Okay. Where?*

"There's only one problem," she added.

Damn! he thought. She's got a boyfriend. "A problem? What problem?"

"I don't drink," she answered.

He chuckled. "No, no. That's not a problem. That's a preference; but that's definitely not a problem."

"It's not a problem that I don't drink and consequently don't go to places that serve people who do?"

"Of course not. Why don't we just meet instead in a place that serves people who eat? Surely you eat, don't you? Why don't we just meet at a restaurant? Will you consider that as a reasonable alternative?" he asked, trying to suppress a smile.

"You're rather a fast worker, Yank, I must confess."

He glanced around. "I don't know of any other way to do this, Miss Whitestone. If I hang around here all afternoon, your boss will eventually come over here and throw me out into the street."

"My boss is a woman," Pamela said, grinning.

"I'll still end up in the street," Flanagan said with a grimace.

Pamela glanced around quickly, then took a pen from the register and scribbled a number on a slip of paper. "Please, let's be discreet about this," she said as she folded and quickly passed the slip of paper to him. "Ring me later, say, after five. We'll talk then. Yeah?"

Flanagan nodded and stuffed the paper into the pocket of his slacks. "After five. Thanks, Pamela."

She smiled again, a warm, wonderful smile that altogether brightened his outlook. She then stepped over and greeted a female customer who stood looking at a countertop display. She glanced over once more.

"I hope she enjoys the Shalimar," Pamela called as Flanagan grabbed his shopping bag and started toward the exit.

"I'm certain she will," Flanagan answered, grinning.

Yep, he thought. I'm *certain* she will.

Flanagan remained sober and awake for the rest of the day, a condition he'd anticipated visiting only occasionally when he had inventoried his vacation needs on the flight down from Da Nang. He wanted rest, booze, beef, and if he could find a female for the other needs, then all the better. He had also wanted to sprawl out on a beach and soak up the sun, maybe drying up the jungle rot on his legs, and he wanted to see those great Anglo women in full figure strutting their stuff up and down the sandy beaches. It had required virtually all of the previous day for him to recover from his encounter with the deserters and others, but he was feeling good again, ready to enjoy the time he had left on his stay.

He called Pamela later, and she agreed to meet him at a pub not far from his hotel, explaining once more that while she didn't drink, she'd make an exception in this case and accompany him to the lounge. He showered and dressed and got there early, braced himself with an Aussie beer, then accepted two more from two other local patrons who had noticed his short hair and then heard his American accent. He felt his heart race when Pamela suddenly showed up in a white cotton sun dress looking every bit as attractive as she had earlier.

They took a corner table and Pamela ordered a soft drink. The crowd was growing, the jukebox was playing the popular *Love Is Blue*. It took several minutes for the opening shyness to wear off before each began to warm to the other. Flanagan explained to her, albeit only briefly, about his Marine platoon-commander responsibilities in Vietnam; about his family back home in Chicago, and their interesting range of endeavors; about his days in college at Northwestern; about his interest in becoming a businessman after his three-year hitch in the Marine Corps had been completed.

Pamela spoke of her family—three older brothers and two older sisters; her retired civil-servant father and schoolteacher mother; her interest in travel; her taking courses at a local college in hopes of one day becoming a teacher of English Literature. She was much more shy and reserved in private, not quite the poised, self-confident saleslady that Flanagan kept picturing from their earlier encounter. Still, there was a discernible warmth and sincerity about her, in her eyes and voice, in her movements, in her smile, that drew Flanagan to her. She smiled easily, unpretentiously, and the soft sound of her laughter was especially appealing. And those eyes—those extraordinary, captivating eyes; those beguiling eyes; those eyes that remained fixed upon him as he spoke, as she spoke, as she leaned and sipped her drink through a straw.

My God, those eyes! he kept thinking.

Pamela gave signs that she was preparing to leave after an hour in the lounge, but Flanagan finally convinced her to stay and have dinner with him. There was a restaurant within easy walking distance, and the closer they got the more the odor of broiling beef prevailed upon Flanagan.

"You can't imagine how good that smells to me," he said as they took a quick glance at a menu in the window. "Like a lot of other things, it seems like it's been forever."

They were seated right away. Flanagan had a steak—the largest offered—while Pamela had a more modest lamb selection. They had coffee afterwards, and by that time much of the new-acquaintance tension had worn off.

"How far are we from the waterfront?" Flanagan asked.

"Not very far—a ten minute walk from here. Why?"

"Will you go there with me?"

"Tom, you've been a delightful host, and I've thoroughly enjoyed myself this evening, but really I must be going."

Flanagan persisted, and soon they were walking along the harbor in an area known as The Rocks, near the large Harbour Bridge. The sun had already set, and a cool breeze combined with the sound of an occasional ferry provided the strolling couple with a comfortable backdrop.

"I want to see you again," Flanagan said as they looked out toward the lights of North Sydney. When he reached for her hand she discreetly avoided his grasp.

"We'll see," was her only response.

"Pamela, I want to see you again. Tomorrow, in the morning, if possible."

She laughed. "Tomorrow's Friday, Yank. I have early classes and then I'm scheduled to work. I'm a working girl, ya' know."

"Can you get the day off. Can you call and ask off?"

"No," she said softly. "I can't do that."

"Then tomorrow night, we can—"

"Tom, please, we're going a little too fast."

Flanagan held up his hands in apology.

"You pushy Americans," she said in jest. "And remember, Lieutenant Flanagan, I'm not one of your soldiers that you can simply boss around when you feel like it."

"I have no soldiers, I have Marines. And I understand I can't order you around, but get this: Tomorrow night you're having dinner with me, and Saturday morning we're going to the park. And we'll find some ice cream and maybe go to the zoo, and then buy some hot dogs—if you even have hot dogs in this country—and have a simply wonderful day, just the two of us. Is that clear, Miss Whitestone?"

She smiled and then laughed softly, and suddenly she seemed far less tense and uncertain. When he reached for her and attempted to kiss her, she moved away slightly. She then reached out and took hold of his hands.

"Tom, please. Let's go slowly."

* * *

They had a lovely day on Saturday at Hyde Park and later The Royal Botanic Gardens.

They were together again on Sunday. They went shopping, took in a movie, and had a quiet dinner together at a Watson's Bay restaurant favored by Pamela. The evening ended early in spite of Flanagan's gentle coaxing, but it was clear their relationship was beginning to blossom. He called her from his hotel on Sunday evening, where they proceeded to talk for two hours about everything from previous relationships to future plans and aspirations. When he finally said goodnight and hung up the telephone, Flanagan remained awake for hours thinking about her.

Something's happening here, he kept thinking.

Good God, he thought. Is this what I need to be doing on my R & R, knowing that I'll soon leave Australia and go back to Vietnam? Do I really need this? Shouldn't I back away from this? Can I afford to become emotionally involved with a woman in a foreign country? And live with all the distractions that would surely follow me back to Vietnam? Do I *really* need this?

But she's beautiful and interesting and a delight to be with. So what if she's not American? Hell, she's close enough.

He kept going back and forth before finally deciding that he would get a good night's sleep and then make a determination in the morning about pursuing Pamela any further.

On Monday morning, Pamela called from work to ask Flanagan if he would care to move into the beachfront home of Pamela's bachelor older brother—an importer of stereo equipment who was away on a business trip to Japan—for the remainder of his stay in Australia. When he hesitated and finally asked if Pamela would be sharing the house with him, she also hesitated, but only briefly.

"Yes," she finally answered. "I've arranged to be on holiday the rest of the week."

They moved in on Monday night and celebrated with a candlelight dinner of take-out Chinese and soft drinks. Flanagan had a bottle of champagne, and Pamela even accepted a glass of the bubbly, though she didn't finish it. The house was tastefully but not excessively furnished, and it was evident that Pamela's brother was well established in his import business despite his relatively youthful, late-twenties age. Afterward they took a walk on the property's private beach and watched the moonlight reflect off the undulating sea and rushing swells. The night air was cool and fragrant, and they soon returned to the nearby house where they made love, with the sounds of the wind and the crashing surf in the background.

She lay close to him afterwards, smoothing the matted hair on his chest. "Why so quiet? Tell me what you're thinking," Pamela asked.

"I was just thinking about how in a few days I'm going to go from being here with you, back to where I came from, and it almost seems unreal."

"Then don't think about it," she said as she moved closer.

He grinned and gave a slight chuckle. "Yeah, right."

"No, really. You don't have to go back for several days. We've got time together, yeah?" said Pamela.

"Yeah."

"Then don't think about it."

"Never happen, dear," said Flanagan. "Vietnam's not a place you can easily put out of your mind."

"Then tell me about it."

"What?"

"Yes, tell me. Tell me what you're thinking. Tell me what it's like over there. Tell me everything," said Pamela.

"I don't think so."

"Please. I want to hear about it. I want you to tell me."

"Not exactly the perfect setting for such a topic, you know?" said Flanagan.

"Tom, please," she said sincerely. "Tell me about it."

Flanagan propped himself up with an elbow and turned toward her. He ran his hand over her smooth shoulder as he sorted through a chronology of images in his head. It all came flooding back—the death and suffering; the heat and the mud; the laughter of his young troops; the mountains and the coastline; the cities, bars, and hustlers; the peasants, villages, and rice fields.

He struggled to condense it all into words an outsider could understand. He swallowed hard and took a deep breath. "Have you ever seen a really bad car accident—a really terrible wreck where people have been horribly hurt or killed—and gotten that sick feeling in the pit of your stomach and that crazy sensation that what you're seeing is a bad dream?"

Pamela frowned, then answered, "Yes."

"That's kinda what Vietnam's like. It's like a terrible car wreck, except it's like that every day. And it doesn't get any better. You finally learn to deal with it—you have to—but it doesn't get better. So trying not to think about it may be next to impossible, I'm afraid. But," he said, leaning and kissing her soft lips, "you're doing an incredible job of keeping me occupied, I have to admit."

"Good," she said, returning his kisses and reaching beneath the covers. "I have my ways, ya' know."

"Yes," he said, responding to her touches and caresses and reaching to administer his own. "I've certainly noticed."

* * *

They spent Tuesday and Wednesday at the beach house, away from everyone and everything but one another. They confided to each other the intimate details of their lives—their deepest fears, their ambitions, their uncertainties. Pamela spoke of her failed engagement, and the heartache that had ensued; of her two roommates with whom she shared an apartment outside Sydney; of her determination to get on with her life.

Flanagan opened up about Jill Rohrbach, of their history together and the subsequent shock of her engagement announcement. Pamela asked about Jill, about her qualities, her background and education, her likes and dislikes, her appearance and demeanor. She noticed Flanagan's always admiring tone when he spoke of Jill, and his still obvious high regard for her in spite of the difficult ending. When Pamela finally asked Flanagan if Jill was out of his system, he hesitated.

"Thought so," Pamela said, smiling sagely.

Flanagan's guilt over his slothfulness caused him to rise early one morning and start off for a conditioning run on the beach. He'd eaten ravenously, drank gallons of beer, and his feeling of pudginess didn't help when, after about a mile, he quickly broke into a major sweat and considered quitting and crawling back to the cool beach house and Pamela's warm body. But when he thought of steamy hot Vietnam, and how in less than a week he'd be back underneath the oven-like, smothering jungle canopy, he prodded himself on to a hard three miles.

It was his singular attempt at reclaiming his top physical conditioning.

By Friday, Flanagan was clearly becoming tense over his scheduled Sunday return to Da Nang.

"Would you prefer to be alone?" Pamela asked when, after awakening from a short nap, she found Flanagan sitting near the water's edge, surrounded by several empty beer bottles.

He looked up and held out his hand. She took a seat in the sand beside him.

"I'm sorry," he said. "I'll be okay."

She sat for a moment before smiling and saying, "Thank you."

"For what?" asked Flanagan with a confused expression.

"Thank you for having come into my life. I'll never forget you, and I'll always be glad our paths crossed. You're a wonderful, considerate man, and I only wish I could spend more time with you. I really wondered if what I was doing was the right thing—being with you, sleeping with you—but now I know without a doubt that if I'd missed you, Tom Flanagan, I'd have missed something very, very special."

He put his arm around her and kissed the top of her head.

"I'll always remember you, Pamela Whitestone," he said, adding with a chuckle, "and if you're ever in Chicago . . . "

They both laughed.

He wiped a tear from her face with his thumb, then held her close. He kissed her gently. "I want you," he said as he pushed her down into the sand.

"What will the neighbors say?"

"I don't know, and furthermore, I don't care," Flanagan answered.

Pamela glanced around quickly. "But I do care. It's fairly secluded, but even still . . ."

"I want you," he repeated.

"Gee, I can hardly tell."

He raised up slightly. "Let me explain the situation to you. Please pay careful attention because I'm only going to explain it once. Here's the deal: It's the sand or the bed. The choice is yours, Miss Whitestone."

She gave a coy smile. "And if I can't bring myself to choose, then we'll just have to give both a go, yeah?"

They both giggled like school children.

"Both it is, then."

* * *

Flanagan sat alone on the porch, amid the hanging plants and the steady breeze, gazing out at the white surf being reflected by the moonlight. It was four o'clock in the morning, and inside Pamela was sleeping peacefully. It was only a matter of hours now before he'd be departing for Vietnam, and sleep for him had come with difficulty.

He thought of Pamela as the sound of the rumbling tides comforted him. He had watched her as she'd slept, remembering how she had turned and reached for him, moving ever closer, her head resting on his chest. Her scent still filled his nostrils, stirring him. He pondered their relationship, about the unlikelihood of its sudden development, about the abrupt conclusion it was about to reach. Pamela was special, he knew. An incredible aura of good fortune had enveloped and guided him when he had ventured into her part of the department store. Perhaps under different circumstances he might have fallen headlong in love with her, as complicated as that could've become. He gave a long, loud sigh, and then smiled slightly.

I'm so glad I found her anyway, he kept thinking.

* * *

On Sunday morning Pamela drove Flanagan to the airport, which was located on the northern crown of Botany Bay, its deep blue waters dazzling against the early morning sun. His ten days in Australia had been a blur, and he was leaving with much more than the normal difficulty that usually followed a pleasant vacation. He kept looking at Pamela, at her face, her eyes, trying to implant as many visual images of her as possible in his mind's eye. He watched her as she drove, as she walked with him into the terminal, as she had coffee with him, and finally as she stood with him, in his arms, at the gate as his flight was called. He had her picture in his pocket; she had his mailing address in her purse. He gave her the bottle of Shalimar as a gift; she gave him a sealed envelope that contained photographs of their time together.

The last call came for boarding.

"Thank you, Pamela. I'll never forget you."

She tried to smile, but as she did so her lip quivered. She grabbed him and clung firmly to him. "Please take care of yourself, Tom."

They eventually parted, and he walked toward the jetway. He mouthed the words, "Goodbye, Pamela," as he gave a final wave.

She waved in return, the tears streaking down her face.

He smiled, and then turned and left.

CHAPTER THIRTEEN
Indianapolis

"We've done it," Kate Flanagan declared in exhausted satisfaction as she watched the late television report with a roomful of her colleagues.

The citizens of Indiana had gone to the polls on May 7 and provided Robert Kennedy with his first primary victory and his initial stepping-stone to the White House. The final tally was: Kennedy-42%; Branigan-31%; McCarthy-27%. Kennedy won 57 of the state's 92 counties; 10 of 11 Congressional districts; all of the major cities except Bloomington and Evansville; more than 85% of the black vote; and a greater than anticipated share among blue-collar whites. Further, Kennedy had lost only two counties where he had personally campaigned in the final two weeks. Almost as an aside, the Washington, D.C. primary on the same day had also been won by Kennedy over Hubert Humphrey by a margin of 62.5% to 37.5%.

The Indiana primary was over; the first hurdle in the series had been overcome. For the Kennedy staffers, there was a palpable sense of relief over what had happened, mixed with a renewed sense of excitement over what was ahead.

The hotel room was crowded. Dan Marinelli and Kate Flanagan were there, along with Goodwin, Walinsky, Greenfield, Dutton, Sen. Hartke, Bill Barry, and Ethel Kennedy. Larry O'Brien, a veteran from the JFK days who had recently come over after resigning from the Johnson administration, much to Kennedy's great relief, was also there. Ted and Joan Kennedy were also present. There were cigars and flowing champagne. Joan Kennedy approached RFK and asked if he would consider appointing his brother as Attorney General when he was eventually elected President.

"No," Kennedy explained with a straight face. "We tried that once."

A few moments later Kennedy leaned toward Kate and said softly, "Thanks for everything you contributed. What you did was important, and I hope you feel a sense of satisfaction tonight."

"I certainly do," she assured, smiling broadly. "I think I'm going to like this job."

Ethel mentioned something about Freckles having soiled the carpet, and RFK immediately turned back to Kate, in whose care the dog had been entrusted earlier in the evening, saying loudly enough for all to hear, "Well, there goes your ambassadorship."

Everyone in the room burst into laughter.

The main party eventually broke up around midnight. Kennedy and his family and several aides headed back to the airport while many of the other staffers merely transferred their mobile partying to this room or that, without leaving the hotel. Dan Marinelli, shirt-sleeves rolled up and tie undone, somehow managed to "liberate" a full bottle of champagne as he and several others, including Kate, headed to his room to continue their revelry. He was humming *Mrs. Robinson*, sometimes singing aloud the lyrics and puffing away on his victory cigar as the elevator reached his sixth floor.

There was talk of what had gone right in the campaign, and about what had gone poorly. There was speculation on what McCarthy's and Humphrey's next moves might be. There was talk of the upcoming Nebraska primary, then Oregon, then the prize California.

"It's definitely taking shape," Marinelli declared to the half-dozen or so staffers in his room. "This is history, ladies and gentlemen. You're a part of history here tonight." Dan brought a fresh glass of champagne to Kate while several of the others gathered at a corner table for a game of poker. "For you, Miss Flanagan," he said, "and I take great delight in knowing that you were a big part of the history being made here this evening."

"I really shouldn't," Kate said as she accepted the glass, "but what the hell, as long as it's history."

Dan touched his glass to hers, then leaned and kissed her on the cheek.

"Careful," Kate said in mock admonishment. "What would Giselle say?"

"Who?" Dan asked.

Kate gave a sly smile. "You know, the one who kept after you in the nightclub. Remember? The Boogaloo blonde with the big boobs?"

"Oh, her," Dan said with a dismissive wave. "By the way her name's Lisa, in case you're interested in another alliteration."

Kate laughed. "Thanks, but I have absolutely no interest in alliterating Lisa, or anything else to Lisa, for that matter. I'll leave that to you."

"What about Lightfoot Lisa with the lovely . . . lovely . . . help me out here."

"Still not interested," Kate said with a frown.

Dan took a step closer. "Then tell me, just what is it that *does* interest you?"

Kate smiled. "Making history."

"Yeah? What else do you enjoy making?" he asked with a barely disguised grin.

"Making tracks," she answered, taking a step back, "if you don't slow down."

"Hell, I haven't even *done* anything," he claimed with an innocent shrug, adding, "yet."

The hour became late, and the combination of the smoky room, the champagne, and the lack of sleep soon got the better of Kate. She said her good-byes over Dan's repeated pleas to stay and party further, and retired to her room, only to be called out of a deep sleep at three o'clock by Dan telling her that she'd left her briefcase in his room.

"I'm leaving town in four hours and I don't want to leave it at the desk. Do you want me to bring it to your room?"

Kate turned on the lamp beside her bed and glanced at the clock. "Crap! Uh, yeah, please. Would you be kind enough to bring it up here?" she asked as she glanced around for her robe.

"I'll be right there," Dan said before hanging up.

Kate's head had already begun to ache, and she was still slightly groggy from the champagne. She slipped into her robe and then sat on the edge of the bed, running her hand through her red hair. She noticed that she was thirsty and hungry, remembering that she had twice declined an invitation to dinner, and she tried to recollect if she still had any aspirin left among her toiletries.

Dan was at the door in two minutes.

"Hello there," he said when Kate opened the door. With a cigarette dangling from his lips, Dan held a serving tray with a hamburger, soft drink, a glass of bubbly Alka Seltzer, and a glass of bubbly champagne all balanced precariously atop it. Her briefcase was on the floor, propped against his leg.

"Grab the briefcase," he said as he moved inside.

"Dan, what the hell are you doing?"

He placed the tray on a table and looked around for an ashtray. "You didn't get any dinner, right?"

"No, but it's after three o'clock in the morning, Marinelli. And I've already been sound asleep, besides."

"You've got a headache, right?" Dan asked.

"Well yeah, but—"

"Take the damn seltzer. Then eat the hamburger. Otherwise, you're gonna feel like you-know-what when you wake up again," he said as he picked up the champagne glass and drank. "C'mon, Flanagan, follow the doctor's orders."

Kate rubbed her eyes and adjusted the black satin robe. She took a seat at the foot of the bed after placing her briefcase on top of the dresser. Dan handed her the seltzer, which she looked at with revulsion before being chided into drinking it. She drank it but then made a child's face at the taste, prompting Dan to hand her the glass of pop. He then handed her the hamburger plate after she'd taken a few sips of the soft drink.

"I want you to know I had to do some pretty heavy bribing to get this stupid thing cooked," he said proudly. "Damn guy wanted another two bucks for a measly slice of cheese. A man has to draw the line somewhere, you know? Anyway, I called you from the kitchen as soon as I got all this stuff collected and placed on the tray."

"You're a calculating scoundrel, Dan Marinelli. You'll do anything and everything to get into my room, not to mention my . . ."

"Just a minute here, Miss Huffy Friggin' Puffy. You could've left your briefcase in any one of a number of rooms, but you chose mine instead. And you got room service, to boot."

Kate gave the burger a quick inspection before taking a bite. It was good and greasy and smelled divine, and she was really famished, so she took several juicy bites with the condiments dripping out the sides before finally handing it back to Dan. He wolfed down the remainder and chased it with the champagne.

"I'm gonna have to get me another bottle of this bubbly," he declared as he held the glass aloft and let the residue drip into his mouth.

"You're gonna feel good yourself when the booze goes away," Kate said.

Dan laughed. "I'll sleep on the plane to Lincoln. Couple of hours, and I'm a new man. In the meantime, I suppose you'd like me to get the hell out of your room and let you get back to sleep, huh?"

Kate smiled sleepily. "That'd be nice, yeah."

He got up from the chair and placed the plate and glasses back onto the tray. "We've had a great day, Kate. And a great night."

"We have, yes."

"And if there's any chance, any chance at all, that you'd like me to stay with you a while longer, then by God we could have ourselves a great morning, too," he said with a chuckle and a glance at his watch. "I have several hours, still."

"I don't think so. We'd both regret it as soon as it was over."

"Like hell we would," he protested.

"We would, for sure."

191

"So you're not tempted? Not even a teensy-weensy bit?" he asked, separating his fingers slightly.

"It's late, Dan. Please."

"I know what time it is. But I want you to tell me that you're not tempted. Look at me, Kate. Tell me to my face that you're not tempted."

She sighed and swallowed before confessing, "I'll admit I'm tempted, yeah. But I'm also more sober than you."

Dan chuckled. "Thanks a lot, Flanagan. It's really comforting to know you'd have to be sideways drunk before you'd consider going to bed with me."

"I didn't say that."

"You said you were tempted, but that you were more sober than me. The latter is statement of fact; and the former is highly flattering, I have to admit."

Kate stood. "Dan, please, it's quite late."

She said nothing when he took her hand and kissed it. He then kissed her face, her neck, then her warm, moist mouth. Kate made only the slightest effort to resist as he pulled her close and kissed her deeply.

"Dan, please," she said almost in a moan.

When he reached for her robe, untying it, she straightened her arms and allowed it to fall to the floor. She felt his warm hands underneath her silk nightgown. He pressed hard against her, and he filled his arms and his hands with as much of her as his reach would permit.

"This won't work," she said after a moment. "We both know it."

"I can't help myself," he said, still kissing her. "I've wanted you for as long as I've known you, and I want you tonight as much as I've ever wanted anyone in my life. God, why don't you leave that hack and come be with me?"

"It wouldn't work. We have to work together; we couldn't hide it for long. It just wouldn't work."

"Leave him, Kate. We can absolutely make it work."

"It wouldn't, we couldn't expect—" she said, pushing away slightly and pausing for a breath. She shook her head slowly, then looked away and said with little conviction, "It just wouldn't work."

"The hell it wouldn't," he said firmly. "We were made for each other, for cryin' out loud. You know that now, and I've known it since I first laid eyes on you. We were *made* for each other!"

He turned her head toward him and kissed her again. She felt him reach for her hips as he continued kissing her. Her tongue was deep inside his mouth, and her brain was as filled with Dan as were her hands. She had quickly warmed to him, her sounds and her moves reflecting her own desires. She moaned once, then again, as he touched her and was touched by her. When he raised the back of her gown and attempted to remove her panties, she gave a sudden gasp and pushed back quickly.

"For God's sake," she said breathlessly. "No, dammit. *No!* We can't *do* this!"

"Why not? We both want it. Why the hell not?"

"Because!"

She straightened things underneath her gown, took a deep breath, and raised her hand to ward off any further of Dan's advances. "I think it'd be best if you left now. Please."

"Are you sure?"

"I'm sure, yes," she said, turning away for a moment and taking a deep breath.

"I want to stay here, Kate. I want to be with you. And I'm not so drunk that I can't help noticing you want the same thing."

"Stop it, Dan. No more. Please."

He hesitated a moment, then nodded and gave a slight shrug. "All right, fine. If that's what you want, then I'll leave. But I want you to know that I meant what I said. And I meant it for all the right reasons. I want us to be together, and when you get ready, when you've gotten rid of that idiot Everett—however you do it and on whatever terms you choose—I want you to know I'll be here. I'll say it again, Kate: I want us to be together. But I'll wait. And I'll give you some room, if that's what you need. And I'll give you some time. Until then, I'll leave you alone and let you decide what kind of life you want for yourself."

Kate took another deep breath, and she noticed Dan doing the same. The tension between them began to ease. They each even managed a quiet laugh as the mood passed like a wisp of smoke in the wind.

"Keep in mind what I've said, Flanagan."

"I will."

Dan smiled warmly. "Sleep well, sweet Katherine," he said as he walked to the door and left.

CHAPTER FOURTEEN
Quang Nam Province, South Vietnam

Tom Flanagan looked out to the front of his sector, across rice paddies and intermittent stands of trees beyond which the village huts and the smoke from the cooking fires could barely be seen. His platoon was near an area the Americans referred to as Dodge City, 15 kilometers south of Da Nang and west of Hoi An. As he scanned the sector with binoculars, he could see nothing out of the ordinary. When he climbed out of the fighting hole he shared with Vasquez and inspected his platoon's positions with Sgt. Douglas, he was satisfied with his fields of fire and tie-in with adjacent units.

It had been a long, arduous but otherwise uneventful day. A helicopter re-supply before dark had included sodas and some of the famous doughnuts from Camp Books. There had also been mail, and Flanagan had received letters from Kate and his mother, along with a letter from Pamela. Pamela's two-page letter was perfumed—Shalimar, no less—and it included an especially attractive photo of her at the beach wearing a white bikini with red polka dots. Flanagan read his letters several times each, and then placed the photo of Pamela in the pocket of his utility shirt. He would resist the temptation to daydream about Pamela until he could later on settle down for the night.

A half-hour briefing on the next day's activities was conducted at the CP by Capt. Tanner, after which Flanagan briefed Sgt. Douglas inside the latter's camouflaged fighting position. It was dusk, and the two men enjoyed a warm can of soda in the still evening air.

"Did I ever show you a picture of my family, sir?" Sgt. Douglas asked.

"No. You've talked about them often, but I've never seen a picture. They're in Los Angeles, right?"

"Affirmative," Douglas said as he handed over photos of his mother and younger sisters. "And here's one of my father, who's deceased."

Flanagan smiled when he saw the picture of the mother and two daughters, dressed in their Sunday finest. Flanagan then looked at the photo of the father, glancing alternately at Douglas and the snapshot.

"Nice looking family. And yeah, you've definitely got a strong resemblance to your dad."

Douglas seemed to appreciate Flanagan's comment as he accepted the photos back.

"You and your father were close, right?" asked Flanagan.

"Very close. I still miss him."

"I'm sure he'd be proud of you."

Douglas shrugged. "He was a good man."

"The world could use a lot more like him," said Flanagan. "By the way, my sister Kate wrote that she's going to be in L.A. working on the California primary for Bobby Kennedy."

"Yeah?"

"Yeah. And didn't you mention that your mother's name is Ruby?" Flanagan asked.

"That's right," said Douglas. "And she lives near Watts."

"Right. I'll drop Kate a line and suggest she give your mother a call while she's out there."

"That'd be great, sir. I'll write my mom and tell her to be on the lookout for the call."

"Oh yeah, I almost forgot," Flanagan said as he dug into his shirt pocket and handed over the photo of Pamela. "This is the girl I met in Australia."

Douglas nodded his approval. "Wow, she's beautiful. How did you manage to come across her?"

Flanagan laughed. "In a department store, of all places. If I'd been looking in a bar, I never would've found her because she doesn't go to bars. We ended up being together most of the time I was there."

"You got lucky, Lieutenant," said Douglas.

"Yeah, well, it was long overdue," said Flanagan, sighing. "Did I tell you that I almost got engaged?"

"In Sydney?" Douglas asked.

196

"No," said Flanagan, laughing. "Back home. I was all set to propose to Jill Rohrbach, the love of my life, and then we had a fight over something silly and it all blew up in our faces. Now she's engaged to another guy."

Douglas frowned. "A fight over what?"

"One of Jill's best friends told her that she had seen me in a restaurant with another girl," Flanagan said, staring ahead blankly. "It wasn't me, and I really think Jill knew it. But then she told me that a former boyfriend from Wisconsin had called and wanted to come to Chicago to see her."

"Ooops. What happened then?"

"We had an argument. I told her she knew me well enough to know that I didn't cheat on her, never had and never would. I didn't know what motive her 'friend' had for telling her such a bullshit story, so I told Jill that her real problem was more with her friend than with me. And I told her that if her ex-boyfriend came to Chicago and started hanging around her, that either he or I or both of us would end up in the ER at Cook County Hospital. And if she was planning on giving her consent to the guy to come for a visit, then our relationship would be finished the moment she told him."

"Did he show up?"

"No. I knew Jill wouldn't agree to it."

"So in the end, you broke up over nothing?" asked an incredulous Douglas.

Flanagan nodded self-consciously. "Yep, it was over nothing."

"Do you still love her?"

"Yes, absolutely," Flanagan answered quickly.

"And do you think she still loves you?"

"I honestly believe that she does, I swear."

Douglas nodded thoughtfully. "And will you get home before her wedding?"

"Yes."

They both grinned.

"You're gonna give it another shot, aren't you?" Douglas asked, nodding. "By God, you're gonna try to get her back."

Flanagan also nodded. "What've I got to lose?"

There was then a silence among them for a moment, a somewhat clumsy interlude with Flanagan coughing and Douglas holding up and glancing at the writing on his soda can.

"Mind if I ask you something, sir? Kind of off the record?" Douglas quickly said as Flanagan got up to leave.

"No, not at all," Flanagan answered, sitting back down. "Fire away."

"I've wanted to ask you this for some time now, but I never got around to it with you being medevaced and all, then with you on R & R and so forth. But what I've really wanted to ask you is this: When we were at Hue City and the shit was the thickest, did you think you'd get out of there in one piece? Did you think you'd survive that fight?"

"No, I didn't," Flanagan answered without hesitation. "My God, I even wrote my sister to take care of my affairs when they shipped my dead ass back in a box. And I wasn't on the best of terms with her at that particular time, either. I didn't quite give up on the idea of coming out of there alive, but I thought for several days in a row that each day would most likely be my last. And I certainly didn't take life more than one hour at a time."

"Okay," Douglas said, nodding. "You *were* like all the rest of us, after all. You did a helluva job hiding it, I have to tell you, because it never showed on you like it did most other people."

"Did you feel the same way? Like you were walking-around dead?" asked Flanagan.

"Yessir. I *knew* I was dead. I just didn't know when or how."

"I didn't notice it on you," said Flanagan.

"You didn't, no kidding?"

"No," said Flanagan. "I actually thought you were about the calmest honcho in the whole platoon, including me."

Douglas' expression showed his surprise. "I wasn't petrified or anything like that, but I expected that any minute some little gook was gonna draw a bead on me and blow me full of holes.

And this may sound strange, but after a day or two of living like that, it was almost like all of a sudden I was at ease with it. Know what I mean, sir?"

"I do, yes. I drew a lot of strength from you, Sergeant Douglas, knowing I had to suck it up and keep doing my job and leading the Marines under my command, Marines like you. I had to keep going no matter what, that I couldn't let you and the others down, even if it meant my life."

"That's decent of you to say, sir," said Douglas.

"It's true."

"Well sir, now that we're doing show-and-tell," Douglas said with a slight chuckle, "mind if I tell you a little something about yourself?"

Flanagan hesitated for a moment before finally saying, "No, go ahead."

Douglas gathered his thoughts for a moment. Flanagan saw him shoot a quick glance in his direction to make certain that he was, indeed, on solid enough ground.

"When you went over the wall that day at the Citadel," said Douglas, choosing his words carefully, "I mean, when you got up and went after Dog when everybody else out there stayed put, well, things kind of changed."

"Changed? How so?" asked Flanagan.

"Well sir, you know how you were tight with Lieutenant Riordan before he got dinged?"

"Yeah, sure. He was a Basic School classmate. Why?"

"He was bad news, sir," said Douglas. "I mean, it was clear to most everyone in Fox Company that he was a prejudiced son of a bitch, simple as that. I saw it myself, and I heard from a few of his own people about some of the cheap shit he used to pull. There wasn't a black person born that he couldn't dislike, and when the word got out among his own people, there weren't many blacks who wanted to be around him, much less in his platoon. These Marines aren't stupid. Some may not be as educated as others, but they damn sure aren't stupid. Anyway, Lieutenant, you got a bad rap just by hanging around Lieutenant Riordan, because you two were seen as being tight and all. And if Lieutenant Riordan was as prejudiced as everybody seemed to think he was—and I damn sure thought he was—then the general feeling among a lot of dudes was that maybe Lieutenant Flanagan's the same way. It was bad news, sir. Number ten, for sure."

"You know better than that," said Flanagan.

"I knew better than that all along, sir. And so did Sergeant Jankowski and the other squad leaders. But lots of other dudes didn't, no matter what I'd tell 'em. That is, not until that day when you went over that wall, went out there alone against those gooks to get a black enlisted Marine who was down and probably already KIA, or very close to it. Anyway, Lieutenant Riordan wouldn't have done that for Dog. Hell, not many of *anybody* would've done that. And when your Marines in Third Platoon saw you do that—black *and* white—why, hell, they knew right then and there they were working for a man they could count on."

Flanagan said nothing.

"Like I said, sir, up until that time a lot of dudes who weren't sure of you could only judge you by the company you kept. They knew you were a damn good platoon leader, and that you seemed to be fair, but they never were sure until that day in Hue City with Dog. Then the word got out. When you were on R & R, Captain Tanner asked me one night what was it about you that caused your people to be so loyal to you. And I told it to him straight, that they saw in you a man they could trust to do the right thing, a man who wouldn't do anything stupid or careless with their lives. I told him that every swingin' dick in Third Platoon counted with you, no matter who he was or where he came from. And every man was expected to do his job like he'd been trained to do."

Flanagan was speechless, and could only nod his appreciation.

"That's what I told the Skipper when he asked, and that's what I meant. Every word of it," Douglas said with uncharacteristic emotion. "By the way, sir, did you ever hear the rumor going around about the deal when Lieutenant Riordan got killed?"

"No. What rumor?"

"He was hit and left out in the open for a good while, and there was a rumor going around that some black Marines were close and could've reached him, but they decided to hold back and let Charlie finish him off."

Flanagan seemed immediately taken aback. "Good God, no. I never heard any such rumor. Is there any truth to it?"

"No," Douglas said, resolutely shaking his head. "I talked to a bunch of dudes from his platoon, and it seems that this whole bullshit matter was started by a white dude who had some problems with a black squad leader right after the firefight. Truth is, there was nothing anybody could've done for Lieutenant Riordan once he got hit and cut off from the main body of his platoon, especially with the wound he had. And I heard the exact same description from several people in the know—squad leaders, platoon sergeant, corpsman, so forth—so I feel like it's good scoop. Not everybody liked the lieutenant, and some guys probably even hated his ass, but I don't think anybody wanted him to end up with his butt in a sling like that."

"What made you want to investigate this yourself?" asked Flanagan.

"I guess you could say I wanted to know if this man's Marine Corps—the Marine Corps that I may stick around in for a good long while—is really what I thought it was when I signed on and came aboard."

"And is it?"

"Yes it is, sir. It isn't perfect, not by a long shot, but it's what I thought it was, what it should be," said Douglas.

"And what would you have done if the rumor you heard had turned out to be true?"

"I thought long and hard about that, sir," Douglas said after a pause. "And I guess the most honest answer is, I don't *know* what I would've done." He then looked squarely into Flanagan's eyes and asked, "Given the exact same situation and if you'd been me, what would you have done, sir, if you'd found out it was true?"

"I'd be pissed, and in a big way."

Douglas shook his head in agreement. "Then based on what we've talked about, what would you have done if you'd been black, and Lieutenant Riordan was down, and you were the closest to him but to get to him you'd have to get out in the open and probably wouldn't take one step before you got zapped yourself?"

Flanagan considered the question for a moment. "I see your point. There's just not a simple answer, is there?"

"No sir, there's not," said Douglas, shaking his head.

"A man has to decide those things on his own, based on his own assessment of the situation, his own principles, and what he views as his duty as a Marine."

"That's right," agreed Douglas.

"But the last time something similar happened to me, I didn't exactly sit around and weigh everything. There was a man down—a green man, not a black one or a white one, or any other goddamn color. A green one, that's all. A green one who furthermore belonged to my platoon. And I could never in a million years explain all the reasons why I did it, but all of a sudden I just decided to climb over that wall and go get my Marine."

Douglas thought for a moment and then nodded. "Good shot, sir. Message acknowledged."

* * *

The point man stopped the column and called Flanagan ahead. 3rd Platoon was patrolling a quilted patch of rice paddies, interspersed with occasional islands of trees, near a village that had long been deemed unfriendly. The remainder of Fox Company was on a nearby sweep of an adjacent village.

"*This* I don't like," explained Monkee with a point at two dense stands of trees to the right-front and left-front of the platoon's avenue of approach. "We walk out there and they kick our ass from both flanks if they're in those friggin' trees."

Flanagan agreed as he stared out at the open rice paddy that would offer little protection if Monkee's instincts were correct.

The two Marines stood in a hedgerow only a few hundred yards from the paddy.

"The village we're supposed to check out is just beyond those trees to the right-front, about half a klick on the other side," Flanagan said as he unfolded his map. He dropped down to one knee and alternately studied the map and the open terrain to the front.

Sgt. Douglas came up and knelt beside Flanagan. "Can we offset?"

"Yeah, but not to where we could get out of range of anything that might be in those trees," answered Flanagan. "They could have ARs and rockets in the trees and mortars to the rear. We can screw with their angles a bit, but we can't slip 'em."

Douglas nodded. "They could aggravate the hell out of us if they're only in one position; they could pin us down if they're in both."

"Where the hell are the binoculars?" Flanagan called.

There was no response.

"Somebody get me the friggin' binos."

The word was shouted back, "Binos up."

Vasquez spoke up tentatively. "I think we may have left them at the other position, sir."

"We did *what*, Vasquez?" said Flanagan.

"I think we may have lost 'em, sir. I haven't seen the binos all day."

"We, Vasquez?"

"Me, sir. I think I may have lost track of 'em."

Flanagan's eyes narrowed. "Somebody'd better shit those glasses, wipe 'em off, and get 'em up here to me ASAP," he called loudly. "I'd better be hearing some little feet running 'em up here, Vasquez, or I'm gonna take the man who was responsible and throw his negligent ass in that famous creek we're all familiar with, and without any paddle."

A Marine suddenly came running from the back of the column and quickly handed the binoculars over to Flanagan. Vasquez, who had been assigned the responsibility for always knowing the whereabouts of the glasses, breathed an enormous sigh of relief after the wilting heat from Flanagan's stare had dissipated.

Flanagan took a look, then Douglas.

"You see anything?" asked Flanagan.

"No sir. Nothing," replied Douglas.

"Can he be in there and we not see him?"

Douglas grinned.

"Yep, you're right. Dumb question." Flanagan then tossed the glasses to Monkee. "Find me something in there, Lupo, in either one of 'em, and I'll blow it away before we ever step out of these trees."

Monkee shifted the glasses back and forth among the two positions, finally turning back to Flanagan. "I don't see jackshit in there, sir, but that don't mean Charlie ain't in there. Should we run some air in there on 'em, just in case?"

"Our mission is to show up at the village unannounced, cordon it off, get a search going and see what's what," replied Flanagan. "If we turn the air loose on these targets, then every VC within five friggin' grid squares knows where we are."

Monkee looked away, thankful those decisions were not his.

"Get the FO up here," Flanagan called in reference to the enlisted Forward Observer assigned to the platoon.

"Yessir?" the corporal said moments later.

"Plot both those tree lines as targets," Flanagan said with a point. "We'll move out toward the one to the right-front, and if we get any fire from either one, we'll drop down and let you call the guns in. The closest is a half-klick away, and the village is another half-klick behind it. If they're in those trees and they decide to hold their fire until we're right on 'em, then you're going to have to work with some tight tolerances, so plot those targets well."

"Sergeant Douglas?" said Flanagan.

"Yessir?"

"Get the squad leaders up here and we'll brief them on what we've got."

"Skipper's on the hook, sir. Wants to know why we're not in the ville yet," said Vasquez, extending the radio's handset to Flanagan.

Flanagan explained the situation to the impatient Capt. Tanner but was nevertheless told to step up the pace so as to keep the overall operation on schedule. Irritated, Flanagan signed off with a terse "Roger, out," and immediately set about briefing his squad leaders on the plan of advance.

One of the veteran squad leaders, a young corporal from Georgia named Hughes, tipped his helmet back and spit a mouthful of dark tobacco juice when Flanagan concluded his remarks. "If he's in there, sir, he might let us pass and then wedge us between the trees and the ville. If we don't stop and check out the trees, we could end up in a real hurt locker."

"We'll check out the one on the right, and we've got targets pre-plotted on the other position and the ville. Our problem is we've got to get to the ville in a hurry."

Flanagan could see that Hughes wasn't happy with the answer, but the corporal nodded his understanding anyway and added a crisp, "Yessir."

The platoon moved out of its tree-covered position as soon as the FO received word that the artillery battery was standing by with the target information on the guns. They moved forward in a V formation, with two squads up and one back. Almost immediately they were in the calf-deep water of the paddy, all amid the scorching sun and the noisy sloshing and sucking sounds made by their boots each time they raised their feet out of the muck. Flanagan was tense and alert, his heart pounding and his mind racing through a laundry list of potential scenarios. He moved his eyes back and forth to the two tree lines, and he, like every other Marine in the rice paddy, expected the enemy gunners to open fire at any moment.

They finally reached the first stand of trees. Flanagan sent a squad ahead to check out the position, but no enemy soldiers were discovered. The other position was off to the hard left, several hundred meters away, and the village was to the immediate front. Flanagan considered for a moment leaving a squad in the trees to cover his flank, but decided against splitting his force. They stayed in the trees only long enough to get a drink from their canteens before they pushed on toward the village. They soon saw villagers in and around the village entrance, and some locals were working in the rice fields. The peasants paid little attention to the Marines and instead went about their business as if nothing unusual was underway.

Flanagan kept glancing back at the position behind him, acutely aware that his back was exposed, but saw no movement in the trees. Once they neared the village, Flanagan called out to his squad leaders to initiate the search plan they had previously gone over in the briefing. One squad went to the far end of the village and took up blocking positions while the other two squads started a hut-by-hut search for weapons, suspects, documents, large quantities of foodstuffs, medical supplies, or anything else that might indicate an enemy presence. When Flanagan reported via radio to Capt. Tanner that his platoon had entered the village and was beginning its search, Tanner reported that weapons and ammo had been discovered at the group of villages being searched by the remainder of Fox Company.

"Keep your eyes open," Tanner warned.

It took almost two hours of careful searching before Flanagan was satisfied that the village of perhaps thirty huts was clean. No tunnels or dugouts were discovered; no caches of weapons or rice. The villagers seemed irate that their thatched huts were the object of the searches, and many protested in the sing-song cacophony of the language only the Vietnamese interpreter could fully understand. One squad found a young male who seemed nervous and suspicious, and Flanagan thought it best that the man be sent off for questioning as a VC suspect, especially when Flanagan noticed the man's grim expression and the way the suspect kept staring at him.

"You VC?" Flanagan asked as he walked over and stood close beside the smaller man, towering over him. "You a VC, honcho?"

The man appeared to be in his early twenties. He said nothing and only stared spitefully at Flanagan when questioned. After a few moments his expression turned into a sneer. The man was dressed in white shirt and black slacks, was razor thin, with soft hands and scratches on his feet and ankles. He glared at his captors as he puffed on a cigarette.

"Can I get you anything? Would you like a Coke and some Raisinettes to go with your smoke, honcho?" Flanagan asked sarcastically. "Look, either you and I can have a conversation in English right now, or I'll pack your young ass off to deal with someone else much less warm and caring than myself. What's it gonna be, hotshot?"

The man remained silent.

"Tie his hands and we'll send him out first chance we get. Tell him we're sending him to a rear area so he can answer some questions. Tell him I strongly suggest that he consider being truthful once he gets back there and starts being questioned."

The interpreter gave the explanation to the man, then began tying his hands with rope. A Marine stood nearby with his M-16 at the ready.

"Fuck you," the VC suspect said as he stared hard at Flanagan.

"Nice meeting you, too," Flanagan said as he reached over and in a rapid single motion snatched the cigarette from the man's mouth and crushed it out with his boot. "The smoking lamp is now out."

* * *

Flanagan and his Marines were back in the field after a couple of days of rest at Camp Lauer. There had been time for mail and hot chow, a swim in the ocean, and a USO show with an unknown female singer pouring out her heart and soul with such popular favorites as *Going Out of My Head*, *The Look of Love*, *Do You Know the Way to San Jose*, and *Can't Take My Eyes Off You*. What the troops had really wanted was some kick-ass rock 'n roll, but since this was the military, since this was Vietnam, since the show was essentially free and the beer cheap, they knew well enough to take anything they could get. And be thankful, at that.

Now it was back to the jungle, patrolling a series of hills and knobs to the west of Da Nang. The company was out in full, with Flanagan's 3rd Platoon in the lead, on the second day of a three-day operation. The weather was miserably hot, and the uniforms of the troops were soaked dark with perspiration in most places, salt-stained in others. The packs, helmets, and flak jackets were heavy and cumbersome, and each man carried as much ammo and as many canteens as he could reasonably manage. The air underneath the triple-canopy jungle was steamy and thick, filled with the putrid odor of decaying foliage and sweaty, apprehensive men.

The heat became debilitating, and Capt. Tanner called the platoon leaders and ordered another rest break. A man from 2nd Platoon had fainted from heat exhaustion, the third heat casualty of the day thus far. When Flanagan went up and down the line observing his troops, he saw that some had sat down and leaned back against their packs, braced against trees, and quickly fallen into deep, fatigue-induced sleep. Others merely sat upright with blank expressions on their flushed faces.

"What I'd give for a cold beer," Flanagan mumbled to Vasquez as he plopped down and pulled out his map for a quick reference check of the location.

Vasquez, who had sat back and fallen asleep, open-mouthed and with his eyes partially open, was oblivious to Flanagan's several questions about the latest radio traffic. When Flanagan glanced over and noticed the young radioman's condition, he said nothing further.

Fox Company moved out after a rest of twenty minutes with Flanagan's platoon in the rear of the formation. Within a half hour after resuming, there was gunfire at the head of the column. The muffled sounds of the firing put everyone on alert, and Flanagan waited in a crouched position in nervous anticipation for the setting to unfold at the front. The point element had a short exchange of gunfire with two NVA soldiers who had been left behind at what turned out to be a fortified bunker complex. The two enemy soldiers were quickly overcome, and by the time Flanagan's men made their way up the column and set up a hasty perimeter around the position, the two dead enemy had been dragged out and left on the ground in front of the first bunker. Both had been shot multiple times, and both were bloody messes of exposed brains and moist, slick intestines. The Marines suffered no casualties.

"What do you make of this?" Flanagan asked Sgt. Douglas. "What the hell's Charlie up to?"

"I don't know, sir. All I know is I can feel 'em. There's a shitload of NVA in this jungle."

Flanagan made sure his men were in place to protect the search of the positions before he found Capt. Tanner standing atop one of the bunkers in the complex.

"We've had an NVA battalion in here recently," Tanner commented calmly as he searched through a batch of captured documents. "This place was full of bad guys."

"Where the hell did they go, Skipper?"

Tanner shrugged nonchalantly. "Beats me, but I'm sure as hell glad I didn't have to throw this rifle company against those godawful bunkers."

There were medical supplies, an aid station, caches of rice, ammo in the form of rockets and mortar rounds, and reinforcing bunkers and trenches that sliced into the freshly-dug earth at jagged, oblique angles. Flanagan dropped down and inspected several bunkers himself, and noted the clear lanes of fire the enemy would have employed against any attacker. The position was situated on a rise such that the NVA would have commanded the high ground, while the attacking Marines would have been exposed to supporting, overlapping fire with precious little cover or concealment. It would have taken a determined attacker to have succeeded against such a fortified position, and only then with overwhelming supporting arms from artillery and air.

"Mother Mary!" Flanagan gasped when he once again visualized a frontal assault against a dug-in enemy.

They gathered all the weapons and gear over the course of the next two hours, set C-4 explosive charges to it, and blew it up. The documents were kept by Capt. Tanner, who tersely noted to his platoon leaders, "There's at least one battalion of bad guys out here someplace, gentlemen," before they once again took up their patrolling of the hills.

They found a suitable piece of high ground before first dark and dug themselves into its crest and slopes. A quick meal of C-rations preceded Flanagan taking out a platoon-sized patrol through some rolling terrain to the northwest of the position. The air was still warm, and the darkness in the foreboding jungle was nearly total. The Marine near the point kept the platoon on course with a lensatic compass while another Marine up ahead responded to the direction and cleared the way with a machete. There was always concern in the jungle—concern over the presence of the enemy and the chance of an encounter—but there was now the concern over the near total darkness, and the chance of losing Marines from the column because they couldn't see or feel the man two feet in front of them.

The men were tired and the pace was slow. The noise and commotion from the hacking through the thick jungle, the stumbling and occasional falling from the tangled vines that seemed to reach out and grab their feet and ankles, and the inevitable stream of foul cursing that usually followed such a tumble could be heard at various points along the column. Flanagan knew their noise discipline was atrocious, and he was about to stop the column altogether and pass along a terse message of rebuke when he himself tumbled and fell over in the dark, dropping his rifle and losing his helmet before a helping hand grabbed him by the arm and steadied him.

"God*dam*mit!"

It was completely dark, and his feet were still tangled. He tried to quickly raise himself, only to fall over again onto his side.

"Here's your helmet, sir. You okay?"

"I'm fine," he finally answered, fearful at first that his shoulder might be dislocated and becoming convinced otherwise only when he could successfully rotate his arm without extravagant pain.

They struggled through the remainder of the patrol and finally covered their preplanned route. They were able to get back into the Fox Company position and catch a quick four hours of sleep before rising once more to start another hot day in the jungle.

* * *

Tom Flanagan's 3rd Platoon was atop a hill in northwest Quang Nam province, serving as security for a 155mm howitzer battery that was supporting an operation being conducted by other units from the 5th Marines. The men had spent the day digging fighting holes, filling sandbags, stringing razor-sharp concertina wire, and setting out claymores. It had been tough, hard work in tough, hard heat, but now they were enjoying the cool sodas and hot chow their artillery brothers had arranged for them to share.

Flanagan had been sitting atop his fighting hole and throwing pebbles into an empty C-ration can ten feet away, remembering his high-school days when he would shoot free throws at the backyard basketball goal to determine if a certain young lady would bestow her reputed passionate talents on him.

Make four or five out of five—She will.

Miss two or more—She won't.

(As best he could recollect, he must have missed two or more.)

Four or more rocks in the can—I go home unhurt.

Miss two or more—I don't.

Miss, miss.

"Well *shit*."

Miss, miss, miss.

"*Shit!*"

He was gathering another handful of pebbles for another round—this time it counts!—when Sgt. Douglas showed up with C-ration meals and took a seat on the ground alongside his platoon leader.

"This is the life for me," Sgt. Douglas said as he and Flanagan propped themselves against sandbags and enjoyed their dinners of beans and franks. "What about you, sir? Are you going to stay with Mother Green the Killin' Machine?"

Flanagan grinned. "Three years, that's my deal. Three years and I'm out the front gate."

"Ah, c'mon, sir," Douglas said, shaking his head in disagreement. "I've got to get you to stay, Lieutenant. You can't leave. This is the job for you, as good as you are. You've got to ship over and stay in the Corps forever."

"No way. Save your breath."

"Think of it this way, sir: Good, satisfying work; great food; exotic travel; free medical care; cheap booze; all the ammo you can shoot; interesting people. You've got to stay, sir. You could never get this kind of deal on the outside."

"Yeah, right. Every day's a holiday and every meal's a feast," Flanagan said with a chuckle.

"There it is."

"Leave me alone," said Flanagan.

"But you've got to stay, sir," Douglas said, becoming more animated. "The Corps needs you. Why, just think what—"

"I said leave me alone."

"Think what kind of future—"

The artillery battery suddenly fired the first two rounds of a fire mission and shook the unsuspecting Flanagan, who proceeded to drop in the dirt the spoonful of beans he was in the process of raising to his mouth.

"Dammit."

"Think of your future, sir," Douglas continued. "Why, when you get to be the Commandant of the Marine Corps, you'd be—"

"Get off my ass about becoming a lifer. There's no way I'm going to stay on past my first hitch. No can do," Flanagan said in a playful tone.

"But sir, you'd do well and fit right in with—"

Two additional rounds were then fired.

"Dammit, will you stow it. You sound like a recruiter, for crissakes," said Flanagan.

Douglas smiled broadly. "That's what I'm requesting for my next duty station. I want to go back to California and be a recruiter."

"Oh? What happened to Officers Candidate School?"

"The Marine Corps may not be able to decide on my application before my tour is up over here. Might not be enough time, I was told. So they may need to put me in a job back in The World until the OCS thing is decided. If I get accepted, I'll get orders for Quantico. If not, then I'll go on being a recruiter."

"Well, stop practicing on me," said Flanagan.

Two more rounds were fired. Flanagan and Douglas stopped and looked up to watch the flight of the two 100-pound projectiles. They heard the characteristic hissing as the shells ripped the air, until the two dark specs quickly disappeared underneath the low-hanging clouds. Far off in the distance, out of view, the two rounds impacted and exploded with dull thuds.

"Wouldn't care to be on the business end of that," Douglas remarked casually as he sipped his soda. "It could definitely screw up your health record."

"Best not tell that to the people you recruit," Flanagan said, grinning.

"What's that, sir?"

"That they might get shot at, maybe even hit."

Douglas laughed. "You sound like a civilian already. I think your pretty young Aussie went and screwed up your killer instinct, Lieutenant."

"Let me assure you," Flanagan said, barely able to stifle a grin, "that my pretty young Aussie did *nothing* to screw me up, and in fact made me a better man in *every* way."

"Right on, sir."

Over the next several days, the duty at the fire base was slow and easy. Flanagan sent out patrols of squad size, but no enemy soldiers were encountered except for a couple of stragglers who were quickly dispensed. The artillery battery fired hundreds of rounds in support of the operations in the adjacent hills and valleys, and several Marine ground units racked up impressive body counts. Marine air was also active in the daylight hours, and F-4 Phantoms and A-6 Intruders, along with Huey Cobras and OV-10 Bronco spotter planes, were frequent visitors overhead as steady doses of rockets and napalm were showered on enemy concentrations.

On the last day of 3rd Platoon's fire-base security mission, deep into the night, the VC sent a team of more than twenty sappers with bangalore torpedoes against the wire of the fire base. They succeeded in blowing a couple of large holes in the concertina, but when the enemy troops rushed forward they were quickly met by Lt. Flanagan's Marines who cut them down with only a handful of VC successfully breaching the perimeter. There was some brief hand-to-hand fighting before the VC inside the wire were quickly destroyed. The Marine infantry troops then got out of the way as the artillery battery fired several point-blank rounds of beehive fleshettes into the VC still in the wire, and the fight was over within thirty minutes.

It wasn't until things had calmed down, however, that Flanagan received word from Doc Fackler that Lance Corporal Lupo, his fellow Chicagoan and the one the troops referred to as Monkee, had been hit in the head with small-arms fire and killed. A medevac chopper came into the position just after first light and evacuated three wounded but ambulatory Marines—two grunts and an artilleryman—along with the limp body of the nineteen-year-old Lupo.

The helmetless Flanagan stood alone on the hillside and watched as the chopper disappeared beyond the green of the distant peaks.

CHAPTER FIFTEEN
Washington, D.C.

I t was raining in Washington when the Braniff Airlines flight from Portland, Oregon touched down on the runway at Washington's National Airport. Kate Flanagan glanced out the window and saw the gray skies and the shiny wet pavement as the jet taxied toward the terminal.

Things were not at all well with Kate. Her personal life was a shambles, and her professional life had taken a sudden and unexpected turn for the worse. On the previous day, May 28th, Sen. Robert F. Kennedy had lost the Oregon primary, marking the first time a Kennedy had ever tasted the bitterness of defeat in 26 consecutive elections. The big showdown in California on June 5th was next on the agenda, but the galling loss in Oregon would linger on for several days.

Kate sat back in her seat and allowed her mind to replay the entire primary effort in Oregon for what was probably the twentieth time since the plane had left Portland. There had been poor scheduling, poor advance work, poor crowds, and consequently poor results. An Oregon congresswoman's sponsoring organization had simply not been up to the task, and in the end Kennedy's own staff had been spread too thin to maintain its edge with six primaries in four weeks. McCarthy's candidacy was supposed to have folded by now, but not only was he still standing, he was actually emerging with unexpected momentum going into California. Oregonians had obviously preferred his quiet, cerebral approach, in large part due to McCarthy's having been in Oregon with his anti-war message early on, earlier than Kennedy. Besides, Oregon's two U.S. Senators, Democrat Wayne Morse and Republican Mark Hatfield, were themselves already anti-Vietnam, giving Kennedy almost no political advantage with his own anti-war stance. McCarthy had attacked Kennedy's record, Kennedy's wealth, Kennedy's ambition, and Kennedy's tactics, all with a biting sarcasm and condescension that had crept into his tone far more often than before. In the end, his remarks had resonated loudly with the electorate.

Kate sighed and shook her head. She could see now in hindsight that the right mix of circumstance and candidate just hadn't been there for Kennedy. There were few ghettoes. The population was only 1% black and 10% Catholic. There was suspicion and in some cases outright animosity directed toward him. And Kennedy had publicly ignored McCarthy's repeated requests for a televised debate, even though several of Kennedy's own staffers, most notably Walinsky, Greenfield, and Kate herself, had urged him otherwise, eventually irritating him with their dogged insistence.

"I lost; I'm not one of those who thinks coming in second or third is winning," Kennedy had said the previous evening from his suite in Portland's Benson Hotel. It had been an odd, awkward time among the inner circle, and Kate had said as little as possible. At one point, Kennedy had put an arm around each of two student organizers and said, "I'm sorry I let you down," when the two youths grievously thought it had been their own efforts that were to blame. A generous congratulatory message had been sent to McCarthy despite the fact that McCarthy had never done the same for Kennedy in the previous Indiana and Nebraska primaries.

In the Republican primary, Richard Nixon had won big over Ronald Reagan and Nelson Rockefeller. It now looked more and more like Nixon was a lock. The stakes were being raised, Kate knew, and the upcoming California primary would go a long way toward determining who would face Nixon from the Democrat side.

Oregon's over and done with, Kate thought as she glanced out the window at the main terminal building. Now it's California and a new chance. We can win, still. We *will* still win.

But first, Everett.

Kate's relationship with Everett had been in freefall for several weeks, and just prior to Kate's most recent departure for Oregon they had both come to agree that a candid, open discussion of their needs and plans was essential. Then they had proceeded to argue, subsequently losing their tempers, and as a result nothing had been resolved. They had spoken by phone only sporadically in the most recent two weeks, but they had agreed that when Kate returned from California in early June, they would sit down and have the discussion they both knew was overdue.

So overdue, as a matter of fact, that Kate had decided on her own to divert from L.A. to come to Washington and get everything out in the open, and hopefully resolved, so she could at least have some peace of mind as she went about her frenetic work in the equally frenetic campaign.

Dammit, she thought, her jaw tightening. I can't go on living like this. I *won't* go on living like this. She had become tense and irritable, and as of late she'd experienced difficulty in concentrating on her work. And she refused to accept this as the status quo. She loved Everett and knew he loved her in return, but something was obviously out of kilter. He nagged and chided her relentlessly about her being away so often, about her need for independence and her search for professional satisfaction, and she resented it. She'd been tempted by Dan Marinelli's overtures, and furthermore had even fantasized making love to Dan the last time she and Everett had been intimate. And, she knew deep within the most safeguarded region of her subconscious, she had liked it all the better as a result.

Something had to give. If they couldn't successfully get things out into the open, if they couldn't deal with their problems and concerns as an engaged couple, then, painful though it may be, their marriage plans would have to be carefully and honestly reviewed.

Kate took a deep breath as the plane came to a stop. The passengers immediately began scurrying out of their seats, but Kate sat quietly for a moment and collected her thoughts. Things were changing at a faster pace than she was comfortable with, and she wanted to be sure the decisions that she and Everett would soon be making about their futures would be made without undue enmity or emotion. She got up and stepped off the plane only when she had determined to herself that she was indeed doing the right thing in coming back home to clear the air with her fiancé, and that she would give this important chance at reconciliation the very best she had within her. By the time Kate had claimed her two suitcases and made her way to a taxi stand, it was pouring rain.

The cab driver dropped Kate off at the Georgetown apartment in the silvery late-afternoon rain. She had packed her small umbrella in one of her suitcases, so she was wet by the time she climbed the steps, unlocked the door, and dragged her heavy bags inside. The lights were off inside the apartment, but as soon as she was fully indoors she immediately smelled smoke in the still, heavy air. She walked down the hall and heard over the noise of the rainfall what she thought to be a human voice. When she turned into the master bedroom, she was stunned to see Everett in bed having sex with a naked young woman who, because of her position atop Everett, Kate could see only from behind. Kate couldn't avoid noticing her long brown hair, her back and buttocks, and the soles of her dirty bare feet. The odor of marijuana still lingered in the air, and the pair was in full copulation on the creaky bedsprings. The young woman, head tilted back and a thin layer of perspiration glowing on her back, was bouncing up and down on Everett's lower torso.

Kate took a deep breath to calm herself, whereupon she stepped into the bedroom and loudly cleared her throat.

The creaking bed fell immediately silent. Everett, his eyes bulging as if suddenly inflated, gasped and nearly sucked enough air into his lungs to make the window curtains blow in the breeze.

"Jesus Christ Almighty, Kate! What are you doing here?" Everett practically shouted as he shoved the young woman aside and then clumsily tried to pull some cover over himself. "I thought you were flying to Los Angeles. What's happened? What the hell's going on? My God, Kate. What have you done?"

The young woman sat upright beside Everett and calmly ran her fingers through her hair, then touched an outstretched finger along the thin line of perspiration above her lip. A slight, almost taunting smile appeared on her face and she made no effort to cover herself. She alternately glanced at Everett and Kate in a curious, almost detached amusement.

"Sorry to interrupt," Kate said with an icy chill in her voice. She then turned and stared hard at the other woman, taking one step closer and bending over slightly as if to get a better look. "Hello, I'm Kate. That's my bed you're in and my fiancé whose brains you're screwing out. And just who in the holy hell might you be?"

"Kate," Everett said, a pleading look in his eyes, "will you give me a chance to explain? For crissakes, please, let's talk this out." Everett nudged the woman and motioned with his head for her to reclaim the dress that lay in a pile on the floor between Kate and the bed.

"I'm Cynthia," she said as she climbed out of bed and picked up her dress, barely five feet from Kate. She was tall and thin, and in one motion she slipped the long flowered dress over her head and shook it into place. She then flipped her long hair, smiled, flashed a peace sign, and walked past Kate on her way out of the room. "See ya' around, Everett," she called as she turned back and took a last look from the doorway. "Nice meeting you, Kate."

Kate's face reddened, her eyes wide and ferocious, and she stared hard at Everett until she heard the door close in the front. She then turned and stormed out of the room.

Everett quickly got up and very nearly leapt into his undershorts. "Kate, wait. Kate. Please!"

When he caught up to her Kate once again had her luggage in hand and was about to open the front door. Everett ran to her, placed one hand upon her shoulder and the other on the door knob in an attempt to keep the door closed.

"Take your filthy hand off me," she snapped as she turned and gave him a disgusted look as he stood beside her in his shorts.

"Please, Kate. Please sit down, and let's talk this out. Don't leave, darling. My God, I've made a terrible mistake, but for the sake of our marriage and all that we've got at stake here, please don't walk out that door until you've heard me out. Give me a chance, Kate. That's all I ask. You can do that, can't you? With all we've been through, everything that we've shared and planned, you've just got to listen to me. You've *got* to."

She still stared, but otherwise said nothing.

"Please, I'm begging you, Kate. Sit down and talk to me before you go walking out that door."

Kate drew a deep breath and, after a long pause in an obvious attempt at reigning in her emotions, turned and walked slowly to a nearby chair and took a seat. "Get some clothes on," she ordered coldly.

"Yeah, right. Great," Everett said, breathless and wide-eyed as if his own execution had just been stayed. "Stay right there. I'll be right back."

He took off in a sprint toward the bedroom. When he returned a few moments later, he was dressed in jeans and polo shirt. He went immediately to the kitchen and got a glass of water which he brought over and placed on the table beside Kate's chair. He took a seat on the adjacent sofa, smiled, and, with an inviting look on his face, patted the seat next to him.

"You've *got* to be kidding," Kate said firmly. "If you have something to say to me, then I suggest you get on with it."

He paused a moment, then sighed remorsefully. "There's an explanation here, but I'm afraid it's a rather long story."

Kate gave a cynical chuckle. "Spare me the details. I saw enough to get the gist."

He sighed again. "All right, then. I'll only ask that you forgive me and give me another chance to be the man I've been in the past, the man you fell in love with and agreed to marry. I know I'm asking a lot, I know I've betrayed your trust in me, and I know I've yielded to a moment of weakness. But I want us to be married, Kate, because I love and cherish you, right this minute, like I've never loved you before. That you've agreed to sit down with me here and now and talk this thing out, after what I've done, well, it makes me love you all the more."

Everett paused and put his hands to his face, lowering his head in humiliation, before looking back up at Kate with moist, sad eyes. "This is the worst, most crushing thing I've ever experienced in my entire life, darling. You can't possibly know how devastated I am at this very moment. And most of it involves my knowing how devastated you are over my behavior. It's killing me inside, *killing* me, and if I could erase it forever there's simply *nothing* I wouldn't do or give to be able to do just that. I need you, Kate, and I want to live the rest of my life with you. But I realize that I've hurt you, and I know it'll take some time for you to heal. I only ask that you give it time, give us a chance to go on with all the plans we've made for our marriage, for our being together for better or worse. Please, Kate, can't you see how utterly hopeless I feel? Can't you tell that this whole thing has broken my heart and shattered my spirit? Let's look at this as a test. Let's use this as a way to deal with our problems. Let's start with the basics, like love and faith and hope and Christian forgiveness. Please, Kate. Please give me some assurance that you're still in this with me."

Kate reached for the glass of water. She fought hard to remain calm but her hand trembled as she sipped once, then again. She then sat back in the chair and crossed her legs, her arms folded across her chest. There followed a period of silence— thick, weighty, lugubrious silence—during which Kate kept her unblinking eyes steadily upon him.

Everett swallowed hard and dabbed at his eyes with his hand. "This isn't easy, darling. Will you at least say something?"

"I feel betrayed," Kate finally said with visible emotion. "I feel humiliated and betrayed. Thoroughly, utterly, completely humiliated and betrayed."

Everett sighed and shook his head. "I understand that, and I feel so very badly for it."

"I feel like something's been cut out of me—against my will, mind you—and that I now no longer have everything I had when I walked into this house a few minutes ago. I've never experienced anything like this before, and I suppose it's numbed me. The shock and the hurt and the humiliation have numbed me. It seems surreal, almost as if I'm dreaming all of this."

Everett started to get up and go to Kate until she said sharply, "Keep your seat."

"I just want to be near you. I want us to comfort each other. Will you let me do that? Will you let me hold you and be close to you?"

"Keep your seat," she said again, firmly, and the matter was dropped.

He sat back and took another deep breath. "I understand that you're hurt. But please, let's try to get through this as best we can."

"What the hell does *that* mean? Are you telling me it'd be better if the circumstances weren't so uncomfortable?" Kate asked.

"Yes, I am."

"Then what do you suggest? Should we just fake the circumstances and pretend they don't exist? Do we just laugh it off and go get a cheeseburger and forget the whole thing?"

"No, that's not what I'm suggesting," said Everett. "I realize what's done is done. I only want to start to put this behind us. Will you meet me halfway on that?"

Kate shrugged. "I'm not sure what you mean by that, either. Do you want me to erase the image in my head of you and this, this Cynthia, soiling the sheets of what used to be our bed and—"

"Don't use the past tense, Kate, please."

"Don't you *dare* interrupt me," Kate flashed, standing up stiffly with eyes afire and fists clenched. "I'll use whatever goddamn tense I goddamn well please, and you will *not* interrupt me again."

Everett used a pleading motion for Kate to take her seat, which she eventually did. "I'm sorry, darling. I won't interrupt you again."

Kate suddenly appeared drained, and she took another sip from the water glass. "I really think the thing for us to discuss is how we go about going our different ways."

Everett winced and became tearful again. "Oh dear God no, Kate. Please, let's not do that."

"I won't deal with this beyond today. I'm going back to the airport and flying to California, and I'd like you to ship my things to Chicago, to my parents' address. I'll have someone come for my car, but if you'll ship my other things to Chicago, I'll get them there," she said, taking another sip and fighting to hold her emotions in check. "That's what I'll need you to do. Just ship my things to Chicago. I'll take one or two things with me before I leave, but the rest you can arrange for."

He leaned back and wept, his shoulders heaving. "My God, Kate, please don't do this to me."

"I'm not doing *anything* to you. You've brought this whole miserable thing upon yourself, and you've left me no other choice."

"You do have a choice, darling," Everett pleaded.

"You're exactly right. And I'm making my choice."

"Please, Kate."

Kate closed her eyes a moment and took a deep breath. "I was just thinking about what the hell *else* could go wrong," she said, following with a slight chuckle, "and then I remembered my brother being in Vietnam and . . . "

She leaned over and started crying.

"Kate, we can get through this," Everett said, leaning forward on the sofa. "We can make a new start, I swear."

Kate raised her hand to her mouth. She looked around for a tissue, and Everett almost tripped as he got up from his seat and sprinted off after one.

"Kate, darling, can't we start over again? Won't you give me just one more chance?" he called as he returned with a box of tissues.

She finally raised her head and dabbed her eyes. "No," she said resolutely, sniffing. "We cannot start over again, Everett. I'm sorry, I really am. I wish there was a way out of this for us, but the plain and simple truth is, there isn't. It could never be the same, never. And deep down inside, we both know it. I'm afraid that we've just got to face up to the truth here, and that truth is, it's over for us."

"Oh Kate, no," he said, weeping.

"Shut up, Everett. You're making me physically sick. I don't want any more of your tears or your sniveling or your miserable pleading. My stomach can't take any more of it, I swear. So stop it, please. Now!"

"Kate, please," he said, his voice full of torment. "Please. I'll do anything, anything at all. Isn't there *some*thing I can do?"

Kate sat up straight and took in a deep breath, her self-control again in evidence. She swallowed and then cleared her throat. "There is one thing, yes."

Everett quickly rose. "You name it. Anything at all."

Kate slipped the diamond engagement ring off her finger and gently placed it on the coffee table. She glanced at her bare finger, at the whiteness and the indentation where the ring had been, and then proceeded to touch the spot almost as if to confirm what her eyes were seeing. She clasped and unclasped her hands, took another look at where the ring had been, and finally pursed her lips tightly together and gave a slight nod. She then looked directly into Everett eyes and, with an expression of unequivocal resolve on her face, said in a calm, soft voice, "You can call me a taxi."

* * *

There was a knock on the door. It was nearly eight o'clock in the evening, and Dan Marinelli was only barely awake, straddling the twilight zone from atop the sofa in his Arlington apartment. When he got up and went to the door and found an exhausted, rumpled Kate Flanagan standing between her two Samsonite suitcases, he gasped.

"My God, have I died and gone to heaven?"

"If you have, I suppose it'd be consoling to know that at least one of us had a successful day," Kate cracked. "Mine has been an absolute disaster. Do you have a spare bed and a washer and dryer, Marinelli?"

Dan quickly walked out and grabbed her bags.

"Or," Kate said, pointing inside, "would I be barging in on the company who's already here?"

"Oh heavens no," Dan said. "Think nothing of it. She's from a large family in Thailand and she'll be perfectly happy to share our bed with you."

"What?"

"I'm kidding, Kate. There's no one here," said Dan, laughing.

Kate waved away the waiting taxi. They came inside and stood clumsily in the foyer for a moment before Dan pointed to a chair. Kate took a seat and glanced around at the sparseness of the apartment's interior. She ran her fingers through her damp red hair and looked at her wrinkled pants.

"So, what's going on with you?" Dan asked with nonchalance.

Kate noticed his probing eyes. "God, it's an awful story."

"I thought you were going to L.A. today?"

"I changed my mind. I had some things to work out with my fiancé."

Dan leaned back. "Oh? And did those things get worked out?"

Kate immediately began sobbing.

"Jeez Kate, I didn't mean—what the hell did I say to cause—here, take this," Dan said, offering a handkerchief. "Good grief, I didn't, I mean I wouldn't—hell, I was just making conversation."

She bent slightly over at the waist with her hand over her face. Her shoulders shook as she finally crumbled under the crushing weight of her emotions. Dan watched in silence for a moment, then got up and started to move to her, but she quickly raised her head and then her hand as if to signal that she'd be okay in a moment.

"I'm sorry, Dan. My whole life's in the toilet. My love life's disintegrated, I couldn't get a flight out, my hair's a mess, my clothes are wrinkled, my—"

"It's okay, Kate."

"My day's been a disaster, and I didn't know what—"

"Kate, dammit, take a deep breath and calm down. It's okay. Everything's okay. You're okay. Okay?"

She took the deep breath and then promptly resumed her sobbing.

"Dear God, Flanagan, do I need to rush you to the Emergency Room?" Dan asked as he got up and ran to the kitchen and brought back a glass of water.

Kate looked at Dan's expression and then the water being held out to her, and suddenly began laughing hysterically through her tears.

"For cryin' out loud, what'd I do *now*?" Dan asked.

Kate finally gathered herself and related the story of her humiliation and breakup with Everett. She was forthcoming and honest in how she described what she had seen and how she had felt. She told how she had then waited on stand-by at Washington National through two flights to Los Angeles with no luck and, finding out that Dan was scheduled to fly to L.A. on the following day, went ahead and booked a seat on the same flight. She told of how she had considered taking a room at an airport hotel, about how she alternately wanted to be left alone but a moment later would desperately need to unburden herself to someone. She talked about how she had considered getting on a flight to Chicago and saying to hell with the life she had so enjoyed in Washington, how she had actually gotten to the point of removing the credit card from her purse to purchase the airline ticket before finally reconsidering. And how she had finally decided to show up unannounced at Dan's door and take a chance that he would be home alone.

Kate appreciated Dan's commiseration, the look of disbelief and disgust on his face, and she especially appreciated his overcoming whatever temptation he may have had to lecture her about Everett. Through it all, Dan simply remained quiet and listened.

And listened.

Kate talked nonstop for nearly an hour, as if the flood of words had been dammed up inside her and then suddenly released. By the time she finished and appeared on the verge of collapsing with fatigue, Dan heated a frozen pizza and opened a couple of beers. She was haggard, and after eating a slice of pizza she took Dan's advice and enjoyed a long, soothing shower. She seemed more refreshed afterwards when she slipped into jeans and t-shirt and joined Dan in the living room for a glass of white wine.

"You look great, Flanagan. You're gonna be just fine."

She smiled softly. "I need to wash my clothes."

"You need to rest. You can wash your clothes when you get to California. What about your stuff at his place? Do you want me to go over there and get it?"

She glanced down dejectedly. "No. He's shipping my things to Chicago."

"What? Why Chicago?"

"I was thinking I'd go home for a while. I figure I'll bring what I need back with me. I mean, good grief, I wasn't thinking too clearly at the time."

"Kate, Chicago?"

"I didn't know what else to do. I just wanted my stuff gone from there as soon as possible."

"We'll bring your things here," Dan said.

"Dan, no. I can't do that."

"Just temporarily. I'll call him in the morning and tell him someone from the Senator's staff will contact him and set up a time to come and get your things. What about your car?"

"I told him I'd have someone come and get it."

"Good. Everything'll work out. I'll send someone from the staff, and we can get the car and your stuff over here where it'll be safe. Then you'll be able to take your time and find yourself another place. I'll take care of everything, don't worry."

The radio from Dan's stereo unit was turned low to *Honey.* They were quiet for a moment as the music played on.

Kate smiled, but not before her eyes teared again. "I really appreciate this," she said in a barely audible tone.

"You turned to me when you needed a little help. That's thanks enough for me," he replied.

She took a deep breath and grinned, her eyes still moist. "I hope things are better tomorrow."

"Ah, they will be, no doubt about it. Tomorrow we start work on the Big Comeback, in sunny California, no less. Things will be much better, you'll see."

Kate gave a dazed nod but said nothing.

"I'm really sorry," Dan said softly. "You've had an all-time lousy day, and I hate it for you."

"If lousy days could be rated with medals," Kate said, her shoulders sagging, "this one would definitely take gold. I just appreciate your being here, I really do. Not to mention letting me barge in on you like this and sleep on your sofa."

Dan shook his head in disagreement. "Of all the people in this world who could show up on my doorstep, you're no trouble, believe me. I'm very flattered, I truly am."

He reached over and wiped at a tear that had streaked down her face. "By the way, you'll sleep in my bed tonight."

Kate sighed and looked down.

"No no," Dan countered. "Don't get the wrong impression. This evening's protocol is completely above board. I'll sleep in here, you sleep in there. Hell, the truth is I sleep on this sofa about as often as the bed anyway."

She looked uncomfortable, still.

"Kate, for crissakes don't worry. You're my guest, and I'm gonna see to it that you get some rest. Period. You'll get a good night's sleep, we'll have coffee and a big breakfast in the morning, and then we'll go to the airport and skip town together. As for everything else," he said with raised eyebrows, "I'll give you as much room as you need. You're gonna need some time, I think, and you won't need me hovering over you like a hungry wolf. You can get some rest here and be ready to leave tomorrow to go work your butt off in California, and the other things will somehow work themselves out, I'm sure."

He held his wine glass toward her. "Deal?"

She smiled and felt genuinely relaxed for the first time in what seemed ages. "It's a deal," she answered, touching his glass with her own.

PART THREE
June – July, 1968

CHAPTER SIXTEEN
Los Angeles

Kate Flanagan relaxed in the living room of the modest single-story home near the Watts section of Los Angeles. Several of her colleagues had advised against her traveling alone to Watts, a mostly black section that had been the focal point of a destructive riot in '65. Dan Marinelli had even volunteered to come along with her, but instead Kate had driven the rental car alone and found the Douglas home on a warm, hazy, laid-back Saturday afternoon.

"I've heard so much about your brother," said Ruby Douglas, her large, friendly face breaking into a grin. "David's written in his letters about how much he's enjoying working with Lieutenant Flanagan. He said Lieutenant Flanagan's recommended him for Officers Candidate School. I guess that'll mean David stays in the Marines. I can't decide whether I like that or not."

Ruby laughed. Kate could see the occasional curious glances from Ruby's two young daughters, Becky and Jessie, ages twelve and eight respectively, from the nearby kitchen table where the two girls were occupied with the remaining half of a large jigsaw puzzle.

"Are you going to tell us about David, Momma?" little Jessie asked when she saw her mother produce a letter from her purse.

"I already did, baby. It's the same letter I read you last night," Ruby patiently replied. She then took from the folded letter several photographs, and held them toward Kate. "Here, I just got these yesterday."

One of the photos showed a grinning Lt. Tom Flanagan, shirtless and holding up a bottle of beer in salute, with other Marines nearby in what appeared to be a cookout at a camp location. Green was the photo's predominant color, from the dark uniforms of the Marines to the hills and countryside in the distance.

"Oh wow, he's so skinny," said Kate as she studied her brother's image. She glanced at the other photos, several of which included David Douglas, then came back to the one that interested her the most. She hadn't seen Tommy's picture in months, and he appeared to her to be at least twenty pounds below the nearly two-hundred pounds he had carried before Vietnam. His color was pale, and his eyes seemed puffy. For certain, he looked older. And he appeared tired. His dark hair was cut short, but he still had that winsome Tommy Flanagan smile, the one consistent likeness that had remained vivid in her memory throughout their long separation. She looked at his familiar face, and as she did she could hear his voice, sense his presence, and remember the words he had written back during the dark days at Hue. He was so far away, living his life in an alien Asian place and experiencing alien hostile things as sure as if he had been sent to Mars. And yet here he was, in her hand, in her eyes and ears, all in the home of this pleasant woman who an hour ago had been a complete stranger.

Kate's eyes were suddenly misty, and she became emotional for a moment as she passed the photos back to Ruby. She gave an embarrassed laugh and then went into her purse for a tissue.

"Does me the same way," Ruby said with a gentle laugh of her own. "It's even worse sometimes when David sends a cassette tape."

"It's been ages since I've seen him," Kate said, sniffing. "I'll be so glad when he's home."

"Did David send us a tape, Momma?" called Becky.

"No baby, not this time."

"Can I get you some coffee, Miss Flanagan?" Ruby asked, standing. "I can put the water on and have a cup ready in five minutes."

"Sure," Kate answered. "And please, call me Kate."

"Then I'll be right back, Kate."

Over the next two hours, the Vietnam connection that had drawn Kate to Ruby developed into a perceptible bonding as each began to feel an affection for, and appreciation of, the other. Ruby was fascinated as Kate talked unpretentiously about her work with the Robert Kennedy campaign, the occasional contact she had with a world-famous dignitary, and the ongoing, routine proximity she had to such important events. Kate spoke of her Chicago family, and of the split that had occurred between Tommy and herself over the war and virtually everything that went with it. She spoke of her fears over her brother's Marine service, and sensed in return that she was talking to someone who was also on familiar terms with those same concerns. When she noticed Ruby's glance at her bare ring finger, Kate mentioned in a matter-of-fact way the recent break-off of her engagement. She appreciated Ruby's sympathetic expression.

"Was he cheating on you?" Ruby asked bluntly in a disgusted tone.

"Yes," Kate replied without any hint of embarrassment. "I gave him his ring back and walked out, and I've never looked back."

Ruby grinned wisely. "Then good for you."

For her part, Ruby took Kate back to the day that husband James had moved his wife and son from a South Carolina mill town to sprawling Los Angeles, light years away in distance and kind; how they had started out in their late-model '54 Chevy Bel Air to cross the country during hot, muggy July; how seven-year-old David kept asking from the back seat, Where are we going, Momma? And how Ruby would tell him, Other side of the world, child, the whole other side of the world. And how David then kept leaning over the front seat and asking, Are we going to China, Momma? And how Ruby answered him, No, baby, California.

Ruby spoke of how they had eventually settled into their home, and how she had gone to work as a server in the cafeteria of a downtown hospital. She described how husband James had taken a job with the County of Los Angeles, working on a maintenance crew and making a decent enough living to have validated his decision to tear his family loose from their deep Southern roots and move them across the country. Their two daughters had been born in '56 and '60, and the family had been mildly prosperous and wholly content until one October day in 1964 when James had suddenly moaned and reached toward a co-worker, after which he had fallen over unmoving and dead on a downtown sidewalk from what was later determined to have been a cerebral hemorrhage.

"Changed our lives forever that day," Ruby said, adding, "and to think James didn't get to see how his boy's been awarded several decorations and been recommended for officer training in the Marines. He would've been so proud of David."

Kate smiled and nodded.

They talked on until early evening, and by the time Kate reached for her purse and mentioned her need to return to her downtown hotel, Ruby countered with a dinner invitation.

"With all we've got in common, Kate, at least you can stay with us a while longer and take pot luck for supper."

When Kate resisted mildly about not wanting to impose, Ruby responded with a dismissive wave. "No trouble at all, really."

Kate glanced over at the daughters, each of whom was sitting alongside Ruby, watching and waiting for the response from the visitor with the red hair. Kate finally smiled and said, "I'd be delighted to have dinner with you and Becky and Jessie."

Ruby quickly stood. "Good. Now I'll have to see what I've got," she said with a loud laugh as she quickly made her way into the kitchen.

Later they all sat down and ate meatloaf together, but only after they had joined hands and little Jessie had graced the food with her "God is great, God is good" blessing. Jessie asked for the umpteenth time if she could have a bicycle for her birthday like sister Becky had received for hers, and Ruby had to answer for the umpteenth time that bicycles were expensive and that new shoes would be far more practical.

"And the way some of these people drive around here, I'd be a nervous wreck every time you went out to ride your bike, just like I am with Becky. Shoes would be better for you, and a whole lot better for me, too."

Kate gave Ruby a preview of several scheduled RFK appearances in the Los Angeles vicinity, to include a motorcade that Kate suggested might be a good way for the girls to get a glance at the candidate. When Kate noticed the girls' confused look, she patiently explained the workings of a motorcade.

"It's like a parade," Kate went on to illustrate.

The girls soon nodded their understanding. Ruby nodded and appeared to Kate to be considering the possibilities.

"Can we go see Bobby Kennedy's parade, Momma?" asked Becky, her own interest elevated.

Jessie chimed in with, "Will he come here and have meatloaf with us?"

"We'll see about the motorcade," Ruby answered, laughing. "But I don't think he'll be coming here for dinner."

Kate finally said her good-byes to Becky and Jessie and walked outside with Ruby into the evening darkness. She and Ruby exchanged addresses and telephone numbers, each promising to remain in touch and to provide the other with any noteworthy news items.

"It's a small world," said Ruby as she walked Kate to her car. "Those two boys are together so far away in Vietnam, and we're together right here in California. I hope you can come back and spend some time with us again."

"I'd like that," said Kate. "After the election maybe we could take the girls to Disneyland."

Ruby smiled. "They'd like that, and so would I."

Kate sighed as she reached inside her purse for the car keys. "I could use some time off myself. The past several weeks have been difficult."

"Please give your brother my regards," said Ruby. "He's important to our family, too. And I hope you get to see him real soon."

"Thanks," replied Kate. "And I wish the same for you and David."

Ruby smiled. "We've both got something to look forward to."

"Yes," said Kate, reaching out for Ruby's hand. "We certainly do."

* * *

It was sunny and warm in Southern California on Friday, May 31st. The cars moved slowly along the wide boulevard, without a police escort. From her seat in the motorcade's lead car, Kate Flanagan glanced behind her and saw Robert Kennedy in an open vehicle with Ethel and Bill Barry. Kennedy was dressed in a gray suit, his coat off and his shirtsleeves rolled up, waving to the crowd, turning to one side and then the other, occasionally sweeping his hand through his hair, the trademark toothy smile there for all to behold.

When Kennedy's car passed directly in front of a group of young people, Kate heard a young man in the crowd shout something to the candidate and then toss a football to Kennedy that he caught and quickly threw back. Kennedy suddenly asked the driver to stop the car, and in so doing pointed and motioned for several people to move toward him. Kennedy stepped toward them in the car and leaned forward, greeting what was at first a trickle of people, then quickly a swarm, with a handshake and a "Hello, how are you?" The crowd surged toward the car, and as Kennedy leaned forward to reach the outstretched hands, Bill Barry held the candidate firmly around the waist for support.

After several minutes, Kate looked out and recognized Ruby and her daughters who were caught in the swell of the crowd. She could see Ruby holding Jessie with both arms and trying to force her way through the crowd. Jessie was clearly becoming frightened by the noise and the excitement, and was beginning to cry. The Kennedy car was virtually swamped by well-wishers from up and down the street, and it was all Bill Barry could do to keep the candidate from being pulled out of the car.

"Over here," Kate called from her car. She climbed into the back seat and was soon leaning out almost onto the trunk and calling to Ruby, "See if you can work your way over here. Hey everybody, clear the way for this lady and her children. C'mon, please clear the way here."

Ruby slowly worked her way against the flow and finally succeeded in breaking out and getting her daughters to the convertible. Inside, Kate lifted the still crying Jessie into the vehicle and gently sat her on the back seat while Becky climbed over the door and joined her sister inside. The driver motioned Ruby to his side where he opened the door and leaned forward as Ruby squeezed into the back.

"Thank you, thank you, thank you," Ruby said in great relief as the perspiration streaked down her face. "I was really happy to look over and see a familiar face."

"It's okay," Kate said, leaning toward Jessie and placing her hand on the child's shoulder. "Everything's okay now, sweetheart. Hey, how would you like to go for a ride in this brand new convertible?"

Jessie looked at her mother for approval. Ruby smiled in return. Jessie looked at Kate and nodded through her teary eyes.

"It's like this everywhere," Kate said with a chuckle. "It's amazing, isn't it? When we start moving again, we'll stop and let you out as soon as we've cleared this part. Maybe a quarter of a mile or so. Will that be okay?"

Ruby nodded. "It'll be fine. If I'd known it was going to be like this, I would've stayed put on that sidewalk," Ruby said, then smiled and added, "but all of us got to shake his hand."

Kate smiled.

The driver of their car gave a quick honk of the horn, stood, and tried to motion to the driver of the Kennedy vehicle.

"We gotta get going," he shouted several times.

It took a while, but after a bit they were moving again, slowly at first, with both drivers sounding their horns in short volleys as a warning to those nearby. It took several minutes of inching forward before the motorcade finally cleared the congested area and resumed its course.

The lead car sped up slightly when the way was clear so the driver could stop and allow Ruby and the girls to disembark without stopping the Kennedy vehicle. Ruby and the kids quickly got out and moved off to the side of the road.

"Thanks again," Ruby called as she and the girls waved at Kate from the sidewalk.

"Great seeing you and the girls. Be sure to vote on Tuesday," Kate called with a wave in return.

CHAPTER SEVENTEEN
Quang Tri Province, South Vietnam

Tom Flanagan first heard the footsteps, then saw the tent flap as it was pushed back.

"You wanted to see me, sir?"

Flanagan looked up from his makeshift desk of ammo crates and plywood and saw the helmetless Sgt. Douglas standing just inside the tent's entrance. "Come in and have a seat," said Flanagan with a point toward a rusty old folding chair.

Flanagan took a sip from a soft-drink can and finished scribbling his signature on the last of a stack of personnel records. He and his Marines had been in garrison for several days now, living in tents and eating hot chow, receiving replacements, washing uniforms, cleaning equipment, catching up on administrative details, resting, relaxing, and generally kicking back and indulging themselves with life in the rear. That same morning Flanagan had savored a long, steamy, comforting shower, and it was the first time in recent memory that he'd actually felt cleansed of the sweat and jungle grime that had become so much a part of his world.

"Do you remember that you might have to remain in-country a little while longer if the decision about OCS hasn't been made by the time your tour's up?" asked Flanagan.

"Yessir, I remember," said Douglas.

"Well cheer up," Flanagan said with a grin. "We just got word today from Headquarters, Marine Corps that you've been accepted for an OSC class that begins next January."

Douglas smiled broadly. "Wow, that's good news, sir."

Flanagan reached across and offered his hand. "Let me be the first to congratulate you. You're going to make an outstanding officer."

"It's hard to believe it's actually been approved," said Douglas. "I tried not to get my hopes up too high just in case I got turned down. Hell, I'm so jacked up I'm already looking forward to reporting in at Quantico and getting started."

"So much for recruiting duty," said Flanagan.

"That's okay, sir, I'll take OCS any day," said Douglas, adding a satisfied "Damn!" as he thrust his fist into his open palm. "I can't believe it. Me, accepted for officer's training. You'll have to give me all the scoop, sir, all the little pointers. I want to be ready when I get there."

Flanagan chuckled at the almost childlike enthusiasm of his platoon sergeant.

"I wasn't sure they'd take me with only one year of college," Douglas said with a sigh of relief. "It must've been yours and Captain Tanner's recommendations that did it."

Flanagan shrugged. "Nah, it wasn't so much what we did. You had enough on your own merit. And by the way, the Skipper wants to see you as soon as we're through here. He wants to add his own congratulations."

Douglas took a deep breath and nodded his satisfaction. "Aye-aye, sir. I'd also like to call my mother back home and give her the good news."

"Good idea," said Flanagan, pausing for a moment as he stared across at Douglas.

Flanagan sat quietly and enjoyed Douglas' evident excitement for a moment longer before finally clearing his throat and announcing, "There's one other thing."

Douglas sat back and placed his clasped hands in his lap. "Yessir?"

Flanagan swallowed and then straightened the papers on his desk. "There's a billet open at Battalion supply. The supply officer's new in-country; he's a friend of mine from Basic School, and he's a good man, a fair man. He asked me if I knew anyone who might be able to come up and join his operation and hit the ground running, to help him square away the logistics mess he's inherited. When I mentioned your name and told him you had a year of college, he said he'd like to have you, no questions asked. Apparently he's got himself a real can of worms up there, and there's a lot needed to get things back on track. He needs the help. And he'd like to have you."

"What happened to the supply sergeant who used to work up there? Why does he need another one?"

"The one who used to be there accidentally shot himself while cleaning his pistol."

Douglas gave a disgusted look, followed by a confused one. "Are you talking about me leaving the grunts, sir?"

"That's right. You'd spend the rest of your tour in supply," answered Flanagan, his tone and demeanor suddenly becoming more detached and businesslike.

"But I'm a platoon sergeant."

"You're a Marine," Flanagan countered sharply. "You'd be going to where a need exists. That's the way you should look at it. Nothing more, nothing less."

Flanagan could still see the look of uncertainty on Douglas' face.

"But isn't there a bigger need for me here, sir?" asked Douglas.

"There's always a need for good people," answered Flanagan. "You'd be filling a need somewhere else, that's all. And I'm sure that a man with your savvy could move over to supply and do them as good a job as you've done Third Platoon."

"So, Lieutenant, are you advising me to take the transfer?"

"I am, yes."

"When would it become effective?" asked Douglas.

"Couple of days, no more," Flanagan answered promptly.

Flanagan watched as Douglas' eyes quickly darted around the interior of the tent, searching, glancing here and there, seeking but not finding. Their eyes met briefly after a pause of several moments.

"You need to know now, sir?" asked Douglas.

"Yes, I want to know now," said Flanagan.

Douglas sighed. "Damn, I don't know, sir. I came in here and got the scoop about OCS, and I was feeling good about that, real good. But then, *this*. I just didn't expect to be hit with something like this out of the blue. It just doesn't feel right, sir. I swear I don't like the idea of leaving Third Platoon. Honestly, I don't like it worth a damn."

Flanagan leaned forward slightly. "Take the transfer," he said in what was nearly a growl. "You've been out in the bush long enough. You've proven to me and to yourself and to everyone else that you're a combat leader. You've earned the respect of every Marine in Fox Company. You've been in some of the hottest action in I Corps. Here's a chance for you to serve out the rest of your tour in the rear and get away from the humping and the mud. You've done your part; you've served the Corps well. Hell, you've earned a Silver Star, a Bronze Star, and a Purple Heart, and you're getting orders to OCS. I say again, you've done your part. Now take the friggin' transfer!"

Douglas expression suddenly hardened. "Have I done something to piss you off, Lieutenant? Am I on your shit list?"

"No, of course not," said Flanagan.

"Are you sure?"

"I'm sure," answered Flanagan. "Why?"

Douglas stared straight into Flanagan's eyes. "Because the advice you're giving me is the exact opposite of what you yourself did when you had your chance to transfer out of the bush. You haven't forgotten that, have you?"

Flanagan swallowed hard and said, "That was different."

"Different? How so, sir?"

"It was just different, that's all," Flanagan snapped impatiently.

Douglas leaned forward, his eyes still fixed upon Flanagan. "May I speak freely, Lieutenant?"

Flanagan hesitated before finally answering, "Yeah, sure."

Douglas took a deep breath and exhaled slowly, looking straight into Flanagan's eyes and sitting ramrod straight. "Seems to me, sir, that you're feeding me some of that 'do as I say and not as I do' bullshit."

Flanagan's eyebrows immediately arched. "I'm not feeding you bullshit of any flavor, Sergeant Douglas. That's not my style and you damn well know it."

Douglas nodded. "That's exactly my point, sir. I know you well enough to know that you'd sooner be sent to the brig in panties and a bra than to transfer out of Third Platoon to a job in supply. Hell, I even know exactly how you would describe somebody who would even *consider* such a transfer."

Flanagan said nothing, his expression stern and his lips pressed tightly together.

"You'd call 'em a candyass," said Douglas. "Straight and simple. Oh, you'd throw in some other words, too, probably some really descriptive ones, but I know good and damn well that the word 'candyass' would be in there somewhere. I know what you'd say and I even know the tone of voice you'd use to say it."

Flanagan stared ahead at Douglas and said nothing.

"Isn't that right, sir?"

Still, Flanagan said nothing.

"Am I right, sir?" pressed Douglas. "Am I right?"

Flanagan finally sat back, and after several moments his expression softened. Still, he remained quiet.

"I know what you're trying to do, Mister Flanagan," said Douglas in a softer tone. "And I appreciate it, I really do. I've known since I first met you that you look after your people as best you can, that you want everybody under your command to have a decent chance of walking away from this thing when their tour's up. And I see this as an example of exactly that. But this platoon is where I belong. And this is where I want to serve out the rest of my tour. I've earned that right, sir. I've earned the right to stay out here in the bush and do what I do best, and not be sent off to some supply job that might be important but nowhere near as important as what I'm doing here. Let those supply types go right on shooting themselves with their own pistols, but don't pull us out of the bush when we want to stay. You've got to let me stay out here, sir, where I belong, and where I can do the most good."

Flanagan sighed. "I'm doing this," he said, choosing his words carefully, "because I think you would do the Marine Corps a great service by becoming an officer and fully developing your leadership talents. I know in my head and my gut that you'll become an outstanding role model as an officer, and I don't need to tell you how important that would be for the Corps and for society in general. And I want to see you be able to have a chance at doing exactly that."

"I understand, sir. And I'll become the best officer I can possibly be. But I need to finish out my tour on my terms, by staying out here in the bush with these Marines and being the best platoon sergeant I can possibly be. This is who I am and what I do, just like you," said Douglas.

Flanagan finally grinned. "I give you a chance to get out of the boonies and you turn it down. You even get all hot and bothered about it. My goodness, the only logical conclusion I can draw from all of this is that you're just plain wacky, Sergeant Douglas. You're boocoo *dinky dao*."

Douglas also smiled. "Right on, sir. All I can say is, it's always good to be around people I can identify with."

They both laughed.

CHAPTER EIGHTEEN
Los Angeles

The phone rang a little after seven in the morning in Kate Flanagan's fourth-floor room at the Ambassador Hotel, site of the Kennedy headquarters.

"Wake up, Flanagan. It's VE Day," said Dan Marinelli.

Kate yawned. "Cute. Victory over Eugene, right?"

"God, I'm amazed at how efficiently your brain works so soon after waking."

"Truth is, I've slept very little. My brain's been working most of the night, to my great aggravation," said Kate.

Dan laughed. "Me too, sweets. Who the hell could sleep with all we've got at stake here? By the way, I'll meet you in the lobby in ten minutes. We'll drive out and get some breakfast at a greasy spoon on the outskirts that serves the most incredible blueberry pancakes you'll ever find, and then we'll take a ride around the city and see how the turnout is."

"Thirty minutes, not ten," said Kate.

"Fifteen," Dan countered.

"Twenty-five."

"Twenty."

"Done. I'll see you in the lobby in half an hour," said Kate.

Kate and Dan walked outside to a sunless, hazy Los Angeles on Tuesday, June 4, 1968, the morning of the California primary. They agreed that virtually everything that could reasonably be done by their candidate had already been finalized in this all-important contest. Saturday's televised debate between Robert Kennedy and Eugene McCarthy had ended with mixed reviews, though both Kate and Dan had generally concluded that Kennedy had not only demonstrated he could go head-to-head with his cerebral opponent, but he had succeeded in emphasizing his broader experience in government and in relating his answers to issues specific to Californians. Both staffers had been with the Kennedy team as it campaigned on Monday for twelve long hours, starting in L.A. and then making stops in San Francisco, Long Beach, and San Diego before finally arriving back in Los Angeles.

Kate began recovering from her fatigue after a light breakfast and the morning newspaper. Later, as she and Dan drove around the different precincts, they noticed that the turnout appeared heavy in the black and Hispanic sections and moderate in the others. They each interpreted the minority turnout as a strong and encouraging signal, since Kennedy's advantage there was expected to be overwhelming. They waved and honked the horn at some of the young volunteers periodically seen holding and raising their Kennedy banners and placards.

"When we win tonight," Dan said as he drove the rented Chevy Impala, "and a lot of McCarthy's key people start to leave him and come over to us, then Gene'll be out there gasping for air."

"You think so?"

"I know so," said Dan. "Goodwin and O'Brien are already talking to some of the McCarthy heavies in New York, and it seems like it's shaping up that if one goes, a lot will go. They may have made commitments, but once they see the handwriting on the wall and their guy starts to unravel, they'll come across. Kind of like the Democratic Party version of the Domino Theory, so to speak. We can win the New York primary and the Democratic nomination on the strength of our victory here tonight. We're even looking at arranging a primary in Rhode Island to make a few more gains. After New York and possibly Rhode Island are all said and done, Bob can get those delegates and Hubert won't know what's hit him."

Kate glanced over at him. "You're certainly not short on confidence, are you?"

"My political instincts are working perfectly today. We've gotten our message out and California's heard us. Your ads were effective and our organization has functioned a hell of a lot better than it did in Oregon. Good grief, it *had* to; it couldn't have been much worse, could it? And our candidate got out and let the people see the real man. McCarthy kept on mouthing off about wanting to debate, and when he and Bob sat down and had it out, McCarthy ended up taking on a lot more water than our guy did. In my considered opinion, Bob cleaned his clock, and that's that."

"I happen to agree," said Kate. "But not everybody may see it that way."

"I know, I know. Just everybody who matters. By the way, Kate, I talked to Ron Phillips this morning and he told me he got all your stuff yesterday from your ex and put it in my apartment. He's even got your car at my place."

Kate smiled. "Thank you Dan and Ron. That's a great relief. Now," she said, rolling her eyes, "all I've got to do is find another place to live."

"Well, I have a suggestion," Dan countered with a quick glance.

"I'll bet you do."

"My rent's two-hundred bucks a month," said Dan. "I'll charge you half and you can share my place. One-hundred bucks a month and you're in out of the rain, Flanagan. What a deal. But look, you don't have to answer now. Take your time. I'll hold your reservation."

"Problem is, there's only one bedroom."

Dan grinned wolfishly. "Exactly. And that's not a problem, by the way. It's perfect—a perfectly suitable solution."

"Wrong on all three counts: It's not perfect; it's not suitable; and it's definitely not a solution."

"Like I said," he said with a smile, "I'll hold your reservation."

Their eyes met briefly before Kate looked away and continued twisting a lock of her hair around her index finger.

Late in the morning they made an impromptu stop at an Alhambra shopping center and browsed through several clothing stores. Dan bought himself a hippie outfit for the victory celebration scheduled that night at Pierre Salinger's jet set discotheque *The Factory*.

"All you need now is a wig," Kate commented.

"Don't tempt me," Dan answered, after which he flashed a peace sign. "Tonight I take on my Haight-Ashbury persona. Deep inside this meek, mild, conformist personality is a free-thinking anarchist."

They had hamburgers for lunch and continued afterwards to tour different parts of the city. The turnout was steady, and their own sampling of voters at several selected polling places was still even more encouraging. By three o'clock Dan was convinced of victory, and by four they were back at the Ambassador. Kate was there to greet them when the Kennedy party arrived shortly after seven to their room on the fifth floor. Room 511 was reserved for the family, while across the hall in 516 a group of journalists, friends, and family members were moving in and out. There was a bar in 516, and the booze was flowing freely by eight o'clock when CBS announced that Kennedy was ahead, followed shortly thereafter by an NBC report that McCarthy was winning.

Kate joined several colleagues in Room 516.

Kennedy had been across the hall discussing strategy with Smith, Sorensen, and Walinsky when he suddenly showed up in 516. The South Dakota primary was also being held on this night, and Kennedy had been receiving reports on the early results.

"Have you heard about the Indian vote?" Kate overheard Kennedy when he asked the group in general, and without waiting for an answer he went on to explain about the overwhelming advantage he was enjoying among Indian voters in South Dakota.

Kate was conversing with a journalist at one point when she heard Kennedy calling to her. She excused herself and joined him in a semi-private corner of the room.

"I understand this has been a difficult few days for you," Kennedy said.

"It's been challenging, yes," Kate answered with an appreciative smile. "And I doubt the last few days have been any easier for you."

"Yes, you're probably right. Will you be okay?" Kennedy asked.

"I'll be fine, Senator. Thanks."

"What is it about love and politics?" he asked, his eyes twinkling. "Each one essential and honorable but at the same time often difficult and painful."

Kate smiled and nodded. "You're very thoughtful. Maybe tonight will be our reward for having stuck it out these past few days."

"Yes, hopefully. Anything from your brother lately?"

"He's doing well," Kate answered. "He should be home before the summer's over."

"Good," he said with a nod as he reached out and squeezed her hand. "Thanks for all your help, Kate, especially under the circumstances. I'll see you at *The Factory* a little later."

Kennedy then disappeared into the crowded hallway between the two rooms to answer some of the rapid-fire questions from the reporters.

Kate listened to the newscasts, and when by 10:30 the black and Mexican votes had come in, it was clear Kennedy was going to be the winner. McCarthy was interviewed at the Beverly Hills Hilton by CBS reporter David Schoumacher, and while McCarthy wouldn't concede that his candidacy was yet doomed, it was apparent that a California defeat would add to its already precarious standing. Kennedy was later interviewed by Sander Vanocur of ABC and Roger Mudd of CBS, both old friends, and then by ABC's Bob Clark and Dan Blackburn on Metromedia radio.

Meanwhile, Kate went down into the Embassy Ballroom and found a happy, animated crowd. "*We want Kennedy*" chants were resounding throughout the room, along with the song *This Land Is Your Land*. There were girls draped in red-and-blue campaign ribbons, and everywhere there were balloons, posters, straw hats, and signs.

"*We want Kennedy. We want Kennedy.*"

"When will he come downstairs?" asked one of the volunteers who recognized Kate.

"Soon, I think," she answered.

Kate returned to the fifth floor and the crowded corridor between 611 and 516. The drinks were still being served in 516, and as she pushed her way through she saw Dan Marinelli standing with a cocktail in his hand, talking to a group of journalists, civil-rights activists, and others. Among those included were Jimmy Breslin, George Plimpton, Theodore White, Pete Hamill, Jack Newfield, Loudon Wainwright, John Lewis, and Charles Evers. Jesse Unruh, Speaker of the California Assembly, came into the room with Olympic athlete Rafer Johnson.

"Kate," Dan called as he saw her and waved. "Over here."

Dan moved aside and guided her into a corner near the bar. "I've been looking all over for you. Can I get you a drink?"

"No, thank you. I've been downstairs. It's rocking down there."

Dan's eyes showed his glee. "It's incredible, isn't it? It's all coming together tonight. The world is about to change for the better whether it realizes it or not."

Television was reporting that the vote in South Dakota was slightly more than 46% for Kennedy and slightly less than 42% for McCarthy. A boisterous cheer went up.

"When is he going downstairs?" Kate asked.

Dan looked at his watch. It was after eleven. "Half hour or so, according to Unruh. Isn't this great?" Dan asked with a sweep of his arm. "Doesn't this make everything seem worthwhile? We're going to the top now, kiddo. Just like the script calls for. The amount of convincing that we'll have to do will become less and less now. Winning is the greatest cure."

He leaned across and kissed her on the cheek. "I'm sorry, but I just couldn't keep from that."

Kate grinned. "It's going to be an interesting night," she said in an amused tone.

"If it's nothing else," Dan said, moving slightly closer, "it will be interesting, yes."

Shortly before midnight, Kate went back downstairs to the Embassy Ballroom with the Kennedy entourage that included Bob and Ethel, Bill Barry, Unruh, Rafer Johnson, and Fred Dutton.

They took a service elevator and came through the hotel kitchen to the narrow gray corridor leading to the Ballroom. Kennedy wore a navy blue suit with a blue-and-white striped tie, while Ethel, who was carrying their eleventh child, was looking girlish in her orange-and-white mini-dress with white stockings.

"*We want Kennedy. We want Kennedy.*"

Kate broke away from the group and found a place in the dense crowd with a small band of volunteers and staffers. Stephen Smith, the brother-in-law who in his understated fashion had so skillfully managed the campaign thus far, was speaking to the crowd. The room temperature was balmy from the crowd and the lights, and there was an electricity surging throughout that everyone seemed to savor.

"You're going to the party at *The Factory* later on, right?" one of the female staffers asked Kate as they watched for the entrance of the candidate.

"Wouldn't miss it for the world," Kate answered, thinking briefly of Dan and his hippie outfit.

A huge roar went up when the candidate started inching his way through the crush of well-wishers toward the podium. The noise reached a crescendo when he and Ethel finally stepped onto the platform and waved to the cheering supporters. Many in the crowd, especially among the young, had the wide-eyed, breathless look of wonderment.

"*We want Kennedy. We want Kennedy.*"

Kate watched in excitement as Kennedy stepped to the microphone and proceeded to thank his supporters, many by name. He then talked about the issues, about the need to seek fair and responsible solutions to the many problems facing the nation, and about how on this same night his candidacy had been awarded primary victories in what were the most urban and the most rural states in the Union. The message was being heard, and the American people were responding.

Kate felt the deep sense of satisfaction among those who had labored so hard to help make this night possible. She had a feeling of momentum, of destiny, that magnified what was already a profound feeling of achievement. Kennedy's powerful presence, along with his graciousness and articulation, rendered a sort of restrained validation to everything they had been striving for. It seemed now that the rest of the world was suddenly catching on to what those in the room had known for some time.

"Mayor Yorty has just sent me a message that we've been here too long already," Kennedy said with his trademark grin as he brought his remarks to a close. "So my thanks to all of you, and it's on to Chicago, and let's win there."

Kate saw Kennedy give a thumbs up as the crowd cheered and the group around the podium closed in around the candidate. Again, as before, movement was made slow by the sheer congestion. She noticed when Kennedy turned and looked around, unsure about the exit route from the Embassy Ballroom.

Kate scanned the room and the still teeming crowd and decided to wait a few minutes before taking the elevator back up to 516.

"What a night!" one of the staffers commented. Her face was drained from the emotion and excitement. "How does he do it? How does he deal with this everywhere he goes?"

"I don't know," Kate answered, her fatigue also showing. "I suppose if he ever leaves politics, he could always be a rock star and keep this kind of excitement around him."

The crowd finally began to thin somewhat after the Kennedy party had made its way off the platform and out of the room. Kate was about to leave for the elevators when she heard a rumbling—a combination of muffled shouts and screams—coming from the direction of Kennedy's exit.

"What the hell's going on?" Kate overheard someone nearby saying.

There were several shouts, clearer now, and when Kate heard the summons for a doctor a cold chill ran through her as quickly as if she'd been submerged in freezing water.

"Oh dear God," a woman screamed. "Oh no. God, please, no!"

Kate then saw that Stephen Smith was back at the microphone in the Embassy Room, calling for a doctor. Photographers and newsmen were making a mad dash in the direction of the commotion, toward the kitchen corridor. A young man came into the Ballroom from the corridor and made a motion with his thumb and index finger of a gun, and pointed to his head.

"It's Kennedy," he was overheard as saying.

Kate turned and saw that several people were now coming back into the Embassy Ballroom, many of whom were pale and wobbly and some of whom required assistance to keep from collapsing. Women were crying; men were crying; there was still an immense amount of shouting and confusion.

Pandemonium reigned throughout the downstairs area. People remaining in the Embassy Ballroom were weeping, cursing, or standing in stunned silence. Others came to the podium to summon help or to make announcements. Kate felt as if she might faint and quickly found a chair in a corner spot. Gradually the reports coming from the scene indicated the worst: Robert Kennedy had been shot and seriously wounded by a crazed assassin. Rosey Grier, Rafer Johnson, and others had subdued the suspect only after an intense struggle of several minutes. There was no information on Kennedy's condition, on whether the wounds were yet fatal, but the prospects were discouraging, in the least.

Kate covered her face with her hands and finally gave in to the sobbing that had been threatening to overtake her.

"Screw this goddamned country, man," a young man screamed in bitterness as he slung a Kennedy banner to the ground.

"No, not again," called another young person nearby. "How could this happen again? How?"

"I'm terribly sorry," Ruby Douglas said as she extended a tissue to Kate.

Kate looked up and, after a moment of bewilderment, eventually recognized Ruby. She nodded and took the tissue, forced a slight smile of thanks, and struggled to regain her composure.

"God, this feels like the absolute end of the world, Ruby," Kate said with considerable effort as she dabbed at her eyes and nose. Her throat was constricted and she felt a generally mystified, almost anesthetized sensation. "I can't believe this. This isn't really happening. This *can't* be happening."

"I got a baby sitter and caught the bus down here just so I could be a part of all this," Ruby said, sighing and shaking her head as she scanned the room. "I had no idea that *this* would be what was waiting on the other end."

Kate glanced over at a banner with the face of Robert Kennedy on it, thought of Ethel and the ten Kennedy kids, and promptly burst into tears again.

Ruby's eyes were moist, and her sad face reflected the hurt she was sharing with Kate and the rest. "It'll be okay again," she said softly and reassuringly, touching Kate gently on the shoulder. "I know it doesn't seem like it now, but it will. I promise."

Kate spoke with her face buried in her hands. "It's just not fair. We were so close. Why now? Why does something like this have to happen now? To him? And when we need him so badly. It's not fair, dammit. It's not right."

There were loud, uncontrollable sobs nearby. Kate glanced up and saw a middle-aged woman in a long flowered dress crying out in agony, her eyes raised toward the ceiling. "Oh God, let him live," she called out in a pleading voice. "Please, take me instead."

"It's not fair," Kate sighed, burying her head in her hands. "It's just not fair."

She felt Ruby's touch again. When she looked up, Ruby was also sobbing heavily. Kate stood, and as she did so, Ruby reached out to embrace her.

They stood there, holding on to one another, their shoulders heaving, both desperately hoping for the best, but deep down both expecting the worst.

CHAPTER NINETEEN
Quang Nam Province, South Vietnam

Tom Flanagan sat at a table with his two platoon-leader colleagues from Fox Company—Second Lieutenants Jay Handley and Frank Lucci. They had that same morning returned from the field after three full days of patrolling, and a shower and change into clean utilities had been a welcome prelude to their search for a cool libation.

They had little difficulty in finding such a place. There were several Marines and sailors in the bar just outside the main gate at Da Nang. It was mid-June, and Flanagan was less than two months away from completing his tour and going home. He was, in the vernacular of overseas Marines, Getting Short. "Fifty-five and a wake up," he had told his junior companions that same morning. The three Marines kicked back in the bar and relaxed, discussing news from home, sports news, world news—any and all news. When the discussion moved to Robert Kennedy's assassination, Flanagan related that while Kennedy's death had been high profile, and his promise considerable, it wasn't a great deal different than the still-daily deaths among the many young Americans throughout Vietnam. "In the end, it's all the same: somebody dies, somebody cries, and somebody's left to pick up the pieces," he told the others.

What he was reminded of, but didn't mention, was how deeply he felt for his sister Kate, whose letter had recently arrived explaining the break off of her engagement to Everett and now her despair over Robert Kennedy's death. She seemed lost, he thought, as disoriented and broken as if she had gone away from a familiar, comfortable place and come back to something she could neither recognize nor reconcile. He had written her a supportive, consoling letter in return, assuring her that the sun would once again shine in her life, much as she had assured him when he had been so filled with gloom during the desperate Tet fighting at Hue. There was hope, he had emphasized to Kate. There was always hope. He would be home soon, and they would

257

then be able to meet in Chicago and drive out to their favorite Dairy Queen and enjoy the simple things once again. As brother and sister; as pals and confidants.

Just hang on, he kept telling her in his letters. Her big brother would soon be there to make things better.

Meanwhile, more beers were served and the focal point of the discussion shifted to Fox Company's new CO, Capt. Trace Lawrence, the twenty-seven-year-old son of a commercial fisherman from Bar Harbor, Maine. Capt. Tanner had only the week before completed his tour and left Vietnam for Quantico, Virginia where he would become a student in the Amphibious Warfare School. They all agreed that Tanner had been a splendid commanding officer—surely he would make general someday, Flanagan foretold—and his officers had dreaded his departure for weeks. But Capt. Lawrence, Flanagan had already discovered, was an ambitious, hard-charging career Marine who had been in-country for three months serving on the staff of the Commanding General, First Marine Division, and who had pulled every well-placed string he could find to get his hands on a cherished rifle-company command.

Flanagan had also discovered that Lawrence was loud and often profane in contrast to Tanner's more refined personal style, but there was something about Lawrence that Flanagan liked, something about his calculated aggressiveness and his coolness under fire that appealed to the warrior in Flanagan. Flanagan knew that the two younger officers were supportive but still uncertain about Lawrence, confounded by his dissimilar style and unsure of the depth of his competency as a combat leader. When they sought the inevitable assurances from Flanagan, they were told bluntly that Lawrence was the boss, and as such it would be *his* duty to evaluate *them*, not the other way around.

"He's not Tanner," Flanagan said firmly. "He'll never be Tanner. And the Marine Corps will never, ever ask either of you for your opinion of a potential commanding officer before they make the assignment and put you under that officer's command. So take it for what it is—a natural change of command from one

Marine to another. Part of your job is to adjust to whatever situation you find yourself in. So adjust, dammit, and stop whining about Captain Lawrence doing this or that different from Captain Tanner."

"Yeah, but he could get us killed by something he does or doesn't do in the field," Lucci protested.

Flanagan's expression instantly hardened. "Look here, princess, did you get some sort of signed agreement before you joined up that specifically prohibited you from being killed in combat under the command of one Trace Lawrence, Captain, United States Marine Corps?"

"Of course not," Lucci said sheepishly.

Flanagan's expression softened. "Then adjust, sweetheart. And cheer up. You got the same deal that I got and everyone else got."

"You heard the man. Cheer up and die like a Marine," Handley said, grinning.

"In your ear, Jay," Lucci snapped in return, after which they all laughed and raised their drinks.

"To death," they shouted.

"Something we all get."

"To death in combat."

"Something we'll all probably get."

"To one Trace Lawrence, Captain, USMC."

"Someone we've got."

"To one Robert A. Tanner, Captain, USMC."

"Someone we had."

"Long live Tanner. Long live the king."

"Screw that. He's back there; we're still here."

"There it is, gentlemen. Now you're catching on," Flanagan said, then turning and shouting, "Bring us another round."

The Stones' *Satisfaction* blared through the jukebox, and some of the male patrons and the heavily perfumed and thickly rouged bar girls could be overheard singing along. Flanagan watched with humor as Frank Lucci made a guitar-playing motion with his hands, even to the point of looking down at his imaginary instrument and offering the contorted facial expressions of a rock guitarist as he played the strings and changed the keys. One of the bar girls came over to Flanagan and abruptly sat in his lap, her arms draped loosely around his neck. Another attractive girl brought three fresh bottles of Ba Muoi Ba "Number 33" beer.

"You love me, yes?" the girl asked of Flanagan.

The young woman had used enough perfume to fill a canteen, Flanagan thought with amusement, and her thick, ruby-red lipstick would have protected her lips from all but an atomic blast. But she was nevertheless cute with her dark, short hair, her smooth skin, her oval face and attractive smile, her tight slacks and sleeveless blouse. She was street smart in an outwardly and endearingly Western way that was clear from her demeanor and her dress.

"I know you love me. You like my big ass. And you like the rest of me. You love me, yes?" she said.

"I do, yeah," Flanagan answered. "Have for months, as a matter of fact. I only wish now that I'd told you earlier, before, uh," Flanagan said, pausing and winking at Lucci and Handley, "before I go home and try to win back my *real* love."

The girl repeated, "I know you love me," and kissed Flanagan on the forehead.

"What's your name, cupcake?" Flanagan asked.

"My name's Kim."

"Well, Kim, you keep that nice butt of yours right where you've got it, and you'll make a believer out of me yet."

"You'll go with me then?" she asked suggestively.

"Go where?" asked Flanagan.

She leaned over and kissed him on the mouth. "We'll go to my place. We'll have a number-one good time, you'll see."

Flanagan glanced over at his colleagues and grinned, his mouth stained by the lipstick. "Young lady, I won't pay a penny more than one-million dollars for your services. And don't try to bargain for more, either. I only have a million bucks worth of piasters in my pocket, and I intend to spend every drop of it here today."

"And by the way," Flanagan said, nuzzling her, "what you're feeling underneath you right now isn't a pistol in my pocket."

The girl laughed and kissed Flanagan again, more a kiss of recognition than romance, a reward of sorts from one con artist to another. "You *dinky dao*. I like you. You *boocoo dinky dao*, like me," she said with a giggle and a point at herself.

She got up and walked away behind the bar, her delightful hips busy underneath the tight slacks.

"Damn!" said Lucci.

"Easy, Frank," said Handley, suppressing a grin and who, like Lucci, was also unmarried. "She may be VC, you know."

"She's got too much ass to be VC," Flanagan commented. "She's making plenty of money and getting plenty to eat. What the hell could the VC do for her?"

"Good point. You gonna tear you off a slice, Tom?" Handley asked.

"Nope. Might get the clap and die. I'll adjust and steer clear of her before I have too much to drink," Flanagan answered to the laughs of the others.

"There it is," said Lucci.

They raised their bottles.

"Adjust or die," Lucci said. "Hey, isn't that the state motto of New Jersey?"

"No, it's Live Free or Die," said Flanagan. "And it's Connecticut."

"Then what's New Jersey's?"

"Pay Up or Die, probably," said Handley. "Or maybe Stay Off the Freeway or Die."

"You ever been to New Jersey, Jay?" asked Lucci.

"Yeah. I almost married the sister of a Basic School classmate, from Trenton. Came this damn close, I shit you not," Handley said, using his thumb and forefinger for emphasis.

"What happened?" Flanagan asked.

"Language barrier," Handley answered with a laugh. "She talked too damn fast and said too damn little. Everybody up there's like that, best I can tell."

"You'd better watch it," Lucci said, looking around. "One of these Navy dudes might be from someplace like Newark, and take your grit ass outside and beat the hell out of you."

"Never happen," Handley said with a loud snort as he puffed out his chest. "*Never* friggin' happen."

"You never know, man. Some guys are sensitive about that."

Handley quickly and loudly pushed back his chair and stood, glaring at the sailors. "Excuse me, gentlemen, but any of y'all from New Jersey?" he called out loudly.

"No," they each responded. "Why?" one asked.

"Never mind," Handley said, taking his seat. "Another round of beers over here, Marilyn."

"It's Kim, you drunk asshole," said Lucci.

When the racy, brassy beat of *Shotgun* began playing on the jukebox, Handley jumped up and grabbed Kim and started dancing with her on the small dance floor off to the side. Lucci then quickly got up and escorted another girl to the floor, and suddenly there were fingers snapping and pelvics thrusting. The music played on. Handley suddenly gave out with a loud Rebel yell.

Flanagan sat back and said to himself with a grin, "I hope the corpsman's got enough Darvon."

* * *

Flanagan returned to the field with Fox Company on a stifling, miserably hot June morning. The mission was the same as always—find, fix, and then destroy the enemy. He and the other officers had been told that the 320th NVA Division had been active in the area west of Da Nang, one element of which had pounded a Marine platoon from the 3rd Marines in an ambush the week before. Capt. Lawrence had passed along to Flanagan and the other platoon leaders the feeling among many senior officers that the NVA were still capable of sustaining a major effort, but there was also a very vocal contingent who felt strongly that the enemy's ability to mass after their horrific Tet losses had been severely impaired. As had been characteristic throughout much of the war with regard to the enemy's true intentions and actual condition, nobody on the American side really knew for certain.

"I think he's damn well out there," Capt. Lawrence had told his platoon leaders in a briefing before the platoon had mounted the choppers. "He may be licking his wounds, and he may be fewer in number than before, but when we find him—and we *will* find him, gents—he'll be as eager as ever to shoot as many round eyes as he can get in his sight picture."

Lawrence had then removed his cigar and spit on the earthen floor in his tent command post. "Problem is, we'll be just as eager to kill his young ass. Right, gents?"

"That's right, Skipper," Flanagan had said with a splitting headache from his hangover.

"Yessir," Handley and Lucci had both echoed, each cutting quick glances at Flanagan and each also suffering from the long session the night before.

"Outstanding," Lawrence had said, smiling. "Let's go get some. Good hunting, gentlemen."

They were soon moving in a column along some densely covered hills and valleys that could easily hide a large NVA unit intent upon refitting and recuperating. Golf and Hotel Companies were also in the field—Golf to the north of Fox Company and Hotel to the northeast—and Lt. Col. Urstadt's command chopper could occasionally be seen overhead. The battalion was out looking for a fight, and just about everyone felt it would only be a matter of time before they found one.

Fox Company took a break in the early afternoon. The men had a C-ration meal along a north-south spine of hills to the west of a shallow stream that the mission's planners had figured as a likely water source. Flanagan's hangover had eased, though the water loss from the exertion of patrolling had only added to his general state of dehydration. He knew better than to go to the field at anything less than his best, and he cursed himself for the stiff but self-imposed penalty he was paying for his mischief. For

Handley and Lucci, venereal disease would now be an additional concern through the next several days. Flanagan had tried to caution them on all the bad things in Vietnam that could befall a careless combat leader or a haphazard lover, but his cool advice had been ignored under the hot circumstances.

Flanagan and his platoon had been on the move again, about an hour after their break, when he picked up a radio report that the first shots of the operation had been fired by Hotel Company at their location three klicks due north of the Fox position. An NVA unit of at least company size had been engaged on Hotel's eastern flank, and when the fighting there quickly escalated to the point that the enemy appeared to be reinforcing, Capt. Lawrence ordered Fox Company to the scene with all due haste.

Flanagan picked up his platoon's pace and closed perhaps half the distance to the Hotel position when suddenly an enemy element to his east opened up with automatic weapons and rockets. The large NVA unit stalled the entire company once its full fire was brought to bear on the Marines. Indeed, it appeared to Flanagan that the enemy unit being engaged by Fox Company might actually be the larger of the two.

"We've got at least a reinforced enemy company stuck in our flank," Flanagan heard as Capt. Lawrence radioed Urstadt, "and it's going to take me some time to break loose."

Meanwhile, Flanagan radioed Capt. Lawrence that the enemy's northern flank, facing Flanagan's 3rd Platoon, seemed vulnerable.

"Then pinch it," Lawrence radioed in return. "Roll it up and we'll keep the pressure on his front."

Flanagan quickly gathered his squad leaders and Sgt. Douglas behind the protection of some thick hardwoods and advised them of his plan to attack the enemy flank. Cpl. Hughes' and Cpl. Hobart's squads would jump off first and attack on line, with a squad following in trace. Flanagan would position himself with the lead squads in the attack, with Sgt. Douglas following from the rear.

"Stay on line," Flanagan advised. "As soon as we push past his forward positions, we'll pivot ninety degrees with Hughes' squad on the outside and then we'll flank their asses. Any questions?"

The veteran Marines posed questions about coordination with the other platoons and about supporting artillery fire, and eventually looked back at Flanagan with determined expressions on their faces.

"All right. We'll jump off on my radio command in five minutes," Flanagan said. "Let's do it."

The 3rd Platoon Marines moved out and attacked across relatively flat terrain. Resistance was far heavier toward the middle of the enemy's position, but when the NVA commanders looked out and saw Flanagan's platoon attempting its flanking maneuver, they moved quickly to reinforce their exposed flank.

It was too late. Hobart and Hughes moved their squads across the fifty meters quickly and expertly, finally turning the enemy's flank and firing along their position's long axis. Handley's and Lucci's platoons kept up the pressure in the middle and on the southern flank, augmented by artillery from a 105mm battery blasting the NVA rear and thereby preventing, or at least discouraging, a withdrawal or reinforcement.

Capt. Lawrence attacked frontally with Handley's platoon once Flanagan's envelopment had succeeded and the northern flank had been sealed. The NVA resisted stubbornly, however, and Handley soon bogged down after taking several casualties. The artillery fire was then shifted even closer in an attempt at breaking up the enemy's middle, but Flanagan screamed in his radio and had it called off after a friendly round detonated near his position and wounded two of his Marines.

The NVA finally broke off and withdrew at dusk. They left behind forty-three bodies and over a hundred weapons of various sort, from AKs to RPGs to B-40 rockets. Fox Company suffered six dead and fifteen wounded in the day's action, with two of the KIAs coming from Flanagan's 3rd Platoon.

The next morning, Flanagan ate a quick C-rat breakfast and then got his platoon on the move to its assigned position. He felt much better after a night's rest, even if his sleep had been spotty and fitful as was typical when he was in the field. Life in the bush was never easy as Flanagan stretched the muscles in his neck and lower back after a night on the hard ground. He had a rash between his legs, commonly referred to as jungle rot, which had caused the skin of his crotch to break open and bleed. Numerous insects had left their marks on him during the night, some causing welts as big as olives on his face and arms. His bowels seemed always fickle, as much from the physical and emotional strain as from the rations and the sometimes dubious drinking water. He made a concerted effort to take care of his feet and insisted that his troops do likewise with frequent drying and changing of socks, but occasional blisters and perpetually tired, sore feet were all too often standard fare for the infantryman. And if that wasn't enough, there was always the heat.

The muffled echoes of the artillery firing could be heard in the distance as Fox Company formed into a column and moved out. Flanagan joined in near the front of his platoon, at the head of the company column. They left the old position in what was already starting out as a hot, steamy day and arrived at the new position after an hour's march. Capt. Lawrence assigned sectors to the platoons and then reported to Lt. Col. Urstadt that Fox Company was in place.

Flanagan and Sgt. Douglas inspected their positions as well as the locations and fields of fire of their machine guns and automatic rifles. They made several adjustments with the M-60s before finally becoming satisfied with the coverage and the tie-in with Frank Lucci's adjacent platoon. Flanagan's position was the company's left flank, facing to the north, with the shallow stream barely twenty meters from his extreme-left position.

"If I was the Skipper I'd set up in a horseshoe shape and let the bastards walk right into it," Flanagan commented to Douglas as he alternately glanced at his contour map and the actual terrain.

"Where would you set it up?" Douglas asked.

"See how that draw funnels right into Second Platoon's position?" Flanagan asked.

"Yessir."

"I'd curl everything around that avenue," Flanagan said with a point. "If he's withdrawing, then the draw's the quickest way out for him. If he comes this way, according to the way Golf and Hotel will attack him, then we should see him in the draw sooner or later."

The ground reverberated from the intensive artillery barrage three klicks away.

"Get some!" Flanagan growled as he glanced at his watch. "Our Golf and Hotel brothers jump off in the attack in ten minutes, as soon as this prep lifts."

Douglas, his M-16 and his helmet in his hands, glanced over at Flanagan and nodded. "Good luck, Lieutenant."

Flanagan nodded in return. "Same, same. Let's do it."

Flanagan and the other platoon leaders were kept apprised of the developing action to the north by Capt. Lawrence, who monitored the radio traffic and remained in touch with Lt. Col. Urstadt. The Marines of Hotel and Golf Companies met stiff resistance at first, but after several hours of fighting and with the help of tactical air and artillery support, the enemy eventually began to buckle under the weight of the coordinated attack. The attack by the Marines from the west and north was designed to push the enemy to the south, into the blocking force, where the men of Fox Company waited in tense expectation.

Flanagan stood alongside Vasquez, his radio operator, in a chest-high fighting hole near the center of his platoon's sector. Their weapons and the PRC-25 radio were close at hand, as were several hand grenades stored along the dirt parapet. The attack by Golf and Hotel was gaining momentum, so contact with the first elements of the NVA force was felt to be imminent.

"Ever worry about dying, sir?" asked Vasquez.

267

Flanagan turned and noticed Vasquez's unusually tense expression. "Sure. I don't dwell on it, but I do think about it sometimes. Why?"

"Just wondering, that's all."

"Are you worrying about dying, Vasquez?" Flanagan asked, looking closely at the young Marine.

"Yessir. Not so much the actual dying part but, you know, about how it might happen and all."

"That's natural," said Flanagan. "If you go to a concert you think about music, right? Well, you go off to war and you think about fighting and maybe even dying. Same principle, I think. When it's all around you, you can't help but think of it. The trick is in not letting it overwhelm you."

"How you do that, sir?" asked Vasquez.

"By remembering two things: One, you have to accept the fact that you don't have full control over your destiny in combat; and two, that you have a job to do and other people are depending on you to do it."

Vasquez sighed. "I'm really having a bitch of a time with it today."

"Get over it," Flanagan said harshly.

"Sir?"

"Get over it, dammit, and that's a direct order! You've got an important job to do, and I can't afford to have you standing around out here waiting to die."

Vasquez was taken aback. He swallowed. "But I was just trying to—"

"I said snap out of it and get ready to do your job."

"I'll do my job, sir," Vasquez said defensively.

"You'd damn well better," Flanagan said with a hard look, "or I'll shoot you myself."

Flanagan stared at his young radioman a moment longer before his hard expression broke slightly, at which point Vasquez started giggling like a schoolboy.

There was sudden gunfire from up ahead as the lead elements of the enemy force ran into the first of the Fox Company positions. The firing was initially sporadic, then quickly escalated. Enemy rockets began exploding in and around the Marines, and soon the area was teeming with NVA. Marine mortars opened up from their positions to the rear. The 60mm rounds were bursting long of the target until an observer corrected the range and brought the rounds squarely onto the enemy.

Flanagan grabbed his M-16 and fired several bursts at the muzzle flashes he could see in the distant tree line. An occasional enemy rocket could be seen flashing out of the trees, followed by the deep, sharp concussion as it burst among the friendly positions. The firing seemed to Flanagan to be confined to the east of the shallow stream, and radio reports from his squad leaders confirmed his observation.

"Stand by for the air," Capt. Lawrence radioed.

The first of the two Marine F-4 Phantom jets came screaming in just over the treetops along an east-west axis. The fast-moving jet dropped a tumbling silver canister of napalm into the 500-meter buffer between the two Marine companies that the enemy had been pushed into. The second jet then made a similar approach and released its load. Both then made another low-level run but this time unleashed a torrent of rockets into the trees. The noise was deafening, the acrid smoke spreading as the two F-4s pulled up and away into the thick, low clouds. Still, enemy muzzles flashed from the tree line.

"We're taking fire from the left, across the stream," came a radio report from Cpl. Hughes on the extreme left flank.

Hughes maneuvered his men into a series of alternate positions along the stream and returned the enemy's fire, then reported to Flanagan that he was facing an estimated enemy squad. Hughes called several minutes later to revise his estimate to that of a platoon.

Flanagan's first instinct was to move out across the stream and attack, but Capt. Lawrence ordered him to keep 3rd Platoon in its position. Several shouts of "Corpsman" were overheard by Flanagan, and on more than one occasion he saw Doc Fackler carrying his medical gear and exposing himself to enemy fire on his way to tend to a stricken Marine. Hughes seemed in no immediate danger of being overrun, so Flanagan radioed his squad leaders and relayed the order to hold fast in the current position.

Flanagan noticed the kerosene odor of the napalm and the pungent smell of the scorched earth as the smoke drifted toward him. Two Huey Cobra gunships showed up overhead and fired rockets and miniguns at specific pockets of enemy troops. Flanagan looked up at one point and saw Lt. Col. Urstadt's command chopper. The NVA were still firing RPGs out of the tree line, one of which detonated close enough to Flanagan's fighting hole that it was several minutes before his hearing returned.

"Damn, that was close!" he read on Vasquez's lips.

The situation remained stable for another hour as helicopter gunships arrived on station to attack the enemy positions on the opposite side of the stream. The Cobra attacks lasted until dusk, after which Marine artillery rounds were fired into the enclave. By the time darkness fell, the sniping from across the stream had ended and the Fox Company position was quiet. The entire company immediately went to work on improving its fighting positions.

After dark, Capt. Lawrence gathered his platoon leaders at his command post—a lean-to constructed from foliage and ponchos—and reviewed under the light of two flashlights the summary he'd been provided by Lt. Col. Urstadt: Enemy losses thus far were 374 dead; over 600 weapons captured; a wide assortment of documents, food, munitions, and medical supplies had been taken. Marine losses were put at 38 dead and 122 wounded.

"We've wiped out an entire NVA battalion," Flanagan commented. "The Old Man's gotta be happy with that."

"He is," Capt. Lawrence replied. "But as usual, he wants more. He thinks we've got 'em by the short hairs now, that we can chase 'em down and finish 'em off."

"So what's next?" asked Flanagan.

"Patrols, patrols, and more patrols," said Lawrence. "Patrols out the friggin' ying-yang. And when we find 'em, we'll all pile on. We're going to push out to the west and try to find the last of the elements we made contact with today, while Golf heads east and Hotel stays in reserve."

"When do we jump off?" said Flanagan.

"Later tonight, after the troops have had some chow and a little more rest."

Flanagan nodded, agreeing that the tactically wise thing to do would be to keep up the pressure, but privately hoping that his weary Marines and their leader would have a chance to rest from the strain of the busy day.

"I can read it in your expression, Tom," Lawrence said. "You agree but you don't like it. Is that it?"

Flanagan shrugged. "Yessir, I suppose so. We're all dragging."

"But think of the other guy. He's not only tired, he's just about beaten."

Flanagan winced. "Yeah, I know. And it's the 'beaten' part that bothers me the most. If we run into him out there in the dark, we'll have our work cut out for us. The little bastards are never easy, but this may be especially difficult."

"I couldn't agree more," said Capt. Lawrence. "But if we can find him out there tonight and fix him and not let him slip away, we don't have to throw everything we've got at him. We can finish him in the morning."

"What if he's reinforced?" Lucci asked.

"Then I suppose we'll find that out in a helluva hurry, Frank. And we'll just have to adjust to the situation."

The three platoon leaders glanced quickly at one another but otherwise said nothing. Handley had a slight grin on his face which didn't escape Lawrence's notice.

"What the hell's so funny, Jay?" asked Lawrence.

"It's nothing, sir, really," Handley answered.

"You were damn well snickering. When one of my officers snickers at something I've said, why, I expect an explanation."

Flanagan quickly spoke up. "Skipper, I just think—"

The rocket exploded in the center of the Fox Company position. Then another blast followed. Then another. Marines could suddenly be heard shouting warnings and instructions nearby. Enemy mortars could be heard in the near distance, firing at the Marines. Automatic weapons began firing from both sides— the sharp cracking of the AK-47 and the deeper popping of the M-16—and an attack by the enemy was being launched at Fox Company's western flank.

"Somebody needs to tell these little assholes they're beaten," Flanagan said as he and the other platoon leaders grabbed their weapons and helmets and took off running for their various sectors.

The explosions were ripping into the position in reddish-orange flashes, followed instantly by the deafening concussion. Flanagan could see tracers carving up the night, snaking into and out of the perimeter. He expected to be shot or blown apart at any moment as he moved toward his sector, but he somehow found the fighting hole he shared with Vasquez even though an enemy rocket went by close enough for him to feel the heat from its exhaust. The dim light from a flare helped silhouette enough of the ground for him to find his way forward. His platoon was facing the brunt of the enemy assault from the west, from across the stream. He could hear shouting amid the gunfire and explosions, and not all of the commands were being shouted in English.

A mortar round fell within ten feet of Flanagan's position and momentarily deafened him. He glanced over to see that Vasquez was still okay just as another round exploded thirty feet behind them. Vasquez looked back at Flanagan and grinned a strange sort of grin, then rose and fired a burst from his M-16.

"We've got movement in the water," Cpl. Hughes radioed from his location near the stream's eastern bank. "Looks like about a platoon on the move."

Marine M-60 machine guns and automatic weapons opened up full blast and raked the NVA wading out across the stream. Flanagan looked up and saw in the light of several grenade explosions enemy soldiers moving toward his positions, some firing and some falling. The attack appeared confined to 3rd Platoon's sector, and there was apparently no enemy fire coming from any other direction. The enemy mortars lifted as the leading elements of their assault force crossed the stream and were met by Flanagan's Marines who remained covered and concealed in their fighting positions. NVA grenades and satchel charges exploded around the nearest friendly positions, but the withering fire was keeping the enemy from penetrating the perimeter's interior in any significant numbers. Vasquez shot an NVA soldier who was running nearby in a low crouch and firing his AK-47 at a target off to the side. The man gave a spasmodic jerk and fell over limply to the side, unmoving. Vasquez fired another burst into him just to make sure.

"They're still coming," Cpl. Hughes called amid the noise of battle only moments before an enemy satchel charge exploded in his fighting hole, killing his radio operator and seriously wounding Hughes. "I don't see any end to 'em yet."

Illumination was supplied by a nearby Marine artillery battery, but the initial rounds were well behind the position and took several minutes for the observer to adjust to where the light was to their front. Several other NVA soldiers who succeeded in penetrating the perimeter were shot and killed. At one point when Flanagan and Vasquez were both bent down changing the magazines in their rifles, an enemy soldier who was running nearby was shot just outside their hole. Flanagan felt and heard the thump when the wounded man fell over hard and moaned. The enemy soldier was still attempting to crawl forward with his weapon at the ready when Flanagan raised his head and noticed the movement. A quick burst from no more than six feet away ended the man's movement.

Cpl. Hughes continued to provide Flanagan with situation reports, though his wounds were greatly weakening him. He was hit in the head, face, and arm. "They're still coming across," he called in a weak voice.

Capt. Lawrence moved two squads forward from Lt. Lucci's platoon to reinforce Flanagan's sector, adding additional firepower at the point of the attack. There were isolated exchanges where Marines and NVA troops were firing at each other at close range, but for the most part the integrity of the perimeter was being maintained. Sgt. Douglas radioed a report to Flanagan that the NVA were no longer moving across the stream.

"Get the heavy stuff on 'em," Douglas called. "They're breaking up and heading back to the west."

The firing lessened considerably as the NVA left behind a small covering force to protect their withdrawal. The first of the artillery blasts came dropping into the enemy within minutes, the deadly explosions in full view of the Fox Company Marines who were still alert and hunkered down in their holes.

"We need a medevac in here," Douglas radioed.

"Roger, it's already on the way," Flanagan replied.

Corpsmen attended to the several wounded right up until the CH-46 was guided into the rear of the position by the light of a flashlight. Thirteen wounded and five dead were lifted out, while another eight lesser-wounded men remained in the field.

Sgt. Douglas found Flanagan after the chopper had left amid a blast of noise and wind.

"Corporal Hughes was still hanging on," Flanagan noted. "Doc says he's got a decent chance."

"He's one seriously tough dude," Douglas commented. "There must be fifteen or twenty NVA piled up within ten meters either side of his hole. They came the wrong damn way when they came across Hughes. He was still firing away, with his head all bloodied up, when I got over there to him."

Later, Flanagan returned to his hole after a short meeting with Capt. Lawrence where he learned that the company would remain in place, at fifty-percent alert for the rest of the night, and then resume patrolling the next morning.

"Get some sleep," Flanagan said to Vasquez. "I'll wake you in three hours."

Vasquez slumped down in the hole and tried to get comfortable. "You know, sir, you're getting too short for this happy horseshit," he said almost as an afterthought. Within minutes he was sound asleep.

Flanagan kept the radio's handset near his ear as he looked out into the dark. You're right, Vasquez, he mused in full agreement. There were enemy bodies nearby whose prostrate forms he could only barely see. There was blood on the ground, and there had been death and violence in this place by the truckload. Yet somehow he had come through again. He was unscathed, apart from some ringing in his ears. And Vasquez had likewise come through it, who hours earlier had foreseen his own death. But there had to be a limit, Flanagan thought. There had to be a ledger, a final settlement. And while it was certainly random and without quantification, there was also the idea of exposure. The more exposure, the greater the chance; the greater the chance, the shorter the average life-span. Flanagan winced, and then set about trying to squeeze out the darker images with the soothing thoughts of home. He could be thankful once again that he was alive, that he would soon enough be boarding the Freedom Bird and flying off to The World. Yep, Vasquez, he thought. You're right. I'm *way* too short for this nonsense.

The remainder of the night passed peacefully.

Flanagan gave the order to move out of the position early the next morning after counting nearly sixty enemy bodies in the immediate area.

"Easy does it, Lieutenant," Douglas advised. "We've got the new guy Murray on the point, and he's boocoo green."

Flanagan looked up from his map and nodded. They were standing off to the side and out of earshot of the others. "What do you think the odds are that we'll make contact today?" Flanagan asked.

"Decent," Douglas said after a moment. "I'd say seventy-thirty, in one form or another. What about you, sir?"

"I feel lucky today. I'm gonna say forty-sixty."

"I hope you're right. Maybe these ornery gooks will drift south today and fight with the friggin' Army. It'd be okay with me."

They had been on the move for perhaps thirty minutes when the point came upon a small path in the thickly overgrown area, and immediately called a halt. Flanagan, who was positioned near the front, quickly moved forward and inspected the trail. He sent two men across who scouted the area to either side and then signaled the okay back to Flanagan, who then started the movement again. The platoon moved across the trail and back into the dense foliage for a hundred meters before the vegetation thinned somewhat and visibility improved up ahead to perhaps seventy-five meters. The point and two others had already moved into a wide ravine when Flanagan looked around at the terrain and had an inexplicably ominous sensation. Something's not right here, he thought, his heart pounding rapidly. Dammit to hell, something's wrong. He held up his hand and stopped those behind him and then quickly moved forward to halt the point in time enough for a quick map reference.

It was quiet. It seemed the quietest place in Vietnam, he thought. What's wrong here? What the hell's wrong?

He kept looking out, scanning, straining to see. Something. Anything. The sweat drops fell steadily off his nose and chin. What the hell's wrong with this place?

"What's the matter, sir?" the young point man asked, eyes wide.

"I'm not sure. This draw's too damned wide, too much like a funnel. Have you seen or heard anything?" Flanagan said.

"No sir. Nothing."

Flanagan kept straining to see ahead. His senses of sight, hearing, and smell were working in overdrive. C'mon, he thought. Show me something. Give me something. Anything. C'mon, you bastards, I know you're there.

"What do you want me to do, sir?" the point man asked, suddenly confused and unnerved by his platoon leader's hesitation.

"This ain't right," Flanagan said, shaking his head. "No way. No goddamn way."

"Sir?"

Flanagan turned and looked at the point man, and as he did so cleared his throat slightly, as if returning from a trance. "Okay, listen up. We'll hold here until we can get a fire team on either side of this thing and see what's what. Dammit, I just don't like the look and feel of it."

Captain Lawrence soon radioed from further back of the halted column and asked about the nature of the delay.

"It just doesn't look right," was all Flanagan could think of to respond. He turned to the nearby fire team leader. "Okay, get 'em across and check it out."

Flanagan waited a moment before starting out across the draw. Nothing unusual was being observed by the fire team, and the column was set to move out again.

The very next moment Flanagan was violently blown into the air by the force of a command-detonated booby trap—a mortar shell—that exploded nearby and severed his right leg above the knee. It also perforated his right eardrum and peppered him in the lower torso with several small fragments. The enemy ambushers then opened up with small-arms fire, instantly killing the point man and two others, then spraying the column from the left side of the ravine. Sgt. Douglas ran forward and began directing a squad in an attempt to flank the enemy soldiers, estimated at first as a squad. Douglas gasped when he looked up ahead and saw Flanagan on the ground, his right leg nothing more than a ragged red stump.

"Shit. *Shit!*"

Another enemy bullet hit Flanagan in the hip, while still another blew off the ring finger of his right hand. Still another burst kicked up the dirt around his missing leg. Flanagan's body shook, his hand then reached for his weapon but it wasn't there. Flanagan rolled onto his side and saw Vasquez nearby, shot in both legs and writhing in pain. An enemy grenade burst nearby, peppering Vasquez with hot fragments. Flanagan managed to crawl to Vasquez's side where he noticed the shrapnel wounds to Vasquez's head, Flanagan wriggled out of his own flak vest and used it to shield his radioman's head and neck. Behind him, Flanagan saw two NVA soldiers moving toward him, firing their weapons as they advanced. Flanagan quickly grabbed the M-16 beside Vasquez, sat up and thrust his bloody stump of a leg into the ground for balance, and began firing at the closest NVA. The enemy soldier toppled forward and fell, barely ten feet from Flanagan. The second NVA soldier stood and fired an aimed shot that struck Flanagan in the chest, between the collarbone and left nipple, driving him backwards as if he'd been hit with a sledgehammer. Multiple gunshots from nearby Marines then killed the NVA before he could fire another shot.

Flanagan tried unsuccessfully to rise and get back into the fight. Sgt. Douglas, who shouted at Flanagan to stay down, got up and sprinted to his downed platoon leader, firing his weapon and being covered by the stepped-up fire of his fellow Marines.

What's happening to me, Flanagan thought as he struggled to right himself. He smelled the odor of burned flesh and rightly reckoned it was his own. He could hear shouting, but he couldn't understand what was being said.

Then he recognized Sgt. Douglas.

Flanagan glanced up at Douglas upon the latter's arrival. He heard the noise and felt the reverberation from Douglas's M-16 as it fired, noticing the spent cartridge cases coming down at him, as if in slow motion, like barrels over a river falls. He wanted to shout at Douglas to get away, but he was gasping and having difficulty breathing. He coughed and frothy pink blood sprayed from his mouth. He felt numbed and in shock. He vaguely realized where he was and what was happening around him, but he had a limited understanding of what had happened *to* him. He continued to smell smoke and blood and burned flesh, he felt nauseated, and when he tried to raise his head and look over the rest of him, Douglas pushed his head down forcefully. Red smoke from a smoke grenade, thrown into the ravine by a Marine to obscure their downed mates from the enemy riflemen, started drifting by.

There was shouting, Douglas was shouting, and then Flanagan saw Douglas recoil when the first enemy bullet struck him in the groin. Douglas ignored his own wound, changed magazines and kept firing, and Flanagan once again saw the spent cartridge cases ejecting.

Get out of here, Flanagan thought he was shouting to Douglas. *Get the hell away from here.*

Everywhere there was firing. Another grenade exploded nearby. Flanagan thought he heard himself screaming over the firing. *What's the situation here? Who else is hit?* Douglas kept firing, his hands bloody from touching his own wounds, the blood smeared across and dripping from the fresh magazine in his weapon. Flanagan heard Douglas shouting, "Corpsman, corpsman!"

Flanagan then heard Douglas shouting, "I need some ammo up here," and noticed when Douglas' head recoiled backwards. He then felt Douglas' body fall across him, heavily, shielding him, as his platoon sergeant was struck in the forehead. Flanagan felt Douglas' warm blood spilling onto his bare arm as he fought to breathe and remain conscious.

"Corpsman," Flanagan tried desperately to shout. Douglas was hit badly, he knew, and needed immediate medical attention. He wasn't certain that Douglas was still breathing, and knew only that his own breathing was shallow and labored. The smoke was so thick now that only Douglas was visible to him. "Corpsman," he gasped once again. *Oh God, is this it? Is this finally it?*

Oh God help me, Flanagan shouted in his mind. He couldn't seem to breathe, couldn't move. Everything was red now, as if he were floating away on a lake of blood.

Dear God help me. Please help me.

There was still firing, lots of firing. But from where? And by whom? There was another frag grenade, then more firing. The ground shook with battle so close at hand.

Where's the radio? Can anyone hear me? Where's my platoon? What's happening to me? I can't breathe. I can't find my weapon. Am I about to die? Is Sgt. Douglas dead? Are we all gonna die here?

Flanagan's eyes rolled back as all the noise seemed to coalesce into a continuous stream, undistinguishable, incoherent. He moaned inaudibly, unaware of any pain and only barely conscious. He wanted desperately to resist, to remain in the fight. He tried to push Sgt. Douglas away, to find his weapon, *any* weapon, but he felt powerless and weightless, as if he were floating. He thought of his men, and of the orders they awaited at that very moment. He then thought of home, and he briefly saw the faces of his parents, sister, brother, and Jill. He tried again to move, but his limbs were unresponsive. He struggled to take a deep breath, but couldn't under the weight of the unmoving Douglas. He attempted to make sense of what was happening—of what had already happened—as he fell deeper and deeper into the darkening red abyss.

Oh merciful God save us!

The last sensation Flanagan experienced before finally losing consciousness was that of Sgt. Douglas' body recoiling at being hit with another burst.

Then suddenly the echoes faded and everything became still and quiet.

CHAPTER TWENTY
Alexandria, Virginia

"The Secretary of Defense regrets to inform you . . ."

Kate Flanagan listened as her mother read through the contents of the telegram and the shocking news of Tommy's multiple fragmentation and bullet wounds, as well as the loss of his right leg. His condition was critical but stable, and he was scheduled for transfer from Da Nang to the naval hospital in Yokosuka, Japan, within a week.

"Oh dear God, *no*!" was Kate's shocked response to the news.

Mother and daughter were both weeping by the time the conversation had ended. At least he's alive, they both agreed in consolation. At least he'll be able to live a normal life.

"Oh Tommy, no," was all Kate could manage to say, almost pleading, after hanging up the phone. She sat down at the kitchen table and went over again in her mind her mother's reading of the telegram. She tried to imagine what her brother was now dealing with, what he looked like, how he was accepting it. Like her nurse mother, she was deeply troubled over the chest and abdominal wounds and their life-threatening potential, far more so than the loss of the leg. She was aware of the war's high incidence of single and even multiple limb loss, and she knew from her mother's comments that the advances in prosthetic devices over the past few years was highly encouraging. If Tommy could only hang on and live, she thought, if he could heal in all the places he still had, he would eventually get over the one he had lost.

Easy for me to say, Kate thought a moment later. A vibrant young man dealing with the loss of a leg would be no easy chore even under the least complicated of circumstances. But he's alive—a gift that so many other young men had been denied. God, if he's not all there, at least he's alive.

He's alive! But he's still in great danger.

Kate had just that week moved into her own place in the greater D.C area and was currently considering job offers from her former ad-agency employer as well as the senatorial staff of Sen. George McGovern, for whom Dan Marinelli had recently gone to work. The McCarthy people had also put out teelers, but her former fiancé was still active in his presidential campaign, and Kate had wisely rejected their overtures. She had been walking out the door of her Alexandria, Virginia apartment for a late lunch with an employment-agency representative when the call from her mother had come.

She canceled her appointment.

Kate called Dan Marinelli and asked if he could help her find out more about her brother's case. She wanted more than a telegram, and her mother was working the same angle with her physician contacts in Chicago.

"I've got to know more, Dan," she said, the pleading in her voice creating an even greater sense of urgency.

"I'll do what I can. Give me an hour or so," Dan replied.

Kate then called a physician friend in Maryland who had been a Robert Kennedy supporter, and went over the news and the likely medical implications and possibilities. Calm down, Kate, the doctor had told her. Let's first find out what we're dealing with and not jump to any conclusions. We can only speculate at this point, and loose speculation is by no means sound medical diagnosis. If you can find out more, call me back, he had suggested. But it's important to remember, the doctor reiterated, that he's alive. Tommy's alive, and right now that's got to be enough.

She agreed. He's alive. We'll know more later.

Dan Marinelli showed up at her apartment barely an hour later.

"He's still alive," Dan emphasized. "He can get through this. He's *gonna* get through this. You've both got the same Flanagan genes, and I know enough about you to know all I need to know about him and his chances of making it. He'll make it through this, Kate, and you'll have him back here again, you wait and see."

"He won't be coming back with everything he left with," Kate said spitefully.

"He *will* come back. Right now that's got to be all that matters."

Kate took a deep breath and announced, "We've got to start calling."

"Calling? Who are you going to call?"

"The Red Cross. The Marine Corps. The Navy medical service. Our congressman from Chicago. Dammit, Tommy's attending physician at the naval hospital in Yokosuka, Japan, if I have to! I want to know exactly what my brother's condition is; I want to know what treatment they're administering and what prognosis they're making; I want to know each and every bit of information related to his case and I want to know it *right damn now!*"

"That may not be so easy," Dan said softly.

"I don't care. It'll be far more difficult to keep me from getting at it."

Dan shrugged and nodded. "All right then. We'll start calling."

"They *did* this to him, and the very *least* they can do is to provide me with a detailed explanation of his condition. I hope they're happy. I just hope the hell they're—"

"Kate."

"Yessirree, I hope they're satisfied. And I want to know the qualifications of those doctors and the whole—"

"Kate, stop! Those doctors have a lot of experience in treating combat wounds. They're seeing it and dealing with it every day with a whole *lot* of people. And nobody's individually responsible for this. Your brother's a Marine infantry officer and his injuries were an act of war. Now stop it."

Kate slammed the phone book down on a table and then said in utter resignation, "My God, Dan, this is what's been happening all over the country for all these years now, to all of those families out there just like mine. All of those families, all over this country, all those young men. And if it keeps up, if it doesn't stop, there eventually won't *be* any young men in this country."

Kate was nearly hyperventilating when she lowered her head and wept.

Dan quickly got up and embraced her, only to be abruptly pushed away. He reached for her again, holding her tightly and eventually calming her. Kate gathered herself after a few moments, and they immediately set about trying to work their way through the labyrinth of Navy administration. After two hours of frustration and seeming obstruction they had produced nothing meaningful. Kate swept a pile of papers off the kitchen table in a fit of anger.

"I've gotta know *more*, dammit!" she said with fiery eyes and clenched teeth.

Fifteen minutes later, Kate's father called to tell her that her mother had succeeded in establishing what would likely turn out to be some important contacts.

* * *

Two days later, a South Carolina relative of Ruby Douglas, having tracked Kate first through Sen. Ted Kennedy's office and then eventually through a series of contacts ending with Dan Marinelli, called with the news of David Douglas' death in Vietnam.

CHAPTER TWENTY ONE
Los Angeles

Kate Flanagan stood underneath the green cemetery canopy at the gravesite of Sgt. David Douglas, USMC, and glanced toward the front row where Ruby Douglas sat with her two young daughters. The Navy chaplain, in his crisp white uniform, spoke in soft tones about sacrifice and dedication, about honor and courage and selflessness and commitment. David's coffin was draped with the bright colors of the American flag, and there was a Marine honor guard nearby in dress blues. The Southern California weather was sunny and warm, with clear blue skies above the puff of white clouds on the horizon. Birds were singing in the background, and a gentle breeze swept along the slight rise dotted with the numerous gray markers. Several dozen mourners were standing respectfully around and behind the family, some of whom had come from as far away as South Carolina to honor this young man who had laid down his life in service to his country.

Kate, in black dress and hat, stood poised and erect as she listened to the words of the minister. She kept glancing at Ruby, with Becky and Jessie beside their mother on either side, leaning on her and holding her arms. Their hiccupy sobbing had finally quieted, their fright eased, and they both looked as exhausted as they were confounded by the circumstances of the past few days. Kate could only barely comprehend how nightmarish those recent days and nights had been for Ruby and the girls.

It just didn't seem possible, Kate kept thinking. But her remembrance of her mother's reading of the telegram announcing her brother's wounding, and now the sight of the flag and the smell of cut flowers and freshly dug earth, reminded her of the hard, irrevocable truth.

Her brother was seriously wounded and Ruby's son was gone.

Ruby had mentioned to Kate at the funeral home on the previous evening about David's last letter, which had arrived that same morning. Ruby explained how he had expected soon to get his official orders to Officers Candidate School, about how bright his future would be with a military career in the Marines. His combat experience and his decorations would help him get ahead, he had related, and his evaluation from Lt. Flanagan had been exemplary. Things were definitely shaping up, David had written, and all that stood between him and a mouthful of his mother's fine cooking was now down to a handful of months.

And then, the dreadful notice that he was Killed in Action.

Kate noticed when little Jessie started to cry again but was calmed with a whisper and a reassuring embrace from her mother. The older Becky was still silent, but Kate could see that she was only barely holding back her tears.

The chaplain concluded his remarks with a reading from Psalms and a brief prayer. Kate watched when Marines of the honor guard came forward and, with white gloves, folded the flag into a tight triangle with the stars up. The flag was then presented by a Marine officer to Ruby, who graciously accepted it, placed it in her lap, then leaned and quietly spoke to each of the girls. The girls nodded and then leaned forward and placed their small hands upon their mother's, atop the flag. Ruby continued to sit up straight, her head erect and her eyes moist but alert.

Tears coursed steadily from Kate Flanagan's eyes as she stood and watched her courageous friend and her two precious daughters cope with their immense sorrow. She ached inside, for a woman and a family she only barely knew and for a man she had never met. But her aching was real, piercing hot and deep within her. She didn't know what to say, what to do, other than to let the tears drip from her cheeks and moisten the ground where she stood, combining with other tears from other mourners in leaving a part of themselves upon the hallowed earth that was Sgt. David Douglas' final resting place.

It was only through Ruby's loss that Kate at last came to comprehend what she and her family had gained.

Marines with M-16 rifles loaded with blank cartridges then formed into a line and made ready to fire their salute to their fallen brother. A tall, decorated Marine gunnery sergeant, the lines and creases of his well-traveled face setting him apart from his more youthful charges, called out the appropriate commands in a voice moderated for the occasion.

"Ready, aim, fire."

"Aim, fire."

"Aim, fire."

CHAPTER TWENTY TWO
Great Lakes Naval Hospital, Chicago

He was home, finally.

"And in one piece, sorta," Tom Flanagan told his parents by phone as soon as he had arrived at the hospital and been assigned to a ward. "A little less agile, mind you, but I'm back in The World."

They had hurried to visit him early the next morning in an emotional reunion at the big naval hospital. The long flight from Japan aboard the specially equipped Air Force C-141 had made a refueling stop in Alaska where, upon landing, the new nursing crew had greeted the returning wounded with an early morning "Welcome to the USA" toast of juice and coffee.

"Thank God," Flanagan had said with misty eyes and a sigh of weighty relief undoubtedly shared by the other returning wounded.

It was late by the time he had arrived by ambulance at the hospital. Even in his exhaustion he had still needed a sedative to sleep, but he had awakened refreshed and alert. There were fellow Marines nearby in the ward—one a lieutenant who had lost both legs at the trunk, the other a captain who had been shot in the lower spine and paralyzed from the waist down.

"You're privileged to be among the ass kickers and the name takers," the paraplegic captain had advised Flanagan on the latter's first morning. "We have to be a little more imaginative with the ass-kicking part, but we still get the job done."

Flanagan had grinned and retorted, "Glad to be aboard, Skipper. I stand ready to take up the march."

"And if you can't keep up with us," the lieutenant had added, smiling, "we'll have little choice but to cut your hair and send you back to Vietnam."

"What a nice thought," Flanagan had said, laughing. "The one all-expense-paid trip to Southeast Asia that I've already been given will hold me for this lifetime, gents. But thanks just the same."

His parents spent a full morning with him and then came back later in the afternoon, this time accompanied by his younger brother, Chris. They brought magazines, newspapers, writing materials, photos, fruit, a transistor radio with ear piece, gum and hard candy, an order of cheeseburgers and fries from beneath the golden arches, and a dozen or so letters from Vietnam from his Fox Company companions who had written to him at his parents' Chicago home. Flanagan quickly looked through the letters to see if one might have Jill's Milwaukee return address, but there was nothing.

Still, it was wonderful to be with family again. He noticed that his mother and father were discreet in their glances at his bandaged stump, but Chris couldn't keep his eyes off it. Chris would occasionally look up and meet his brother's eyes, then quickly turn away in embarrassment only to cut another quick glance at the stump a moment later.

"It's okay, Chris," Flanagan finally said.

"I'm sorry, Tommy," he said sincerely. "I didn't mean to stare."

The parents shifted uncomfortably.

"Chris," Flanagan said softly, "and you too, Mom and Dad, if you want to look at my leg, if you want to ask me about it, if you want to look at my chest or my hand or my gut or my butt or any place else, then for cryin' out loud go ahead and look."

"Tommy, really, we—"

"It's okay, Dad. It's just me down here. I'm the same, honest. I just look a little different. And I'm not bothered by the fact that you guys can't help but notice it. Heck, if I could look down on myself, I'd probably stare too."

His mother leaned over and tearfully embraced him. His father and brother also moved closer, and the tension and awkwardness lessened considerably.

His mother Elaine scrutinized his bandaged hand with her nurse's critical eye, then pushed the sheet back and examined his hip. "Gluteus-max tissue only, right? No damage to the pelvis or coccyx?"

"No, none," said Flanagan. "It got me flush in the cheek, and it couldn't have been better placed, except for the stigma attached to it. You know, the stuff about a Marine getting shot in the ass, and all that," he said, drawing a slight smile from his father and a loud laugh from his brother.

"How many intestinal punctures were there?" asked Elaine.

"Couple or three, I think. No biggie. They closed 'em all and then treated for infection," said Flanagan.

Elaine's eyebrows raised. "I was told eight punctures. Are your ears healing okay? Can you hear all right?"

"What's that you say, nurse?" he said, holding his cupped hand to his ear.

"And the collapsed lung? Any more problems there?"

"Nope. The docs inflated it back like a balloon. It's working like a champ."

She smiled and ran her hand through his hair.

Flanagan smiled. "Did you call overseas, Mom?"

Elaine smiled back. "One of our physicians on staff knows a surgeon down at Cook County who's in the Navy Reserves, and he was kind enough to get us in touch with the right people."

"Would you believe your mother orchestrated your entire treatment plan, son?" John said with a wink.

"Yeah," Flanagan said, laughing, "Now I know why they shipped me home a week ahead of schedule. They got me out of there before that Elaine Flanagan lady called again from Chicago with a clipboard full of instructions."

They all laughed.

Father Mike visited later and brought Flanagan a small Bible, a Cubs cap, and a get-well card signed by members of the church staff. Before leaving, he glanced around quickly and then slipped Flanagan four small airline bottles of whiskey.

"I thought you might enjoy these," the priest said in a lowered voice. "Anyway, you've certainly earned them, my young friend."

Flanagan smiled and thanked the priest.

After Father Mike had left, Flanagan summoned a nurse and requested three glasses of water for himself and his two nearby companions. When the water had been delivered and the nurse had returned to her station, Flanagan grinned at the captain and the lieutenant and tossed each a bottle of whiskey.

"I've been instructed by a family friend to enjoy these," Flanagan said in an exaggerated whisper. "And I prefer not to drink alone."

"Honest to God," the lieutenant said, "I was just this minute thinking that what I really needed was a little liquid refreshment."

The two men emptied their bottles into the glasses, stirred it with their fingers, then paused and looked toward Flanagan.

Flanagan took a deep breath and held up his glass. He said in a voice that suddenly began to fill with emotion, "Gentlemen, to the finest Marine I've ever had the privilege of serving with; to the man who saved my life and lost his own in the process; to Sergeant David Douglas, United States Marine Corps. May God rest his soul."

The others raised their glasses. "Sergeant Douglas."

With tears already forming in his eyes, Flanagan took a sip and then leaned back on his pillow.

* * *

Flanagan had been moved outside in a wheelchair, underneath the morning shade of an oak tree, dressed in blue pajamas and robe, along with the Cubs cap from Father Mike. There were several other patients nearby, some with visitors, but it was mostly quiet. Except for the stiffness in his hip and the dull ache in his chest, he was reasonably comfortable as he listened to the birds and enjoyed the mild, steady breeze against his face. He had immediately noticed the wind blowing against the empty leg of his pajamas, but he decided to enjoy what he had, rather than dwell on what was gone forever. The blue waters of Lake Michigan were shimmering, the white-sailed vessels dotting the surface and trailing their wakes in what appeared to be a distant slow motion. He turned his radio on low to his favorite Chicago AM station and heard for the first time the hit song *This Guy's in Love with You.*

He was home, finally. He couldn't breathe enough of the magnificent Chicago air or enjoy enough of the lake or the radio stations or all other things Chicago. Not quite all of him had returned, and certainly not in the ideal manner in which he had visualized his homecoming during so many lonely days and nights in Vietnam. But he was home and, given what he had so recently experienced and somehow survived, given the condition of his two new, uncomplaining friends in the ward, given the fate of Sgt. Douglas and so many others he had known and served with, he was content to be home at all.

He had been wrapped inside a blanket of dark melancholy on the previous evening. A disheartened Flanagan had related to Father Mike how he had prayed often and hard about following the will of God, only to conclude that His apparent will had been a trip to Vietnam to be blown apart and nearly killed in what was now a divisive and unpopular war. Father Mike had given Flanagan a piece of paper at the bottom of which he had written "Romans 8:28" and "II Corinthians 12:9-10," with his suggestion to drink in the passages and trust in the message.

Tears had formed in Flanagan's eyes when Father Mike had smiled and clasped his hand. "It's a bonus, Tom," the priest had told him with a wise nod. "Your being here, your being spared is a bonus. Look at it that way for the rest of your days."

And he was so right, Flanagan concluded as he looked out at the dazzling lake. It really is a bonus.

Father Mike had also spoken about adversity, about the resiliency of the human body and the profound capacity of the human spirit to endure and overcome. Especially the human spirit, he had emphasized. Flanagan had lain awake for hours considering the words of Father Mike and the scriptures he had provided, and how those words so aptly fit the circumstances of his life now. Flanagan felt in his robe for the piece of paper Father

Mike had given him. On it were written the words of Theodore Roosevelt.

"It's not the critic who counts; nor the one who points out how the strong stumbled, or where the doer of deeds could have done better. The credit belongs to those in the arena; who strive valiantly; who fail and come up short again and again; who know great enthusiasm and great devotion; who at best know in the end the triumph of high achievement; and who, at the worst, if they fail, at least fail while daring greatly, so that their place shall never be with those timid souls who know neither victory nor defeat."

He folded the paper and slid it back into the pocket of his robe. He took a deep breath and let his thoughts drift back to Vietnam, to his men, to their unselfishness and sacrifice. He thought briefly of the causes of the war, of the politics, but then his thoughts returned to his men—the young Marines who had bled and wept and hurt. And as he thought of Sgt. Douglas, he pondered how some of his Marines had also given their last full measure.

"Lieutenant, could I bring you a cup of fresh coffee?"

An attractive Navy nurse of the same rank as he walked up alongside his chair. "Might help cut this wind a little, huh?" she added softly.

He took a refreshing breath and gathered himself, coughing slightly to allow the lump in his throat to ebb.

"I'd love some coffee, yes," he finally answered, then slipping into his best accent and adding, "and would ya' be so kind as to put a wee drop of Irish whiskey in it for me, darlin' dear? It's the old bones, ya' know."

"I'll bring you a blanket, Tom, but no booze."

"You're a hard woman, Ellen," he said, reaching out and taking her hand. "A good woman, yes, but a hard one. And from the faint whisper of that delicate Southern accent, probably a Baptist one, at that. But listen, dear, can't you make an exception and take a little pity on a broken down old Marine who'll be sitting up there on a sidewalk on State Street in the freezing cold, selling pencils from an old tin can, as soon as you and your people have finished with him and thrown him out the door?"

"I'll do the same for you on State Street as I'll do here: Coffee, yes; a blanket, yes; but definitely no booze."

"Coffee will be sufficient, nurse," Flanagan said in mock stiffness. As she walked away grinning, he felt for the small bottle in the pocket of his robe. "Use my own, then," he mumbled, adding a defiant sniff.

Flanagan glanced over and saw Lt. Henry Lambright, the double amputee from his ward, spending time with his wife, Sharon, and their two-year-old daughter, Lily. Henry was holding the young girl in his lap as he sat in his wheelchair, his lovely wife watching alongside from a folding chair.

Wonder how that'll work out? Flanagan thought. Not all of these stories, he knew, would have happy endings. An attractive, vibrant, healthy young woman might have to reconsider being with a man whose limbs had been blown away, maybe other parts of him blown away, important parts. Nope, he thought. Not all of these cases will be the "happily ever after" sort. But, he thought as he watched the Lambrights enjoy their visit, it would be great if this little family could somehow remain intact.

His mind wandered as he thought of the grievously wounded men in this and other hospitals, and of the thousands of war dead already resting in cemeteries across the nation. When would it all end? *How* would it all end? And *then* what? He wondered if a memorial to their sacrifice and service might ever be constructed, like the ones he'd seen on the Civil War battlefields when he'd been stationed in Virginia. If a Vietnam obelisk was ever erected in downtown Chicago, he pondered, would the bums and the anti-war types urinate on it, albeit for different reasons, but still defiling the place and leaving it smelling of piss? *Thanks for your glorious service . . . (unzip) tinkle, tinkle, belch, fart (zip) . . . you baby killers and misguided fools.* He chuckled softly at such a thought before dismissing it with a shake of his head.

Then the nagging returned. It was deep within him, dark and deep, and he was only able to suppress it during parts of the day, but very little of the night. It crept up and ate at him like a virus, especially when he saw a beautiful woman or heard a soft female voice. The temptation to do little more than constantly think of Jill was always strong, but coincidental with any thoughts of Jill were those abysmal doubts that seeped up out of the cracks of that bleak, foul pit of self-pity he tried so valiantly to keep tightly sealed. Self-pity could destroy him, he could already see, and the examples of the two brave men in the ward had been nothing short of a blessing. But, he also greatly feared, pursuing Jill further would likely be an exercise in futility, given his current circumstances.

"Here's your coffee, Lieutenant."

He pulled the bill of his cap down low and stared out at the lake, fearing his reddened eyes might expose him. He accepted the Styrofoam cup with a nod of thanks, but he realized there was something different—the voice, the sleeve, the faint odor of the perfume—and when he turned and looked up, he saw the most beautiful smile he had seen in a very long time.

"Kate!"

The coffee spilled as Kate grabbed and hugged him. Flanagan laughed and held the cup away from him, then reached for her and held her with one arm, tightly, until he could feel the moisture from Kate's tears against his face. When they separated and he leaned back and got a good look at her, she was smiling and crying and laughing and beautiful.

"I didn't think you'd be here for a couple more days," he said while she fumbled through her purse for a tissue.

"I couldn't stay away. I caught the red-eye first thing this morning," she said with a giggle and a point at her eyes. "I grabbed a cab at O'Hare and came straight here."

The nurse Ellen brought a folding chair for Kate and a towel with which Flanagan could dry himself. Flanagan introduced the two women.

"He's told me all about you," Ellen said, "and about how you worked in Bobby Kennedy's campaign. You must've seen so much in the past few months."

"Yes, I did," Kate said, smiling and then nodding toward Flanagan, "but nowhere near as much as my favorite older brother."

Flanagan reached for Kate's hand after Ellen excused herself and left. "God, I'm glad you're here."

They made small talk for several minutes, about the weather, the family, and the hospital, until they finally paused and looked at one another in silence.

Kate smiled. "I'm glad you're finally home, big brother. Those were some long days while you were away."

They embraced again.

She glanced at his bandaged leg. "I'm so sorry. I can't imagine what that must be like. But I hoped and prayed for so long that you'd make it home, I don't care what's missing or damaged as long as you're back here alive."

She leaned across and rested her head on his shoulder.

"I'm glad you got rid of that hack Everett, sis," he said in a benevolent tone. "Smartest thing you could've done."

She snickered. "I knew that was coming. And I can just imagine how you took *that* little piece of news."

"I really wanted to kick his ass."

"I'm well aware of that. Always was, to be honest."

"I'd still like to," Flanagan said with a defiant cock of his head.

She raised up and gave him an odd look. He glanced first at his missing leg and then back at her, finally grinning and causing them both to laugh loudly for several moments.

"Thank God it's still you," Kate said, reaching out and hugging him once again.

Nurse Ellen brought two more cups of coffee and then discreetly slipped away. Flanagan sipped his coffee but otherwise sat quietly for several moments, enjoying his sister's presence.

"So," he said after a deep breath and a shift in his chair, "tell me everything that's gone on in your life for the past year."

Kate grinned and then began with, "Well, let's see," before starting the chronology of her life's most recent major events. She spoke of her ad-agency work, and then of her recruitment by the Kennedy campaign and the long hours and excitement of the primaries. She talked about her meeting and developing a friendship with Ruby Douglas. She spoke sorrowfully of the dreadful events of the assassination and the end of the campaign. And finally she turned upbeat over the news of her recent decision to accept a position with the Democratic National Committee, and how she will continue to remain in Washington.

"So you've decided to stay involved in politics?" Flanagan asked.

"Yeah," she said, cocking her head sideways and smiling. "I've had a taste of it and now it's in my blood. It's tremendously satisfying."

"Will you be disappointed when Nixon goes to the White House?"

She slapped at his arm in mock anger. "If that happens, hell yes, I will. But don't worry, dear, the only way he'll see the Oval Office is when he's called up there by a Democrat president for a social visit."

"Will it be Humphrey?" Flanagan asked.

"Yeah, it looks like it now."

"And the convention will be here in Chicago in a few weeks, right?"

"Right here in the Windy City," Kate said.

"Will you be coming back?"

"You bet. I wouldn't miss it for the world, especially now with you being back home."

He glanced up at her, his eyes becoming misty again. "Mom told me about your going out to California for Sergeant Douglas' funeral. I can't tell you how much that meant to me, to know that you were there."

Kate nodded, smiling softly. "Ruby's a remarkable lady. I'm sure her son was equally exceptional."

"He was, yes," said Flanagan, staring out at the lake but with the image of his platoon sergeant firmly fixed in his mind. "He was the best Marine I ever saw. Maybe someday I can meet his mother."

There was a long silence as Flanagan sat with shoulders slumped, staring out emptily and remembering only disjointed fragments of a day that ended one life and forever changed another. Finally Kate reached over and ran her hand along her brother's arm.

Flanagan took a deep breath and managed to break the spell. He swallowed hard and took another deep breath, then turned and looked at Kate. "So," he said with a sudden grin, "how's your love life?"

She stared into his eyes a moment before shrugging and grinning. "It's okay, I guess. I mean, I don't have a fiancé or anything, not after I dumped the last one."

"No boyfriend?"

"Well, not really. Nothing formal, anyway."

"Nobody you're dating regularly?" he asked in mock amazement.

"Well, there is one guy, yeah."

"Oh?"

She grinned again. "Dan's really sweet. You'll like him, I know you will, and I want you two to meet. He's also a Vietnam vet, so you'd at least have that in common. I suppose it's safe to say that we've become quite close."

"Yeah?"

"Yeah. So what about your love life, hotshot?" she asked in a husky voice.

He tensed slightly and looked away. The smile left his face in gradations, like a curtain being drawn. "So? What about it?"

"So tell me about it. You asked me about mine and I told you. Now I'm asking you about yours," she said with a nod in his direction.

"Not much to tell, I'm afraid," Flanagan said softly.

"Have you written Jill about, you know, about . . ."

"About my leg getting blown off? Is that what you're trying to say, Kate?"

"I guess so, yeah. Have you notified her?"

"No," Flanagan said curtly.

"Why not?"

"Because she's an engaged woman, dammit. And oh by the way, it's not me that she's engaged to. She doesn't need to hear from me any longer."

"How do you know that? Did Jill tell you she doesn't want to hear from you anymore?"

"No."

"Would you feel the same way about contacting her if you hadn't been wounded, hadn't lost your leg?"

Flanagan looked away but Kate immediately shifted around in front of him so she could still see his eyes.

"Well?" she pressed.

"I don't know," he said in a voice filled with uncertainty.

"So you're going to leave her in Milwaukee with no idea about what's happened to you?" Kate asked.

"This might be the perfect time for you to back off, in case you're wondering," he snapped impatiently, then immediately became regretful over his tone.

Kate sipped from the cup of coffee. "Okay, so get all mad and huffy with me," she said calmly.

"I just want you to back off, that's all," he said after a pause.

"Do you think you'd be asking her to accept you as a cripple? And that she might even look at you that way?"

"No, Kate. It's because she's engaged to another man. *Good God!*" he said with an exasperated sigh and an uncomfortable shift. "You really are subtle, aren't you? I appreciate your delicacy, sis, I really do."

Kate leaned over to within inches of his face. "Okay, Tommy, I'll knock it off. But I swear I never thought I'd see you like this."

"Like *what*?"

"Like this," Kate said with a nod toward him as she backed away. "Full of hesitation and self-doubt, crawling all over me about my lack of subtlety and delicacy. I mean, c'mon, you were always a knight in shining armor to me, even when I didn't agree with a whole helluva lot of what you were saying or doing. You were strong and brave and intelligent, a constant, a *rock*, and I always admired you for it because I never, *ever* felt that way about myself growing up. But because I knew I had a big brother with all of those great qualities, I always had hope that maybe someday I might have them, too. And the fact that I can now claim some of those qualities is as much a credit to you as anyone else."

He took a deep breath and tried to compose himself.

"I won't let you do it, Tommy. I won't let you feel sorry for yourself. You may hate me before this is all said and done, but right now you need me. Nobody else on the face of God's green earth will talk to you this way, and you need to hear what I'm saying. And you need Jill. And," she said, nodding, "we need *you*, the same Tommy Flanagan that we all know and love. Not some pitiful shell in a wheelchair."

He raised his head brazenly, his jaw firm. "Pitiful shell? *My God*, just who the hell do you think you are, coming in here and talking to me that way?"

Kate looked squarely at him, unblinking. "Mom and Dad told me you were doing great. Father Mike told me you were doing just great, in great spirits. Couldn't be better, just doing great. The staff here told me you were doing great. Everybody I ask says you're doing just great. Just great! But I knew when I asked you about Jill and saw your reaction, that would be the litmus test; *that* would be the big truth-teller. And it was, Tommy. You're not doing great, not yet, and I can understand how you might feel like I've hurt you by saying what I've said. I didn't come here to hurt you, you know that. You know that as surely as you know you're back in Chicago."

"Then why did you do it?" he asked, suddenly feeling beaten and vulnerable.

"Because I read your letters, and because I know you almost as well as I know myself. You wrote and told me that you wanted to see Jill when you got home. That told me that you'd thought about it long and hard, that you knew what you were going to do and how you were going to do it. And so then I knew full well that you hadn't given up on her, even though she was engaged. And I know that deep down you thought you could somehow fix things with her, and get her back. But even if you couldn't work it out with her, at least you were going to see her and try your damndest."

Flanagan lowered his head in resignation. "She can do better now. She deserves better."

"No way can she do better than you, Lieutenant Thomas Michael Flanagan. No *way!* And I'll bet you a steak dinner and an expensive bottle of red that she *knows* she can't do better."

Kate reached out and gently placed her hand on the back of his head and began stroking his neck. He looked at her for a moment and then leaned his head against her bosom, a role reversal they both quietly but instantly recognized.

"You've gotten a lot smarter since the last time I saw you," he said admiringly.

"Thank you," she said with a slight chuckle. "We may as well share some of our hard-earned wisdom."

"I'll write her today. I'll get a letter off to her today."

Kate smiled, then leaned and kissed her brother on the cheek as she enveloped him in her arms. "She'll come to Chicago to see you. Don't worry. I know."

"How do you know?"

"I just know."

He turned and faced her. "I appreciate your coming here and," he said, pausing and grinning self-consciously, "helping me to see things a little more clearly, even if you were just a wee bit brutal."

Kate laughed. "I accept both your thanks and your critique, and I'm glad I could help."

"You did, sis. You certainly did."

The inviting aroma of lunchtime drifted out across the yard from the nearby galley. Flanagan noticed when Kate stole a quick glance at her watch. It was nearly noon.

"How's the food here?" she asked.

Flanagan shook his head and made a disgusted face. "Hardly fit for a cripple," he said with a twinkle in his eye.

They both laughed.

"Nah, the chow's really okay here," he said. "Would you be kind enough to join me, Miss Flanagan?"

"The pleasure would be all mine, Lieutenant Flanagan."

* * *

They had a pleasant lunch outdoors with help from a nurse. Kate stayed on a while longer, talking, laughing, and reminiscing.

"That's the third time you've done that," Flanagan said as they remained outside for coffee after their lunch.

"Third time I've done what?"

"Looked at your watch," said Flanagan.

Kate swallowed. "It's a habit. Sorry about that. It's just a habit, that's all."

"Some other place you've got to be?"

"No hurry, no. Well, actually there is, dear. But I have a few minutes, still," said Kate.

They visited a while longer before Kate finally kissed him goodbye and left him outside where she'd found him, underneath the trees, still wearing his Cubs cap.

She didn't travel far. Kate was sitting in the hospital's front lobby when she saw an attractive young woman in a mid-length, sleeveless blue-and-white dress approaching. Kate recognized her immediately, and got up and started toward the doors. Once inside, the young lady waved and smiled broadly at Kate. She was fit and slender at five-foot seven, with long blonde hair and striking blue eyes. Her radiant smile, her rounded face, and her generally soft features projected an aura of friendliness, of authenticity. She moved about with an easy continuous flow, a natural grace that, when combined with her raw physical beauty, drew the inevitable head-turning stares.

Kate reached to embrace her. "Thank you for coming, Jill. I can't tell you how happy I am to see you. I've missed you so much."

"And I can't tell you how happy I am to be here," said Jill Rohrbach. "Thank you so much for contacting me and letting me know what's happened."

Kate could see that Jill's hands were trembling from her nervous anticipation. "C'mon," she said as she led Jill into the lobby. "Let's go inside and find a place to chat. I've just come from visiting Tommy, and I need to fill you in on his condition."

Jill immediately stopped and appeared frightened. "Is he all right? Is there something else wrong, Kate?"

Kate gave a soothing smile and reached for her hand. "He's fine. And no, nothing else is wrong. Believe me, he'll be overwhelmed to see you."

There was a coffee shop nearby. They got a couple of fountain sodas and took a seat at a table furthermost from the entrance.

"Did you drive here from Milwaukee?" Kate asked.

Jill gave a long sigh, then grinned and said, "Yes. I really don't think I slept at all last night. I've been on pins and needles for the past twenty-four hours. My stomach's in knots and my brain feels like it's in a fog. Honestly, Kate, I must look like a dirty dishrag."

"You look terrific. My brother's always had great taste."

"Your brother," Jill said in a soft tone, smiling and shaking her head, "has had me worried sick for weeks. How is he today?"

"He's doing well, under the circumstances. We've just had a good visit, and I won't mislead you and tell you that he's not struggling with what's happened to him. He'll need some time to get over it, both physically and emotionally, but there's no doubt in my mind that he will. He's seen a lot since he left for Vietnam, and he's been very seriously injured, and I can't help but think that he's been changed by it all. But there's plenty left that you'll be able to recognize as soon as he smiles and laughs and makes a joke, and if you can get past the fact that he doesn't look exactly the same as he did the last time you saw him, then it'll be fine."

Jill took a deep breath and nodded, but otherwise remained silent.

"And you'll need to understand that he's probably terrified that you won't be able to get past it, that it'll be too much for you to handle. He won't expect you to act like nothing's happened, but just understand that he'll be watching closely."

Jill nodded again.

"Just thought I'd let you know," Kate said as she sipped her soda through a straw. "And be sure to listen for his humor. That's the giveaway."

Jill reached over and touched Kate's hand. "I could never thank you enough for contacting me. And I can't begin to tell you how much it means to me to see Tom again, after all these months."

Kate smiled and nodded. "I think I understand," she said as she stood. "Well, it's time you two got re-acquainted."

Jill stood and quickly tried to smooth the wrinkles from her dress. "How do I look?" she asked with obvious anxiety.

"You look wonderful, Jill."

Jill placed both hands over her heart. "Oh Kate, my nervous system is an absolute disaster right now. I think I might be sick."

Kate reached out and took her hands. "It'll go well, trust me."

Jill smiled and took a deep breath, then started out of the coffee shop with Kate.

* * *

"Lieutenant, there's a visitor here to see you."

Flanagan looked around from his wheelchair as he watched a game show on the television in the ward's common area. "Yeah? Who is it? Someone from my family?"

"I don't know," the nurse answered as she moved behind his chair and started to push him. "You can see for yourself."

"Who is it, Ruth?" said Flanagan.

"Let's go see."

"Ensign Fortunato, would you be so kind as to tell me who the hell it is?" he called gruffly as he turned back to look at her. "Stop right now and answer me. That's an order, a *direct* order. Ensign, are you deaf? Stop!"

They pushed past two swinging doors and rolled part of the way down a long narrow corridor, stopping outside a private room whose door was closed.

"Ruth, what the devil do you think you're—"

The tall, brunette nurse held an index finger to her lips and gave a "Ssshhhh". She then pushed open the door and wheeled him inside. Flanagan glanced inside the room, but saw no one.

The nurse tapped him lightly on the shoulder and pointed to his left before leaving and closing the door behind her. Flanagan looked over as Jill, seated in a nearby chair, stood and gave him a nervous smile. He gasped, his eyes bulging and his mouth suddenly opening with surprise. With little hesitation, Jill stepped toward him and leaned to embrace and kiss him. He thought he might hyperventilate, prompting him to separate his mouth from hers so he could take in a large gulp of air. He could then see that she was crying slightly, after which she started giggling.

He tried to speak but his tongue failed him. He looked at her several times, up and down, back and forth, before his brain caught up to his eyes.

"Hello Tom. It's wonderful to see you," she said after wiping her eyes with her fingers.

"Jill, how did," he said, stopping to swallow. "When did you, how in the world," he paused for a breath, "God, why didn't you just drop in on me and surprise the living hell out of me?"

She looked at him apprehensively. "Are you upset with me?"

He kept staring at her, as if to convince himself of her actual presence. "No, of course not."

He reached out to her again, and again they kissed. He caught the familiar scent of her perfume as he held her close, and he could feel his heart pounding inside his chest. Is this really happening? he kept thinking with his arms wrapped tightly around her. Is she really here? She had the same soft feel, the same scent, the same taste, the same powerful affect upon him.

He was still breathless when Jill finally broke away and took a seat in the chair.

"Well, as you can see," Flanagan said self-consciously after another deep, clearing breath, "I'm a little, uh, surprised. Delightfully surprised, though. But surprised. Uh, can I get you something to drink? A snack or something? A sandwich? A soda? When did you get here? *How* did you get here? How did you know where I was?"

He stopped and attempted to compose himself. He felt a warm flush of embarrassment.

Jill grinned. "Are you disappointed?"

"No, *no!* Of course not," Flanagan said with obvious sincerity. "I've never been so pleased in all my life," he said, hoping he didn't look as boiling hot as he now felt. He nervously cleared his throat. "Wow, I really didn't expect this, Jill. I'm sorry if I appear a little dazed."

"You look fantastic. I had to see you. So how are you? How are you feeling?"

He quickly glanced down in the direction of his missing leg. "I'm doing well. I'm much better now, thanks. And yourself?"

"I've never been better."

Flanagan nodded and grinned slightly.

"Why didn't you write and let me know?" she asked gently. "I didn't know what to think."

He sighed and shook his head slowly, glancing away for a moment. "You're about to be married, Jill. I'm sure you're busy with a million details. Honestly, I just didn't want to intrude." He sighed. "I assume you found out about me from Kate, right?"

"Yes. She's been an absolute angel. And please don't hate me for showing up like this."

Flanagan hesitated a moment before finally moving close to her and reaching for her hand. "Hate you? This is the best surprise I've ever had in my life, I swear. I still can't believe I'm not dreaming all of this."

He reached his arm around her as she leaned across and kissed him on the cheek, then on the lips.

"You're not dreaming," she said softly.

She sat back and took his hand and examined it, after which he watched her eyes and measured her expression as she looked him over completely.

"My dear Tom, it must've been dreadful."

"It's okay," he said, still watching her eyes. "I'm fine, really."

"I was so frightened when I found out. And I was so relieved when Kate called finally to say you'd been sent home to the States."

He frowned. "Well, *most* of me made it back okay. It's not a very pretty picture, I'm afraid."

"I've never seen anything quite so lovely."

"What would your fiancé say if he heard you say that?" he asked, still observing her carefully.

Jill grinned slightly. "Can I tell you something?"

He paused a moment before finally answering, "Sure."

Jill looked down briefly and cleared her throat. "After I wrote and told you of my engagement, and then received your letter in return, I knew in my heart that I still loved you. I never stopped loving you, even though I admit I tried as hard as I could to forget about you after you left school for the Marines. But I could never forget you. And I also realized that I'd be making a huge mistake if I married Branson. It just wouldn't have been fair to go ahead with the marriage, and I think he finally came to see things through my eyes. It was hard—it's been hard ever since the day you and I separated—but I just couldn't go through with it. I just couldn't."

Jill paused and wiped away a tear. She then held up her left hand, sans engagement ring. "So I called it off," she said as her voice broke with emotion. "And even though it's been a long time, I'd like to have you back in my life again. I'm not sure where we'll end up this time, but I *am* sure that I want to give it another try."

He stared at her in silence for a moment, studying her face, her eyes, drinking in her entire presence. As long as he'd dreamed of her, as desperately as he had wanted her, as fearful as he had been of losing her, she was here now, in the flesh, as bright as ever, and for him alone. The very thought of it took his breath away. The sight of her was at once so appealing and invigorating that he could suddenly visualize himself fainting and falling out of his wheelchair. Very few such long-anticipated events ever exceeded the preceding imagery, he knew, but this would clearly be an exception.

"I've thought about you constantly during some of the darkest days of my life these past few weeks. The thought of seeing you and being with you again was the only thing that kept me going. That probably saved me, Jill, along with a Marine sergeant who I'll tell you about later. I was laid up for days, my leg gone, my lung punctured, my finger gone, holes punched in me, tubes stuck in me, people pricking me with needles, people waking me when I tried to sleep. And when the pain was really bad, when I thought it might be too much for me to take another hour, I'd think of you. Then, when I'd feel better, I'd think of you. When the mail was delivered, I'd think of you. When I'd go to sleep and dream, most of the time I'd dream of you."

He reached over and wiped a tear from her eye. He smiled, and when she smiled in return, it was as if all of the pain had gone, all of the suffering had ended.

"I just couldn't give up," he continued. "There was too much to lose, too much I wanted to say to you, too much time I wanted to spend with you again. Then, after I started getting better, I wasn't sure if things would be the same as before. Will things still be the same with you? Am I the same? I just didn't know. I honestly wasn't sure for a time whether I was lucky to have been spared, or cursed."

He reached out and took her hand, then drew another deep breath that seemed to calm him. "The answer's clear to me now, as clear as anything I've ever known," he said, adding with a huge smile, "I love you, Jill, and right now I feel like I've gotta be the luckiest damn guy in the whole damn world."

When Jill began crying again, he maneuvered his chair around to be at her side, where he then reached out and held her and kissed her and gently wiped away her tears. He eventually calmed her, and later they were laughing and joking when there was a sudden knock on the door.

"Yeah? Who's there?" he called.

Kate opened the door and peered in. "Am I disturbing anything?" she asked, grinning mischievously.

"No," Jill answered.

"Yes," countered Flanagan.

Kate remained only partially inside the door. "Oh? Well, what?"

Flanagan grinned. "We were about to, you know, we were going to, uh, we were right on the verge of . . . "

"Yeah? Doing what?"

"Well, if you must know, we were just about to put on some soft music and dance," Flanagan said with a straight face.

Flanagan saw Kate glance at Jill a moment before both women erupted in laughter.

* * *

The infection in his damaged lung had greatly weakened Flanagan, and he was unusually quiet and listless as Jill Rohrbach sat with him in the early afternoon at his naval hospital bedside. He had been bedridden for two days, immobile and lethargic. He coughed often, sometimes uncontrollably. He was short of breath, with pain underneath his breastbone, along with a dull aching in his leg and hip. Antibiotics dripped steadily from the nearby plastic bag into the intravenous line attached to his hand. Jill fed him a soft drink through a straw, and felt his warm, sticky forehead. She stroked his head and smoothed his hair, which by now had grown slightly longer than the typically short, regulation-style Marine Corps look.

"Did I tell you already that you look fabulous today?" Flanagan asked in a weak voice as he leaned back and smiled at Jill.

She was dressed in a sleeveless red blouse with black slacks, her blonde hair pulled into a ponytail. "Yes, you did. But I won't tire of it, I promise."

Flanagan showed Jill the letter that had arrived that morning from Capt. Trace Lawrence, his former company commander who was still in Vietnam, advising Flanagan that he had been recommended for the Navy Cross, the nation's second-highest decoration for valor. Capt. Lawrence indicated that the approval might take some time, but the battalion and regimental commanders had enthusiastically added their endorsements. With his previous awards of the Silver Star, the Bronze Star, two Purple Hearts, and the various other campaign and service medals, Capt. Lawrence suggested the addition of the Navy Cross would no doubt make Flanagan one of the most decorated Marines in the Corps.

Jill finished the letter, then leaned and kissed Flanagan. "I'm so proud of you," she said with emotion.

Flanagan grinned. "And I promise *you* that I'll never tire of hearing *that.*"

It was July 4, 1968. Jill had brought a small American flag that Flanagan had attached to the movable tray beside his bed. He sat up in bed, turned, and saluted the flag before falling back onto his pillows, exhausted.

"Are you okay?" Jill asked when she noticed his pale color.

"Yeah, I'm fine," he replied in a raspy voice and with a shortness of breath.

He coughed for several moments, then asked for another sip of the soft drink.

Jill reached for and held his hand. Flanagan's struggle to breathe intensified. She became alarmed when she slid two fingers over his wrist and felt his rapid pulse.

SHALL NEVER SEE SO MUCH

"I'm getting the nurse," she said. "I'll be right back."

Flanagan then coughed and seemed to gasp for air. He looked directly at Jill, his eyes wide and his expression uncomprehending, and as he did so he reached his arms toward her. "Jill," he called out weakly.

"Tom? Are you all right?" Jill asked as she leaned to embrace him. She could feel his hurried, shallow breathing on her bare shoulder. "Tom, talk to me!"

Flanagan coughed again, and this time there was blood visible inside his mouth. He made an inaudible sound and seconds later went fully limp in Jill's arms.

"Somebody help me. I need some *help* here!" Jill called out loudly.

She held onto him, supporting his head, and as she looked into his vacant eyes she noticed he was no longer breathing.

"I need a doctor here!" Jill called out loudly. "Help me, please! He's not breathing! Please, *for God's sake I need some help here!*"

"Tom, please, talk to me. Tom, *please!*"

A nurse, followed quickly by a doctor, immediately arrived at Flanagan's bedside. Their sudden words and actions had an unsettling urgency to them as they set about attempting to revive Flanagan. The doctor leaned over and shined a light into Flanagan's eyes while a nurse felt for a pulse before wrapping a blood-pressure cuff around his limp arm. The doctor then pressed his stethoscope to Flanagan's chest and listened intently.

"Check his airway," Jill heard the doctor command while he still listened for Flanagan's heartbeat.

"What's happened to him?" the frightened Jill asked as she kept her eyes fixed upon the unmoving Flanagan. "Please tell me what's going on."

Another nurse came and quickly escorted the shaken Jill to a nearby waiting area as the medical team worked frantically over Flanagan.

"They're doing all they can," the nurse replied patiently.

"I need to be in there," Jill said as she started walking back toward Flanagan's room, only to be restrained by the nurse and guided back to the waiting area.

Another doctor and nurse arrived at Flanagan's bedside.

"*I need to know what's happening in there!*" Jill called loudly to the clinicians.

The nurse finally coaxed Jill into a chair, where almost immediately she began quietly weeping.

After nearly twenty agonizingly long minutes, the attending physician finally appeared in the waiting area, a somber look on his face, and spoke quietly to Jill. She heard something about deep-vein thrombosis, about a likely pulmonary embolism, but heard little else after receiving the news she so desperately feared.

Tom was gone.

Just moments later a smiling, buoyant Kate Flanagan turned the corner and entered the waiting area, where she saw a near-hysterical Jill Rohrbach being consoled by a nurse as the solemn physician walked slowly away.

"Oh God, *no!*" Kate said, stopping immediately and instantly becoming breathless and panic-stricken.

EPILOGUE
Chicago

It was Memorial Day, Monday, May 26, 1975, only one month after the fall of Saigon to the North Vietnamese Army. The old baseball park at the Arlington Heights high school where Tom Flanagan had performed as a prep star was overflowing with students, faculty, parents, former students, area businessmen, and a host of local politicians. The aluminum bleachers were full, and dozens of folding chairs had been added on the playing surface to provide enough seating. A podium had been established near home plate, facing toward the playing field. It was an absolutely gorgeous day in Chicagoland—warm, sunny and clear, with the large American flag proudly snapping in the steady breeze from its center-field pole.

Kate Flanagan Marinelli sat at the podium and looked out over the assembled crowd as the school principal drew her remarks to a close. Kate's husband Dan, along with their daughter Rachel, age three, and their son Douglas, age five, sat in the front row. Her parents, John and Elaine, and her brother Chris, sat alongside Dan and the kids. Further back, Kate saw Jill Rohrbach Davison sitting with her two-year-old son on her lap.

Kate smiled when she turned around and glanced once more at the press box and saw *Tom Flanagan Field* freshly painted across the front. A plaque would later that day be placed at the entrance to the facility, reading:

Tom Flanagan Field
In memory of Lieutenant Thomas Michael Flanagan, USMC, who died July 4, 1968, as a result of wounds received in Vietnam, and who graced this playing field with his athleticism, his sportsmanship, and his competitive spirit.

The principal closed her remarks by introducing Kate as the sister of the honoree and the driving force behind the memorial. The crowd stood and politely applauded as Kate, dressed in a

313

navy-blue suit with white blouse, approached the podium. Kate began her remarks by introducing her family members in attendance, and then by thanking all the various city and county officials who had helped give life to the memorial. She also introduced a group of twenty-two of Tom's high-school and college teammates, who received an enthusiastic ovation when they stood together and waved to the crowd.

Kate quickly glanced down at her parents before continuing. They were composed, but she could sense that the emotion of the day was weighing heavily upon them.

"I would like to report to you that, as a result of the generosity of numerous local business establishments and other private donors, a fund has been established that, with the addition of public funds, will be used to transform this facility into a modern, fully equipped, concrete stadium. The current capacity will be doubled, and the facility will be first-rate in every respect. There will not be a finer high-school baseball facility in this state, and I am anxious for all of you to see the plan for yourselves. An architect's rendering will be unveiled for your viewing immediately after this ceremony."

Kate waited for the applause to wane before continuing.

"Several of my brother's teammates from high school and college approached me and asked my suggestion on what they could do to honor Tom. I told the guys about Sergeant David Douglas, a Marine hero from Tom's unit in Vietnam who, without hesitation, went to Tom's assistance when he was critically wounded. Sergeant Douglas gave up his own life as a result, and left behind his mother and two younger sisters. We unanimously decided to honor Tom by providing full, four-year scholarships to Sergeant Douglas' sisters to the college of their choice. This gesture was extraordinarily well received by the Douglas family, and I thank all of you gentlemen for your equally extraordinary kindness and generosity."

Kate blew a kiss to the group of teammates as the applause grew.

"Now I'd like to tell you about another American hero," Kate began after the ovation. "I'd like to tell you about my brother, Tom."

Kate felt a lump in her throat and paused briefly, glancing down at Jill who was wiping her eyes with a tissue while softly bouncing her young son Michael upon her knees.

"He was here," she continued. "He walked the halls of this school. He played ball on this very field. He drove these streets and shopped these stores and dined in these restaurants. He worshipped here and went to the movies here and when he got sick he went to the doctors here. He was from us; he was one of us. He was born to parents who are here with us in this audience, and when he died, he died in the arms of the only woman he ever truly loved, who is also here. I had the great good fortune to be his sister, and it is with immense pride and heartfelt appreciation that I represent our family in this tribute to our beloved Tom.

"That my brother was an American war hero is undeniable. He was awarded the Navy Cross for his valor, the citation of which reads, in part, 'Lieutenant Flanagan, already seriously wounded, removed his protective vest and placed it over the upper body of his wounded fellow Marine, all while continuing to provide accurate protective fire. His indomitable courage, his utter disregard for his own safety, and his relentless fighting spirit inspired and rallied the troops under his command.'

"His citation for his Silver Star award reads, in part, 'Under intense enemy small-arms and automatic-weapons fire, Lieutenant Flanagan unhesitatingly left his protected position within the Hue Citadel compound and moved out alone to retrieve his gravely wounded Marine.'

"And his citation for the Bronze Star award reads, in part, 'Lieutenant Flanagan's skillful leadership, his intrepidity under fire, and his aggressive maneuvering of his platoon resulted in the decisive defeat of the numerically superior enemy force.'

"While there was no formal award for this deed, the eyewitness is seated on the front row here today, as a special guest of my family. Former Marine Matt Wenrick was my brother's radio operator before and during the battle for Hue, in 1968. When Matt was wounded and lying exposed in a Hue City street, he tolle of my brother racing to his side and pulling him out of the line of enemy rifle fire. Matt also tells of how Tom shielded him with his own body when enemy mortars began exploding nearby. Matt has spoken to me more than once of how he truly believes Lieutenant Flanagan saved his life that day in Vietnam. He also told me how he would have willingly followed my brother on a frontal assault into and beyond the very Gates of Hell, and he vaguely remembers telling Tom something to that effect just before being evacuated out of Hue to the hospital. It turned out to be the last time he ever saw my brother. Matt left his pregnant wife, Janie, and his twin children, Megan and Mark, in Portland, Oregon to be here for this ceremony today."

Wenrick, a telephone-company service technician, looked up, smiled, and winked at Kate when the applause began spreading through the crowd.

"My brother was a hero to me for his many wonderful qualities," Kate continued. "He was a brave, tough Marine, for sure, but he was also a kind, loving, forgiving person. He was wise and mature beyond his years. His loyalty to his family and friends, and later to his Marines, was done out of love and unselfishness. My brother and I didn't always see eye-to-eye on many of the issues and events of those turbulent days, but it was only after his passing that I fully grasped all that his service and sacrifice had meant. His motivation for serving our country was done out of his sense of duty, the same sense of duty that sent other young men in other generations off into harm's way. Tom helped me understand that military service and devotion to one's country, even at a time of bitter divisiveness, is a high and honorable endeavor. Political perspectives aside, the people who fought in Vietnam sacrificed the most of any of those of the Sixties generation. It is their service and their collective sacrifice, honored in part here today through my brother's memory, that I'd like to recognize."

The applause multiplied again. Kate nodded and then smiled slightly.

"My brother would be uncomfortable with this sort of thing being done in his honor. As accomplished and articulate as he was, he was never at ease when being recognized for his individual achievements. When he was awarded the Most Valuable Player trophy at the baseball banquet his senior year at this school, he rose from his seat, stepped quickly to the podium, received his award, nodded and said 'Thanks a lot,' and promptly returned to his seat. When asked by my parents on the drive home that night why he had been so uncomfortable being recognized as his team's MVP, Tom replied, 'Because it's embarrassing, for cryin' out loud.' If he were here today, if he were sitting on the front row listening to and blushing from everything being said about him, he would be restless and fidgety, looking up at me with that unmistakable Tom Flanagan look of annoyance on his face. I can see him in my mind's eye, clearly, and I swear I can almost hear him telling me to finish up my remarks and get this whole thing over with, that it's embarrassing, for cryin' out loud!"

Kate glanced down amid the laughing crowd and saw her parents smiling for the first time that day.

"But I also know that if he could choose to be recognized in a certain way, that a baseball field named in his memory would be the most satisfying of all. Especially this field, the field of his youth that gave him so many treasured memories. I began my remarks by saying 'He was here' and I close by saying he *is* here. He is here in the hearts of those who knew and loved him, who went to school and played sports with him, who served our country with him, who took great joy in his presence and deeply mourned his passing. He is here for those like myself who remember him every single day that passes. He will always be here. In name. In spirit. In our hearts. He is here with us today."

Kate saw Jill, her eyes reddened and her tears flowing without restraint, sitting ramrod straight with her son close to her bosom.

"And so it is my distinct privilege today, with the grateful and humble acknowledgment of our entire family, to dedicate this wonderful facility to be henceforth known as Tom Flanagan Field."

The crowd stood and applauded loudly. Kate stepped back and finally let the tears stream down her cheeks. She turned around and looked at the sign once more.

Tom Flanagan Field.

The applause grew. Kate wiped at her eyes, then smiled and breathed a sigh of immense relief. She felt a comforting peace settling over her, much as she did when she and her mother shared a warm blanket during one of Tom's chilly, early season baseball games at this very location. She glanced down at her husband, who nodded enthusiastically and gave her a thumbs-up. Kate noticed Matt Wenrick when he stood at attention and gave her a crisp military salute. She watched her father reach his arm around her mother's waist as they both looked up and smiled proudly. She saw a still-emotional Jill slipping quietly away with her son in her arms.

"We did it, Tommy," Kate mumbled under her breath. "We did it! Welcome home, big brother."

THE END

Breinigsville, PA USA
02 June 2010
239093BV00005B/71/P